RISING
LIKE THE

TUCSON

DOUBLEDAY
New York London Toronto Sydney Auckland

RISING

LIKE THE

Tucson

. . .

Jeff Danziger

PUBLISHED BY DOUBLEDAY
a division of Bantam Doubleday Dell Publishing Group, Inc.
666 Fifth Avenue, New York, New York 10103

DOUBLEDAY and the portrayal of an anchor with a dolphin
are trademarks of Doubleday, a division of
Bantam Doubleday Dell Publishing Group, Inc.

Excerpt from *Safire's Political Dictionary: The New Language of Politics* by William Safire, copyright © 1978 by William Safire, reprinted by permission of Random House, Inc.
"Different Drum" by Michael Nesmith copyright © 1965, 1967 Screen Gems-EMI Music Inc. All rights reserved. International copyright secured. Used by permission.

Library of Congress Cataloging-in-Publication Data
Danziger, Jeff.
Rising like the Tucson / Jeff Danziger.
p.   cm.
1. Vietnamese Conflict, 1961–1975—Fiction. I. Title.
PS3554.A584R57   1991   91-7496
813'.54—dc20   CIP

ISBN 0-385-41866-3

BOOK DESIGN AND ORNAMENTATION BY CAROL MALCOLM

· · ·

For
my
Father

· · ·

"Vietnamization—*a plan for the extrication of U.S. ground forces from Vietnam, with the concurrent buildup of South Vietnamese forces, so as to provide the South Vietnamese people with what President Nixon called 'a reasonable chance for survival.'*"

—*William Safire*
Safire's Political Dictionary:
The New Language of Politics

PART

ONE

...

C H A P T E R

O N E

TOUCHHOLE

Lieutenant Starret lay with his
face in the dirt, pretending he was dead.

The dirt smelled bad. In fact, it stank. You never knew where
latrines had been moved in these artillery bases, or how many
times. He might have his nose pressed down in soil previously
used as a latrine. That was something to think about. But if he
were supposed to be dead, what would he care what things
smelled like? He wasn't supposed to be breathing, was he? And if
the North Vietnamese saw him breathing, they would shoot him.
So what was the problem?

Firebase Touchhole was being overrun. Something had gone wrong with the intelligence. Something had gone wrong with the radio relays. Something had gone wrong with all of the things that were supposed to arrange for the defense of Firebase Touchhole. Touchhole was a lonely little place, blown out of the jungle just months before. It had forty men and six guns. Not much.

When the fighting started in the late afternoon Starret saw some of his men killed, a sight that enraged him, and he fired madly into the trees with the others. No one seemed to have a good idea where the little bastards were. The artillery fired wildly. Starret and the rest of his men fired.

But where? Into the mass of trees that ringed the base? The trees were dark, dense. Mortars dropped out of the sky on Starret and his men and bullets crackled by. More of his men were shot. The light was failing, and the sky turned a dull red. The forest turned black. Then another barrage of mortars. Then a brief period of waiting. Then the North Vietnamese cut through what little fence there was around the firebase and invited themselves in.

Why weren't the radios getting through? Where, for Jesus' sake, were the gunships? What was going wrong? Murder them, that's what he'd do. Not the North Vietnamese—the fools at division headquarters. Fools! Inattentive fools. Like Lieutenant Kit, for example.

Starret wondered if Lieutenant Kit was the cause of all this. Maybe Kit had been left in charge of intelligence operations that night. Or maybe he was hiding. What a fool! God, he hated Kit just at this moment, and would kill him if he got out of here. Lieutenant Kit should not have been in Vietnam. If there were a right way to fight a war, Kit shouldn't have even been in the army. He certainly shouldn't have been an officer. The army had made a great many mistakes in its pursuit of a victory in Vietnam. Making Lieutenant Kit an intelligence officer was just one of them.

Endless mistakes. The mistakes in the late 1960s had built upon the mistakes in the early 1960s, all on top of one another, so that the war teetered like a rotten tree waiting to fall. But nobody knew *when* it was going to fall or *which way* it was going to fall. Lieutenant Starret was not schooled in history, and he could not judge the staying power of wars. But if you could believe Lyndon Johnson, and if Richard Nixon were any guide, the thing must end!

Yet the war went on. Starret had led his men well for six months, bringing to his command a creativity and carefulness his men appreciated. Six months is a long time in a war. They appreciated Starret's sense of his own survival. He did not get reckless. He did not yearn for medals. Some lieutenants wanted to take no prisoners, but Starret wanted to take no chances. *No decorations and no perforations.* He was a rare find—a careful officer. His men loved him. At least they didn't try to kill him, and for officers that counted as love in this war.

But no matter how careful he had been, after six months, his sense of survival had grown into a solid, continuing dread. At last he had opted himself out of the war. Lyndon Johnson had done the same thing. And no one was shooting at him. And now Nixon was opting out, and if Nixon could do it, Starret decided, while playing dead on Firebase Touchhole, he could do it, too. Regardless of the consequences, if he weren't discovered playing dead here and killed, then he, William Starret, first lieutenant of the 1st of the 27th Infantry, had no further interest in the war. Certainly it had no interest in him.

• • •

Shooting bounced around among the bunkers on Firebase Touchhole and bullets pinged off the howitzers themselves. It was the scariest kind of fighting, crawling around in the red dirt in the dying light of the afternoon, looking for someone to kill.

Starret had crawled over to an ammunition trailer where he saw two other Americans huddled, with the hope that he could make some sort of position out of it. When he got there he discovered they were dead.

There was a lull in the firing, and he heard men running. He heard Vietnamese voices coming closer. Several voices. He dropped his rifle and lay facedown next to the dead soldiers.

He lay there for a few minutes getting used to playing dead, breathing slowly. Then he opened one eye and peeked out. He

could see small figures darting about in the dark. Occasional shots were fired. What could those shots be? Were they running around shooting the wounded Americans, perhaps? How amusing. He closed his eye again and lay there listening, smelling the stinking dirt.

He heard footsteps, shuffling footsteps. He held his breath and lay rock still. The footsteps were coming closer. He cautiously drew in air and held it. Perhaps, he thought, this wasn't such a good idea after all. The shuffling footsteps came closer yet. They came right beside him. Whoever it was kicked Starret.

I am dead, Starret thought. *Leave me alone.*

A rifle muzzle sniffed around among the dead men and Lieutenant Starret. Starret wanted to open his eyes. Plenty of dead men lay with their eyes open. His lungs were bursting, searching through the air they held for any remaining oxygen.

He could breathe in, he told himself in a small, squeaky internal voice, and risk being shot through the back of his neck, or he could hold his breath further and commit suicide by self-asphyxiation. Or he could jump up and knock over the North Vietnamese. Or maybe be shot before he could get up. His mind raced through the options over and over, hundreds of times. In ten seconds more he would act or be dead. He began to count backwards.

Ten—nine—eight—

The rifle muzzle grazed his cheek slowly and came up under the lip of his helmet. It jerked up, pulling the helmet away. The seconds were running out. He must breathe.

Three—two—one.

Something exploded very close to them. Starret, in terror still, but sufficiently sure of death either way, exhaled and drew in fresh air. The North Vietnamese had looked toward the explosion, as anyone would, and Starret knew this was the moment to raise himself up and overpower the man. Then he would pull the North Vietnamese down, take his rifle, and shoot him in the head or the heart.

But Starret lay still.

The North Vietnamese ran off at a slow, shuffling trot. The sound of helicopters came closer. Starret opened his eyes and saw the man go. He could have rolled over, taken his own rifle, and emptied it after the soldier, filling his back with bullets, killing him certainly. But he lay still, listening and thinking. No one cared what he did. He closed his eyes again and made himself think about what he wanted to think about—his wife, his children, his car.

Something moved next to him.

One of the two Americans he thought were dead was moving. He was still alive. The second man was alive, as well. They were both moving.

Starret scrambled over to them, his hands going over their bodies, searching in the gloom for the damp warmth of an oozing wound.

"Hey, hey," Starret said under his breath. "Don't move now. Where are you hit?"

He rolled one man over.

"I . . . uh . . . I'm . . ." the man said softly.

"Where're you hit?" Starret said louder as the sound of the helicopters increased.

"I'm . . ."

Starret pulled open the man's shirt. He ran his hand up to the man's neck, feeling for a pulse.

"Where're you hit? Tell me!"

"I'm . . . uh . . . not."

"What?"

"I'm okay. I'm not hit. I'm all right."

And so was the other man. They were both all right.

"Fuck d'you mean you're all right?" Starret asked.

"We're all right. We're not hit."

"Not hit at all?"

"Uh . . . yeah. We're all right."

"Really?"

"Yeah . . . really . . . not. We're all right, L-T."

Both of them were all right.

Well, actually, all three of them, Starret reflected, including himself, were all right.

"I see," he said.

• • •

Later, back at the main base at Phuoc Vinh, he felt very calm and reassured about the entire incident—calmed by the real knowledge that he could have done such a thing. Real knowledge is the hardest thing to come by in a war zone. But now Starret could see how it was.

It was the end of 1969. What was going to happen? Innocence was gone. No one was innocent anymore. Not the troops, not the politicians, not even the taxpayers. And the war was lost. It kept going, yet it was lost. Starret would have fought on if there had been a reason. But anyone with any brains could see there no longer was a reason. He had to wait now until those without any brains came to the same conclusion. Or got themselves killed. And he had to make sure they didn't take him along.

He found himself being much nicer to the men and the other officers. Even that incompetent fool Lieutenant Kit, whom he now decided he would not murder. He could have murdered Kit, but it wouldn't have made any difference. Kit was useless. Everybody knew Kit was useless. But it wasn't their fault. It wasn't Kit's fault, either.

Lieutenant Kit was simply no good at this kind of work.

CHAPTER

TWO

LIEUTENANT STEVENSON

Lieutenant Stevenson sat naked in his hot, cramped room in his hot, cramped bunker on Phuoc Vinh army base, hunched over his tiny desk, reading letters from his mother. It was late and every cell in his body wanted to sleep. Some already were.

Every week, his mother (his stupid mother!) sent him the stock tables from the *Wall Street Journal,* just as he had ordered her. These, together with statements from his broker, were the only things Stevenson lived for. The most unbearable thing about this war was that other people were getting rich. People he knew. Friends who had not gone to West Point, who had been smart enough to go to regular colleges and get fake draft deferments, were getting rich. They lied to stay out of the war. They got doctors to lie for them. They paid the doctors, and the doctors lied. Stevenson cursed his luck. He had wanted to be a doctor before he had decided to go to West Point. If he had become a doctor he could now be making huge amounts of money, lying for people who wanted to get out of the draft.

His eyes rested on a headline. He smote his brow.

"Christ!" he hissed.

On the back of one of the stock pages was an article about someone getting promoted to vice president of a division of some corporation. *But this was someone he knew!* His eyes fastened on the name in disbelief. Why did he have to see this?

"Christ!" he said again, in the agony of helpless envy.

He *knew* this person who was getting promoted. This person was a *friend* of his, now making a fortune! Which just went to show you how stupid his mother was. Couldn't she have had the brains to look through the goddamn newspaper and make sure that no articles about friends of his (actually former friends, although they didn't know it yet) were in there?

God! What a mistake it had been to go to West Point! Even if it had been free! He thought he was being smart, getting something for nothing. Why couldn't he have been smarter and seen that you get what you pay for in this world? There's no free lunch. If you go to a free military academy, you're going to pay for it by being forced to watch other people get ahead of you. The best thing you could hope for was that you could wind up being a general.

Like his general. His pain-in-the-ass general.

Lieutenant Stevenson was the general's aide-de-camp, a position of nagging responsibility and detail. He didn't like the job and he didn't like the general. Of course, being the general's aide did give him a little more clout than the average lieutenant. It gave him some rank over sorrowful items like Lieutenant Kit, for example. He could dare to be obnoxious to walking duffel bags like Major Bedford.

But Stevenson hated the job. General Walker was a fat pain in the ass. And the war was a pain in the ass. And the fact that he

was falling behind financially was a pain in the ass. Everything was a pain in the ass.

"Christ, Christ, Christ . . . what a fool I am!"

But despite this momentarily low opinion, Stevenson was smart. He may not have been the nicest person in the world, but he made up for it, somewhat, by being smart. Even though General Walker was a pain in the ass, he was a powerful one. And Stevenson could handle men of power, such as the general, even if they were pains—even if they were querulous old bastards. This trait made him invaluable as an aide-de-camp. *Someday,* Stevenson thought, *I will get out of the army and I will go to work for a powerful man on Wall Street, and I will succeed. I will succeed where others fail because of what I have learned in the army. And it will turn out that this was all worth it.*

Oh, Christ, he thought. *This better be worth it!*

Being a general's aide is not difficult work, but it is a time-consuming post. An aide must always be bothering his own mind to anticipate what the general will want next. Stevenson had three more months as General Walker's aide, and his next assignment would assuredly be with an infantry line company or something equally dirty and distasteful. The worst thing about a line company, besides the obvious danger of being around heavily armed and foul-tempered enlisted men, was that his mail would be even slower. He would be out in the woods somewhere with the North Vietnamese and the mosquitoes and the explosives. His mother's letters and the stock tables would be delayed even further. And what would happen to his investments?

Stevenson was a good officer, so far as most things went. He was punctual, neat, clean, orderly, intelligent, brave if necessary, and able to bear hardships. And most important, he looked good in a uniform. His sense of loyalty, however, was almost nonexistent. At West Point he had failed to develop a love for the army and had little affection for the people with whom he worked. He was dedicated to the furtherance of his own fortunes. And while self-dedication was not an unknown character trait in an American army officer (and even less unknown in the air force), in Lieutenant Stevenson, it rose to unusually persistent levels, which was why he hated being stuck here wasting valuable time while the rest of the world was making money in piles.

Now Stevenson sat in his tiny, gloomy room in the bunker for lieutenants and read down the list of stock figures by the small electric light on his desk. His head hurt and his eyes hurt from long days of work in uninterrupted succession. He wanted to sink into mindless sleep, the only escape there was.

But these numbers held a mean fascination. His eyes crossed. The numbers blurred and fogged. He fought off the weariness and tried to concentrate. Who could know where the fortunes lay? There was a secret in these numbers. His holdings, his portfolio, pathetic as it was, was posted on the wall. Nearly dead from fatigue, he faithfully looked up his stocks and made notations as the prices went up and down or stayed the same. It was all the fault of the war, people said. Of course it was. Stevenson agreed with them. Everything was the fault of the war.

Here, in the year of our Lord nineteen hundred and sixty-nine, after billions had been spent, victory was still in doubt. Victory in doubt! It looked as though there might not be a payoff. No payoff!? But what was it all for? Billions and billions of dollars spent to make this sad, waterlogged country fit for human habitation, and now what? Peace talks? A negotiated victory? A negotiated settlement? A negotiated defeat? What would happen? What would Nixon do? Could you trust him? *Would Nixon give away the store?*

Peace meant inflation. The market shivered. War meant taxes. The market reeled. One thing was for certain. You couldn't trust Nixon. You couldn't trust the Republicans. That was for certain. And another thing was for certain. You couldn't trust the Democrats. In fact, you couldn't trust anyone! That was for *certain* certain.

What would happen? What?! The numbers drifted without confidence. The sectors didn't know what to do. Guns or butter? Guns and butter? Guns? Buns? Buns and Gutter? Stevenson's head fell forward in exasperation and exhaustion. He massaged his eyes violently until the glittering images inside them rose in the blackness and exploded.

In four short hours he had to be back on duty with General

Walker—on duty, looking as if he had just stepped off a parade ground, when he got to the morning briefing. At the morning briefing, the staff got the latest military intelligence. The latest death and destruction. Bodies strewn all over the countryside around this cesspool of a town. Blood and death. Numbers of dead Americans. Numbers of dead South Vietnamese. Numbers of dead North Vietnamese. Every morning they heard about the dead of the previous twelve hours, briefed by that fool of fools, Lieutenant Kit.

Wait a minute! Lieutenant Kit! Stevenson's weary mind caught on something.

There was something about Lieutenant Kit. Just the other day, or the day before. What was it? Something the fool had said about money. Lieutenant Kit, whose hair hung down in his eyes and who appeared to be scared out of his wits most of the time. Lieutenant Kit, who hid behind his boss, Major Dow, or who hid somewhere else when he couldn't find Major Dow. Lieutenant Kit, who supposedly was a Vietnamese translator, but whom no one had ever heard actually speak any Vietnamese. Lieutenant Kit, who couldn't read without moving his lips. Who had said something to Stevenson, just the other day—something about money. Yes. About making millions of dollars . . .

But what was it? Stevenson couldn't remember. He was now so tired his brain hurt. He half rose from his chair and fell sideways into his sodden bunk. He fell through the bunk into a black pool of sleep. His thoughts swirled around and around—Lieutenant Kit . . . millions of dollars. . . .

C H A P T E R

T H R E E

LIEUTENANT KIT

Major Dow watched Kit's face. They were in Major Dow's office—a cramped, messy little place, lined with messed-up maps—listening to the North Vietnamese on the radio.

Major Dow was the division intelligence officer, and Kit worked for him because he was, as mentioned before, theoretically an interpreter. Kit liked Major Dow because Major Dow seemed wise and easygoing, but mostly because he seemed to like Kit.

"Can you understand what he's saying?" Major Dow asked,

shifting his roly-poly body in his chair, squinting his dark eyes at Kit.

Kit pushed the hair out of his face and listened for a few more seconds.

"Not exactly, sir," he said, which was true. Kit wouldn't have lied to Major Dow. And "not exactly" was the truth.

But to be completely honest, he should have added, "and not generally, either."

• • •

Kit was an officer only because he supposedly understood Vietnamese. In the late 1960s the United States was desperate to Vietnamize the war—something it had neglected to do until it was too late. Nixon had promised to do this, and he told the army that they better get cracking on this project. The army's first problem was to tell the Vietnamese.

Vietnamization was not good news for the Vietnamese government, and thus no one was in a hurry to tell them. The American army looked around for officers, preferably in the lower ranks, who could speak Vietnamese. Regrettably, there weren't many. Then they looked for enlisted men who could speak Vietnamese and made them into officers. Kit was one of these.

How much Kit understood of the Vietnamese language had never been seriously tested. Among his other fears—and there were hundreds, with new ones popping up every day—was the fear that it would someday be discovered exactly how little he really knew. From time to time he had to speak to a Vietnamese in front of another American. He relied on the most basic sentences, and then, when the Vietnamese he was speaking to finally took pity on his attempts and switched to English, no one was the wiser. The only person who really knew how little Kit knew of the language was Sergeant Xuan of the National Police, who was an agent for Major Dow. And Sergeant Xuan was too polite to betray what he knew.

Kit had studied at the Army Language School as an enlisted man on a lonely air force base in West Texas. He had no interest in languages, but the course was a full year long. After he was drafted, this seemed like a good way to avoid the infantry.

How to avoid the infantry! Theories abounded in those days about the best way to avoid the infantry once you were caught in the draft. The usual dodges, such as quickly bribing a doctor or an air force or navy recruiter, or best of all a coast guard recruiter, had all been proscribed by the time Kit got his notice. Unfortunately, Kit was not married. Unfortunately, he had no physical afflictions, no religious objections, and no history of mental instability. He was not, unfortunately, a homosexual or a felon.

He had bumbled through college, learning as close to nothing as possible, remaining in the background of most activities, with few social entanglements. Two girls he met and dated intermittently continued to write to him after he was drafted, but they provided little comfort. He got several letters from his grandmother, in whose mind the Vietnam war was an extension of the war in the Pacific and who thought she was still writing V-mail, but only one or two from his mother, who was less patriotic. His father, a real estate developer in Connecticut, never wrote. Not at first, anyway.

The two girls he had known in college were more or less dutiful in their correspondence for the first two months. One of the girls, named Marlene, told him that he should refuse to pick up his rifle in basic training, an action which, she claimed, could be explained in terms of conscience. The result would be his dismissal from what she called "deeds of blood."

Certainly Kit had no desire to do "deeds of blood," especially if anything of an equal and reciprocal nature were in the offing. But when the time came to take up weapons and march off across the frozen wastes of Fort Dix to the rifle range—the moment when, if his conscience were really all that repulsed, he should have balked—he was unable to refuse to do what all the others did. Marlene became involved with someone else and didn't write anymore.

• • •

The contractors who ran the language school in Texas told the army that their system would teach the most dull-witted soldier to speak Vietnamese. The secret ingredient in this system was

time. And since the contractors got paid by the hour taught, there was, happily, no shortage of this secret ingredient. Students would learn the Vietnamese language, the contractors claimed, in the same natural way they had learned to speak English—that is, by endless, childish repetition.

The teachers, who were French–Vietnamese, loved this system. They resolutely refused to explain anything, insisting instead that crazily untranslatable blocks of vocabulary be repeated endlessly. It was, for Kit and the others, a mass of silly codes to be memorized, words such as *do* and *da* and *dong*. Impossible to take seriously.

Vietnamese, Kit learned, is a tonal language—a fact that any American could live a long and rewarding life without ever knowing. The words, like Chinese words, had tones. The word *do*, for example, has six tones, and six separate meanings. The word *da* also has six. The word *dong* has six tones, as well. In fact, every word had six tones. Sentences—nay, whole paragraphs—could be written using just *do* and *da* and *dong*. And there were eleven vowels, and several extra consonants. Thus, the number of permutations on a basic word was staggering.

Kit worked hard at memorizing sentences such as:

Da dau dau dong da dong do dau dong da.

His mind boggled. It seemed like an odd way to prepare for war. But it was better than being in the infantry. He sat in the barracks in West Texas at night, sometimes all alone, preparing the next day's lesson. He repeated over and over:

Da dau dau dong da dong do dau dong da.

Da dau dau dong da dong do dau dong da.

His fellow soldiers did not work hard at trying to remember *Da dau dau dong da dong do dau dong da*. They went to Juarez and got sick on mescal and infected with gonorrhea, which was a much better way of preparing for war. Most of them had no idea what was going on and never studied. In class, when a word was said wrong, the instructor insisted that it be repeated until someone, without being allowed to check in the book, and without any assistance from the instructor, figured out what the mistake had been. Or until the class time ran out.

This went on for a year.

But when the course was nearly over, Kit realized he again faced shipment to the war. On the average, 150 Americans a week were being killed in the war when the language course began, and the figure had risen to 175 when it ended. During the year, Lyndon Johnson had added his own name to the casualty list and announced the beginning of Paris Peace Talks. The Peace Talks fooled very few people, but they sure fooled Kit, who very much wanted to be fooled.

All he needed was something else to stall going overseas. He applied to medical technician's school, which would take seventeen weeks. He was rejected. He applied to heavy equipment school, eight weeks. He was rejected. He even applied to projectionist's school, a mere three weeks, but he had no luck there, either. In desperation he applied for Officer Training School. This was six months long, but no. A regulation said you had to use your language training overseas first. Kit was shaken. There was no escape.

But a rumor reached his ears that the army was suddenly eager for intelligence officers who could speak Vietnamese. He could apply for an intelligence commission directly.

Kit laboriously completed the forms. This time the application wasn't rejected. Instead, it disappeared. He heard nothing for weeks, then months. Then he began to make emergency plans.

He considered other ways of avoiding the war. For example, he could have injured himself purposely. He could have feigned illness or madness. He could have committed some violent act that would have resulted in a court-martial and an undesirable or dishonorable discharge.

But he stumbled in the slightest lie. He was not a violent person. He didn't know enough about illness or madness to act either convincingly. He could have committed some sort of crime which would have given him the delay of a court-martial, but he didn't know what crime to commit. He had no idea how to steal a car—for example, a military police cruiser, which he was sure would have been serious enough. He couldn't really think of any crimes beyond that, and he reasoned that anyone for whom car theft was a mystery was probably incapable of worse things.

There were other possibilities. There was drug addiction, heavy drinking, homosexuality, and being a general wiseass. But gross habits and perversions had grown so common of late that they might well be perfectly acceptable. In times of war, all sorts of things were allowable. He had no way of knowing. He thought of writing to his father, who had been in World War II. But his father had always been such a busy man that he probably wouldn't have written back.

There was only one sure thing, and that was to go AWOL. There were thousands, more probably tens of thousands of men AWOL at any given time from the army. It surprised Kit to find this out, but he decided that it was his last best hope. He planned that he would simply not show up for his flight overseas. This plan appealed to him because it put off any overt action until the last possible minute, and it put his mind at rest until that time.

And with his mind at rest, he was able to do quite well, graduating with the highest score in his class. He was helped in achieving this position by the fact that no one else sought the honor.

• • •

In Pentagon doctrine, the language school was becoming desperately important. Someone had to tell the South Vietnamese that the war was being turned over to them so they could be blamed for the upcoming defeat. Generals delegated this to colonels, colonels to majors, majors to captains, and so on. Telling the South Vietnamese seemed like a good job for lieutenants. The South Vietnamese, quite reasonably, did not want to Vietnamize the war. They didn't want the Americans to leave. They knew what was going to happen. They had known from the beginning.

Kit didn't know much history—not much more than the milky version he had been presented in school. This led him to the vague conclusion that the United States was being forced, surely against its fundamentally peaceful nature, to mount a war effort to save some defenseless people from dictatorial aggression. In every war so far, America had met and mastered the forces of evil, beaten them back, and ensured the survival of democracy. The war in Vietnam must surely be much the same situation. Wasn't it?

But people his age were in the streets screaming about this

war, refusing to be drafted or sent to fight. Rightness or wrongness of the war was hardly the question. If so many of his countrymen refused to fight on the grounds he now began to suspect were their real grounds—that is, that they simply didn't want to do it—well, then, he didn't want to do it, either.

The language course ended. Kit saw his name on the roster destined for overseas shipment. The Paris Peace Talks had done nothing. Now he feared only that his resolve to go AWOL would disappear, and he would obey the orders after all.

Then, suddenly one day, he was called to headquarters by a major and told that his application to be an officer had, by some process of military mysticism, been approved. He was dumbfounded. The good parts of this promotion—the increase in pay and benefits—paled beside the best part, which was that he would have to take *three more months* of training stateside.

And so he accepted the commission, and stuck his right hand up in the air and swore to another abstract and confusing oath, and got some new uniforms, the glaring hatred of his former friends, and a few salutes. And with no motive other than avoiding the war, he became Lieutenant Christopher.

Lieutenant Christopher. Or as the Vietnamese teachers had always called him, because of their inability to wrap their mouths around the name Christopher and because of their predilection for monosyllables—Lieutenant Kit.

He was given three months of training, which included the scantiest basics of being an officer, of which he retained the scantiest amount. He learned that there were some people who liked being officers, and there were some who didn't, and there were some who were utterly indifferent. He learned that he was in the third category.

Then a most surprising thing happened.

From out of nowhere, he got his first letter from his father, who was suddenly very proud of his son because Kit was no longer an enlisted slob.

And, with all the things that were now on his mind, by the time he was actually sent to Vietnam anyway, Kit had forgotten nearly all of his Vietnamese.

And thus, in the hot, dank, crowded intelligence office in

Phuoc Vinh, three months later, when Major Dow made him monitor the North Vietnamese on the radio, he listened carefully. The voice of the North Vietnamese said:

Da dau dau dong da dong do dau dong da!

"Can you understand what he's saying?" Major Dow asked him.

Kit thought a moment and said: "Not exactly, sir."

And this was true, since he understood it not at all, which included all degrees of exactness.

C H A P T E R

F O U R

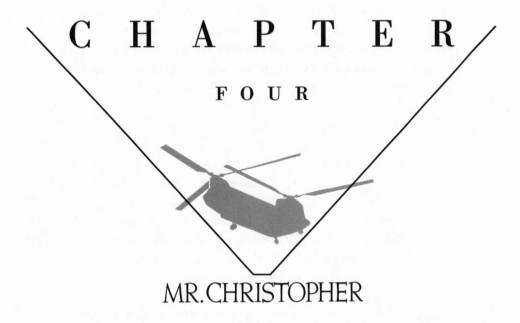

MR. CHRISTOPHER

When Kit had been an enlisted man, his father had never written to him. And back before that, when he was still in college, his father had been barely aware of Kit's existence.

But when they made him an officer, Kit wrote and told his mother, and his mother told his father, and a letter suddenly appeared from his father offering hearty congratulations.

I always knew you were officer material! I'm proud of you!

His father had been an officer in the South Pacific, in a war so popular that the enemy was immediately forgiven in appreciation. Kit's being an officer seemed to cement a bond between them. As a student Kit had been a disappointment to his father. As a private, he had been an embarrassment. But as an officer, Kit was an equal. Mr. Christopher's letters were comradely, exuding manly fortitude. He wrote Kit advice about being an officer—knowledge gained in the Second World War. Such as:

Remember. Your men come first!

Kit read this in the air-conditioned library trailer on Phuoc Vinh army base. The library trailer was air-conditioned to keep the books from rotting. Outside it was 101 degrees. Inside, with the air conditioner unit beating its brains out, it was a cool, comfortable 92 degrees. Kit looked nervously around to see if anyone had noticed he had been there two hours already. No one was watching him. He went back to his letter.

Yes, of course his men came first. But he didn't have any men. If luck held he would never have any men. If *their* luck held, he would never have any men.

Discipline is a two-way street, son, remember that!

This was slightly more cryptic. Kit didn't know what it meant. But he committed it to memory.

Generals put their pants on just like lieutenants. One leg at a time!

The only general Kit had met was General Walker, of whom he was terrified. Every morning Kit gave the morning briefing to General Walker and the other staff officers. He would try to think of General Walker as more of an equal if he could. But he didn't think so.

His father's letters, which he dutifully answered, had gone on like this for the first few weeks he was in Vietnam. Kit happily wrote back a few of the details of his war experience so far. Actually, there were only a few details, and he wrote them all.

Then, to keep the letters going, he made up some more. He left out his afternoons sitting in the library trailer.

It was nice to be writing letters back and forth to his father, especially when they had never been close. His father had always seemed so busy, so full of enterprise, quick to judge, dismissive and preoccupied, while Kit had been shy—more like his mother. But now things were changed. Maybe something good would come out of this war. *Dear Father,* he would begin, and end with, *Your son, James.* His father was taking an interest in him, giving him advice, worrying about him. Some weeks his father wrote twice—two letters in the same week!

But quite suddenly, in the second month he was in Vietnam, his father's letters took a different direction. An abrupt change of mood. It was as if something had occurred to Mr. Christopher. Something that could not be denied. The letters became more excited, more insistent, more detailed. More commercial.

There is no time for opportunity like being in a war zone after the war is won. You could be lords in the land!

Lords in the land! What could this mean? Dimly, Kit remembered.

At the close of the Second World War, Mr. Christopher had been in the Philippines. In the Philippines, opportunity abounded for Americans with enterprising spirits. Mr. Christopher got out of the navy there and purchased three surplus PT boats. He turned them into rapid transport boats to run mail and kerosene between the islands. He had bought land and influence and set up three casino nightclubs for the entertainment of naval personnel. Until he was nearly machine-gunned in the streets of Manila by the various warring factions of Filipino politics, he had made money at an alarming rate, sending it back to the States in bundles.

He never forgot those days in the Philippines, when the victorious Americans were, as he wrote, *like lords in the land.* This condition, he wrote Kit excitedly, was reproducible in Vietnam. Once the victory was secure, by negotiation or however, the country of South Vietnam would be established as an American

satellite or colony or whatever. And then, he wrote, *You will all be like MacArthur—like lords,* etc.

His letters bounced along, describing post-victory South Vietnam, dictated to his secretary between real estate deals. He painted for Kit a picture of pampered and privileged living unknown since the days of British India. Kit was unfamiliar with the Raj, as he was with most of history, but he read on.

Unlike British India, his father wrote, the great servant class would not be Indians, whose women reeked of curry and had red spots on their foreheads, nor would they be Filipinos, whose women were ill-tempered and lazy, but rather, he wrote as one man to another—not as father to son, but as men of the officer class, men of the world—they would be Vietnamese, whose women were dainty and small and pretty. Kit thought about this tentatively. The Vietnamese women certainly were pretty. *Especially those with some French blood,* his father pointed out salaciously. Kit wondered which of the village girls who worked on the base might be partially French. He couldn't tell.

Kit's father's activities now in Westchester County and southern Connecticut included the building of shopping malls and buildings for professional offices and corporate headquarters. In his vision of what would happen in Saigon after the inevitable American victory, the need for this type of real estate was endless. There was little doubt that the American victory would signal the cessation of the domino theory in Southeast Asia. It meant that the American sphere of influence would be established in Indochina along an axis that ran from Bangkok to Saigon, and that of the two cities, Saigon would be the more prominent.

It would mean, he assured his son, that not only would there be a renewed flood of money into the Saigon metroplex, but an equal flood of private investment. Aid and investment would rush in on a scale that would make the Marshall Plan look like a Red Cross picnic. Kit froze at the next line. His father wrote:

What luck that you speak the lingo!

But to be ready for this tide in the affairs of men, preparation had to be done now. He urged Kit to study maps of Saigon and its surrounding areas as if he were looking at, say, Stamford, Connecticut. Where were the major highways? Where was the air access? Where was the railroad? Were there construction unions to be worried about? How much did bricklayers make in Vietnam?

Kit had no idea. Maps? He didn't know how to read a map very well. He could find the places on the map in the briefing room, for the morning briefing, where Major Dow had placed the little numbered stickers. But beyond that he needed help.

"What are you looking for, sir?" asked Specialist Five Harrison, who worked in the order of battle section and kept all the maps updated with known and unknown enemy positions.

"Well," Kit said. How to explain this? "I'm looking for somewhere in Saigon that would be good for . . ."

"What, sir?"

"Well, a place that might be good for . . ."

". . . getting laid?" Specialist Harrison asked helpfully.

"No, no," Kit said, "I don't . . ."

"Don't wanna get laid?"

"No. I wasn't looking for that."

"Oh, come on, L-T."

"Actually, I am looking for land. Umm . . ."

"Land? What kind of land?"

"Good for building . . . uh, you know, hotels and shopping centers. Things like that. You know?"

Specialist Harrison didn't know. Maybe they didn't have shopping centers where Harrison came from, Kit thought. Or maybe he was playing stupid, which enlisted men did sometimes.

"Some areas that are high and dry, not swampy. You know?"

"Sure," Harrison said. "Look here. What, is the army going to build some hotels?"

"Umm . . . Yes," said Kit.

Look at the map, his father had said, as if you are looking at a medium-sized American city like Stamford. Kit looked, trying to think of southern South Vietnam as if it were southern Connecticut, where he had grown up. Unlike Stamford, most of the area around Saigon was flooded or swampy much of the year, suitable for nothing more lucrative than growing rice, but there were some higher areas where, Specialist Harrison pointed out, the combination of dry ground and sparse population might be right. For example, there were the suburbs of Bien Hoa.

"You can build shopping centers all over there, L-T," Harrison said, laughing.

"You really think so?" Kit asked.

"You can get laid, too," Harrison said.

• • •

Kit had seen Bien Hoa once, when he first came into the country. Bien Hoa was a crowded, cacophonous warren of wartime overpopulation. But according to the map, the slightly higher land surrounding it was dry, ideal for construction. The main highway from Saigon had been expanded conveniently to four lanes by the Corps of Engineers. The U.S. Air Force Base at Bien Hoa could handle overseas flights. The old French railroad tracks, even the ones that ran through Phuoc Vinh, were still there. It was, in short, a developer's paradise.

Kit wrote a brief description to his father. He mentioned the highway, the railroad tracks, the air base. He mentioned that Specialist Five Harrison, who he described as a map expert, but whose rank he didn't mention, also thought it might be a good area for shopping centers and hotels and so on.

Yes! Yes! his father wrote back. *Good God! The very place!*

All you needed was a little foresight and you could see it clearly. Bien Hoa was the place. The next step was to get the property and get it now, while the prices were low. Owing to the war and all.

Mr. Christopher's letters crackled with anticipation and excitement as the weeks went on. He had, he told Kit, spoken to his moneyed friends and they shared his zeal. The money was waiting —in fact, it was champing at the bit. They were talking of millions!

Who do we talk to? Can you contact a legal firm in Saigon? Let's get somebody on a retainer, dammit, and have him get to work

locking up options. Do you need some cash? I can send some cash. There's nothing like cash in hand to get people moving. We need action on this, son. Action!

Action? Kit stared at the letter. A legal firm in Saigon? What action?

His father's letters became more insistent. Should he transfer earnest-money funds to Saigon? Should the money be in Vietnamese piastres? Hong Kong dollars? Should he open an account in the Bank of Hong Kong or the Chase Manhattan Saigon branch? Should he contact friends in New York who were international lawyers? Did Kit not realize that the war was nearly over?

Mr. Christopher had sent advisory letters from his broker friends, clippings from business magazines, and finally, a letter from a law firm in New York offering to go on retainer for the purpose of setting up a development corporation. They were talking of millions. He was working at his end! How were things progressing at the site?

The site? Kit hadn't even seen the site. What should he do? Get a jeep and drive down to Bien Hoa? To do what? First of all, he didn't know if he could find Bien Hoa. Second, it was dangerous. Third, it was dangerous. Fourth, it was dangerous.

Suddenly, Kit felt terrible. He felt as if he had lied to his father. And when his father found out, he would be disappointed. He would be disgusted. Everything would be over. Kit wanted to give up, but he couldn't. He wanted to write back to say it was impossible, to plead helplessness. He shouldn't be an officer. He couldn't speak much Vietnamese. He had forgotten so much. He could say hello and how are you, but most of the vocabulary was gone. If he got into a business deal with the locals, he would have to trust them. But could he?

He needed advice. He needed someone he could trust. Somebody who was smart and would tell him what to do. Someone who thought about money all the time, like his father.

Kit sat in despair in the air-conditioned library trailer and read his father's latest letter.

I can't say this strongly enough, son. You are in a position to make millions. I made money in the Philippines, but just think about how much I could have made if I had been in Japan! And that's where you are. After the war, Vietnam is going to grow just like Japan! Just like Korea! With American help, the whole damn country is going to rise like a Tucson from its ashes!

At the next table, jammed against the wall, reading a two-month-old copy of *Forbes* magazine, Lieutenant Stevenson sat watching Kit in disgusted amazement.

"Christ!" he said at last.

"What?" Kit said, looking up, brushing the hair out of his eyes.

"Can't you read to yourself? You're whispering. You're driving me crazy."

"I'm sorry, sir."

Stevenson released a loud wheeze of annoyance.

"What did you say?" he whined at Kit.

Kit looked up at Stevenson. Stevenson sounded just like his father used to sound when he was disgusted.

"I'm sorry, sir."

"You don't have to call me 'sir,' you idiot. You're a lieutenant, too. Or haven't you figured out that part yet?"

"I'm sorry."

Kit went back to the letter.

. . . just think about how much I could have made if I had been in Japan! And that's where you are. After the war, Vietnam is going to grow just like Japan! Just like Korea! With American help, the whole damn country is going to rise like a Tucson from its ashes!

"Jesus!" Stevenson exploded.

"Sorry, si . . ."

"What is the matter with you?! You're still doing it! You need someone to read your goddamn letters to you?!"

"No, sir."

"And for Christ's sake, will you stop calling me *sir!*"

"Yes."

"It may come as a brilliant revelation to you, but we're the same rank!"

A wave of utter despair washed over Stevenson. The same rank! Could it be believed? Four years at the goddamn Point, beating his brains out, to wind up the same rank as Kit! A man who couldn't read without moving his lips!

"This is the only place where I can get fifteen minutes reading and I don't want to be disturbed," Stevenson said.

"Yes. I won't do it anymore."

But the afternoon was getting late, and the library trailer was cool only if you sat perfectly still. Stevenson could do little more than look at Kit, who now sat staring at his letter, his lips pressed tightly together.

"Oh, Jesus! Can't you read without moving your lips?" Stevenson burst out.

"No. Yes. No."

Suddenly, Stevenson felt hopeless. He was robbed of the few minutes he had to do some reading. And he felt guilty, which was odd for Stevenson. Kit was pathetic, but the mail was a special case. Mail was a sacred thing in a war zone. Mail was what you lived for.

"Go ahead!" he ordered. "Go ahead! Read the damn letter! Read it *out loud!*"

"It's all ri . . ."

"That's an order! Lieutenant! I'm giving you an order!" He wagged his finger at Kit. "Don't you know that? I'm a goddamn lieutenant! And you're a goddamn lieutenant! *We're both lieutenants! See?* And when one lieutenant gives an order to another lieutenant, the other lieutenant *has to obey!* Didn't you know that?! That's why we have lieutenants and captains and majors and colonels! That's why we have all *this shit on our shirts! Now read it!*"

Stevenson rolled up his magazine and got up to leave.

Kit began reading out loud.

You are in a position to make millions. I made money in the Philippines, but just think about how much I could have made if I had been in . . .

Stevenson bolted angrily out of the library trailer, slamming the door behind him, from the 92-degree coolness into the 101-degree heat. Reflexively he closed his eyes against the glaring sun, walking with his head down, barely aware of what was ahead of him.

He had gotten about fifty paces when the phrase *a position to make millions* made him stop. Stevenson stood, blind in the sunlight, and turned around slowly. The library trailer floated in the waving heat currents.

. . . *a position to make millions* . . .

Had he heard correctly? *You are in a position to make millions.* Millions? Lieutenant Christopher?

What millions?

C H A P T E R

F I V E

PHUOC VINH

Lieutenant Stevenson was right about Phuoc Vinh. If you were an American, it was a disgusting place. Even by Vietnamese standards it wasn't very nice. But life hadn't been kind to Phuoc Vinh.

Back when Kit was still a boy in Connecticut in the 1950s, people were fighting and killing one another in the greater Phuoc Vinh area. Back before that, when Major Dow was still a boy in New York in the 1940s, and even back before that, when General Walker was still a boy, wherever and whenever that was, people had been fighting and killing one another all around Phuoc Vinh, up and down the Song Be River, in and around the smaller villages of Bo Mua and Nuoc Vang.

In the years since the war with the Japanese, plenty of blood had been shed. The French and the Viet Minh had chased one another around through the fields and forests. Then the Viet Cong and the South Vietnamese had squandered time and lives in the early 1960s. And now the Americans and the North Vietnamese contested the place.

The town of Phuoc Vinh was sixty kilometers north of Saigon, more or less, and in 1969 it was still the nominal capital of its district. A rutted main street with an open ditch sewer ran through the village up to the side of the old French-built administration building, which stood in the center of a weedy field at the end of the French-built railroad tracks. At the other end of the street was the Catholic church, a homely affair, creatively built of found and donated items, corrugated tin, yellow brick, and blue tile. Its bell tower was done in Indo-Chinese Art Nouveau, and there was even a bell.

The other buildings of the village were situated here and there, straggling along the street. There was an open restaurant, a place that fixed Honda motorbikes, two barbershops, and an indeterminate number of laundries that did a starchy, moldy trade with the American army, whose officers required starched uniforms in order to be able to fight in the tropics. Nearly all of the buildings had bullet pocks. Out in front of the Xua Honda shop, a child sold red gasoline in wine bottles neatly lined up on a small folding table. In the early mornings, when there was sufficient mist to blur the outlines, and the church bell was ringing, the village was almost attractive, but at any other time it was not.

The old administration building was supposedly the seat of district civil government. It had a two-story tower of leprous stucco in the center with mismatched one-story appendages to either side, scarred by age, stray bullets, and mold. Its red tile roof over the years had admitted mortar shells and the monsoon rains. Repairs had been made with anything available. The building sat like a blind sphinx, staring through its glassless eyes down the rusty, crooked tracks to Saigon. No trains ever came to

Phuoc Vinh. The cars were full of squatters living in the Long Binh switchyards far to the south.

The daily work of administering what civil law was left in Phuoc Vinh was done here by a painfully unhurried and informally appointed staff of clerks who were empowered to do very little except set their own hours, which they did individually. Authority for doing things came from the executive officer of the district, a fat South Vietnamese army colonel who roared through with a convoy of two or three jeeps every few days, as the spirit moved him. He would scream at the clerks and turn over some desks, scattering papers. Then he would leave. He preferred to hang around the U.S. Army base which sprawled next to the town, where there was an air-conditioned officers' club, and where, as a member of an allied force, he could charge drinks. In his absence, the district clerks were left to make and keep their own counsel, in whatever way they saw fit, and at whatever pace. Or no pace at all.

•   •   •

Phuoc Vinh U.S. Army base—with its helicopters and hospitals and trucks and service clubs and officers' and enlisted clubs; its bunkers, PXs, chapels, snack bars, basketball and tennis courts; and all the rest of the things needed by Americans at war —was to the east of Phuoc Vinh in an enormous compound of several square miles. To the north was a mine field, another gift of the French.

The tactical operations center for the division, where Kit and Lieutenant Stevenson worked, was well inside the base, and well inside its own compound. The operations center was a large, squat fortress made of heavy lumber, steel runway planks, and sandbags, flanked by several house trailers for the commanding general and his deputies, all surrounded by chain-link fence and concertina barbed wire. Everything was packed in sandbag walls and connected to the outside world by crazy webs of wires, some strung overhead, some on the ground. On top of the operations center, in hills of sandbags, grew a spidery forest of radio antennae and a radar tower. In back was a lumpy tennis court where Major Dow and the general used to play each evening. One night a mortar landed on one of the baselines, digging a sizable hole. The tennis playing stopped. Next to the tennis court were the surgical hospital, the officers' club, and the graves registration morgue.

The troops lived in bunkers set here and there, at any angle that happened to occur to the minds of the various builders. There were bunkers for the officers, bunkers for the enlisted men, a bunker for the military police detachment with a small stockade for prisoners of war, a chapel, a post office, a service club where movies were shown, an engineer detachment with a zoo of equipment, innumerable showers and latrines, barracks bunkers for the infantry brigades, a horror of a mess hall, and a series of collapsing canvas sheds that served as a motor pool. To the west, where the ground was slightly higher and firmer, the engineers had built a short airstrip, a fuel depot, an ammunition dump, and some buildings for helicopter repair.

All around this area ran a perimeter of perhaps three miles or more, studded with bunkers and towers, paralleled by barbed wire and defended by sloppy rows of claymore mines and flares. The shape thus defined was of a kidney, more or less, with the village and the main gate in the indent.

At the four compass points of the base were artillery batteries with 105-mm guns and sometimes larger cannons. Behind, and a respectful distance from the guns, underground storage bunkers had been dug for the ammunition. From the bunkers to the guns ran miniature meandering boardwalks so that gun crews, carrying shells during the roaring and flashing madness of a standoff attack, would have sure footing.

A maze of wires and cables ran between the buildings. Communications and power supply were as chancy and inexplicable as in any Oriental city, and depended on the weather as much as anything else. When a line failed, a new line was simply strung and the old one forgotten.

In fact, nothing was done or built except on a temporary basis, in the knowledge that the deterioration of the dry heat in the dry season and wet heat in the rainy season was constant. Sandbags fell apart, buildings tipped when the ground washed away, telephone poles leaned and hung on their wires. The rot worked its way up through the floors, which first became springy, then broke through. Poor Major Bedford fell through a floor once and hurt himself. He asked if he qualified for a Purple Heart for this wound. Everyone laughed, and he decided to pretend he had been joking.

Even the more massive, fortified buildings were kept standing only as a result of perpetual maintenance. The walls were supported with random props installed as needed, and the roofs were covered with layer upon layer of moldy canvas drenched in oil. The rest of the buildings, from the bunkers in which the men lived to the flimsy house trailers of the commanding general, were all held together in a state of suspended disintegration, constantly rebuilt and strengthened against the ravages of weather and wandering explosives. A near miss by an incoming mortar round or the shock of outgoing artillery could bring an entire structure down on the heads of its inhabitants—the humans, the dogs, the rats, the bugs, everybody.

Why were things this way? Because everyone believed in the early 1960s that the war would soon be over, a belief replaced in the late 1960s by the hope that the war could not last forever. By the time Kit got to Vietnam, the only hope was that you would be able to leave in one piece, and the hell with everyone else.

Most of the building materials were diverted to the black market. The Americans had to make do with what they could scratch together or steal back. Construction varied between extraordinary overbuilding and ghostly flimsiness—sometimes both in the same structure. Kit's shower hut, for example, was roofed with solid steel planking meant for runways for twenty-ton bombers. But there weren't any bombers around; the bombers were in Thailand. The runway planks had been delivered to Phuoc Vinh. A mistake. So they were used as shower roofs and covered with three layers of sandbags to protect against falling mortars. The uprights were rotten two-by-fours from the Pacific Northwest, bought by the Japanese, who then sold them back to the Americans at a riotous profit. One evening, after several days of rain, when the moon was full and there was no chance of a mortar attack, the entire thing collapsed sideways, water tank and all. Kit's boss and friend, Major Dow, placidly shaving inside, received a painful wound. The steel planking fell away from the rotten studs and struck him a hard glancing blow on his pudgy right shoulder. Major Dow was a moderately heavy man, but he could move quickly. He made a miraculous escape amid the falling sandbags and was able to stagger in the beautiful Asian moonlight, nude and half shaven, to the hospital for treatment.

Kit lived in a hunched wooden bunker with a tin roof close to the rear of the mess hall. Kit had been told that this was an advantage, and he had believed it at first. Then, as the garbage odors grew worse, he saw how he had been lied to.

The mess hall was regularly sluiced down with a strong chlorine mixture designed to kill bacteria. It also killed all the plant life under and around the building. The plant life might have been able to absorb the waste water and grease from the kitchen, but it could not survive the chlorine. A sullen fog of odor grew until it was as close to a living thing as a gas can be. No one could mistake its warning. The food served here was rich, heavy, and unimaginative, and only career soldiers could eat it in a hot climate. Most of it was thrown away. A crowd of ten or more garbage cans of uneaten, putrefying food stood in the sun every day, waiting to be sold to the pig farmers from Bo Mua who paid the mess sergeant.

"If you don't like the goddamn food, don't goddamn eat it," the mess sergeant told anyone who complained. "I don't give a good goddamn. If you pigs don't eat it, the other pigs'll eat it. Ha! Ha!"

Even closer than the mess hall was a generator shelter housing two large diesel units that alternated in service without ceasing. The exhaust stack went through the roof of the shelter and took a crooked turn toward Kit's bunker. His sleeping quarters reverberated like the engine room of a ship.

• • •

Kit spent as little time in his bunker as he could and as much as possible in the operations center. He also spent a good deal of time in the library trailer. Because he was an officer, the enlisted guy who was the librarian could not kick him out. And because he was supposed to be an interpreter, he could pretend to be reading something in Vietnamese, when actually he was trying to compose a letter to his father about buying real estate in Saigon.

He opened his notebook and tried to write.

Dear Father,
I don't think we should

He stopped. Deflecting his father's commercial excitement was going to be harder than he thought. He tore the page he had written on out of his notebook and crushed it into a ball. He began again:

Dear Father,
Everything is going well, but I think maybe it would be better if we waited until

He paused, then covered this letter with his hand and crushed it into a ball, as well.

Dear Father,
I don't know how to tell you this exactly but what you want me to do is going to be very hard. I am not very good at this kind of thing. I would really just like to come home as soon as I can and see you and Mom. Maybe I could work for you and do real estate stuff back in America. I am sorry that

He stopped again. If he told his father the truth, he would never hear from him again. His father would be disgusted with him, thinking him a commercial coward. Even if he simply suggested waiting, his father wouldn't want to wait. Money wouldn't wait. His father wanted to send him cash now to start hiring people.

He tore out the third attempt and crushed it into a ball.

Then for a while he sat dejectedly with the three balls of crushed paper on the table in front of him, without the slightest idea of what to do.

CHAPTER

SIX

LIEUTENANT TOOMEY

On the wall inside General Walker's trailer was a secret chart showing the declining number of American troops in Phuoc Vinh as the disastrous policy of Vietnamization took effect. Stevenson's job was to keep the chart current. General Walker glared at Stevenson, wattles aflame. Walker had been drinking whiskey with Major Dow, which made him prolix. It was not yet two in the afternoon.

Now, by accident, Stevenson knew another secret. The general concluded in his graveliest voice:

"And what I mean by that, Lieutenant, is if I ever hear, or if it ever becomes known, or if I hear it spoken of or mentioned by

any other person, I shall come after you and I shall remove your soul from your body. Do I," the general paused to drain the remainder of his glass, "make myself clear?"

You pompous windbag, Stevenson thought.

"Yes, sir," Stevenson said.

"You will not speak of this to anyone. You will not remember anything of this. If there ever is a court-martial, you will say to yourself isn't that interesting, and might that not resemble an event which I dimly remember speaking of with General Walker, one hot day in his trailer in darkest Phuoc Vinh?"

The general wiped his lips.

Whom does he think he is threatening? Stevenson thought, restraining his lip from its desire to sneer. *I heard the whole horrible story. So what?*

Major Dow sat on the other side of the tiny table in the trailer, drinking whiskey as well. His fat face was still, but his quick eyes moved all around the room, and up and down Stevenson's long frame.

The general's speech had come to an end.

"I will speak to no one about this, General," Stevenson said in a level voice. "I understand the severity of this case."

"I hope you do, Lieutenant, because I never meant for you to find this out. I . . ."

"Sir," Stevenson interrupted. "You have my sacred word as an officer and a gentleman."

General Walker stared at him. He said slowly:

"If you meet Lieutenant Toomey in the street, you are to say nothing. If you meet Lieutenant Toomey in the club, you are to say nothing. If you meet Lieutenant Toomey years hence, you are to say nothing. I cannot make you keep your mouth shut, but I can make you wish you had."

"Yes, sir."

"Lieutenant Toomey will be here every day. I haven't decided what to do with him."

"Yes, sir."

"That's all, Lieutenant. Matthew, give me another drink." He held out his glass to Major Dow.

• • •

Stevenson left the general's trailer in a mood of dead anger and vicious hatred for the man. This kind of treatment! He wanted to slam the trailer door behind him, but he wisely held himself. Even when he heard the mutter that followed him through the door, "Officer and gentleman—my God!"

The heat outside was unbearable. He had a hundred things he was supposed to be doing. But the hell with them. He headed back to his room in his bunker. He sat down immediately to reconstruct everything he had heard before he forgot any of the details. The man's name was Lieutenant Toomey—an infantry officer whose actions, whose crime, the general was going to bury. A horrible thing. Lieutenant Toomey had been sitting there for the past hour telling them all the details, explaining his acts as if there were some reasonable excuse.

Stevenson tried to remember it all—the names of the dead men, the unit identifications, the commanders, the operations officers, the dates, and the times. Thank God he had a head for gossip and tale-telling. Walker had asked him to be there as a witness before he realized how bad it was.

Stevenson wrote several pages of cramped detail—what Toomey had claimed as his reason for the killings, how he claimed the thing had happened. He wrote a short prefatory note to a friend at the Pentagon, a friend he had known from West Point, a man on whose lack of principles he knew he could rely. Then he folded the entire mass of paper and wedged it into an envelope. He addressed it to his friend, licked it, and propped it up on the little shelf above his desk. He looked at it. *Now that I have written this, I will think no more about this,* he said to himself, *even though I know a man cannot order himself not to think about such things. They will try to cover up the truth, but it will come out. This is worse than My Lai.*

And as he sat staring at the envelope, the flap curled spookily back by itself. A frisson of fear went through Stevenson. The truth was coming out! The glue on the envelope had been ruined by the humidity, as everything got ruined by the humidity. The envelope would not stay shut. He looked in his stationery box for

some tape. There was none. For want of an envelope, the secret would be lost, he thought. He would have to walk to the post office for a good envelope.

He wrote a mailgram to his mother, with some instructions to his stockbroker, and signed the letter of buy and sell orders *Your son, David.* Then he amended it to *Your loving son, David,* for the purpose of giving her a thrill. He put both letters in his pocket, put on his hat, and started off through the heat for the post office.

The sun beat down ruthlessly. The odors of Phuoc Vinh rose to his nostrils with equal ruthlessness. Stevenson hated this part of the day, especially being outside. It was the army's practice in Vietnam to burn human waste with diesel fuel. Every morning, after the first flood of quinine-induced diarrhea, the cans in the outhouses were dragged out into the sun, splashed with diesel, and ignited. A dirty black smoke rose over Phuoc Vinh and hung there to be inhaled by all who had the misfortune to be outside. Stevenson tried to breathe as little as he could as he walked to the post office, but some breathing was unavoidable.

Lieutenant Starret, who had played dead on Firebase Touchhole, hailed him from behind.

"It's Loo-tenant Stevenson! Out in the sun? Jesus!"

Stevenson turned.

"You're still here? What are you doing?"

"Going to the O-club. For a drink."

"You're always at the O-club."

"You have a keen sense of the obvious, Lieutenant." Starret grinned. "No wonder you're the general's aide. It's because they have beer at the O-club."

Stevenson said nothing. Starret was always at the O-club these days. And nearly always drunk at the O-club.

"Come on over to the O-club for a beer, Lieutenant," Starret said.

"I've got work," Stevenson explained tiredly. "The war, you know."

"Just a beer. Jesus, it's so hot."

"No. I've got to do things. Walker's on my back."

"Fuck Walker. Just a beer."

"No."

"Okay. Then buy me one?" Starret said with a pleading look.

"You're broke?"

"A keen sense of the obvious. And a subtle flair for the obscure."

Stevenson dug out his wallet and gave Starret some scrip.

"Thanks, Lieutenant. I'll pay you back maybe."

"How can you drink this early?"

"I'm drinking all I can."

"Why?"

"Oh . . ." Starret smiled and looked around at the collection of twisted buildings and bunkers that sat broiling in the sun. The engines on the refrigerator trailers at the graves registration morgue pounded away in the heat. "Just depressed, I guess."

• • •

The mail came up by helicopter from Tan Son Nhut in the morning and was sorted by the enlisted clerks, who first looked through for their own mail, then for anything that looked like pornography, which they read or stole. Then they sorted the mail and distributed it to the unit boxes, if any time remained. There were two enlisted men in line ahead of Stevenson. Stevenson waited patiently. For him.

"I need an envelope to send a certified letter," Stevenson said at last to the clerk.

"It's too late today, sir," said the clerk sweetly.

"Too late?"

"That's right, sir."

"Well, take it today and send it tomorrow."

"Can't, sir. You have to bring it in tomorrow, sir."

"Why can't I mail it today and *you* send it tomorrow?"

"Can't, sir. You have to come back tomorrow, sir."

Stevenson was in the mood of anyone who has just been waiting in line behind enlisted men after inhaling air laced with incinerated human waste, some of it unavoidably from enlisted men.

"I'm General Walker's aide. I can get you assigned to the Cambo border. You'd like that?"

"Sorry, sir, I'm just telling you what my sergeant tells me to tell people."

"I can get him assigned to the Cambo border, too."

The mail clerk blinked.

"That's different, sir. In that case, I'm sure I can take your certified letter today and make sure that it gets sent tomorrow."

Stevenson hated to throw his weight around like this. But the alternative was not throwing his weight around. The mail clerk gave him a nice new envelope.

Regular mail was free, but for certified mail there was a slight cost. Stevenson pulled out some military scrip, little colored bills for coins and dollars. Real money wasn't allowed in Vietnam. He peeled off a few blue twenty-five cent bills. On one side of the bill was an engraving of a nuclear submarine. On the other side were two American astronauts floating in space. The most profound and the most ethereal of American projects.

He made a quick count of his remaining scrip, his wad of worthless paper, trying to remember what he had given Starret. It wasn't money. It didn't look like real money. It didn't feel like real money. Nothing felt like real American money. Soldiers spent the scrip crazily and gambled it away as fast as they could. It was, after all, the ultimate insult. You were risking your most precious possession and you were paid in the least convertible currency. Real American money was forbidden in the war zone because it contributed to inflation.

He addressed the envelope and pushed it under the grille to the clerk. The clerk smiled and pushed it back.

"Please put it through the slot, sir."

Stevenson squinted at the clerk, trying to understand the enlisted mind, trying to understand why he hated enlisted men so very, very much.

"Put it through the *slot?*"

"Yes, sir. See that slot on your right. Next to the window?"

"I see the slot."

"Well, that's where you should put your letter, sir."

"Thank you, Specialist," Stevenson said through his teeth. He put the letter through the slot.

It fell into the box, next the mail clerk's elbow.

"How was that, Specialist?"

"That was just fine, sir. That was well done, sir."

Stevenson tried to think of something he could do to make life more unpleasant for the mail clerk, but nothing seemed to come to mind. And remembered he needed a favor.

"Is there any mail for me, Specialist?"

"I don't know, sir."

"Could you look?"

The mail clerk looked at him like a puppy.

"If you promise," he said.

"Promise what?" Stevenson hissed.

"Promise not to send me to the Cambodian border."

It was amazing, *amazing*, the shit one had to put up with, Stevenson thought. Even regarding this little incident as a minor phenomenon worthy of scholarly observation, it was still amazing.

"I promise," he said.

The mail clerk handed him his mail. Virtually nothing. Nothing worth the phenomenon he had endured to get it. Junk mail. A flyer from the Reserve Officers' Association heralding a new breakthrough in retirement benefits. He turned to go.

"L-T?"

"What?"

"Would you do me a favor?"

"Of course, Specialist," Stevenson said. "My heavens. Why wouldn't I?"

"Would you tell Lieutenant Kit he has a registered letter here?"

"Kit?"

"Lieutenant Christopher?"

"I know who he is," Stevenson said peevishly. "Just deliver it."

"Can't, sir. He has to come in and pick it up. It's registered."

Stevenson thought a second. "Give it to me. I'll give it to Lieutenant Christopher."

"Can't, sir. He has to sign for it."

"I'll sign for it."

"Can't, sir. He has to sign for it himself."

Stevenson thought a moment.

"Officers can sign for other officers."

"They can?"

"Of the same or lower rank."

The mail clerk paused. He hadn't heard of this policy. Actually, no one had.

"Are you sure?"

"I am the general's aide. Do you think I'm making this up? Of course, I'm sure. Besides, Lieutenant Christopher is a very busy man. I'll see him tonight."

The mail clerk gave him the letter. Stevenson signed the log. He took Kit's father's letter and looked at it briefly. Then he shoved it in his pocket unconcernedly.

"Have fun in Cambodia," he said to the mail clerk, and left the post office.

Back in his room he took Kit's letter out and examined it closely. Fine corporate stationery. From *Howard Christopher and Associates, Stamford, Connecticut.* A letter from dad. There was some writing paper in it that seemed to be wrapped around a wad of other paper. It was a thick wad. Even through the envelope he could feel the unmistakable thickness and heaviness of the paper inside, many sheets of it. He felt its shape and dimensions. He held it up to the light. Only one thing felt like this when it was stacked up in an envelope. Only one thing was this shape.

Money. Real American money. He was sure of it. He ran his thumb tenderly against the flap.

The glue held fast. Damn.

"Hmmmm . . ." Stevenson hmmmed, thinking about other things he knew about Kit.

On the other hand, he reflected as he propped the envelope up on the little shelf above his desk, it was an exceedingly humid day, and in all this humidity, you never could tell.

C H A P T E R

S E V E N

MAJOR BEDFORD

To the rear of the mess hall that Kit avoided three square times a day was a muddy and foul-smelling field across which the wash water from the mess hall oozed down to a filthy, narrow creek. Here it joined other efflu-ents from the American base—diesel from the fuel depot, leach water from the garbage dump, and a variety of other military fluids. This combination gave off an odor that probably violated the Geneva Convention, especially when combined with burning shit, garbage fumes, and diesel exhaust. Even the nearby village of Nuoc Vang, on the hottest day, with piles of dung drying by the side of the road, was never able to generate a smell to match the American base.

Kit's bunker was on one side of this field. On the other side was another bunker, slightly larger and better appointed, for higher ranks—captains and majors and above.

Major Bedford lived here.

It looked like any other bunker, set in a nest of barrels of sand, concertina wire, sandbags, ammunition boxes, and itinerant trash. One wall of the rocket box revetment had keeled over and had been replaced by sections of steel runway planking that leaned against the building to deflect the evening mortars. The telephone pole on top slanted toward the greatest number of wires. Some flags hung from it in shreds. There was a South Vietnam flag, and Confederate flag, and, most tattered of all, the flag of Puerto Rico, from when the bunker had housed some enlisted troops.

Major Bedford's bunker looked as damp and cramped as any of the others. Seven rooms were connected by a narrow zigzag hall copied from the trenches of the First World War. The design would diffuse the blast of a grenade, should one be lobbed in by anyone—for example, a passing enlisted person seeking to redress some fancied injustice.

Major Bedford had talked the other officers in the bunker into assigning a small room to their houseboy, Thi Tuan, so he could stay overnight. This was a violation of the regulations. But they didn't agree with those regulations, so they ignored them. They thought Thi Tuan, being a Phuoc Vinh boy, would know about upcoming deviousness among the locals and could warn, either directly or by his absence, that some sort of sapper attack was planned. In truth, Thi Tuan knew nothing. He thought he would be safer living with American officers.

Thi Tuan was effective, however, against the rats in the bunker. The rats, which during the night swarmed over the garbage cans and under the mess hall, hid during the day in the enlisted and officers' bunkers. Above the ceiling they slept and raised their rat young. Thi Tuan had invented a tilting box trap that was ingeniously simple. Major Bedford was sure it would have made Thi Tuan a rich man in a more highly developed economy. After the rat was caught, Thi Tuan pounded it to death with a length of steel pipe and then threw the corpse into the drainage ditch.

He was working on other traps that operated on the principles of drowning, electrocution, spring-loaded razor blades, and other lethal combinations. He could have been even more effective if they had allowed him some ammunition, but that was also against the regulations—in this case, regulations with which they agreed.

Thi Tuan swept the rooms out every morning, tidied things up, tended to the laundry, and even went to collect the mail. He paid special attention to Major Bedford's room. He knew Major Bedford was his protector. He decorated Major Bedford's room according to his own sense of what a field officer's quarters should look like in a theater of war. He painted the walls solid red. He added carefully accomplished scenes of Vietnamese village life; girls on bicycles with long, flowing traditional dress; water buffalo in rice paddies; religious grave markers; and his favorite subject, the Black Virgin Mountain, which dominated the horizon to the north. He also tried some war scenes, but he came to the conclusion that Major Bedford, who was a gloomy sort of man, had probably seen enough war outside. So he painted them over with more red.

Over Major Bedford's little field desk he arranged a military display. He made a crisscross of two Chinese rifles, which Major Bedford had bought as war trophies. He draped a bandolier of ammunition from one rifle butt to the other. Above this display he tacked a picture of Major Bedford's wife, an American flag, and a picture of General William C. Westmoreland cut from *Time*. To Thi Tuan's mind it was the essence of the victory to come—swashbuckling bravery under the aegis of Old Glory and two prominent jaws.

Major Bedford realized that his room now looked ridiculous, but he could not summon the cruelty to take the decorations down. He liked Thi Tuan and liked to watch him pattering around in flip-flops and thin shorts. Thi Tuan was bright, hard-working, and cheerful in the face of his problems. The war had robbed him of nearly everything, but his good humor remained.

He had lost his family, his boyhood, and certainly anything re-
sembling an education. Yet he was still cheerful. *The Vietnamese
are amazing,* Major Bedford thought.

But Thi Tuan still did not understand certain things. He did
not understand starched fatigues, for example. Major Bedford
paid Thi Tuan to re-starch and re-press each set when they came
back from the village laundry. Using a piece of plywood stored
under Major Bedford's bed, an iron sent from the States, and
spray starch bought in the PX, Thi Tuan pressed them crisp and
crackling, just like stateside. But secretly he thought it was very
silly.

If he had not been as ready to excuse Major Bedford's behav-
ior as he was, Thi Tuan might have thought him a vain man.
That would have been a cruel misjudgment. In fact, such a misjudgment would have been possible only by someone unfamiliar
with the realities of the American military. In these realities,
Major Bedford had schooled himself with the concentration of a
sailor studying the escape hatches when his ship is sinking. Because the truth was that Major Bedford's army career was, if not
yet sinking, at best dead in the water.

It had been a sobering day when he finally made the rank of
major—a sadly disappointing day. He had been passed over
twice, and in the army scheme of things, the third chance is the
last chance. When he had finally made major, he had breathed a
short sigh of relief, cut shorter by the immediate realization that,
without a marked slaughter of lieutenant colonels, this was to be
his last promotion. The army had subtle ways of communicating
its intentions. A begrudged promotion was scarcely a promotion
at all. It meant you could pin on your badge of rank, but you
shouldn't get used to it.

Even as he had been celebrating his promotion, buying drinks
for the bar, he had been inwardly miserable, suspecting that everyone knew how close to full rejection he had come. But he was
not ready to admit defeat. In the first place the war might get
worse—it certainly wasn't getting any better—and his prayers
would be answered. More lieutenant colonels might get killed. Or
the lieutenant colonels' prayers would be answered and more full
colonels would get killed.

The second reason was even more compelling. He had nowhere else to go. He wondered if the army ever realized how dedicated an adversary they created in a man with nowhere else to go.

And that was the worst part. A man like himself needed something from the army. He needed the volume, the meaning, the authority, the grounding, the ballast, whatever it was, of a *position*—something solid and recognizable behind him. In short, he needed the army more than it needed him. He was no longer young, but he didn't look old. He was experienced in the army, but not actually in war. He had thought that being a major would mean something, but so far, it had meant very little.

General Walker had offered him the job of civil affairs officer, dealing with the locals, supplying them with things to win their hearts and minds, dropping leaflets on them, running psychological operations. The general said all this civil affairs stuff was important. But the general lied. He didn't care about civil affairs. Nobody did. Hell, not even Major Bedford. It wasn't the real war. The real war was fought like all real wars, by killing people as rapidly as possible.

Major Bedford understood now that he was on his own to make whatever career points he could out of this foolish job. It was a depressing proposal, and depression came easy to Major Bedford. Only by comparing his lot in life with that of less fortunate and lower-ranking people could he rise each morning and go to work.

But he did rise each morning. He was awakened regularly by a small bell that hung over his bed which Thi Tuan rang by means of a string that ran out to the hall through a hole in the wall. Thi Tuan was completely reliable. Thi Tuan would keep ringing until Major Bedford was completely awake and had grunted his permission to stop.

• • •

On the day after Lieutenant Stevenson found out the secret of Lieutenant Toomey, Major Bedford was awakened by the bell. His clock said ten minutes after two, but his watch said five thirty-five. The generator had failed in the night. He was on time, thanks to the reliability of Thi Tuan, which was in turn his own reliability. He rolled into a sitting position and indulged himself in a self-review and planning session as he waited for the blood to equalize itself throughout his body.

From the shelf he took a small stainless steel mirror. The mirror was too small to reflect the entire expanse of his face, but what he could see was enough to show that no miracles had taken place overnight—further confirmation that they never would. It was a round face of much flesh. Virtually no sharp angles, no dramatic chiseled planes, no clefts, no overhangs or promontories —not even clearly defined jowls. The lower line of his face was a firm arc with a slightly protruding chin. His cheeks were round and soft, with a healthy glow nearly as red as a birthmark.

His eyes were dark, but if he tried some of the expressions necessary for a commander—the sadistic arch of the eyebrows, the discerning squint, the quizzical grin, the accusatory fleer, the long-suffering stare into the middle distance—any of these brought his eyes into an Oriental narrowness. He stared at his nose, the nostrils of which flared at just slightly too great an angle outward. He knew that men could go very far in the army on just the right flare of nostril.

In plainer, more painful terms, he did not have a military face, and to be consistent, he did not have a military body. His shoulders were wide but the trunk of his body was thick, and despite heroic bouts of dieting, his stomach would not recede. Appearance was everything. In his solid, round-faced, slow-moving way, he looked like the very thing he must not look like. He looked like a sergeant.

Sergeants, after years of drinking mess hall coffee and eating mess hall food, years of tolerating orderly room boredom, years of swilling beer at fetid NCO clubs, took on a stolid appearance that they maintained with more coffee, heavy food, and beer. He must not look this way.

But what could he do? The only way you could get the army to do what you wanted was to beat it into a corner. He needed something to make him look like he must be promoted. He had to look as if he had been there for the bloody work that protected the nation. Something to show that he had stood where the fulcrum of history groaned between the weights of right and wrong.

Something to show that he had seen all this, because the truth was . . . well, the truth was he hadn't seen any of it.

Perhaps a wound, he thought. *And a Purple Heart medal to wear.*

This wasn't the first time he had thought about this, but so far, the closest he had been to actual combat was the nightly mortar attacks. His closest experience with death was taking a village boy from Nuoc Vang, who had been run over by an American personnel carrier, to Cong Hoa Hospital in Saigon. The boy was crushed and was actually dead when they left in the helicopter, but Major Bedford was uncomfortable about taking the dead body back to the boy's family, so they had continued with the corpse to the hospital.

A Purple Heart would be a visible sign to all that he was a soldier with a history. Not just an overweight major in a dead-end career. And as corrupt as this sounded, Major Bedford thought that really, it was not his fault. He would have been a good soldier if only someone had let him. It was not his choice that he had to posture with starch and medals and so on. He would gladly fight whoever had to be fought. God knew he loved his country; he'd have been a fool not to. *Show me what to do and I will do it,* he thought. *Show me the enemy and I will kill him as fast as you can say Jack Robinson. Never mind the reason why. I just want the goddamn promotion. Why does a man have to beg?*

Perfection would be an injury to the arm or leg, one of the places where people who wrote movies always wounded their heroes, or people they intended to use later in the plot. He reached down and stroked the thick round muscle of his calf. And the feel of the solid muscle in his hand reminded him that there was a difference, a painful difference, between thinking out such a plan and actually going through with it. He would not only have to injure himself, but he would have to do it in the middle of an attack in order to qualify for a medal. Fortunately, the North Vietnamese attacked every night.

But sitting here with the solid, soft white mass of living leg muscle in his hand, he began to wonder. Could he really gash himself? Could he force himself to puncture himself, spurred on by the knowledge that it was a necessary career move, knowing he was only minutes from some of the best medical treatment ever provided to an army in the field?

He imagined himself in a mortar attack, the usual confusion, with dirt and pieces of buildings flying around, himself running for cover, spotting a jagged edge of steel runway planking or a steel post. He would run toward it. He would trip.

The injury would be over in a minute, the flesh parted and the bone exposed, hopefully. But could he do it? This act of throwing oneself against sharp steel would require not the abandon he had originally supposed, but an incalculable amount of self-control. He would have to control the involuntary lurch away from his purpose, let his body fall toward the steel, give fate its direction, and let it take him where it would. It would require exactly what the citations for bravery always said—*a complete disregard for his own personal safety!*

What about a wound to the face?

He took the mirror again and held it before his face. Then, with his other hand, he squeezed the red flesh of his cheek so that a deep crease ran vertically from just below his right eye to his jaw. He squeezed hard for ten seconds and released the flesh. For a few seconds a white track blazed across his cheek, disturbing the rosy symmetry, and down the middle of this mock scar tissue ran a dark red line. What could have done this? A bayonet? A few millimeters higher and he would have lost the eye.

Then the blood rushed back in, pumped by his healthy and well-nourished heart, and the dramatic white streak was lost. The effect was gone, and in its place was the fleshy face of a man whose best attribute was his reliability.

• • •

He had to get going. He knew that his thinking was mad. Perhaps if he let himself go completely he would be visited by the kind of genius that usually accompanies madness. He was suddenly extremely hungry, and there was no time for breakfast.

He got off the bed and put on his robe and shower shoes. He barely had time to shower and shave before the morning briefing. He picked up his toilet kit and stepped out into the narrow hall. At the far end of the hall, Major Ponchuso and Major Daugherty

were talking about arresting village girls from Phuoc Vinh caught whoring on the base.

As he flip-flopped along the boardwalk to the shower, he looked across the mud field and caught sight of Lieutenant Kit leaving in an awkward hurry to prepare for the briefing. For some reason Kit was wearing a helmet, although no mortar attacks ever took place in the morning. Major Bedford wondered if some new intelligence had been received that indicated mortar attacks in the morning. He went through his entire shower with this nagging fear in his mind, when in fact Kit was wearing his helmet only because, as often happened, he couldn't find his hat.

C H A P T E R

E I G H T

THE MORNING BRIEFING

There were two briefings every day—morning and evening. All the information of the past twelve hours was presented—the intelligence, the operations, problems of supplies and logistics, the civil affairs stuff, even news on the chaplain's office. The officers mounted a small, brightly lit dais in the dark theaterlike room in the operations center and addressed the general and the staff.

Outside the operations center was chaos, heat, and dirt; the noise of armored vehicles, trucks, and helicopters; men yelling and things exploding. But inside was air-conditioned order and officers reporting calmly the confusion and violence of the war as if they were discussing the affairs of a corporation. The really interesting information, of course, was about the fighting, collected by Major Dow's intelligence office. Major Dow had given the briefing job to Kit, hoping it would be something Kit could do. So far Kit hadn't screwed up utterly, but he had come close.

Major Bedford, wearing a helmet, was early and hungry. He walked through the communications area on his way to the briefing room. Nobody said anything to him. The only person who greeted him was a strange new lieutenant named Toomey. Lieutenant Toomey was sorting casualty Polaroids, searching for duplicates. The table in front of him was strewn with Polaroids of dead North Vietnamese all puckered with bullet holes.

Lieutenant Toomey's head was shaved very close. He gave Major Bedford a quirky smile, and a loud, nervous, "Morning, SIR!" which Major Bedford was loath to acknowledge. He hurried past to the briefing room and took a chair in the back row.

Major Bedford hated giving his part of the briefing because he thought his own information was boring and tame. All he could report was giving away food and dropping psychological warfare leaflets, all of which was supposed to make the locals love the United States, which gave them food, more than the North Vietnamese, who took food away from them—usually, the same food. In effect, the Americans were feeding their own enemies. Even worse, rather than looking like munificent saviors whose advice and counsel should be heeded, the Americans looked like fools who deserved to be bilked.

"Makes us look like goddamn fools, Bedford!" the general had growled.

"Yes, sir, I suppose so," Major Bedford had agreed, cursing his luck.

"I'd rather be thought a murderer than a fool any day!"

"Yes, sir," said Major Bedford. *It's not my fault,* he thought miserably, but he felt that he was being blamed.

The briefing room was filling up. Major Bedford sat in the rear and went over his information. Today he reported the installation of a rice polishing mill in the village of Phu Trach. The machine was made in Japan, bought with American tax dollars, and would make the Vietnamese rice compete with rice grown in Arkansas, also paid for by American tax dollars, shipped here free. It was staggering nonsense, but what could he do?

He was also trying to get a helicopter outfitted with loudspeakers to play psychological warfare tapes, but he hated to talk about that. The other officers snickered. He would report that church attendance had improved in Phuoc Vinh, which was taken as a sign of a growing confidence in the government. This late in the war, it didn't seem to make much difference. Anyway, the priest had lied, but Major Bedford pretended not to know that, because General Walker was a Catholic. So this would be his report—lies, foolishness, and boredom. Besides which, he looked like a sergeant.

Kit stepped up on the dais now and stood to the left-hand side of the map, with his briefing cards in his hand, awaiting the general's entrance. Lieutenant Stevenson strode through officiously. Major Bedford found himself in contemplation of Kit's physique and manner of leaning against the map. The brilliant lights came down across Kit's face at a steep angle, accentuating his features, making his eyes look deeper and older, at the same angle that would make Major Bedford's jowls look rounder and heavier. Major Bedford stretched his own neck and reached up to feel the layer of fat that went from his chin to his breastbone. His breakfastless stomach rumbled and he felt miserable.

His contemplation continued down Kit's body until he realized, with a sudden start, that he was imagining the inside planes of Kit's thighs, covered with curly blond hair. He was shocked at the path of his thoughts. He put his head down and violently massaged his forehead. He thought of the inside of his own thighs, which he had studied for years in the latrine. They were fat, white, and nearly hairless—in short, disgusting. Good God! Men, soldiers, did not think about the insides of each other's thighs—not, for God's sake, in the middle of a war.

Kit reviewed his briefing cards again, terrified of making an error in a location or a unit name. Major Dow, who liked Kit despite Kit's uselessness, gave him a reassuring smile, just as he did every morning. The briefing cards were arranged by location of each skirmish, from west to east. Behind Kit the map spanned the entire area of operations for the division, from north where

Lieutenant Starret's men had been fighting to the more peaceful areas to the south where the Australians took responsibility. To the far west, the U.S. 17th Division and some ARVN units took over; and to the east, where the notoriously inept U.S. 112th Division and some notoriously cruel Korean units shared the fighting.

Kit's briefing covered all of the contacts with the enemy, the deadly and explosive events that made everything else necessary. The general had liked Kit when he had first met him; Major Dow had noticed that. Kit looked good in a uniform—young, tractable. But he had become so terrified of losing his place, or giving the wrong information, or worst of all, being asked a question. He was afraid of embarrassing himself, but more afraid of embarrassing Major Dow.

The sergeant major came through the door and called everyone to attention. General Walker slumped across the room to the empty chair. Then everyone sat down, and Kit walked forward on the dais.

"Good morning, sir," Kit said.

"Is it?" the general grunted.

"Sir?"

"Nothing. Go on."

The first report was the final figure on an incident the previous day.

"At this location Tuesday, sir," Kit started nervously, "uh . . ." he looked down at the card.

"Tuesday?" the general interrupted.

"Yes, sir, these are the final figures, from the contact Tuesday, here." He touched the map with his pointer.

"Go on."

Kit dreaded interruptions.

"Alpha Company, 1st of the 9th Infantry, made contact with enemy unit of approximately twenty individuals, resulting in a final count of fifteen enemy line one and three line two and no U.S. casualties. Two enemy remanded to MP compound."

A *line one* was a dead soldier; *line twos* were wounded. The general gave a thin smile and held his arm up with a thumbs-up sign. Lieutenant Stevenson leaned forward and smacked his palm with his fist and said, "All right!" Kit knew this was good news and smiled back tentatively, although that was the one thing Major Dow had instructed him specifically not to do.

If he had had more experience, if he had witnessed the hellish events he had just described, he would have been better equipped to follow Major Dow's instructions against smiling, and he certainly would have found Lieutenant Stevenson's words and gesture revolting, as indeed they were.

What had happened was that on Tuesday afternoon, two platoons of Alpha Company had discovered the twenty North Vietnamese sleeping in an overgrown graveyard. They had circled to get between the graveyard and the nearby forest and then begun firing. In the confusion, the North Vietnamese ran, most unarmed, into the rice field nearby, where those who remained standing were shot down. They danced around in the water with their hands above their heads in an attempt to surrender, but no order to cease firing could be heard over the noise. The two who had the presence of mind to play dead remained as prisoners of war in the MP compound.

Kit's next item was a reversal of American luck.

It was the nature of the fighting in Vietnam late in the war to seek the enemy on foot but not to fight him by hand. When an enemy unit was found, the American units would draw back and call in artillery, and only after a murderous barrage would the American infantry go into the enemy area. This attempt to keep American casualties to a politically acceptable level meant that American units were never to hike farther than the guns could reach accurately. The accurate range of the 105-mm howitzers was as much as six miles, and platoon leaders inscribed their maps with the range and azimuth of the battery protecting them. This area, known as the artillery fan, was also known to the enemy, who entered it at considerable risk. The North Vietnamese had great respect for American artillery, which was reasonably accurate and certainly plentiful. There seemed to be no end to the supply of 105-mm shells the Americans would send out to destroy an enemy unit, or a suspected enemy unit, or the rumor of an enemy unit, or just for the hell of it.

But a platoon of the 52nd Infantry had *not* been careful. Two days before, they had sighted three enemy soldiers, who stood and looked at them and then disappeared. Neither the platoon leader nor his sergeant had great experience, but they made up for this lack with a lot of enthusiasm. They moved in the direction of the sighting, but found nothing. The next morning they spotted seven more enemy at a distance away who stood and looked at them and then disappeared. The American unit gave additional chase until they made a third spotting, this time only five soldiers. The platoon leader was beginning to enjoy himself. He urged his men on at a faster rate.

When they had been lured outside the range of their own guns, the North Vietnamese turned on them with mortars. From invisible positions in the forest, but so close that the Americans could hear the thunk of the shot leaving the tube, they fired mortar after mortar. The Americans could not fire back with their rifles to any effect in the underbrush, but the enemy mortars' high arcing trajectory cleared the trees easily.

There were officers in the briefing room who could imagine the interval between hearing the mortar round being fired up and the explosion as much as ten seconds later when it came down. But Major Dow could imagine in greater detail than that. He could see the platoon leader in white panic when the realization of his recklessness dawned on him. He could imagine the frenzied attempts at communication and the pleading for transport and artillery, and the time running out, and more mortars coming down.

It had taken nearly half an hour to get any helicopters up in support, and then the enemy had compounded the trap with a clever deception.

They stopped firing. The platoon leader, who had not been killed, and by this time was crazed with anger and fear, begged for help and for medical evacuation helicopters. Eight of his men were dead and most of the others were seriously wounded. One man had been hit directly with a falling mortar round and had been blown apart.

On the reasonable assumption that the enemy had run out of mortar shells, the men in one helicopter tried to land in the midst of the carnage. They were wrong. Three additional mortar rounds were fired in rapid succession that landed near the ship, knocking it over on its side. Other helicopters armed with rocket artillery were in the area, but the forest was dense, and by this time the daylight was fading. Two of the wounded died on the ground from loss of blood—something that wasn't supposed to happen in this war. Not to Americans, anyway.

Then the confusion and disaster moved into a new league. A second medevac ship attempted to make a landing in the dark. The mortar fire had stopped for nearly an hour, but this was also an intentional pause. In the dark the enemy had moved up into the very area in which they had trapped the Americans, and were able, with rifle fire, from the midst of the dead and wounded, to bring the second helicopter down and kill all of its crew.

The general now sat slumped in his chair and waited for Kit to give him the latest figures on the chaos and destruction. He knew part of the story and realized that the trap had been nearly flawless. He had called the air force to bomb and napalm nearby. The air force didn't like to do this in twilight. They had only the hope that the threat of napalm and the sound of jets would make the North Vietnamese quit for the day.

The scene of the battle, if it could be called a battle, was lit with flares. The general had ordered the air force to abandon its customary caution and send jets with sticks of small bomblets out to ring the area. These crackled through the forest almost as ineffectively as rifle fire, but they were enough to make the enemy quit. And by the light of the flares, two helicopters were able to land and get out the wounded and the dead. Thirteen were dead by that time and nearly all the others were wounded in some way. One had been blinded. The lieutenant was intact but was taken to the hospital in Saigon.

And still the enemy had not left. After the last casualty had been taken off they had returned to set fire to the two helicopters.

Kit now tapped the map with his pointer and described this disaster in the dry terms of the briefing report.

"A platoon of Echo Company, 52nd Infantry, made contact with enemy group of undetermined strength resulting in thirteen U.S. line one, twelve U.S. line two medevac."

A result like this was sad and maddening at the same time. It was inexperience and stupidity, it was youth and inattentiveness, lack of control and insufficient training. It was an American trait —a childish belief that mistakes didn't really matter and that one could always count on some magical extricating power, who was partial to Americans, to intervene at the last minute.

More men were being landed this morning in an area to the north of where the slaughter had taken place. General Walker slumped in his chair, thinking of the cost, not only in human life, but in money. Probably three or four million dollars had been wasted last night. His face fell into an expression of tired helplessness and he looked without focusing at Kit's boots. Everyone waited noiselessly. Kit had read everything on the card and stood waiting for a signal to go to the next incident.

Kit saw something now in the general's face he had never noticed before. He remembered what his father had written, about generals being just like regular people. He saw that his report of all the men getting killed by the mortars had filled the general with true sadness. The general's face had taken on a pitiable sag.

The general looked up at Kit, and Kit, because he suddenly felt responsible for having caused the man what looked like genuine grief, felt sorry for what he had done. Once again, without thinking, but from the very best of intentions—that of comforting his fellowman, regardless of rank—he violated Major Dow's rule about smiling during the briefing. He looked back at the general and gave him a small comforting smile.

There was an immediate altering of the general's expression.

"You think this is funny, Lieutenant?"

His words hit Kit like cold water. The room was dead quiet.

"No. No, sir."

And now Kit smiled in supplication and growing bewilderment. He thought it was anything but funny. How could anyone think he could think that?

The general shifted in his chair and continued.

"Well, I'm glad you find it amusing, Lieutenant. I would think a *combat veteran* like yourself would be able to see the humor here."

"I . . ."

"What would you have done, Lieutenant? Does some masterful tactic occur to you?" His voice was low and even, but rising slowly.

"No. I'm sorry, sir."

"Any more jokes for us today? Any more funny stories? Anything else happen out there that struck you funny?"

"I didn't mean that . . ." he said in a small voice that cracked.

"What *did* you mean, Lieutenant? Tell me. I'd like to know how you can find something amusing in the death of . . ." He paused. "You stupid ass. What do you think this is? What do you think is going on here?"

"Sir . . ."

"You know what your problem is, Lieutenant? You haven't seen this crap up close! Shit! I suppose you have some clever thing you'd do?"

"No, sir."

"I oughta send you home. They'd send me some other fool. God! Goddamn it, Matthew!" the general exploded to Major Dow.

Suddenly he got up and stamped over to the door and through it. Major Dow jumped up and followed. Lieutenant Stevenson followed, and all three went out.

Kit was left on the dais, in the lights, in front of all the assembled officers of the division, without knowing what to do. Echo Company, of the 52nd Mechanized Infantry, was all shot up. Men were dead. A man was blind with a portion of his face blistered away. Three medics had been wounded so seriously in the helicopter crash that they would never walk again. The platoon sergeant had a bullet in his stomach.

The general and Major Dow's conversation could be heard through the open door. Then Major Dow came back into the briefing room alone. He stood in front of Kit and faced the assembly.

"Gentlemen, that's it. We'll continue this evening. Thank you."

The division officers got to their feet and, mumbling and complaining, shuffled out of the briefing room.

Major Dow walked over to his seat to pick up his papers. Kit followed him out and down the hall and into the intelligence office.

In the back row, Major Bedford sat and waited until they were gone. He felt sorry for Kit. He looked at the map, and he could still see, in his mind's eye, the figure of Kit leaning against the western part of the province.

But he caught himself. Once again his thinking was wandering off dangerously to forbidden areas. Once again it had gotten completely out of his control. He looked at his watch and saw that as a result of Kit's screwing up the briefing, he now had nearly an hour to spare. He could still get breakfast.

Lieutenant Stevenson came back through the door on the right and busied himself around the general's chair, looking for something. And from the other door, to the left of the map, another figure entered. It was Lieutenant Toomey.

He watched Lieutenant Toomey saunter over to bother Lieutenant Stevenson. Toomey was thick and muscular and had a bullet-shaped head with close-cut hair. He wore yellow sunglasses and his skin was pale. Stevenson looked at Toomey for a split second, then, acting as unaware as he could reasonably manage, went back to searching the floor beneath the general's chair for something. Lieutenant Toomey rocked on his heels.

"Lieutenant Stevenson," he said, and he smiled his bright, squinty smile at Stevenson, who was now looking directly under the general's chair.

"Go away," said Stevenson back to him.

Toomey wore a pistol belt with a holster and army .45 automatic on his hip.

"Glad I'm not that poor bastard," he said, referring to Kit, rocking back and forth, smiling.

Stevenson returned complete silence, but he had found what he was looking for—the general's pen. He stood.

Lieutenant Toomey continued talking. "I wanted to ask you something, Lieutenant Stevenson. In this area," he pointed to the eastern side of the map, "who's going to move in? I'd like to get assigned there after . . ." He gave Stevenson a squinty, knowing smile. "See this village here? I'd . . ."

Lieutenant Stevenson said nothing. He walked quickly away, toward the general's door.

"Well, but, what's the unit going in there? Stevenson?"

Stevenson was gone.

Lieutenant Toomey stood for a minute and looked at the door, his features working oddly.

Major Bedford stood up as quietly as he could. But the riser creaked and Lieutenant Toomey's head snapped around.

"Major Bedford, sir! Good morning to you, sir!" He took three long steps toward Major Bedford, blocking his way. Major Bedford could not avoid his smile, and he noticed that Toomey's face, in the glare of the lights, had a sick yellowy color.

"Excuse me," said Major Bedford.

"What did you make of the briefing, sir?" asked Toomey, following him toward the door.

"Nothing," Major Bedford said.

He walked as fast as he could past Lieutenant Toomey and out through the crowded operations office. Clerks were cutting orders and typing up operation plans.

At the end of the row of desks General Walker stood, surrounded by three staff officers. The general looked up, saw Major Bedford.

"Major Bedford, a moment," the general said.

Major Bedford stopped, and was suddenly aware that Lieutenant Toomey was pulling up right behind him. The general looked at Major Bedford and then at Lieutenant Toomey.

Major Bedford didn't know what to do. The general looked at both of them as if to say, "Is he with you?" And Lieutenant Toomey stood there as if to say, "I'm with him." And Major Bedford felt miserable.

"Major," said the general, "will you see the priest from Phuoc Vinh?"

"Yes, sir," said Major Bedford. "I'll see him today."

"Good, good. Tell him I want to see him," and with one more strange look at Lieutenant Toomey, he turned back to the three officers. Major Bedford gritted his teeth as he walked on, knowing that Lieutenant Toomey was right behind him.

Toomey followed him all the way to the mess hall. Major Bedford said nothing, but Lieutenant Toomey kept up his side of the conversation with little or no response. Toomey followed him into the mess and down the serving line to the coffee urn. It was too late for breakfast, but there were always doughnuts and corn bread in a flat pan. Major Bedford grabbed some pastry without looking, but as he went to the coffee urn, he found Lieutenant Toomey in front of him.

"Let me get coffee for you, sir. Milk and sugar, am I right, sir?"

It was time to do something about this, Major Bedford decided.

"So," Toomey rattled on as they went toward a table, "in the area south of the river near Mau Than, I would cordon the village. And where would they go? Where? There's only one place. Right? Sir?"

"Go away," Major Bedford said, sighing.

"Right! Across the river, obviously. I mean, they will go right across and we would be waiting for them. And there's no field of fire like a river. Like shooting ducks. Are you a duck hunter, sir? I thought somebody said you were an old duck hunter."

"No. Could you leave me alone?"

"You'd probably be pretty good at it. You must be a pretty good shot, sir."

Maybe, Major Bedford thought, *if I throw hot coffee at him . . .*

"Lieutenant," he said in a tired voice, "I have to do some work now, so if you wouldn't mind getting lost."

"I could accompany you today, sir, when . . ."

"That won't be necessary, Lieutenant."

"Are you sure, sir? Well, if you need any help, be sure to just give me . . ."

"Yes," said Major Bedford, "I'll remember that."

"And if you need help later, sir, I'll be here this afternoon. I'll probably see you at the briefing."

Major Bedford saw the terrible future now.

"Lieutenant," he said, "why are you here?"

"Sir?"

"Why are you always hanging around here? What are you waiting for? What did you do?"

Lieutenant Toomey paused a while and his face worked. His right eyebrow went up at an alarming angle, and his eyes seemed to go out of alignment.

"Well, I was . . . I mean, I am assigned to headquarters for . . . reassignment."

"But what did you do?" Major Bedford said. "Are you waiting for an *award* or something?"

"Award?"

Major Bedford looked at Lieutenant Toomey. For the first time in the last two weeks, the lieutenant avoided his eye.

Lieutenant Toomey was silent.

"Well. Maybe you can tell me later," said Major Bedford, rising, "perhaps sometime soon." He drained his cup. "I'll look forward to it."

He put his dishes on the tray rack and walked through the door, out into the brilliant sunshine, munching his corn bread. And then he turned and looked back at Lieutenant Toomey through the screen door. All he could see was the back of Lieutenant Toomey's bullet-shaped head.

• • •

In the intelligence office, Major Dow was trying to explain to Kit why he should not take the morning's experience personally.

"Just don't worry about this anymore. Shit things happen sometimes. That's all there is to it. So let's just forget all about it and figure out what we're going to do next."

"Maybe he'll send me up to a firebase," Kit said nervously, thinking about playing dead like Lieutenant Starret.

"No. Come on, now, I don't think he'll do that. And so what if he does? Listen, it's great duty out there."

But Kit knew very little about the artillery firebases, except that they were all over the map and that they were attacked every night.

Firebases were built by blowing a hole in the jungle with some large jungle-clearing bombs. Then the engineers airlifted in a few small bulldozers to flatten the space and push up a berm. Then they cut down trees and flew in three or four guns. Then they built bunkers and erected fence and did other improvements. In short, it was miserable, dirty, and very dangerous work. And all the while, the North Vietnamese shot mortars in or rocket grenades, or anything they happened to have. The North Vietnamese also dug up unexploded howitzer shells and turned them into mines. They ringed the entire battery firebase with these mines and other booby traps, so that fairly soon there was no way off the firebase except by helicopter, which they shot at with their new heat-seeking rockets.

The firebases were named for girlfriends and parts of girlfriends. Firebase Touchhole had the worst record. It had been overrun three times, and the stories that came back amazed Kit. Lieutenant Starret told him of being overrun in a midnight raid, and of playing dead while the North Vietnamese walked right over him. Starret had been very drunk when he told this story, but still. Stories like this kept Kit awake at night. He could not fall asleep when he thought about such possibilities. Even when he practiced playing dead in his bed, he could not sleep.

"I'm the one who should be worrying," Major Dow said with his hand on Kit's shoulder. "If you go, he's going to give me what's-his-name for a briefing officer. That weird guy."

"Lieutenant Toomey? He's weird?"

Brisk footsteps came down the hall and Lieutenant Stevenson's head poked around the corner.

"Major Dow? Ah! And the famous performing Lieutenant Christopher."

"What is it, Stevenson?" Major Dow asked in a flat voice.

"Well, General Walker has asked that . . . well, this is awkward. It's like this. The general wants to see you. He's decided something *in re* Lieutenant Christopher."

Lieutenant Stevenson looked at Kit for just a few seconds too long.

"You must have other errands to run, Stevenson," Major Dow said coldly.

"Oh, I do, indeed," Lieutenant Stevenson said with a bright smile, and he withdrew. His quick footsteps went down the hall.

"Well," Major Dow said. "Don't spend any time worrying

about it. Whatever happens, happens. I'll try to see what I can do."

He picked up his hat and his papers and left.

Kit sat alone in the cluttered intelligence office. He found a peanut brittle block on Major Dow's desk and began to eat it, wishing as usual that he were home, that he had someone to talk to, that . . .

"Ah, Lieutenant Christopher!"

Stevenson had appeared again in the door.

"Yes?" Kit said in a sticky voice.

"I nearly forgot," Stevenson said. "You have a letter. A *registered* letter. I did you the favor of picking it up at the post office." He smiled at Kit. "I believe it's from your father."

"Oh," Kit said. "Thank you." He began looking at Stevenson's hands for the letter.

"Ah! No," Stevenson said. "I don't have it with me. It's in my room. You can get it later. Stop on by. Stop by, and I'll have it for you. You know where my room is? Good. At about sixteen hundred hours. I'll be there."

"All right," Kit said, still wondering if he were going to be sent out in the jungle.

"I'll see you at my room then. At sixteen hundred. Right?"

"Yes," Kit said, wondering if he would live through the first month on a firebase.

"Lieutenant? Sixteen hundred is four o'clock, you understand?"

"Okay," Kit said, wondering if he'd make the first week.

Stevenson looked at Kit.

"Lieutenant, that's when Mickey's little hand is on the four, right?"

"What?"

C H A P T E R

N I N E

A PARTNERSHIP

At sixteen hundred hours—
four o'clock in the afternoon—Lieutenant Stevenson was waiting
in his room with Kit's letter, massaging it gently.

At seventeen hundred hours—that is, when Mickey's little
hand was on the five—Stevenson was still waiting. Kit hadn't
showed.

"Idiot!" Stevenson whispered to himself. Stevenson decided he
had waited long enough. He had other things to do. Lots of other
things to do. He didn't have to sit here and wait for that idiot Kit
to show up and open his letter.

He went to the door of the bunker and looked out across the filthy expanse of the base, now a dusty orange sprawl in the receding sunlight. No Kit to be seen.

He held the thick envelope in his hand. There was no doubt of its contents. Curiosity raged throughout his entire body. Obviously, Kit had simply forgotten.

"Idiot!" he whispered again.

• • •

But Kit hadn't forgotten. He knew what the letter was. He had been writing lies to his father. He had tried to write the truth, but then he couldn't, instead writing some pleasant fiction about their real estate venture. He had written all about how well things were going, which they weren't, and about how he was making progress, which he wasn't, and about how he had hired a Vietnamese agent to go to Bien Hoa to see the land they were going to buy, which he hadn't. And now he wished he had never written those things, and was thinking of joining the North Vietnamese Army.

His father simply didn't understand. This wasn't like World War II. The war in the Pacific had simply been the Americans against the Japanese. But here it was the Americans against the North Viets, the Viet Cong, the locals, the National Police, the rotten government, the Buddhists, and, not incidentally, other Americans. The American army didn't get along with the air force. In fact, the army hated the air force, thought them cowards. The air force hated the army right back as dirty and foul. The enlisted men hated the officers. The senior noncoms hated the lower enlisted. Staff officers hated the line officers. Regulars hated the reservists. Flyers hated nonflyers. Combat troops hated the rear. Enlistees hated the draftees, and the draftees hated everyone.

If that weren't enough, in some units, racial hatred made order impossible. Black troops trashed white bunkers. Whites trashed them back. Mess halls were destroyed by fights; orders to stop were completely ignored. The enlisted quarters fell into conditions of such disrepair and squalor that the officers no longer even went near. Graffiti on buildings and vehicles betrayed the

Americans' fractured desperation. Howitzers had "White Power" painted on the barrels. Trucks had raised black fists. Outhouses were scrawled with "White Man's War," which was answered by the unanswerable "Nigger."

In the middle of this, his father wanted him to launch a real estate venture? It was impossible. Impossible. Every morning he decided he would write to his father and tell him so. And every evening he wrote more lies. Because if he had told the truth, things would go back to the way they had always been. He would get no more letters.

So he had to write lies. His father, after ignoring him for years, was asking too much of him. Kit couldn't do these things. There were no days off in the war. It went from day to day without a break. He didn't want to be here. He hadn't wanted to be an officer. He was a terrible officer. He knew it. He couldn't arrange a real estate deal. He couldn't remember the language. He had no head for business. He wanted to go home. He knew what would be in his father's letter. He felt miserable. He hid in the library trailer.

"Ah!" said a voice.

Kit looked up.

"Ah-hah! *There* you are!"

Lieutenant Stevenson had just come in in a gust of hot air, and was standing before him, smiling.

"I just happened to be passing by!"

"Oh," Kit said.

"I thought you were going to stop by my room at sixteen hundred and get your letter."

"Yes, I'm sorry."

"No problem!" Stevenson drew up a chair. "You probably forgot. Hah-hah! Well, guess what! I brought it *with* me. Just thought I *might* run into you."

Stevenson pulled the letter out of his pants pocket.

"And here it is!"

Kit took the envelope listlessly. All along the flap a ragged condition had set in, as if someone had been scratching at it. Little nervous tears, here and there.

"I almost opened it myself by mistake. Hah-hah!" Stevenson said.

"Well . . ." Kit began to put it in his pocket. "Thanks."

"Open it!" Stevenson said, smiling. "I mean, God, aren't you going to open it?"

"It's not important . . ." Kit said.

"Not important! Not important? Hah-hah! It's a registered letter! Of course it's important! Jesus Christ! Come on!"

Kit looked at Stevenson as if seeing him for the first time. Stevenson's smile was bright and demanding.

"No," Kit said. "It's just . . ."

"Open it!"

"All right."

"God, yes, I mean, I signed for it. I troop that thing all over the base looking for you. I'm getting curious. Know what I mean? Hah-hah!"

Stevenson smiled some more.

Kit ran his thumb down the envelope flap and peeled it back.

"It's from your father!" Stevenson observed helpfully.

"Yes."

"A letter from dear old Dad!"

"Yes . . ."

Kit pulled the letter out and unfolded it. Stevenson's face froze.

"Holy Jesus! *Look at that!*"

Inside was money. Quite a bit. A wad of American money in twenty-dollar bills. Many twenties.

Kit dropped them on the table in resignation.

Stevenson gasped, *"Sweet God!* What is this?"

He turned around to see who else was in the trailer. There was just the enlisted clerk.

"My father . . ." Kit began. "He thinks that . . ."

Stevenson picked up the money and began to count.

"Jesus, Mary, and Joseph, and all the ships at— Twenty, forty, sixty . . ."

Kit forced himself to look at the letter.

Dear Son,

I can't begin to tell you how proud we all are. I hope this money reaches you and is enough for you to start paying your man. Everyone I talk to is behind us. These are people who know how things get done in this world. We've opened an operational account here . . .

"Christ! I think there's a grand here!" Stevenson whispered loudly, hunching over the table. *"Did you know this?* What . . ."

"It's my father. He wants me to . . . Oh, I don't know . . ."

"What?! WHAT?!"

"I can't explain. It's too . . ."

Stevenson stared at the letter in Kit's hand, frantic with curiosity. Then he regained control. He moved his chair closer to Kit.

"May I?" he said musically.

He calmly took the letter from Kit and began to read.

As soon as the account is opened, (the neat typing marched across the page) *I will be able to wire funds direct from New York. We have formed a corporation registered in New York with an initial capitalization of three million. There are twelve partners besides your mother and me. I put you in for a share, as well. And of course if you want to let any of your army buddies in on the thing, it's okay with me.*

Only make sure they are people who can keep a secret. This whole idea is only valuable as long as it remains a secret.

Stevenson stopped in shocked amazement and gave Kit an appraising squint. Kit looked at his hands. Stevenson continued reading, now moving his lips.

Remember, Son, there is no time in history like the time right after a war when you are on the winning side. It is the time when the victors make the laws and take what they like.

What fools we were in Japan! Why did we not just annex the whole damn country? Why did we not treat them like the little rats they were? We would now own the entire island of Japan! An entire colony of hardworking little Japs all making things for us. American boys died in the Pacific so their sons could pay money for Japanese cars? I tell you, Son, when I think of it, it makes me so damn mad! We won the war—the entire place should have belonged to us!

But we won't make that mistake in Vietnam, Son, not if you and I have anything to say about it. But we have to act. The war may be over soon. Remember, fortune favors the bold. There are millions to be made.

Stevenson looked up, his eyes like hubcaps.
"What IS all this?"
"I don't know. It's my father's idea . . ." Kit said sadly.
"You don't know?! He says there are MILLIONS to be made. Listen to this!" Stevenson read on:

I'm very impressed with the caliber of man you plan to hire as our agent.

"What agent?"
"I don't know. There's no agent."
"No agent?"
Stevenson's eyes raced through the text.

He sounds like the perfect man-on-the-spot for our operations. We'll make a rich man of him for certain. I'll never forget Eddie St. Thomas, the little Flip who was the first person I hired in the Philippines. I always thought he was a Jap, but there was no way of proving it. Well, son, he's a rich man today, if he's still alive, and all thanks to me. Just like you'll be able to do for your friend in the police force.

"What's all this Philippines stuff?"
"I don't know. My father thinks . . ."
"Who's your friend in the police force?"
"Well . . . Sergeant Xuan. I thought he . . ."
"Jesus!"
Kit fell silent.
Stevenson picked up the wad of money again. He stroked its curious spinachy texture.
"Jesus Christ! A thousand dollars. I haven't seen this stuff in months."
American green money, strange and wonderful, Stevenson

thought, as he looked at the twenty-dollar bills. When you hadn't seen American money for a long time, it had a curious beauty.

"Listen, can I ask you something?" Stevenson said, drawing himself closer, "something personal? I mean, seeing as how we're friends and all?"

"Okay."

"Is your father . . . *rich?*"

"I guess so."

"Lieutenant Christopher," Stevenson said slowly, looking at the money, "I think you had better tell me everything."

And so Kit told Stevenson everything. All about the real estate consortium. All about Mr. Christopher's triumph in the Philippines and his grandiose plans for Vietnam. All about the partners back in Connecticut who were putting up money to buy Saigon real estate out from under the war refugees to build shopping centers and golf courses for Japanese businessmen after the war. All about the millions to be made when the price of land in Saigon went through the roof after the armistice.

Stevenson listened, staring at the money, studying the intricate engraving. "THE UNITED STATES OF AMERICA" it said across the top of the bill. Powerful words. Wonderful money. Of course, buying Saigon made sense. Of course, the price of land would go through the roof. Of course, Japanese businessmen would want to come to Saigon and play golf. Of course, there were millions to be made. That's what the war was about. Stevenson was lost in the future.

"But . . ." Kit paused.

"But what?"

"But, I don't know."

"If you say 'I don't know' again I'm going to smack you. *What is wrong with you?*"

"I can't do this. It's impossible. My father is just . . ."

"What?"

"He doesn't understand. I've written all kinds of stuff back to him. Now, I don't know what to write."

"What? Tell him everything's fine! Everything's going to be great!"

"I can't . . ."

"What do you mean, we can't. Of course we can!"

"We?"

"Look, you've told me everything, right? And don't you feel better?"

Kit thought a moment. Actually, he did feel better.

"Well, yes . . ."

"See? You were just lonely before. You needed help. You needed a *partner*. Someone you could *trust.*"

"Yes, well." And he did feel some relief.

"Now," Stevenson said under his breath, "let's get out of here."

Stevenson folded the letter, put it in his pocket, and scooped up the money.

"Listen. I've just had a brainstorm. I'll put this money in my safe. It'll be safe in my safe. Okay?"

Kit stared at him. He felt even more relief.

"Okay. If you don't mind."

"Not at all. You don't want this lying around, you know. It's illegal."

"It is?"

"Of course. You can't have American green in Vietnam. It contributes to inflation," Stevenson explained as they went through the door of the library trailer. "Didn't you know that?"

"No."

"Yes. Absolutely. And we don't want inflation, do we?"

"No."

"Not now, anyway. Not yet."

"No."

"Hah-hah!" said Stevenson. They crossed the street to the operations center.

A mortar fell out of the sky and exploded to the north. It was the time of day for mortars. Kit froze.

Stevenson, oblivious to the mortar, put his arm around Kit's shoulder.

"HAH-HAH!" he said.

And his laughter rolled out to dare the incoming mortars.

CHAPTER

TEN

POLAROIDS

Starret had run out of money again. He had been playing cards with his men—the few who had survived the overrunning of Firebase Touchhole—and they had cleaned him out, the bastards. He needed some more to drink to while away the hours on stand-down. He wanted them to give him some of his money back. He threatened to turn them in for playing dead on Touchhole. They threatened to turn him in for the same thing. Real bastards. He went through his meager horde of possessions, looking for something to sell.

He had sold his radio to Sergeant Matthews and his stereo to the jerk lieutenant who ran the ammunition dump. No one wanted his camera, a piece of junk he had brought from the States. Everyone else was buying new Japanese stuff from Hong Kong. But now Starret had no money, not even enough to buy film. Or beer. His pay went home to his wife. He was broke in the middle of a war. His most salable possessions were two Chinese pistols. They were pretty rusty, but they might bring a fair price.

He tried a sale to Major Bedford in the civil affairs office. Major Bedford was working on a request for a loudspeaker system that would be installed on a helicopter. Psychological appeals would then be made over enemy territory, urging the North Vietnamese to surrender before they won the war or something.

"So, you wanna buy a Chinese pistol, Major? You can take it home as a war trophy." He put the pistol on the table.

"You've been out in the jungle," Major Bedford said, interrupting his pistol sales pitch. "Do you think this is a good idea?"

"Do I think what is a good idea?"

"If we play psychological warfare tapes over the jungle to make the NVA give up. You think it'll work?"

"Do you want to buy a Chinese pistol?"

"No," said Major Bedford.

"It won't work," said Lieutenant Starret summarily. He picked up the pistol and left.

"Listen," he said to Kit, whom he found in the Officers' Club drowning his morning sorrows in Coke, and whom he wrongly suspected of having money. "Listen, you want to buy a Chinese pistol?"

Kit had great respect for Lieutenant Starret. Starret, while drunk, had told him in confidence what had happened on Touchhole that terrible night. He also told Kit how he had suspected that Kit was at the bottom of the screw-up. But Kit hadn't even been on duty that night. And Starret apologized for having suspected him.

"So, I can sell you this pistol, and you can take it home as a trophy. You can tell everybody you got it off a dead gook. I mean, a dead enemy soldier." He held up one of the pistols, drawing it out of a bag of things he had decided to sell for beer money. The rust was growing around the cylinder. *Dammit*, Starret thought, *the humidity here ruins everything.*

"I don't really have any money until next pay," Kit said.

"You can borrow some. I need some now."

"I don't really want a pistol."

"What? What are you going to take home for a trophy? You know, to show your grandchildren?"

Kit hadn't thought about that. It did seem that he should have something to show somebody. Maybe he should use some of the illegal American money. But his money was in Stevenson's safe.

"How much . . ." he asked Starret vaguely.

"For you, Lieutenant, seeing as how I held such unjust opinions of you for so long, and seeing as how it wasn't your fault, and seeing as how I told a lot of people that you were responsible for getting me damn near killed, and seeing as how I'd like to make it up to you . . . uh . . . fifty dollars."

Which wasn't a bad price. Down at the air force base in Bien Hoa, air force colonels would pay two hundred for something they could claim they had taken off a dead enemy soldier. The air force never got near enough to any dead enemy soldiers to take any weapons. They had to pay through the nose to get war trophies from the infantry. But, as Major Dow observed, life was unfair even in the air force.

"I don't have fifty dollars," Kit said, hating to be the source of disappointment. "To tell you the truth, I only have five dollars."

"Shit, I've gotta get some money," Starret fumed to himself. His credit at the Officers' Club was dead.

"I'll lend you the five dollars," Kit said.

Starret looked at him.

"You will? No. I couldn't take it. Here!" He fished out his camera. "Take this for five dollars. It's a great camera. A Kodak!!"

"No, just take the five bucks," Kit said, handing it to him.

Starret held the money, a damp piece of military scrip with the engraving of two spacemen floating in space. "You're right. This camera is a piece of shit." He threw it across the room. It smashed against the wall.

"What's that?" Kit said, noticing something in Starret's bag.

"What?" Starret asked.

"That," Kit said, and drew out a plastic snowstorm globe.

"Oh, Jesus, that. You want that? My daughter sent that to me. Look at that. Snow."

Kit shook the globe and the snowflakes swirled up around a figure of a snowman and a Christmas tree.

"I'd sure like to see some snow," he said, and thought of snow, so peaceful, so far away, so cold, so clean, so everything Phuoc Vinh was not.

"I know," Starret said.

Kit looked at it wistfully. Starret said:

"Jesus, my daughter sent that to me. I couldn't sell it."

"Oh, I understand . . ."

"Twenty bucks. Five now."

Kit felt silly.

"No, I was just . . ."

"Sold! Gimme the five."

Kit protested a few times, but finally took the snowstorm globe and stuck it in his pocket.

Starret ordered himself a beer and then another and rapidly went through Kit's five dollars. An hour later he was cadging drinks from some infantry platoon leaders and trading Polaroids. Kit watched.

For years the army had been lying about the number of North Vietnamese it had killed. Lying about the number of enemy killed in a popular war is fine, since it amounts to telling people what they want to hear. But in an unpopular war, such lies are quickly found out. Then they abet the enemy. The TV and newspaper reporters thought the army was lying about everything. If the army had to lie about how many Vietnamese it were killing, it probably wasn't killing enough. The news people had made a big deal out of the false casualty claims. Several journalistic careers were advanced, and several military careers suffered.

But just about then Polaroid had perfected a cheap model of its sixty-second camera. The army bought thousands and issued them to platoon leaders with plenty of film. From then on, every enemy kill reported had to be substantiated with a Polaroid.

It was a grisly business. The location and date of the kill were written on the back and the Polaroids sent up through the chain of command. Kills were reported to company commanders, then collected and sent to battalion, then to brigade, and finally to division. Finally they wound up in Major Dow's office. The Polaroids were filed with the order of battle reports. Any nosy reporters who wanted to shame the army now would be taken to these file cabinets and allowed to peruse the actual living proof of the dead. Few had the stomach for such research, and the issue seemed ended.

Claims of enemy killed went down for a while. But then they began to climb again. The platoon leaders began to take duplicates, triplicates, and so on, and trade them like baseball cards. No one had thought to limit the supply of film.

Kit watched now as Starret and four other infantry platoon leaders traded Polaroids.

"You got this guy?" Starret held up a picture of a dead body lying in the grass with the front of his shirt saturated with blood. The man's eyes were open.

The others looked at the one Starret held and checked through their stacks of dead.

"I got him," said one.

"I got him," said another.

"Hold it. Guy with eyes open?" said a third. "I don't got him."

Starret flipped this third officer a copy of the picture he was missing, and said: "Where's the other one? The guy stuck in the hole?"

"You don't have him?"

"No," Starret said, checking through his stack.

"Shit, I don't got another one of him," said the officer. "I guess I ran out of film."

"Shit," said Starret. "Then you gotta buy me a beer."

The Polaroid system to keep perfect accountability of enemy dead was a failure. Even Kit could see that from where he sat at the table. The problem was that all Vietnamese look pretty much alike to Americans, and they look even more alike after they're dead.

Major Dow put out a disposition form to commanders, warning that the filing of duplicate enemy dead Polaroids would be treated as a falsification of kill reports. He even tried to take the matter seriously. But one twisted body half naked in the grass with bullet puckers all over it looks pretty much like another. Unless there's something else to distinguish it.

"Hey, you know what?" one of the platoon officers said to Starret.

"What?"

"Look at this one."

"What about it?"

"See this?" he pointed to a chest wound.

"What's the matter with him?"

"Look at that."

Starret leaned beerily over.

"Do I have a copy of that one?"

"It ain't a *him*, that's what's wrong with him."

"It's a him. Fuckaya talkin' about?"

"I'm tellin' you, that ain't a bullet hole. That's a nipple."

Starret squinted.

"Really?"

"Really."

"He's right."

"That's a tit. I'm telling you. It's a *her*."

Starret went through his Polaroids. He pulled out his picture of the corpse in question. The others studied their copies. Kit didn't have a copy so he had to look on with Starret.

"Hmmm, I don't know," Starret said.

"I'm tellin' you. It ain't much of a tit, but it's a tit."

"Maybe she's a nurse."

"Shit."

"What?"

"What? We don't shoot nurses."

They looked at each other.

"All right, pitch that one," Starret said and ripped his picture into small pieces. Some of the others did the same. But not all. One lieutenant objected.

"You're crazy. What are you ripping them up for?"

"You can't turn in dead nurses," Starret explained.

"I know," said the other, "but them pictures would be worth some money over at the air force."

Starret's face clouded as he realized the truth of this.

"Dammit!" he swore. "Shit! I forgot."

"I'll bet twenty bucks!" said the other lieutenant. "You know how sick those guys are."

"Shit!" Starret hit the table. "Goddamn it!"

"A dead nurse. Twenty bucks, at least!"

"Shit, man, fifty bucks like this!"

"How could I forget like that?!" Starret went on. "God! What a fool I am!"

C H A P T E R

E L E V E N

FATHER TRAN

Major Bedford's driver was
Sergeant Swanson, who never said more than was absolutely necessary.

Swanson had been in the army thirteen years, and all he had
ever done was drive vehicles. First it had been trucks; now it was
jeeps for officers. He didn't read. He didn't listen to the radio.
During his time between driving assignments, he sat still in a
chair in Major Bedford's civil affairs office and waited.

Over the years, Major Bedford had made a private, inexact
study of odd cases in the army for the purpose of comparing
them to himself. Men like Sergeant Swanson had struck a bargain

with the army—a bargain of minimums. Swanson expected both
to give and get the minimum, and if he had been offered more
money, he probably would have turned it back in, figuring the
army was trying to trick him. When Major Bedford considered
his own messy little ambitions—how he struggled for recognition
to advance to the rank of lieutenant colonel, for no other purpose
than to avoid the shame of being heaved out as a major—he
found Swanson's approach to rank intriguing. Maybe Swanson
had the right idea.

• • •

The jeep jumped and clattered through downtown Phuoc
Vinh, bouncing along, followed by its own dust cloud across the
field to the front of the Catholic Church. Sergeant Swanson
brought the jeep to an abrupt stop. The dust cloud continued on
gracefully without them.

Major Bedford got out of the jeep and stretched his back muscles. He looked up at the church for some minutes, trying to
decipher its message. The Phuoc Vinh Catholic Church was one
of humanity's more inexplicable attempts to put its faith into
architecture. It looked like Cardinal Cushing had opened a cus-
tard stand. Father Tran's battered red Honda 90 leaned up
against the front door.

"I'll be a few minutes," he said to Swanson, who said nothing.

The sides of the church roof were steep and made of roofing
steel. Inside the temperature was enough to bake bread, and Major Bedford immediately felt the perspiration start down his
back. There were signs in Vietnamese on the wall, and the cast
plaster statues were decorated with beads and pieces of fabric. A
row of about seven candles ran across the front of the altar.
Behind the altar, there was a crèche sheltering a white plastic
baby Jesus doll in a bed of red velvet.

Major Bedford stood in the hot darkness of the church, smelling the petroleum smell of the candles. It was rumored that the
North Vietnamese used this church as a post office.

"Hello?" he said loudly, unsnapping the strap on his pistol.
"Anybody here?"

He waited.

"Hello?"

No one answered.

When he was back home, his wife pestered him every Sunday, and he went to church only under protest. But he wondered now if God would take a greater interest in churches in a war zone, in a poor country, than He did in, for example, churches back home in California. The church his wife made him attend in California was a huge, expensive, glistening building with a sweeping roof and modern steeple that floated in a glittering sea of parked cars. The people who worshiped there would never have been able to get any serious worshiping done here in Phuoc Vinh. It was too hot, for one thing. His wife would have been very uncomfortable. Her church, the name of which he couldn't remember, was air-conditioned to a deliciously cool sleeping temperature.

Above him in the darkness, hundreds of tiny lights twinkled, like the stars in the heavens—a wonderful effect caused by bullet holes in the tin roofing. The flickering candlelight cast moving shadows against the back of the altar. The baby Jesus doll lay on its back, and the shadows of its little plastic fingers waved on the wall like seaweed.

Father Tran must be around somewhere, he thought. He sat down in the front row of little chairs. The heat made him woozy.

What I want, he said to God solemnly, *is to hear someone call me Colonel Bedford. Somebody like . . .* and Kit's face appeared in his thoughts. He shook his head. He couldn't think about Kit. He had a career to think of. *What I want is for more lieutenant colonels to get killed so the army has to promote majors.* Wait. You can't pray for that. On the other hand, the war will go on and someone has to be killed. Why not lieutenant colonels? Someone has to do it.

The dark heat radiated from the sloping steel walls of the church. He sat baking like a potato. His fatigue blouse was soaked in perspiration.

Why was everything in life so difficult? People tried so hard. They worked and slaved all their lives. They fought for things—for land they couldn't possess, for ideas they barely understood. They went out and got wounded and killed following the orders of people they didn't even know. They blew up homes and towns.

They ruined the land and wasted one another's irreplaceable time. They ruined the lives of their children and their enemies' children. Nearly everything they did wound up worthless, hopeless trash, cast aside, forgotten, no matter how hard they tried to do the right thing. And they died, forgotten by the hordes of other people trying to do the same.

All this under the eyes of God, Major Bedford thought. *God, who looks down here, as in California. Or maybe not as much here.* He looked at the plastic doll for some minutes. Then he closed his eyes and saw Kit reaching out to him, smiling, slender and muscular, and naked, except for a helmet.

Father Tran had come up outside, walking back from the center of Phuoc Vinh with the day's mail and a newspaper. He saw the jeep and he stopped. A wave of fear washed over him.

Well, there was nothing to do but go over to say hello to Sergeant Swanson. Sergeant Swanson looked at him.

"Hello. You are well today?" Father Tran asked in his nearly perfect English.

"I'm okay," Swanson returned loquaciously.

"And can I help you?" asked Father Tran.

"Mmmmm, nope."

"I am just going to make tea. Please come in. Tea is good on a hot day."

"None for me."

"Ah, well, I fear there is no mass until much later today. You are a Catholic?"

"Mmmmm, nope."

"Well, then." Father Tran forced a smile. "Good-bye."

He walked a few steps up the dusty path. Then he stopped and turned back to Swanson.

"You are sure I cannot help you in any way?"

"Nope."

"You are alone?"

"Nope."

"Well, then . . ." He looked at Swanson with a doubting squint.

• • •

Father Tran went into the church very slowly, not wanting to be surprised or surprise anyone. He could never be sure who might have entered the church and be hiding in the shadows. Inside the door he stopped.

The Viet Cong and the North Vietnamese had used his church for many purposes. Sometimes they hid here, left guns and ammunition here, or caches of rice and other food. Sometimes they posted orders under the seats. Sometimes they even brought unwanted babies here for the priest to find homes for—babies that were half dead and would have died for certain if kept out in the jungle. And babies of the South Vietnamese army troops sometimes stayed here, even with the babies of the North Vietnamese.

He scanned the church as his eyes grew accustomed to the gloom. He stopped. He saw that the person sitting in the front row was a large man, which meant it was an American. First he was afraid it might be General Walker, but no. Father Tran knew Major Bedford, from whom he had gotten rice and cooking oil. Now he recognized his form in the dim light, but he wasn't sure he remembered his name correctly. He had never thought that this man, who had so much to give away, would need the relief of prayer.

He crossed himself and sat down quietly next to Major Bedford.

"You must forgive me, *dai-ta*, " he said softly, not sure of Major Bedford's rank, and erring on the side of promotion. "You must forgive that I was not here to meet you."

Major Bedford's stomach rose and fell rhythmically. His hand twitched.

"You must forgive me that I have never thought to ask you to pray here in my church," Father Tran continued.

Major Bedford was dreaming.

It was a horrible nightmare. He had been found out. He had been caught. He was being forced to work in a mess hall. He was forced to cook and serve food to other officers he knew, who now ridiculed him. Stevenson was there making fun of him, and even Kit was there laughing at him, and . . .

He woke with a start.

"Jesus!" he said, looking into Father Tran's narrow little face. "Oh, Jesus! Where am I?"

"It is all right," Father Tran assured him. "We will pray, *dai-ta.*"

"Oh, Jesus!"

"It is all right."

"Who . . ."

"It is I, Father Tran. You know me, Colonel Bedford."

Major Bedford realized that it *was* all right. He had not been caught and reduced to the rank of private and did not have to work in the mess hall. Kit was not laughing at him.

"Oh, God!" he said, with such sudden conviction that Father Tran was alarmed. Major Bedford had grabbed his arm.

"We will pray?" Father Tran said hesitantly.

The nightmare of his demotion and shame faded away, leaving him still a major.

"Oh, yes."

And he fell out of the chair and onto his knees.

• • •

Later, as they walked out into the sunshine, he told Father Tran that General Walker wanted him to come to the base.

"I . . . have many things to do," Father Tran said edgily.

"Well," Major Bedford said. "He wanted to see you."

"Ah. Maybe tomorrow."

"Okay."

Father Tran stood in front of the odd church, with the stars that shone inside.

"You do not have a priest there?" he asked.

"I don't know. Maybe we do. I'm not Catholic myself."

"It is nothing," Father Tran said at last. "I will come."

C H A P T E R

T W E L V E

MAJOR DOW

As the afternoons wore on at Phuoc Vinh base toward the end of the dry season, the orange sunlight slanted through the clouds of dust that rose through the day, making them nearly opaque. By five o'clock the atmosphere was thick with smoke and fumes, the stench of diesel, burning shit, incinerated garbage, and other miscellaneous odors and wastes. It was the dying part of the day.

The sun lingered as a sullen red oval mass on the horizon as it has in all wars. The elongated shadows made it difficult, if not impossible, to determine, from a helicopter, who was shooting from the ground. It was a good time to fire mortars at the Americans. The gunship pilots could not see very well to shoot rockets back. The North Vietnamese, who made up in cunning for what they lacked in ordnance, positioned themselves during the day, and as the sun lowered, started their mortar barrages from the forest.

Some evenings they only fired three or four shots at random into the Phuoc Vinh base. Other nights they lofted hundreds of the little pear-shaped 82-mm rounds into the air. There was no way of knowing how long an attack would last. The mortars were aimed at the helicopter pads and the airstrip, but sometimes they fell on the headquarters buildings, sometimes on the main gate, and sometimes on the village. If they had any, the North Vietnamese shot 122-mm rockets into the sky. The 122-mm rockets were made in China, particularly crude but devastating devices that had all the accuracy of a meteor. They carried a canister of explosives about the size of a small wastebasket, with enough power to flatten an entire compound or put a ten-foot hole in a runway.

Mortars were bad, but the rockets were murder. One afternoon a rocket landed nearly half a mile away from Kit. It hit the ground near three empty trucks, making a rushing, punishing, loutish sound. Kit stood shocked, looking around. Seconds later a piece of truck body fell out of the sky near him, which would have killed him if it had hit him.

Kit began looking for a safe place to position himself around four in the afternoon, but that wasn't as easy as it sounded, in part because everyone was doing the same thing. He was usually on duty in the operations center.

"Go get something to eat," Major Dow would suggest, not realizing Kit's terror of the outdoors, "and get me something, too." And Kit would have to walk down the length of the division street to the mess hall in abject fear, pretending that he wasn't worried. It was completely within Major Dow's power to send one of his enlisted clerks. But, Kit thought, what if one of the clerks gets blown up or blinded while he's on his way to get me something to eat? It would be a hard thing to have to live with. He would have gladly skipped the evening meal altogether, but Major Dow liked to eat.

On his fifth week in Phuoc Vinh, he had been caught out in the middle of the street when the first mortar of the evening landed in between two of the enlisted bunkers. The roof of one was lifted up and turned over on the other. Sandbags and lumber flew all over. Two young infantry soldiers came running out in the street, swearing and carrying on. They saw Kit, frozen in place from the blast, staring at the damage to the building. They ran over to him and knocked him down. They grabbed him by his uniform and pulled him across the street to the shelter of the post office, just as additional mortars reached the ground.

Mortars were loud when you were outside. They were very loud. More pieces of building and shreds of screening flew around. Eight or nine more explosions followed in quick succession. An incredible amount of dirt was in the air. Somebody was yelling. Kit was useless, and the infantry sergeants were disgusted with him.

When this attack had been in progress about three minutes, the two howitzer batteries on the east side let loose. The army had a new radar system that supposedly could figure out the source of incoming shells and calculate a target. It was not, however, a very accurate system, and sometimes gave map coordinates that were way off. But some target was better than no target. The artillery batteries let fly fifty or sixty shells into the lowering darkness. The outgoing was louder than the incoming. The earth shook, and Kit pressed himself against the sand-filled barrels that ringed the post office.

"That's our stuff, Lieutenant," said one of the infantry sergeants, in a voice with less respect for authority than normal.

"What?"

"That's our artillery, Lieutenant. They're ain't gonna shell our own fuckin' post office."

• • •

The force and viciousness of incoming mortar bursts and outgoing artillery fire had the effect of destabilizing Kit's sense of up and down. The incoming mortars exploded with a crumbling explosion, like a bat hitting a bag of ice cubes. He felt the force of it in his stomach; it seemed to get in between his joints. Artillery had a crackling sound—a sharp, snapping, treble ripping blast followed by high-pitched rushes of air as the shell raced off into the sky. The batteries fired over and over, perhaps dozens of times, bracketing a target. Kit cringed for the duration of these attacks. He could only wonder what it would be like on the other end, out in the dark jungle, surrounded by deafening eruptions of dirt and water and trees.

He wished he could be like Lieutenant Toomey, who seemed not to hear the explosions, and who always walked around outside during mortar attacks. But Kit was stunned by the experience of explosions. If something exploded near him, he was left immovable for a time. It was very embarrassing.

"Don't worry," Major Dow said. "You don't worry about the explosions you can hear. You hear them and they won't hurt you. See?"

"Yes, but then what about . . ."

"Then you get out of the way. Kit, do I have to explain these things to you? When you hear something explode, you run for it. You dive for cover. You understand? Just like a submarine. Ah-ooh-gah! Dive, Dive, DIVE! *You won't hear the one that kills you!*"

"I won't?"

"No, don't worry. You'll be dead immediately. They come *faster* than sound."

Good God, Major Dow thought to himself, *it's all so obvious.*

"It'll be all over. No problem."

"Really?"

"That's right. One second you'll be alive and the next second you're dead. You're nothing. Poweee! Just pieces. It doesn't even hurt."

He waved his pudgy hands around to describe an explosion.

"You know the expression, 'You'll never know what hit you'? Well, that's what it's like."

"I guess that's what it must be like," Kit said.

"Yes," Major Dow said cheerfully. "Actually, it's not a bad way to go, when you think about it. Unless, of course, something goes wrong."

"Wrong?"

Major Dow's expression darkened.

"Yeah, like you live through it," he said. "That's not too good. That's pretty bad, actually. I mean, you're all blown up but you're still alive, with your ears stickin' out of your ass. Well, let's not think about that."

But Kit was thinking about it.

"Sir?"

"I said we weren't going to think about it."

"Yes, but this isn't exactly the same thing. Do people still do things like . . . uh . . . like they did in the other wars? Do they still jump on grenades? You know, if one comes in a fox-hole?"

Major Dow thought a minute. He had been raised to think that during the Second World War it was pretty much expected procedure that if a German potato masher came rolling into a trench there was a mad rush to jump on the grenade, get your legs blown off, and thereby save your buddies. This idea was based on some facts, to be sure, and he had read the accounts of the Medal of Honor awards in *Reader's Digest*. But in Vietnam he had only heard of one such incident.

"Yes, sometimes they do," he said.

"What happens to them?"

The one story Major Dow had heard wasn't too impressive. An air force clerk-typist had thrown himself on a grenade tossed into a window on Bien Hoa Air Base. What the clerk-typist did *not* know was that the grenade had been tossed by an embittered young black staff sergeant. It was destined for a lieutenant colonel who had interfered with an affair between this young black staff sergeant and a beautiful Vietnamese cleaning maid. The clerk-typist who jumped on the grenade had dislocated his shoulder in the action, but the grenade hadn't gone off because the sergeant had left the pin in place. He had only meant to scare the colonel, who hadn't even been in the room. The operation was a flop all around. The sergeant was convicted by his fingerprints on the side of the grenade, the clerk-typist did not get a Medal of Honor, and the colonel was free of any further interference in his pursuit of the girl.

"The kid did get some sort of medal. He got a Bronze Star, I think. And maybe a promotion."

"But that's not fair," Kit protested. "How did he know the grenade wouldn't go off?"

Major Dow was tired of talking about this.

"Look, Kit, I don't know. If you're in the air force, you have to expect weird things like that. The air force is weird top to bottom. And I have to go see Walker."

"It's weird?"

"Yes. It is. Believe me."

Kit was about to ask if the army was weird, too.

"The army, on the other hand, is not weird," Major Dow said, getting up and crossing to the locker where he kept his own supply of toilet paper. "The army is fucked up. As fucked up as a football bat. But it's not weird."

• • •

That night in his little room in his bunker, Stevenson read all of Mr. Christopher's letters. Kit had given them to him, some of them unread.

"If I'm going to help you," Stevenson told him, with an arm around Kit's shoulder, "I have to know what's going on, don't I?"

"I suppose so," Kit agreed.

"You'll feel better," Stevenson told him.

"Yes, maybe . . ."

And it was true. Kit did feel better.

Honoring his new business partner's privacy, Stevenson skipped over the personal parts of the letters. They were boring, anyway. Mr. Christopher hardly knew his son. There was also a lot of flamboyant stuff about fortune following the flag and the role of the businessman in the conflict. Some of it was a little crazy. And yet, when Stevenson reread all this, it made a kind of sense. Did anyone ever consider the possibility of the United States owning the entire island of Japan, dominating it the way Russia dominated Poland? Good question. Why did we not oc-cupy and keep Japan after the Second World War as a colony making things for us? We won the war, so what did we get for

winning? Why did we let them get away with their freedom? In short, why were we such saps?

You will be like lords in the land, Mr. Christopher had written.

Stevenson liked that. A lord in the land. He liked outranking people. In fact, that was the only thing he liked about the army. But being superior to a few thousand smelly enlisted men was nothing to being a victorious savior to an entire nation.

He took the envelope of American money out of his safe— actually, out from under his mattress—where he was keeping it for Kit. The stack of twenty-dollar bills was soft and leathery, imparting the feel of intrinsic value. The sight and feel of it made him think, with even more longing than usual, of the peaceful hills and winding roads of America; of big, beautiful houses and sedate suburbs and quiet vehicles and the clean, orderly attractiveness of American things and people. He thought of girls— clean, soft, and estrous girls, and how much one could get away with on a weekend in New York City if one had pockets full of money.

The bills were beautiful. Hypnotic. He studied the odd but familiar icons and antique flourishes, the official lettering, "THE UNITED STATES OF AMERICA" on the rippling ribbons and spidery lace, Andrew Jackson with his hair tossed in the wind, his face abnormally long. In Phuoc Vinh, you could forget there actually was a United States of America. And on the other side of the bill was the White House, done in green, a scene of placid Southern charm, rendered so carefully. He held one bill up and peered closer at the little windows in the White House. Behind one of them, he imagined, even at this moment, Richard Nixon was discussing events with his advisers, or perhaps he was plotting politics with his California friends, or upstairs having dinner with his homely wife and his ditzy daughters.

He stared for a time at the money. Slowly, as he concentrated on it, the pile of twenties rose into a misty column to the tens of thousands, to the millions, all from the flat little stack on his desk. Slowly it grew into the kind of fortune that gave men the standing to have universities named after them.

Fortune favors the bold, Mr. Christopher had written.

Yes. There was a tide in the affairs of men. The war would end

and the American speculators and Japanese industrialists would flood in. They would throw money at him. *Vietnam will rise like the Tucson from its ashes,* Mr. Christopher wrote. Think of it!

Obviously, it could be done. He had enough money here. He would hire an interpreter. He would hire Sergeant Xuan away from Major Dow. He would send Sergeant Xuan to Saigon to buy land. He must hurry. The war could end at any moment. Xuan was smart. Xuan would understand. And being smart, he would want to be in on the ground floor with some future lords of the land, even if it were, regrettably, Xuan's own land. That was inevitable. If Xuan were smart enough he would happily agree. After all, Xuan was Vietnamese, and the Vietnamese must be getting good at accepting the inevitable by this time.

He read Mr. Christopher's most recent letter.

"As a result, son, I have decided that as soon as you can arrange it, I will come to Saigon for an on-the-spot inspection of what we are buying.

Stevenson sat bolt upright.

Good God! Obviously, Kit hadn't read this. He'd have filled his fatigues for certain.

It's hard to sell land to people that I haven't even seen. I'm bringing Al Hart, our corporate counsel. Nobody knows more about these real estate syndicates than Al does. He has been so much help in this, you can't imagine. I want him to be there to look over the papers and the deeds or whatever there is. There's nothing like on-the-spot observation.

Jesus! Mr. Christopher would be coming here with what's-his-name the lawyer, right in the middle of the war?!

Al says he can take a trip sometime soon, so let us know as soon as there will be something to do there. We're going to start to get visas as soon as possible . . .

Stevenson sat and thought about what to do.

It was one in the morning again. Zero one hundred hours. There were some muted explosions in the distance, and a soft crackle of machine gun fire. The distance and the cushioning quality of the damp night air made the sounds of explosions and gunfire sound harmless, almost like a child's game. It was one minute after one o'clock in the morning, and somewhere near Phuoc Vinh base, or on it, someone was throwing grenades and shooting.

He pulled off his jungle boots and threw them out the door for the mama-san who polished them. He pulled off his socks, which stank, and his fatigue shirt, which also stank. He pulled off his fatigue trousers and his green underwear. Everything stank. He jammed them in his laundry bag, together with the rest of his clothes from the week, in a large stinking olive green clot.

Buck naked, he flopped down on the bed. He lay there for some minutes thinking about what to do, holding the roll of money in his hand, savoring its smooth leathery surface. He stroked it tenderly.

Magically revived, he rose and sat at his desk.

He took out a piece of stationery and began a letter:

Dear Mr. Christopher,

But there was a problem. There was the problem of Kit. Kit was sort of in the way. He would have to be managed. Walker wanted to send Kit to an artillery firebase where he would as- suredly walk in front of a howitzer and get his head blown off. Then Mr. Christopher would get depressed and the land deal would be off. Well, Stevenson thought, he would have to see to that. Things had to be managed. Anything could be managed.

Business management. That was the key.

You see, he thought, *it's so simple.* This war was like all other wars. It was not about communism or capitalism or any other *ism,* and not about the moral right of the pathetic Vietnamese to self-government. Not about Marx or Jesus or hearts or minds. This war was about the same thing that all other wars had been

about from the beginning of time—wars between men, animals, and even insects. It was about that most fundamental of causes.

It was about real estate.

He took out a fresh piece of stationery and started again:

Dear Father,

C H A P T E R

T H I R T E E N

THE RUBBER PLANTATION

"**I** am moving Lieutenant Toomey," General Walker said to Lieutenant Stevenson. He was studying the chart of troop strength on the wall of his trailer.

"Yes, sir."

"You are one of the three people who knows why."

"Yes, sir."

"I remind you that you are sworn to *forget* why."

"Yes, sir."

"So I can assume that, pursuant to my orders, you have forgotten it already?"

Stevenson paused a moment. The trailer smelled like the old man.

"Forgotten what, sir?"

"Don't push it, Lieutenant."

The chart on the wall showed even fewer Americans left on the base as Vietnamization was forced forward.

"Get rid of what's-his-name," said the general. "Send him to Echo Battery on Armpit. He makes me sick."

"Lieutenant Christopher?"

"Him."

Lieutenant Stevenson frowned at his clipboard. He wrote Christopher to Firebase Armpit.

General Walker looked sideways at Stevenson and rubbed his unshaved wattles. His eyes were red and puffy. He rubbed them, as well.

"Something bothering you, Stevenson?"

"He's a fuck-up, sir. You know that."

"So?"

"He'll get someone killed. And considering . . ."

Stevenson was right. Army unwritten policy was to keep known or suspected fuck-ups at headquarters. It wasn't a very good policy, but it was better than having them out where they could get people killed. But too many people knew about it.

"Where, then? I can't stand him."

"Well, there is one thing, sir."

"What?"

"Well, he speaks Vietnamese, sir."

"So?"

"We might have a need to speak to the Vietnamese."

General Walker looked at Stevenson levelly.

"What the hell for?"

"The National Police. The district. Something like that."

"Shit."

"Civil affairs. Psy ops. Something like that."

"I can't stand civil affairs. I can't stand psy ops."

"And you can't stand Christopher."

"Shit," the general said, wanting a drink.

"Yes, sir," said Stevenson, knowing that he had won.

"Just remember what you're supposed to forget."

"It is erased from my memory."

"Shit," said the general, thinking that it was probably too early to have a drink.

"Sir?"

"I said *shit!*"

Here, sir? Stevenson thought, but did not say.

• • •

Lieutenant Toomey had been in the division seven months. For most of that time he had been in the 4th Battalion of 15th Mechanized Infantry Brigade, a unit known for bloodthirsty sloppiness. The commander, a Colonel Warren, was dead now, but when Toomey joined the battalion, Colonel Warren had just come out of the hospital, where he had been treated for burns to his legs. Warren was a large man who had come up through the ranks. He had been shot down in an observer plane, and when the plane skidded in and caught fire, he had been thrown clear. But his trousers had burned, and he had been in the burn center offshore. When he came back to his command, a feat possible only by ignoring his pain and keeping himself doped up, he was in a mood more murderous than anyone could have imagined. His legs hurt him constantly. He had trouble sleeping and stumbled around most of the day and night in a rage. He harangued his troops in language so flamboyant and vicious that most of them ignored him as a crazy man.

But it's not easy to ignore the commander of an infantry battalion when you are *in* the battalion. Warren's orders, issued vocally and with wild death in his eyes, had to be followed or contended with. There was no reasoning with him. Warren ordered villages burned and buildings knocked down. These orders were tempered by the company commanders. A few buildings would be burned and some brickwork would be demolished. They never burned whole villages. He ordered prisoners brought to his headquarters and questioned in his presence. His executive officer, who had grown to hate him, refused to allow violent treatment of the prisoners, and Warren knew, even in his frenzied thinking, that if he laid a hand on a prisoner, his exec would raise hell, not

because the exec cared about the prisoners, but because he hated Warren. But Warren could scream at them and smash his steel walking stick on the table in front of them. He could swear horrible things at them and show them his burned leg where the blisters still ran.

The 4th Battalion had taken Lieutenant Toomey under its aegis toward the end of the previous rainy season and placed him as a platoon leader in one of its line companies.

Two days later, the battalion started a sweep through three villages in which the CIA had determined, through its secret sources, that there were all manner of Viet Cong leadership. The operation was to start at dark, when it was assumed these leaders would be filtering back into the villages. Colonel Warren was there himself.

In the darkness, most of the operation was lost in confusion. The battalion's wheeled vehicles roared into the center of each village and the tracked vehicles bounded out into the fields around the villages. The theory was that the people they were looking for would be caught in the village or shot while trying to make a run for it. Colonel Warren's burned legs yearned to catch someone.

Lieutenant Toomey was carried along by his men, since he had only the slightest idea of what was going on. But he learned quickly from them. They were all experienced troops, having seen a number of these operations and plenty of killing.

His platoon was not in the lead. More experienced platoon leaders went before him. He and his men followed, entering the village after the main charge. They went house to house with powerful flashlights, escorting the inhabitants—fathers, mothers, old people, terrified children, and squalling babies—out into the street. They then began going through the little houses. They turned beds over, emptied drawers, knocked over kitchen pots and storage boxes, and generally made a mess. This was all done without much system, in an impressively sloppy and cruel manner.

And during all this confusion and uproar, over the rumbling truck engines and the crackle of the radios and the crying of the children and the sound of things being upended, Colonel War-

ren's bellow could be heard in an endless stream of hateful profanity.

"FIND THE BASTARDS. FIND THE SLIMY, SCUMMY
BASTARDS. I WANT THE YELLOW BASTARDS, GET
THEM, DRAG THEM OUT HERE!" and so on and so on, at
the top of his lungs.

The men in Lieutenant Toomey's platoon knew that Warren
was a madman, and although they went through the motions of
the search, their hearts were not firmly behind the disruption of
this village in the middle of the night. Searching villages seldom
turned up anything. Colonel Warren may have been a fearless
warrior of use in another place and another time, but he was not
the kind of man they wanted to follow.

But in spite of the lack of commitment, one Viet Cong was
found. In several of the houses, the searchers discovered tunnels.
Lieutenant Toomey's men discovered a tunnel that only went a
few feet. And at the end of that few feet, they discovered a
slender young man, dressed in black, crouching, holding some
papers. The papers turned out to be aiming charts for mortars in
Chinese, clear enough proof that the young man was up to no
good. He was bound tightly and brought out into the center of
the village and made to stand in the glare of the truck headlights.

Colonel Warren had an ARVN interpreter with him who gave a
malefic oration to the villagers, strutting back and forth in front
of the prisoner. The interpreter held a switch of rice grass in his
hand and whipped the prisoner's face as he passed.

"WHO KNOWS THIS MAN?" he screamed in Vietnamese.
Smack! with the rice grass.

"WHO KNOWS HIS NAME? TELL US NOW!" Smack!

Children cried softly. The truck diesels idled.

Smack! Smack!

"WHOSE HOUSE IS THIS?" screamed the interpreter,
pointing to the house where the prisoner had been found.

Lieutenant Toomey stood by the side of one of the trucks. He
was fascinated by the tension in the air. He bit his lip with every
stroke of the rice grass switch; his facial muscles jerked involun-
tarily. Warren was standing right in back of him.

But this process was going too slowly for Warren. He was tired and angry, and his legs were on fire. He pushed Toomey out of his way and went over to the prisoner.

"YOU HAVE ONE MINUTE!" he roared to the villagers. "TELL THEM!" he yelled at the interpreter. And while the interpreter was screaming, he took his enormous hand and put it around the young man's neck, picking him off the ground. The prisoner, with his hands bound behind his back, struggled and kicked. His bare foot kicked Colonel Warren's burned leg.

"God DAMN you!" he bellowed and threw the young man on the ground hard.

"You SHIT!" he screamed. "YOU YELLOW SHIT!" He drew back and kicked the prisoner with his large black boot, sending him skittering sideways, rolling over and over. Warren came after him, jumped and landed on him with both heels, sinking deep into the prisoner's chest. The thin body absorbed the full blow and rolled slightly out from underneath Warren, who barely regained his balance. He hobbled off, cursing.

On Warren's orders the prisoner was to be brought to the battalion headquarters for questioning. Toomey directed two of his men to pick the prisoner up and put him in the nearest truck. But as they did so they noticed that he was dead.

"What?"

"He's dead, L-T."

"You're sure?"

Toomey's men looked at each other.

"Maybe if you kiss him he'll come back to life, L-T."

Toomey had never seen a dead person before. Not even back in the States.

"Should we take him in anyway, sir?"

Toomey held his flashlight in the man's face. The man's mouth ran blood and other fluids, and his eyes were open and apoplectic. Warren, who weighed over two hundred, had landed on him full force with his heels, crushing his ribs and collapsing his heart. Toomey was surprised at his own curiosity at what had happened to the slender young man who had been standing there alive just minutes before.

"Well . . ."

"He's sure dead. He won't be any use. Warren ain't going to want him now."

• • •

The general had gotten several reports the next day of how the operation had come off, and several renditions of how Colonel Warren had kicked a prisoner to death in the middle of the village. It was a sickening situation. He had made a mistake sending Warren back to his command and he would have to relieve him. But that would take a few days, and other operations were going on that occupied his time.

The 4th Battalion was in the thick of fighting in an area of tunnels and underground hospitals. Warren pushed his men deep into a heavily tunneled area, calling in air strikes uncomfortably close. Lieutenant Toomey could hardly believe the way the ground jumped under his feet from the bombs and how he had to gasp for oxygen after a napalm strike. They had dragged roasted bodies out of the tunnels, some dead, some still alive.

"If they're alive, shoot them!" Warren had said.

"We're to shoot these enemy, if they're still alive," Lieutenant Toomey told his men.

And they had. They shot them all. It seemed a merciful thing to do in certain cases. Some after they were dragged from the hospital tunnels, some while they were still in their earthen beds. The operation went on for a week, during which Lieutenant Toomey lost track of how many men he had seen die. Despite the danger to himself, he felt he was working in the middle of a harvest. The napalm-burned and shell-shocked North Vietnamese they pulled out of the holes and killed were part of a collection they would continue all the way north to the DMZ. And all they had to do was keep it up and the war would finally be won.

He himself had shot only one man, a badly burned young man who crawled out of one of the tunnels, stumbled to his feet, and began to stagger toward him. The man's clothes were in shreds, and Toomey could see the burns on his arms, chest, and face. On his face was an expression of painful wonder, as if to ask, wasn't it bad enough being burned? Was he to be shot, as well?

But Toomey shot him three times before he even had time to

think about what he was doing. The rifle noise was barely audible in all the other noise. The man fell over to the side, and Toomey went quickly on without looking at him further.

In this short period of time his sensibilities had been shocked out of all proportion. He told himself he really didn't know what he was doing. But he wondered if his men had ever been this deep in blood before. Nevertheless, there was a perverse elation that came with all this fighting. He began to understand the overall nature of the operation, the relationship between the use of the various weapons. He saw how the infantry fit into the scheme of overhead bombing and artillery missions. He began to see that despite the confusion and horrendous noise, there was a system to all this. And he began to see that even the death of the men who died made sense. Otherwise, there was no way of measuring success.

He directed his men carefully, but with increasing confidence and aggressiveness. And they obeyed, even though they knew what aggressiveness in lieutenants meant.

Warren thrived on this kind of operation. All the rules were suspended. He lived for the moment, screaming orders, moving his companies about, arriving in the middle of the fighting in his jeep, tongue-lashing his commanders, and all the while, chewing pills to keep the pain in his legs under control. The enemy they found fought desperately, sometimes grenading their own wounded in an attempt to kill Americans.

At one end of the tunnel complex, Toomey's men found a small group of enemy soldiers who held out for a day and a night. Warren took a special interest in this problem, urging Toomey to push his men into the tunnels themselves. He ordered gas grenades thrown into the tunnel, then concussion grenades, and then gas and concussion grenades together, but each time the Americans attempted to enter the tunnel, they were greeted with rifle fire.

In no time this tunnel had become an obsession for Warren. He ordered Toomey to send three men farther in the tunnel with more grenades. The men looked at Toomey as if he were crazy.

First they pretended they didn't hear him.

Then they pretended they didn't understand him.

Then they refused.

Toomey wanted to tell his company commander, but he wasn't there. Then Toomey made a mistake. He told Warren.

"Make them do it, Lieutenant. That's a goddamn ORDER," Warren bellowed, his mouth twisted to the side, and then he left for another part of the battle. Toomey stood and thought about what to do.

He went back and told his men, who were crouched by the side of the logging road that wandered through the tunnel area. There were five of them, experienced troops, who had seen a lot more action than he had.

"It's an order," he said.

"Well, eat the fucking order, L-T," they replied.

Toomey tried to reason with them. Warren would come back, he told them, and would want to know what was going on. He would have to tell him they had refused the order.

"He'll court-martial all of you," Toomey told them.

"And if he tells *you* to go up there, what are you gonna do, L-T?" asked Blackwell, his radio operator.

The opening of the tunnel gaped not thirty yards away. He heard Warren coming back, the jeep motor at full throttle. He saw Warren get out of the jeep and talk for a second to the driver, telling him to radio his location. Warren looked over through the foliage at Toomey's men, who were still crouched there. Warren's face was malice made flesh. Lieutenant Toomey didn't know what he was going to say. In the noise of rifle fire and other explosions he could not think straight. He thought he would say they had tried, or that they were getting ready to try, or something. He left the five men and crouch-walked over to the road.

Warren walked toward him.

Then he took a little hop and stopped, his face cleared, and he fell forward in a heap. The driver jumped out and hugged the ground. Toomey ducked and looked around. But three of Toomey's men stood and came over to inspect.

Warren was still alive so they shot him again in the head.

• • •

There had been five men with Lieutenant Toomey when the killing of Colonel Warren had taken place. Toomey hadn't seen the shot fired, and he hadn't really seen who had shot Warren the second time. Warren's driver hadn't seen the first shot, and he had been under the jeep during the second one. Lieutenant Toomey had wondered if they meant to shoot the driver, as well, and he wondered briefly for his own safety. But Blackwell told him not to worry.

They told the driver to take Warren's body back to the command post where the executive officer was, and one of Toomey's men went back with him. After the jeep had left, Blackwell radioed in that Colonel Warren had been shot, and that they were staying there to see if they could flush out the area where the shots had come from. Then they sat by the side of the road and waited. The order to pull back came half an hour later. It was getting dark, and they had no luck fighting in the dark. Whoever was at the end of the tunnel was spared.

From then on Toomey had lived in a state of awkward intermittent fear. His men, he knew, had shot Warren, and he was just as sure that they would shoot him if he tried to do anything about it. But as the days went on, the shooting of Warren began to make sense to him. His men had acted, he began to think, not out of a sense of self-preservation, but simply because a limit had been reached. If anyone was at fault, it was Warren. Or had been Warren. The events of the past weeks had brought Toomey to the point where he could regard killing as a solution for most annoyances, and regard it even as a reasonable solution.

Blackwell seemed to sense most accurately what Toomey was thinking. Blackwell was black, and taller than Toomey by a head. He was thin and meanly handsome, but his perpetually pursed lips and drooping eyelids gave him a sullen, derisive aspect. Blackwell was in the annoying habit of smiling at him and telling him that everything was all right. He would greet Toomey every morning with the same reassurance.

"How's it going, L-T?"

Lieutenant Toomey would mumble something.

"Good, good, everything's going to be all right. You'll see, L-T. Everything's gonna be fine."

And the death of the hated Warren seemed to fade among all the other death. No one seemed to care very much. Warren had no close friends who cared. That same week another battalion commander had been killed, so it had not seemed like an unlikely occurrence.

The secret, however, didn't go away. It was there among them. Sometimes Lieutenant Toomey wanted to curse out at Blackwell that everything was most certainly not all right, that he was going to turn them all in. He came to hate Blackwell's assurances and attempts to drag him into their crime. His mood in the evening was the most unstable and fearful of all, when he was in camp and had to review orders for his men, or talk to them, or inspect their gear. He began carrying a pistol all day. When they were on base he moved to another part of the officers' bunker without telling anyone.

But Blackwell was right. It was turning out all right. No one seemed to care about Warren. He had been a monstrous man—a crazy, bloody bastard. Warren had killed at least one defenseless man that Toomey knew of—the prisoner in the village—by stomping him to death. And God knew how many other incidents there had been before that. So, the reasoning went, the hell with it. People were getting killed in all sorts of illegal ways in this country. What difference did one more make?

Three weeks went by. Warren's replacement was a younger man named Fox, with a squarish head and gray crew cut hair. Lieutenant Toomey liked Fox. Fox looked like an infantry commander. He was soft-spoken, thoughtful, and intelligent. He planned operations to make the greatest use of artillery and air raids and minimum use of infantry. The sloppiness in the 4th Battalion was brought under control. Orders were written out, plans were followed by the book. Fox stayed behind the action, traveling by helicopter. He didn't wander from skirmish to skirmish as Warren had done. He got along with his executive officer and his noncoms. He got along with everybody.

More men were added to Lieutenant Toomey's platoon. He felt himself getting used to the job. He still wore the pistol nearly all the time, but additional fighting pushed the death of Warren to the rear of his mind.

• • •

Lieutenant Toomey had told the general and Major Dow and Lieutenant Stevenson all about this. He told them how he had become better at his job. He told them how he had gotten so he could give orders that required risk and produced death. He told them everything.

Toomey said that he began to develop an odd affection for the enemy's guns. He began carrying a captured AK-47 in place of the American M-16. The M-16 seemed like a toy, made of light castings and black plastic, a silly thing, prone to jamming and plugging. The AK-47, on the other hand, was heavily built with a scimitar curve to the magazine. It fired larger, heavier bullets— bullets that tumbled along through the air and could knock a man off his feet. The M-16 was made to be easier for the troops to carry in hot weather, but Lieutenant Toomey didn't mind the heavier rifle; in fact, he rather liked it. The Russian rifle felt like something substantial; it felt like a weapon, made to a design based on the task of heavy, brutal killing.

He had bought the AK-47 from a soldier in another platoon, and had spent a great deal of time polishing and oiling it. And thinking about it. He thought about the person in Russia who had made it, and about the last North Vietnamese who had owned it. He stroked it lovingly and coated it religiously with a fine spray of oil every night. After he had the barrel cleaned he would hold it up to the light and view the reflections off the hypnotic spirals inside. He tried to imagine the explosive rush of the powder forcing the bullet along, sliding and rotating under thousands of pounds of force, finally bursting out of the muzzle on a wave of flame. He was transfixed by the chemistry that made gunpowder explode. How could it happen? How could it be a still, gray powder one second and a mass of angrily expanding gases the next? How could the bullet remain in one piece with such power applied to it? You had to slow time down to think of it. It was nothing short of incredible.

And the trajectory of the spinning bullet, racing through the air and coming to rest in a stomach, or a heart, or piercing a skull and lodging in the folds of brain tissue. Splintering bones. Think

of that in slow motion. He was amazed at the way different things from different parts of the world came together in a war. This weapon, for example, made of steel smelted in northern Russia somewhere, worked and manufactured into the various parts of a rifle, carried here over the Trans–Siberian Railroad, then given to a North Vietnamese soldier to use against Americans from the other side of the world. Then the North Vietnamese is captured and the rifle winds up in the hands of Lieutenant Toomey from Illinois, who cleans and oils it and takes it out and shoots another young man from North Vietnam. The young man had been a boy in North Vietnam, and before that a child, and before that a baby, the same way Lieutenant Toomey had been a baby. And all those things were going on leading to the minute when the bullets were borne on the exploding gases out of the barrel of the Russian rifle and through the air, and into the young man from North Vietnam, where it tore apart his heart. Because of a dispute that neither one of them understood or cared about.

Lieutenant Stevenson had written all this down and mailed it to his friend. But there was more.

• • •

The area the 4th Battalion was assigned to patrol seemed to have been cleared of its main body of enemy. Colonel Fox said the North Vietnamese had most probably gone back into the thicker woods north of the Bo Rang rubber plantation. And Fox said the 4th was not going to go and chase them unless they were ordered to do so.

The mahogany forest north of the Bo Rang rubber plantation was old forest. The owners of the plantation would not let the logging trucks get to it for fear they would damage the rubber trees. The parallel rows of towering rubber trees left the road at a right angle, stretching at least a mile before they ran up against the forest. There was a fence between the rubber trees and the forest, but it was as unnecessary as it was ineffectual. The forest was its own protection.

The undergrowth and confusion of fallen trees and branches was extraordinarily dense, a perfect place to hide. Colonel Fox

said that they would find nothing in those woods, not because it wasn't there, but because they would walk right by it.

But the rubber plantation itself was a different situation. The rows were perfectly straight and about twenty feet apart. The crowns of the rubber trees met at the top, screening out all light. At the bottom of each tree were rows of V-shaped scars and a small cup into which the latex dripped. The little collecting wagons, some pulled by donkeys, some motorized, went up and down the rows slowly, ceaselessly, all day. The crews of sad, slow-moving women emptied the cups at the bottom of each tree, and poured the white latex sap into the tank on the wagon. At the end of the day, when the tanks were full, they would begin the long trek back to the processing plant near Bo Rang Village. When night fell, the plantation was deserted and extremely dark, and the North Vietnamese could do whatever they wanted. But to get out they had to cross the plantation.

The manager of the plantation, LaPorte, whose family had worked for Michelin for three generations, bribed the North Vietnamese with food and medicine, even as his father had bribed the Viet Minh, before Dien Bien Phu. LaPorte had also bribed the Saigon government. The word had come from somewhere that no artillery was to be lobbed into the rubber plantation. It had taken fifty years to develop this plantation, and Michelin wasn't about to let it be turned to wreckage if they could help it. The North Vietnamese agreed to leave the trees alone. And the Americans were prevented from shelling it.

But Colonel Fox decided to put squads in the roads between the rubber trees on a twenty-four-hour basis, hoping the North Vietnamese would get hungry enough to reveal themselves. They would have to fight or starve, or so the thinking went. Lieutenant Toomey's platoon and two others were given the western end of the plantation to patrol.

They were dropped off from a convoy of trucks in the late morning. Between the main road and the plantation was a narrow field and then a dirt road for the collecting wagons. Once they had crossed the dirt road they were in the dark, cool tree caverns of the plantation.

Toomey's platoon went into the first row ahead of the other

two platoons, making them closest to the forest. They began moving slowly forward, from row to row. When they came upon the first collecting wagon, the women stopped and stared at them as they went by. Blackwell gave them a little wave, but got nothing in return.

Blackwell came up behind Lieutenant Toomey.

"L-T," he whispered.

"What?"

Toomey was watching the dark line of the forest.

"L-T, look at those rubber bitches. They know what's going on here. That one. She looked at me like dead meat. You see that one there?"

Toomey looked at the woman he pointed to. And she looked directly back at both of them.

Eight rows farther they came upon another wagon, this one behind a small truck. But the women here didn't stop their work, and Blackwell watched them carefully.

"L-T, hold up," he said quietly. "There's somebody under that wagon."

Toomey looked, and there certainly was. A man with a rifle was under the latex collecting wagon they had just passed, doing a not-very-good job of hiding. And as they turned to watch, the man scampered from his hiding place and made for the forest.

Toomey's heart leapt in his chest. He yelled to the four men to his left to go after the scampering figure. Then he sent another four from his right. They began walking back in the direction Toomey pointed, but the man had disappeared. They waited, moving forward cautiously.

Suddenly, the man darted between two trees in a farther row.

"There he goes," Toomey yelled. "See him?"

But they hadn't seen him. Or maybe they had.

"Ah, the hell with it, L-T," Blackwell said beside him. "They ain't never gonna catch that monkey."

"I know right where he is. I saw him."

"Well, the hell with it. It's just one monkey, L-T. Forget it."

"Get over there!" Toomey yelled to the rest of the squad.

"Oh, fuck it," Blackwell said angrily, "the hell with him."

Toomey fastened his eyes on the tree he had last seen the man run to and began running toward it, pointing with his rifle.

"This way," he called. "Right over there."

When he was within two rows of the tree, he hit the ground in the shallow ditch beside the road and motioned the others to do the same. Eight of them lay waiting for the man to make his next move.

They waited for two minutes and nothing happened. The soldier on Toomey's left called to him softly,

"What do we do now, L-T?"

"Move up," Toomey told him. "Go on."

"Move up?" the soldier returned.

"Up to that next row, goddamn it!"

"Which row, L-T?"

Toomey recognized the incipient back-pressure to an order, and it made him furious.

"Move, dammit."

But no one moved.

"Look over there, L-T."

Toomey had made the assumption that the man was alone, and that he had been hiding under the trailer because they had trapped him. He saw that Blackwell had raised his head and was looking around. He was watching the boundary of the plantation where the darkness of the forest started.

"Open your eyes, L-T," said Lawry, the machine gunner, to his right. Along the edge of the woods there was all manner of activity. He could detect at least fifty men moving in the trees, maybe more.

"Let's skedaddle, L-T," Lawry said. "There's a whole bunch in there."

"You move up, Lawry," Toomey told him, and called back to Blackwell, "get up here."

"Move up for what?" Lawry hissed. "We ain't got enough men here," and then he added the universal word of warning: "Sir!"

Blackwell scampered up and threw himself down beside Lieutenant Toomey.

"Call the other platoons, and call battalion," Toomey told him.

The man behind the tree broke for the boundary, from tree to tree, in intermittent runs.

"There he is," Toomey called out, rising to his knees. "Fire!"

In his next run the man was hit by fire from six rifles and gave a brief cry for help. Then he tumbled and lay still. No shots came from the woods, but the silence was considerably altered. Lawry watched the tree line, his eyes wide.

"There's hundreds . . ."

"Let's get out of here, sir," Blackwell said under his breath, "before you do something else stupid."

Toomey turned and looked at him.

"We are not getting out of here."

"They are going to cut us up."

"I told you to radio, now do it."

"I'm not gonna radio. I'm leavin'."

"Blackwell, I'm telling you just one more time."

"We're going to pull back, sir, and we can talk it over in a safe place."

"Talk it over?" Toomey said. "I told you what to do!"

"Pull back!" Lawry called to the men to his right.

Blackwell rolled himself around and got up in a crouching position.

" 'Bye, sir," he said, and ran back to the next row of rubber trees.

Toomey ran after him and caught up in a blind rage. He pushed Blackwell against a rubber tree. The weight of the radio nearly made Blackwell fall over.

"Listen to me," he spat out, holding Blackwell's shirt, "I give the order and you do what I say. Now . . ."

Blackwell pushed him aside. Toomey was shocked. Blackwell ran to the next tree. "Pull back!" he yelled.

The rest of his men scurried back from the road and made for the rubber trees. Toomey was left burning with rage and mortification. He raised his rifle, or rather it seemed to raise itself, and he did what he did not mean to do.

He fired at the retreating Blackwell.

Blackwell's arms went out and he tumbled forward under the weight of the radio.

Toomey stared at him.

He looked around. He saw no one. He took a few steps forward and saw Lawry. Lawry was huddled behind a tree, his machine gun across his knees. He stood up. His eyes widened.

Toomey swung his rifle around at Lawry, but Lawry dived for the next tree. Toomey fired the rest of the clip at the tree, tearing up the bark.

Toomey leaned against a tree and struggled with another clip.

"Lieutenant!" Lawry screamed from behind the tree.

Toomey pulled back the charging handle on the rifle.

"Lieutenant!" Lawry bellowed.

Toomey stepped out in the open.

Lawry threw himself on the ground, and the machine gun clattered before him. He raised the barrel and pulled the trigger. Toomey waited. Lawry hit the top of the gun, pounding it with his fist. He yanked the lever.

Toomey waited. For bullets. For explosions. For a sign. The machine gun was jammed.

From then on the North Vietnamese, watching from the comparative safety of the forest, saw the spectacle of an American lieutenant at war with seven of his own men. Blackwell was killed immediately. Lawry had seen him die. Toomey shot Lawry as he lay on the ground struggling with the M-60. Lawry pounded on the gun and tried to crawl into his helmet at the same time.

Toomey's men would have killed him without doubt if they had all realized at the same time what was going on. But it became apparent to each at a different stage. And Toomey, now crazed with fear that they were all out for his life, was able to kill all seven. Only then did the North Vietnamese come out of the forest and chase the rest of the battalion off the plantation.

The North Vietnamese came running at a slow lope, fifty or sixty men. Fourteen other Americans were killed before they could get out of the rubber trees.

In the afternoon, the battalion came back with armored personnel carriers with machine guns on them and pushed the North Vietnamese back far enough so the dead could be retrieved. The fighting had been intermittent and furious and stupid. The North Vietnamese knew they wouldn't be chased into the woods. They fired rocket grenades and mortars at the armored carriers. They stopped firing only when they feared that the Americans would be driven to the use of napalm, which would have destroyed their hiding spot and violated their agreement with Michelin. Even so, the rubber trees suffered terrible damage.

• • •

The spectacle of a court-martial of an American lieutenant charged with killing eight of his own men would have eclipsed even the celebrated Lieutenant Calley case, which the army had barely survived. Toomey had told them only because he thought they already knew. It was a powerful piece of information. Enough to destroy whatever little support remained back home. It was powerful in many ways, enough to make a man very careful how he used it. It could put an end to the war. It could put an end to real estate deals. It could happen either way.

C H A P T E R

F O U R T E E N

MISS TUYET

Three-quarters of a kilometer from the Phuoc Vinh base, down the road toward Phu Loi, which eventually led to Saigon, was the National Police barracks for Phuoc Vinh. The building was left from the French colonial era, a low structure made of odd-colored brick, with a tile roof. The walls were crusted with mold, and the brick walls that surrounded it were covered with a sickly vine. The main entrance to the yard was glorified with a brick arch supporting a metal sign bearing the shameful legend, "CANH SAT QUOC GIA," The National Police.

The National Police were the most misunderstood unit in all of

South Vietnam, except as they were understood by the North Vietnamese, who understood that they were an autonomous gang of thieves and opportunists answerable to no one. Their daily trade was to govern the flow of traffic throughout the country. And as they did so, they exacted a steady tribute from the long-suffering Vietnamese motoring public. They were called the White Mice because they dressed in white shirts, dark trousers, and white visored hats. Most of their senior officers were local tyrants, like Captain Lam in Nuoc Vang. And like Captain Lam, they tended to be fat and sweaty, two notably non-Vietnamese characteristics.

The National Police generally didn't bother Americans, of whom they had a sullen fear, but they were a cruel annoyance to their own people. Police forces are much more impervious to reform than armies. Major Dow had to deal with the local National Police because they knew Binh Duong Province much better than the army. They knew Phuoc Vinh as only the local leeches can know an area. When dealings came up with the woodcutters, or the farmers, or the merchants, Major Dow called the National Police.

His most recent problem was to stop the supply of rice to enemy troops. The American infantry found that when they were able to surprise an enemy platoon in the jungle enjoying their morning meal, the foodstuffs shot out of their amazed fingers were, more often than not, American grown and processed. Strewn on the enemy campground, or jammed in the enemy packs, or filling the enemy gut were rice, beans, dried meat, and so on all shipped over at American taxpayer expense. It was bad enough that the North Viets made land mines from unexploded American projectiles, that they healed their sick with stolen American medicines, and even ran their radios on stolen American batteries, but when they fed their faces with American food, something had to be done.

North Vietnam discovered that, in supplying their troops, it was far easier to send them south along the arduous Ho Chi Minh Trail carrying American money than the actual food and medicine itself. For American money, the South Vietnamese Army and the National Police happily supplied their enemy from their own plentiful stolen American stores in a program of suicidal greed unmatched in the annals of war.

The food was stolen from depots in Saigon or Long Binh or at Newport, right off the incoming ships, or requisitioned for refugees and then diverted. Tons of American rice were transported to the countryside under the very eyes of the National Police. Thus, when Major Dow wanted to find out what was going on, he went to the only person he trusted in the garrison.

Sergeant Xuan's full name was Nguyen Van Xuan. Xuan was pronounced *swan,* and it meant "spring." He was making a career of the National Police because it kept him out of the South Vietnamese Army. It wasn't hard duty; he spent some time doing regular police work and more time dealing with the Americans. He got along well with the Americans, partly because he spoke English fluently, and partly because he understood what made the American army operate. He could read the American newspapers and follow events back in the States on Armed Forces Television. Major Dow was appreciative of his grasp of American politics.

"Laird is, with all respect, a windbag," Sergeant Xuan would offer respectfully.

"Yes," Major Dow agreed.

"Kissinger is, with all respect, a criminal," he said.

"Well, yes, possibly," Major Dow agreed.

"But Nixon," Sergeant Xuan concluded, "Nixon is a mystery."

• • •

Kit's transfer from being the briefing officer to the lonely depths of Major Bedford's civil affairs office was a sad experience. He was very ashamed.

"I saved your ass," Stevenson told him.

"You did?" Kit said.

"Walker wanted to send you to a firebase."

"I should have gone."

"You can still go," Stevenson said. "I can unsave your ass."

"Uh. No."

"Now, then. Here's what you should write to Pops."

He handed Kit a draft of a letter to Mr. Christopher.

"I never called him *Pops,*" Kit said.

"Yes, well, *whatever the hell* you called him," Stevenson whined.

"Okay."

"See? Here is what we're going to do. Here's a whole list of suggestions you're going to make to Dad. See? We're going to hire somebody."

"Umm-hmm," Kit said, reading Stevenson's letter to his father.

"What about your friend Sergeant Xuan? I mean, we could pay Sergeant Xuan five hundred American. I could send him to Saigon. He speaks French and English. He could negotiate the deal. He could arrange for the lawyer. He does speak French, doesn't he?"

"He does?"

"I think so. You said so."

"I don't know," Kit said.

"You *told* me he spoke French."

"I don't know. I can't speak French."

"Well, do you think five hundred is enough?"

"I don't know."

"You think it's too much?"

"I don't know."

"It's wonderful having you as a partner, you know that?"

"I'm sorry. I . . ."

"Never mind," Stevenson said, preparing to go. Then he stopped. "Oh, and when Dad gets here . . ."

"What?"

"Your father's coming here. Didn't you read that letter?"

"Here?"

"You must have missed that part. Ah, well."

"What do you mean?"

"Well, Dad is coming here."

"What?!"

"He wants to. He's bringing his lawyer. I told him it was fine."

"Here?!"

Another intelligent discussion of business affairs, Stevenson thought.

"See?" Stevenson took the letter and pointed to his own writing. He read: *"So, Dad, we'll be waiting for you. My friend Lieutenant David Stevenson says hello. I don't know what I'd do without him . . ."*

Kit looked at Stevenson, aghast.

"But you can't write that! My father . . ."

"What's wrong now?"

"He can't come *here!*"

"Look!" Stevenson's voice dropped to a level denoting logical seriousness. "Dad was in the Second World War, wasn't he?"

"Yes, but . . ."

"And he lived through it, didn't he?"

"Yes . . ."

"And the Second World War was a hell of a lot worse than this war, wasn't it?"

"Yes."

"I'm not worried. *He's* not worried. *His lawyer* isn't even worried. So what are *you* worrying about?"

"But he's my *father.*"

"You're right." Stevenson's face cleared. "Take out the word *Dad* wherever I used it. Put in *Father.*"

• • •

"Of course, the truth is . . . he's useless," Major Dow advised Major Bedford.

"I see."

"But, what the hell. And harmless."

"That's okay. I don't mind," Major Bedford said.

"You've got to give him something to do."

"I'm sure there's something."

Finally, Major Dow and Major Bedford agreed that Kit should become involved in the plan to stop the flow of stolen rice.

"I'll give him everything we have so far. He can start a file on the project."

"Good," said Major Bedford, happier than he had been in months.

Kit thus became the "Rice Denial Officer" for the entire division. It didn't really mean much except that Kit was responsible for keeping a secret file on the Rice Denial Project. The file had nothing in it, but even that was secret.

The new Rice Denial Officer was briefed by Major Dow.

"Well," said Major Dow, starting the briefing, "there really isn't anything so far," he said, bringing the briefing to a close.

Kit said, "Maybe Sergeant Xuan might . . ."

"Good thinking, Lieutenant."

Kit thought Major Dow was probably making fun of him. He fell silent.

"No, really, Kit, I mean it. That is a good idea."

•   •   •

Sergeant Xuan was a neat, compact man, the most intelligent, confident Vietnamese Kit had yet met. Any fool could get promoted to sergeant in the army, but in the National Police, one needed cunning and a sense of survival.

One had only to look at Xuan to at least feel confident in him. And he was good company, so competent and humorous, so cool and yet full of life, so respectful and yet two steps ahead of everyone else, a family man and yet a man of the world. Kit felt he had known Xuan for years, although it had only been a few weeks.

And Xuan did know something.

A girl in the village of Nuoc Vang had seen something suspicious. Sergeant Xuan had found out about it. She had told someone who had told someone else who had told one of Sergeant Xuan's men. She said she had seen some men who might have been enemy soldiers cross the road three miles south of the village and then recross shortly thereafter, carrying what might have been bags of rice. It might not have been bags of rice, and they might not have been enemy soldiers, and it might not have been three miles. Miss Tuyet wasn't sure. The only thing to do, Sergeant Xuan suggested, was to take her out along the road to see if she recognized the spot.

The suggestion immediately became the plan. The location on the road might be a valuable piece of military intelligence, and they certainly needed some. Sergeant Xuan suggested to Major Dow that he and Kit start out early in the morning so they could

see what they could see before the rain started. The dry season had ended, and there was plentiful rain now every afternoon.

• • •

They had gone in a jeep to the village of Bo Mua very early, and Xuan presented his demands to the girl's father. But the rest of the morning hadn't gone well.

The girl had been on her way to school. She didn't want to go with Kit and Xuan. After some heated discussion, Xuan had been forced (against his natural inclinations, surely) to pick Miss Tuyet up bodily and place her in the back of the jeep. Keeping her there was not an easy task because the jeep had no top, and there was nothing to lash her against. She couldn't have been more than twelve. She called to her father in a childlike, plaintive voice some words of pleading Kit could not understand, but her father turned away. This touched Kit, and he felt momentarily mean. Xuan had to turn from the steering wheel and raise an open hand to her. That had been enough. She kept still.

She remained quiet as they bumped along the road south. Kit turned and gave her his most understanding smile. He saw how young she was, and how pretty, and how terrified. He reached around and gave her a pat on the knee. And then, because he realized that she was only a child and because he liked children, he reached up to pat her on the head. She drew her head back then and made a quick move to bite his hand. But not quick enough.

Sergeant Xuan hit the brakes, and they slid to a stop at the side of the road.

"She thinks we are going to rape her," he said, turning and getting up on his knees in the seat facing her.

"Tell her we aren't," Kit said, and he prepared to listen carefully to what words in Vietnamese Sergeant Xuan would use to convey this delicate negation. Xuan, he knew, was a gentleman and would be tactful and convincing, but Xuan spoke so quickly. Xuan smiled at Kit, a reassuring smile, looked back at the girl. Then, like lightning, he gave her a stinging slap that turned her head.

Kit was surprised. He hadn't expected this. Xuan was still smiling. Kit looked away, and the realization flickered across his mind that this was the first violence he had seen close up in this country.

Miss Tuyet began to whimper quietly. It was still very early in the morning. The fields on either side of the road were green with new growth. In the distance, smoke from the morning fires in Nuoc Vang drifted placidly up into the azure sky. A few clouds were forming in the west where they would grow into monstrous thunderheads by noon. Two small brown birds chased each other through the grass at the side of the road. The muddy water in the puddles and ruts glittered in the sun.

It pained Kit to hear the girl whimpering, but he kept himself from looking at her. He looked sideways at Xuan, who gave him the same reassuring smile. Then, like lightning, he gave the girl another slap in the other direction, a harder slap that raised a row of four welts. She cried aloud. Kit squirmed in his seat. He outranked Xuan, he thought, and if he disapproved he ought to say something. But he waited. Maybe that had been the last slap. Maybe Sergeant Xuan had made his point, and they could drive on now. Maybe this was as hard for Sergeant Xuan as it was for Kit.

"Ask her if we are close to the place," Kit said, hoping it sounded like an order.

Xuan sat back against the wheel with his hands on his hips.

"Do you want me to smack your face apart?" he asked in Vietnamese, too fast for Kit to follow.

Kit tried to understand. He waited for her answer. She should say yes or no, which he would be able to pick up, but she said nothing.

"Ask her again," he ordered, more or less.

"Do you want us to tie you behind the jeep and drag you to death?" Xuan asked in the mercurial southern dialect. This time the girl shook her head and mumbled.

"What did she say?" Kit asked.

"She says she does not know," Xuan said, "but I think she is lying. Don't you think so, *trung-uy?*"

"Well, I . . . ask her if she recognizes anything," he said,

"like a tree or a rock or anything." He looked up and down the road. There were no trees and only a few small rocks.

"Do you want us to leave you naked in the jungle?" Xuan spat out in Vietnamese, raising his voice. The girl cried out and shook her head violently.

Kit looked at her now. Her face was contorted with grief, and she held her fists against her forehead.

"Wait," Kit said. "Tell her we will pay her some money. Tell her I will give her three hundred piastres if she can tell us the place."

Sergeant Xuan smiled appreciatively. He raised his eyebrows in admiration.

"We will fine your father three thousand piastres," he told the girl in Vietnamese, and the words went by so quickly that Kit only caught the three and the piastres. What was the word for hundred? He couldn't remember exactly. This singsong, monosyllabic language was impossible to follow—a frustrating dribble of bits and pieces strung together on a moan.

He would show the girl some money, he thought, and that would demonstrate his good faith. He took out his wallet, but he had no money. He went through his pockets while Xuan watched him. In his shirt pocket he found a candy bar, one of Major Dow's peanut brittle blocks.

"Here," he said. "I'll give this to her." He held out the candy to the girl.

"We will give you rat poison," Xuan told her. She drew back. Her face was red and pitifully swollen, wet with tears and perspiration. She looked at the candy in horror. Kit tried to entreat her with a smile and held the candy close.

"Here," he said, "for you." He smiled more broadly—all children like candy. "It's very good."

The girl began to cough and choke. She put her hands to her throat, then pushed Kit's hand back. Her coughing grew worse, violent and rapid; her eyes looked wildly in all directions.

"Here," he said again. He reached around to pat her on the back, but she ducked away. She tried to stand up and fell toward him. She closed her eyes and screamed, a broken choking scream. In a spasm she knocked the candy away and struck out now, blinded by tears and fear. Her fingers, narrow and clawlike, amazingly strong, with sharp nails, grazed Kit's face, close to his eyes. Now entangled with her struggles, he put one hand over his face and tried to hold her away with the other. He felt her scratch at his face. He swung, catching her on the side of the face with the heel of his palm, knocking her sideways against the antenna mount. She bounced back dazed, eyes closed, with some blood in the corner of her mouth. This last blow, more blunt and substantial than Xuan's, was enough to quiet her. She held her thin little fists in front of her face.

Kit gathered his wits. Xuan had retrieved the peanut brittle from the road. He dusted off the sand and unwrapped it. He stood by the side of the jeep and took a bite.

"We will go on now," he said, smiling and chewing. "Maybe she will see something."

He got back in the jeep.

"Very good candy," he said.

• • •

They drove up and down the five miles between Bo Mua and Nuoc Vang while the monsoon clouds grew overhead. Xuan repeatedly asked Miss Tuyet if she recognized anything, but she shook her head dumbly. Her eyes were swollen, and Kit wondered if she could see anything at all. This mission would end in failure, he became convinced. He would find nothing, no intelligence, nothing to put on the map.

He was painfully ashamed of himself for striking the girl. It was a mean, horrible thing to have done, and he burned with mortification. Xuan had hit her with a purpose, dispassionately, as one strikes a child. But he had swung in confusion and fear. He felt brutal, and he looked down at his hands. They were long, muscled, and heavily proportioned. The girl was so light and thin he might have knocked her head off if he had wanted to. He turned in his seat to look at her.

She was a pitiful sight without doubt. She had been on her way to school that morning, he thought as he watched her nod with the motion of the jeep. She had never expected all this. From nowhere had come a ride and a beating.

There was a canteen of water in the jeep. Kit took out his green handkerchief and moistened it, then wrung it and held it in the wind to cool it. He turned to her. She shrank only a little when he gently began to wipe her face in a manner that begged forgiveness. She let him wipe away the tears and the dirt, not looking up. He gently wiped her cheeks, her forehead, and even more gently, her lips.

Her face was very swollen—one eye had completely closed, and her lip hung loosely on the side Kit had struck. He brushed back her hair with his other hand, and she raised her head and looked at him through one eye. Xuan drove more slowly, watching him.

Kit touched her swollen lip gently. She was still, even in this state, extremely pretty, and when she finally gave him only the faintest smile, his heart dropped. He picked up her limp hand and brought it across his face in a mock slap. He made her hand into a fist and brought it up against his nose. He feigned being punched. Then his theatrically pained expressions softened into a pleading smile, and Miss Tuyet could resist no longer. She succumbed to the appeal of Kit's silliness, and even though her face still hurt, she gave him a crooked grin. Kit kissed her hand and patted her head and saw that he had been forgiven. Xuan, who missed nothing, stepped on the gas, and the wind picked up Miss Tuyet's long black hair.

"She is Catholic," Xuan told Kit as they sped along. "She will tell the priest she was beaten. But do not worry. I will tell them I had to beat her because she tried to bite you."

"No," Kit said quickly. "Tell them what really happened. Tell them . . ." He stopped. Tell who? A priest? What priest? He wasn't worried about the Phuoc Vinh priest. Or should he be? He hadn't even met the priest, and what could a priest do?

"The priest will raise hell," Xuan said. "He will say we tried to rape a village girl."

Kit's uneasiness bloomed into new dread. It would look that way. They had taken a girl from the village, and they would bring her back with her face beaten. What was Xuan smiling about? He was already in trouble. This was a crime. He looked back at the girl. She was happier now, but her face was still marked. If the

priest complained to the army, the general would court-martial him. They would throw the book at him. He was sure of that. The army loved to make trouble for lieutenants.

"Wait," he said, putting his hand on Xuan's arm. "Stop."

Xuan pulled the jeep over. Monstrous clouds lung low, and the air was heavy with the threat of rain.

"Tell her I am very sorry," Kit said, looking at the girl. "Tell her I meant no harm. Tell her we just want her to help us. And we want to help her. Tell her . . ."

"You are an evil girl," Xuan said in rapid Vietnamese. "You want an American husband to take you to U.S.A. We will tell your priest. Then you will never marry. We know your father is VC so you lie to us. We will tell the priest everything."

Miss Tuyet's swollen face fell. She began to mumble and then to sob.

"Tell her we only want to help," Kit said, "and I will give her some money as soon as we get back."

Xuan looked thoughtfully at her. Then he took the girl's hand.

"Ah. We will not tell the priest," he told the girl. "You are a good girl after all. Come here. I will let you drive the jeep. Hurry, before I change my mind."

The girl looked at him in surprise.

"Hurry, you can drive the jeep, but you must hurry."

She looked at the wheel. This was a treat the Vietnamese children prized.

"Come on, then, don't you want to drive?"

Miss Tuyet paused a moment more, then scrambled forward into Xuan's lap and grabbed the wheel.

Xuan pressed on the gas and the motor roared. He let out the clutch with a snap, and the jeep sprang across the yellow road and down the ditch on the other side. Miss Tuyet hadn't the slightest idea of what the steering wheel was for.

Xuan was indeed a genius, Kit thought; he would not be court-martialed, and everything would be fine again. The jeep caromed around off the far side of the ditch and mounted the road at right angles. The girl's knuckles were white on the wheel. She pulled it back and forth, and her teeth clenched as they headed back toward the scene of the almost court-martial and off the road again into a muddy vegetable field. Buried to the hubs, the jeep groaned and strained. Xuan ground the jeep into reverse. He was a genius and there was no doubt about it. The jeep bucked backwards, up onto the road, and they lurched off toward Nuoc Vang at great speed.

Miss Tuyet, like all Vietnamese, loved to drive, even though this was her first time. Xuan kept the jeep at an alarming rate, and her driving skill deteriorated joyfully. It was a good day again. The engine screamed, and then her long black hair flew back into Xuan's face, blinding him. Kit had to grab the wheel a second before they would have plunged into a culvert ditch. She tired of road travel and wanted to go back into the field. She pulled at the wheel, trying to turn off the road at full speed. Kit grabbed the wheel again and pulled it the other way, and Xuan hit the brakes so hard the jeep slid sideways, went up on two wheels, and came crashing back down with a rattle of loose parts. Miss Tuyet laughed, and her laughter was a wonderful sound. Kit laughed because he would not be charged with rape after all. And even Xuan, who usually only smiled, joined in.

Miss Tuyet banged on the wheel. Xuan brought the jeep around then gave it gas. Still in third gear, it bucked and made painful mechanical sounds, but went forward, picking up speed, throwing muddy clumps of the yellow road high in the air.

• • •

It occurred to Kit in the midst of all this hilarity that Miss Tuyet's driving lesson might be clouding the supposed goal of this morning's mission. But she was enjoying herself so much, and after the earlier unpleasantness, they certainly owed her some fun. The significance of the spot of the road where somebody, maybe the enemy, maybe not, may or may not have crossed, bearing whatever they were bearing, to other enemy or whoever the hell it was, all seemed less important than ever. He did not forget about it, he reflected, as they zigzagged down the road, but after all, who really cared?

They would fail in their mission, but it couldn't be helped. It was going to rain and that would put a stop to their search. A few drops fell. Xuan pulled the jeep up under an enormous mahogany

tree by the side of the road. He turned off the engine and began
to talk to the girl in a cheerful and entertaining manner. She had
a sweet little girl's voice, and when she smiled her teeth were
perfect and white. Kit was glad she was enjoying herself, but he
could not understand very much of their conversation. A slight
breeze preceded the dark clouds.

Like a hammer, the first wave of the afternoon rain fell and in
seconds they were drenched. Kit's hair streamed down over his
eyes, which Miss Tuyet found very funny. Her black clothing
stuck to her slender body, and her hair ran with water. Kit gave
her his helmet to wear, which she thought was even funnier. She
waggled her head back and forth so the helmet went around like
a top. Sergeant Xuan gave her a mock interrogation.

"You are VC, isn't it true? You are a spy?" he shouted over the
noise of the rain.

She loved wearing Kit's helmet. She was still on Xuan's lap,
and he bounced her up and down so the helmet went at crazy
angles. She laughed in a delightful way. She found it even more
hilarious when Kit began arranging his plastic poncho over her
head, even though she was already soaking wet. Her laughter
became joyful shrieks. Fresh bursts of rain pounded down, roaring through the tree and clattering off the hood of the jeep.
Nearly solid waves of rain brought down leaves and twigs from
above.

Xuan decided he wanted to smoke. He put his head under the
poncho and tried to light a cigarette.

"You are VC, *phai khong?*" Kit shouted at the girl. He held the
poncho up to make a little tent so Xuan could smoke. The girl
threw back her head with laughter, nearly breaking his cigarette.
Xuan pushed her forward against the wheel. She pushed back at
him. Kit watched them, thinking how adept Xuan was, and what
a good, stern father he must be.

Suddenly he saw the cigarette fall out of Xuan's mouth and
Xuan's face contort in pain. Xuan gave a high, short grunt and
arched backward, his eyes protruding, his mouth open in horror.
His hand grasped Kit's arm like a talon, and he fell forward
against the girl's back. The girl laughed and struggled.

A second shot stitched through the windshield, splintering it

into thousands of jagged lines, and two more went into the hood. Kit heard them.

With the strength and skill that is born of panic, Kit pulled the girl from Xuan's lap and threw her sideways out of the jeep, where she, still laughing, danced on one foot off balance and fell sideways into the yellow mud. Xuan collapsed against the wheel. Kit raised one foot against Xuan's hip and pushed frantically. Xuan tumbled out sideways, but his legs tangled over the sidewall of the jeep, his boots caught under the pedals.

Another shot splintered the steering wheel, and bits of black plastic hit Kit's face as he scrambled to the driver's seat. He kicked furiously at Xuan's legs and stamped on the foot starter. The jeep lurched forward and then stopped. He pulled Xuan's legs upward and threw him out of the jeep. He stamped on the starter again. The jeep, still in gear, jumped forward and turned stupidly toward the side of the road. Kit, now floating in terror, wrenched the wheel around and pressed on the gas. The motor roared and the jeep bucked violently. Another shot thudded into the passenger seat, and out of the corner of his eye he saw the girl, now on her feet, blinded by the poncho swaddled around her head, standing in the roaring rain. He ducked forward, attempting to crouch behind the wheel, the engine wailing. He heard nothing but the shots—not the rain, not the motor, not the muffled cries of the girl. Nothing but the pop of the sniper's rifle, which he remembered, like crystal whiteness, quite clearly, Major Dow had told him would not hurt him. The shot that would kill him he would not hear. Nearly blind with rain, he aimed the jeep and drove wildly out into the road.

When he was about a hundred yards from the tree, he swung the jeep around and rolled out of the seat into the mud.

In the downpour he could see the enormous outline of the tree and the tiny figure of the girl standing in the road. Xuan's body had fallen against the tree as if in siesta. The girl stood there waiting, either not understanding or too terrified to know what to do. He watched her walk slowly toward Xuan and then back to the center of the road.

He was soaked and now covered with mud. It was still raining, but not as hard, and Kit did not want it to stop. In the rain,

things seemed less real. His terror had abated, and he lay in the mud behind the jeep, trying to get his breathing under control and to figure out what he should do.

Xuan was dead under the tree, the girl was too stupid or too frightened to know what was happening. And he was lying in the mud in the middle of the road to Nuoc Vang. There were only a few minutes of rain left. When the rain stopped he would have to do something. *They won't shoot her,* he told himself. *She's just a girl. Xuan's the one they wanted. They hate the National Police. And now Xuan's dead, so the thing to do now,* he thought, *is to get back in the jeep and get the hell out of here before the rain stops and they can see to shoot straight.*

He could tell them back at the base that they had been ambushed, that there had been seven or eight enemy. He could tell them that he had exchanged fire or something.

He crawled closer to the jeep so that his head was under the body. The engine was still running. Why had they stopped shooting? Maybe they thought he was dead. Maybe he should play dead, as Lieutenant Starret had done. Maybe they would be coming down for him now. Maybe they wanted to steal the jeep. Maybe their plan was to shoot the drivers of vehicles and then steal the vehicles. That meant they would be coming for him any moment now.

But there was a rifle in the jeep, he remembered, in a clever little rack by the door. He crawled backwards through the squishy mud and reached his arm up for the rifle. It was stuck. In order to get it out he was going to have to sit up. He wasn't going to be able to play dead and get the rifle out, too. This rack wasn't so clever after all. In fact, it did not allow a soldier playing dead under a jeep to arm himself.

The rain was tapering off slightly—a panicking realization. He brought the rifle down to mud level and tried to prepare it for firing. What a stupid, complicated, unwieldly thing an M-16 was, cheaply made like a toy. He struggled with it up on his elbows, pulling the charging lever back to load a round. The little spring-loaded door on the side popped open. He released the lever so that the recoil spring would send the bolt forward. But when he

looked in the little door he saw that the bolt had not completely returned.

He hit the bolt plunger with the heel of his hand. The rifle slid out of his grasp, landing on its side in the mud. Christ! When he turned it over the chamber and the bolt were covered with yellow mud. He pulled on the lever again. This time the bolt returned, ejecting a live round and a quantity of mud. Then it would do no more. He tried to scoop the mud away with his finger, and he hammered on the side of the rifle with his fist. It fell again from his hands; this time, the muzzle dived into the mud. He tried to clear the mud from the flash suppressor. Maybe if he held it up to the rain, the mud would be washed away.

But the rain had trailed off to nothing.

The sun was returning rapidly, and immediately he could feel its warmth. Brilliant rays were coming through the parting clouds. They would come for him now with their rifles that *did* work. They would come walking over to see if he were dead, and they would find out that he certainly wasn't. And then they would shoot him and drag him back into the field.

Steam began to rise immediately from the road. It was horrible to think of being shot here in the middle of the steaming road, here in the steamy, bright sunshine, covered with mud, with a rifle that didn't work. Would they say anything before they shot him? Could he go back to playing dead? Had they seen his struggles? He could jump up and get in the jeep and still make an escape. God! The jeep was still running. If there was a chance at all, it was to get in the jeep and get the hell out of this place. Leave Xuan and the girl.

Jesus! He heard a movement in the road. Footsteps sloshing through the puddles. They were coming for him! It was time to play dead. There was nothing else left to do. He was terrified. He put his head down, slowly, slowly. Right into the mud. Surely that would convince anyone.

Oh, Jesus, and God, too, he thought, *I want to live through this.* I should never have stopped. I should have kept on driving. I didn't want to be here. It wasn't my idea. Let me get through this and I will do anything. This is not the way to die.

Miss Tuyet walked around the corner of the jeep and saw Kit

lying in the mud. He was very still, and his face was in the mud, but she could see, even in her fright, that he was still breathing slightly. He was still alive, but she had no idea how badly he was hurt, and she could not see any blood. She reached down and touched his shoulder lightly. He quivered, but he did not move. She tried to think of what to do. Her brother had looked like this when he had been shot in front of the church in Phuoc Vinh, and they had brought him home to Bo Mua and waited three days for him to die. She must go and tell someone, she thought. She must do what she could to save Kit.

It was miles back to Bo Mua, provided she could even figure out the direction. The sun was getting hot, and the steam was rising from the road in stifling clouds. In either direction it was going to be a long, miserable walk.

She looked again at him lying in the mud in the hot sunshine. She still had his poncho around her shoulders. She took it off and put it over him, to shade him from the sun, the same way they had put a cloth over her brother in Phuoc Vinh. Then she turned and began walking to the south.

When she had gone about fifty yards she heard the jeep motor race, and heard Kit shout to her. She turned and saw the jeep coming at her, with Kit driving and waving, in a wild confused way and covered with mud. He reached out to her and grabbed her arm, pulling her into the jeep. She looked at him in amazement. He noticed the bruise he had given on her face, what seemed like centuries ago. Then he kicked at the gas. The machine bounded forward, and they were off for Bo Mua, splashing through the ruts, driving as never before.

•   •   •

A mile down the road the jeep ran out of gas. Kit made one or two attempts to get it going again, then gave up. He put Miss Tuyet on his shoulders and carried her the rest of the way. As they went along, she tried to explain something to him in Vietnamese.

"The man in the tree," she said, "he told me to go home with you."

By the time they reached the two stubby brick pillars that

marked the village limits, Kit had invented a game he hoped would get Miss Tuyet's mind off the day so far. He allowed Miss Tuyet to steer him like a car by turning his head by the ears.

He set her down on the road just inside the village.

"Well, you are home," he said in his not very fluent Vietnamese. He patted her head. "You are home. *O nha.*" He wanted to tell her that he had brought her home safe, but he couldn't remember the word for *safe.* He remembered the word for *sick.*

"Bi binh, khong?" he asked her.

"Khong," she said, *"khong bi binh.* I am not sick."

"Well, then, *Toi phai di.* I have to go."

He turned to go.

"I hope I see you again."

Miss Tuyet looked at the ground, and finally spoke.

"I have to go to school now," she said.

"What?"

"I have to go to school now."

"Oh, school. Yes."

She turned and began to walk away.

"Good-bye," he called.

She turned back and gave him a slight smile.

"Chao, trung-uy." A silvery little voice.

"Yes," he said, *"chao . . ."*

Kit watched her walk away toward the open pavilion that served as a school and wondered what she would tell them.

Then he started off, back in the roasting sunshine, to the National Police barracks to tell them about Xuan.

CHAPTER

FIFTEEN

SERGEANT XUAN

But Xuan was not dead. Because the sniper had been directly overhead, the bullet had gone into his shoulder and down the right side of his back. He had blacked out from the shock and the pain. When that wore off he had awakened where Kit had thrown him, collapsed against the tree. He had been able to crawl into the middle of the road and then collapsed again. A patrol from his own police found him there. They took him for a bouncy, excruciating ride back to the National Police barracks, where they called the American base to report the disappearance of Kit and the girl.

• • •

Major Dow was in the middle of another disaster. The 1st
Battalion had shot some Phu Trach Village Popular Forces,
thinking they were enemy because they were dressed in black.
They were dressed in black because all villagers dressed in black.

The Popular Forces were tiny local units set up by the South
Vietnamese government. They were paid a little bit and given
guns. And sometimes they organized safe little patrols out around
their own villages. There they were, armed with rifles from America, out patroling the fields around their beloved villages, just like
the minutemen.

But by mistake an American patrol of the 64th Infantry had
killed most of them. The villagers were, after all, villagers. Their
training was negligible. They had no idea what was happening.
After returning a few shots, they lay down and returned no fire.
The Americans warily approached and saw the mistake they had
made.

It wasn't really the Americans' fault. Americans shot at everything these days. The American units were smaller now, and they
were scared. But Major Dow had the problem of determining
what should be done.

In the middle of all this, Major Daugherty delivered the news
that Sergeant Xuan had been shot and that Kit was missing.
Major Dow called the 12th Armored Cavalry Regiment, which
owed him countless favors, and asked for two personnel carriers
to go out and look for Kit. Then he called the Aircraft Company
for a helicopter. He commandeered Sergeant Swanson to drive.

"Want me to go with you?" asked Lieutenant Toomey, who
wasn't allowed to leave the base alone.

"No," said Major Dow. He saw Toomey standing there with a
sandwich and a pistol and his Chinese submachine gun.

"I mean, yes," said Major Dow.

Stevenson walked out into the late afternoon steam.

"Where's Major Dow?" Stevenson asked Sergeant Swanson,
meeting him by his jeep.

Swanson shrugged.

"Where are you going?" Stevenson asked.

"Don't ask me," Swanson said, starting the jeep.

Major Dow came out with a helmet on, which he rarely wore. And a rifle in his hand, which he rarely carried. Toomey was behind him. They climbed into the jeep.

"What's going . . ." Stevenson said.

"I'll be back. Tell the general."

"What?"

"Xuan's shot. Christopher's missing. Go."

Sergeant Swanson gunned the jeep.

"What?!" Stevenson said.

The jeep took off.

"Wait!" Stevenson hollered, running after it, and clambering in. "WAIT!"

The tracked personnel carriers barreled down the muddy road until they came upon Kit's abandoned jeep and his mud-encrusted rifle. Speculation and deduction had reached a fine edge. Sergeant Sill of the 12th ACR was sure Kit had been captured.

"He's probably a prisoner for the rest of the war, sir," Sergeant Sill said.

"Shut up," Major Dow said.

"Sorry, sir, but that's probably what happened. They'll probably drag him back up the trail."

"Sergeant . . ."

"Sorry, sir, but that's what happens. If he don't get malaria and die first. A buddy of mine . . ."

"Just shut up," Major Dow said.

He wanted to send the two personnel carriers out into the fields to search for evidence of a trail, but he knew they wouldn't find anything. He could hear the approach of the helicopter he had asked for. He stood in the steaming sunshine, in the middle of the road, surrounded by the two jeeps and the two carriers, their motors idling, in a fog of humidity and diesel fumes, with the helicopter overhead, buzzing around in circles, looking for something.

"What do you think?" said Lieutenant Stevenson, who had been composing a condolence letter to Kit's father, just in case.

Major Dow thought of Kit as a captive. He pictured Kit being pushed along by the vicious North Vietnamese, perhaps wounded and his wounds untreated, his uniform torn, his hands tied behind his back so that when they pushed him he was off balance and fell forward and then had to struggle to get back on his feet in the awkward way a man with his hands behind his back has to get back up. Major Dow saw Kit's shocked and uncomprehending expression; his disheveled blond hair; his long, gawky physique; his light gray eyes now frightened and pleading.

Sergeant Sill wandered off down the road a little. Lieutenant Toomey wandered with him, thinking about disappearing, something he had been thinking about for some time. He looked down the road. If they organized search patrols now he could just fade away. He wondered how far he could go. Then down the road he saw someone. Damn.

"Hey, look, Major," Sergeant Sill called. "This your man?"

A tall person, with gawky physique, was walking toward them from the direction of Bo Mua, covered head to foot with dried yellow mud.

"Is that him, Major?"

Kit stopped for a second to take in the entire assemblage. He saw Major Dow and waved.

● ● ●

Not until they were in his office, out of the sight of Sergeant Swanson and everyone else, did Major Dow let himself show Kit any of the relief he felt. Then he threw the door shut and grabbed Kit in a violent bear hug. And then he swore at him and called Kit names of such ferocity that Kit was completely confused. Major Dow would have explained, but at that moment Sergeant Swanson barged in with the vehicle trip log for him to sign, and then sat down, immovable, because, in fact, he was assigned to Major Dow for the rest of the afternoon.

● ● ●

Sergeant Xuan was taken to the MASH at Phuoc Vinh base where the doctors, led in their efforts by a Captain Barks, removed the bullet and sewed up the long, torn wound down his back. Captain Barks said Xuan was lucky, nothing serious had

been hit. But because of its length, the wound was an especially painful one, and Xuan had to lie motionless on his stomach. The slightest movement brought an involuntary cry to his lips.

Xuan lay very still and wondered what would happen to his job in the National Police. Things didn't work the same way they did in the American army. A wounded policeman or soldier was not necessarily a hero to be preserved and honored. The living remains of soldiers could be seen, with limbs missing, eyes gone, horrible facial deformities, and the like, wandering aimlessly around Saigon streets begging from the heartless Saigonese, who never gave anything to anybody.

Xuan's career was based on his ability and brains. He knew French, English, Chinese, and some Japanese. He was a useful person, not only in the solving of crimes (on the rare occasion when anyone wanted to solve one), but also in the management of foreign elements. No one was better than Xuan at managing Americans and getting money from them. This, in the eyes of his superiors in the police, was a skill with a future. The greed of his superiors was an unthinking kind. He kept himself out of their most blatant schemes. But someday, he thought, an opportunity would present itself, and he would be able to act with impunity. Such was the nature of war. If you could avoid getting killed or maimed, there were great opportunities.

His immediate superior, Captain Lam, had a career built on sheer cruelty and force. Against such men there was no defense except equally violent and forceful acts. Lam was short, heavy, mean, and greedy, not to be trusted. But in dealing with other people, Lam, barely conversant in his own language, needed Xuan, at least as long as he was healthy. These days there was a purpose to Captain Lam's life, which was to get as much as he could from the Americans before the war was over.

Lam had learned his extortion procedures in the National Police under the French and later under the Dien government. But no times had been as good as the present times. The French had been stingy and the Saigon government was usually broke. But the Americans begged to be robbed. They demanded so little in return. A few patrols up and down the roads, a few roadblocks, a few supposed Viet Cong shot every so often. Lam got vehicles from the Americans; he got small arms and ammunition; he got radios and trucks and uniforms. He got water coolers and generators and electric fans. And if he had wanted air conditioners, he could have gotten them as well, but air conditioners used too much electricity and thus had little resale potential, so he had no use for them. Lam's normal tactic was to demand whatever he wanted, to pound on the table with his stick, and if that didn't work, to punch people. But he couldn't do that with the Americans. He needed Xuan's subtle touch and gentle friendliness, such as one used with children.

"No air conditioner! No goddamn air conditioner!" he screamed at Xuan.

Xuan agreed with him.

"We need more roof metal! Tell them!" Captain Lam screamed.

"All right," said Xuan. "More . . . I will tell them."

Every month, through Xuan, Captain Lam requisitioned a shipment of corrugated roofing steel from Major Bedford's civil affairs office. And every month a truck from the Engineer Battalion showed up at National Police headquarters with a load of the gleaming metal shipped from Wheeling, West Virginia. And from there the metal went into a sales and distribution system known only to Captain Lam. Surely, sooner or later, someone would notice that the National Police had no legitimate use for this stuff, not even for one load in a year. Why did Major Bedford or Major Dow not investigate? Captain Lam was suspicious about this. He suspected Xuan might be skimming money somehow in cahoots with Major Bedford. He had badgered Xuan for an answer. Xuan explained as well as he could.

"They have so much," he said, "that they don't even think about it. They are happy to be giving it to you."

"Ah," said Captain Lam, squinting, not convinced.

"They think they are winning your heart and mind," Xuan told him. To himself he admitted that only the Americans could be so careless as to spend money trying to win two things that obviously did not exist.

But Captain Lam was a man of intricate suspicions. The only safe position in this war was to be on both sides. And that's where he was. Xuan had no doubt that Lam was, if not in league with, at least on terms with, the North Vietnamese. He gave them rice. Xuan had proof. His own eyes had seen Lam turn over bags of American rice to LaPorte, the French manager of the Michelin plantation in Bo Rang, where Lieutenant Toomey had shot his own men. LaPorte, in turn, delivered it to the North Vietnamese in the latex wagons. Xuan had seen the trucks—American five-quarters, loaned to Captain Lam for his patrols—leave the National Police compound, laden with bags of rice from Arkansas, and head out in the middle of the day for the rubber plantation. Captain Lam even had these convoys escorted, front and rear, with machine gun jeeps, which he had also gotten from the Americans, to protect it from raids by . . . whom?

Who, indeed? Even in his pain, lying immovable on his stomach in the hospital bed, Xuan found this amusing. The rice was destined, it was supposed, for hungry refugees from the free fire zones. But it was going to the enemy. No one would try to raid these convoys. The refugees might have, if they had known, and could have run fast enough.

Xuan's first two days in the hospital provided him time to think, although most of the first day he spent worrying. His back felt as if it were split open. He was immovable and helpless. But on the second day the pain subsided a little, and he began to arrange things in an orderly fashion.

The body took a very long time to heal. So quickly ripped apart, so slow to heal. He would be here at the American field hospital until he was well enough to move, perhaps another day or two. Then he would be moved to the military hospital in Saigon, or perhaps the provincial ward in Phu Loi.

• • •

Lieutenant Stevenson made his way to the hospital through the afternoon monsoon on Sergeant Xuan's second day of recuperation. Stevenson's poncho kept him fairly dry on top, but his trousers were soaked from the splashing puddles. He hoped that, in the nearly solid rain, no one would see him. The sound of the deluge on the tin roofs of the buildings was deafening.

He reached the squat, dark brown field hospital and went in-

side. No one was on duty except the nurse, who had the same characteristics as the building, and who looked at him suspiciously.

"You have a Vietnamese police sergeant here?"

"Yes," she said.

"I want to see him right away."

"What for?"

Stevenson tried to see things from the nurse's point of view.

"That's none of your goddamn business, now, is it?"

"You can't see the patient unless the doctor says you can, just like I told the other guys."

"Look, I'm the general's aide. I'm General Walker's aide. I've got to show him these papers." He held up some of the letters from Mr. Christopher.

"Like I told the other guys! Don't you listen? The hospital policy is you gotta see the doctor first," she said. "Why do I have to take all this shit from you people?"

"What other guys?" Stevenson asked warily.

"The police guys," she said. "If they could go find the doctor, so can you."

Stevenson looked around. He saw the door to the ward and went over to look in.

"Hey," the nurse protested, "You can't go in."

"Shut up. I'm just looking."

Through the clouded plastic window he could see, at the far end of the ward, Xuan's bed. And seated at the end of his bed were two Vietnamese in white National Police shirts.

"I'm the general's aide," he said, turning back to her. "I don't have time to go running after doctors. You go find the doctor and send him here."

"I can't leave," she said. "You can't order me around."

"You better move your ass, troop." He looked for her rank. She was a lieutenant, just like he was. Goddamn it! His lord in the land status couldn't come a moment too soon.

But the contentiousness drained from her face.

"I don't care," she said, giving up and turning back to her desk.

Xuan was asleep. Captain Lam and another policeman sat still

at the end of his bed, waiting for him to awaken. They nodded to Stevenson as he approached. Stevenson smiled his tightest smile. Then he pointed slowly at them and to the door.

"You have to go now," he said in a level voice. "Get out."

Captain Lam's eyes narrowed and he looked at the other policeman.

"Out," Stevenson repeated. "Get out."

Captain Lam began to say something in his harsh Vietnamese, but Stevenson held his finger up to his lips.

"I'm a doctor. Doc-tor? And I say get out."

"Bac si," said the smaller policeman. Captain Lam's face went red around his eyes, and he stood up, for a second looking murderously at Stevenson. Then he turned on his heel and strode to the door, with the smaller man in tow.

The rain roared outside with such violence that the spray made its way through the large louvers on the windows. Xuan was feigning sleep. But now a new mystery had arrived. What could the general's aide want with him?

Stevenson began clearing his throat loudly. He moved a chair around to make enough noise to wake the wounded man. Xuan didn't move, even when Stevenson had clattered the two chairs together so loudly that an American sergeant, three beds down, woke up and swore viciously at him to cut out the fucking noise.

"Oh, fuck you, too," Stevenson muttered at the wounded man.

At last Stevenson gave up, sat down, and waited. He watched the rain cascade from louver to louver in nearly solid sheets. The cool spray drifted into the room. It was like being behind Niagara.

"Trung-uy?" Xuan said softly after a few minutes.

"Ah," Stevenson said. "Sergeant Ex-you-un. How are you feeling?"

Xuan's voice was barely there. It hurt like hell even to breathe.

"I am better—okay, I guess."

"That's good, that's just fine." Stevenson paused. "I just stopped over to see how you were getting on and to see if there was anything we could do to make your stay easier. Anything at all?"

"That is kind of you," Xuan replied softly.

"Ah, well . . ."

Stevenson had thought this might be awkward.

"Yes?" Xuan asked him.

"Ah, well . . . let's see. How long will you be here, Sergeant?"

"A few days more."

"And then they will send you to Cong Hoa Hospital?"

"I would hope," Xuan said, "to go somewhere else."

"Of course. Maybe we can help in that regard."

Cong Hoa was the military hospital in Saigon—a dirty, miserable place whose halls resounded with the screams of the wounded, and whose grounds backed up to a military cemetery.

Xuan realized now that some sort of deal was afoot. He sensed the American trait of not wanting to do something chancy unless it met with favorable judgment from everyone.

"There is something you want to discuss, *trung-uy?*" he asked after Stevenson's uneasiness reached a critical state.

Stevenson cleared his throat again. He drew his chair close to the bed, leaned forward, and began to speak rapidly.

"Of course, anyone with vision, as I'm sure you are a man with vision, has no doubt thought of the end, which will come, as it has, I'm sure you realize, to every war in the history of the twentieth century, and other centuries, as well. Now, when I say the end of the war, which will be, make no mistake, an American victory, and a time which we are thinking about because, as I'm sure you have realized, when this happens, it will be like so many other wars, and the price of what we call the consumer market will rise, and I mean rise . . . ah . . . astronomically."

Phrases from Mr. Christopher's letters came and went. Stevenson leaned down close to Xuan's ear.

"What I am talking about, Sergeant Xuan, is that I represent, I am the agent for, as well as being one of the members of, what we call a *syndicate*—a real estate syndicate. Do you know what I mean?"

"I think I know," Sergeant Xuan said softly.

"Good. (Stevenson barely knew, himself.) Do you know what is going to happen to real estate after the war, Sergeant?"

Stevenson lowered his voice.

"Do you know that the price of real estate in Saigon is going to go through the roof? See, not only does the upcoming American victory mean that there's going to be prosperity, but there will be peace. Saigon will become the leading metropolis for all of Southeast Asia. And the American government will want to show the world that democracy is the best system. You follow me? That means they will pour money into this country. Like you have never seen."

"I see," Xuan said.

"We are going to do to this country what happened in South Korea. Have you ever seen South Korea, Sergeant? Seoul is a showplace for . . . uh . . . you know, democracy. And you know what Koreans are like. Just think what Saigon will be like!"

"And that's because, when we win a war, we are going to show why we started it. I mean, why we got involved. See? This is where we stopped the march of communism. This is where the dominoes stopped falling!"

"Yes, *trung-uy.*"

"Here." Stevenson's voice was an excited hiss and his eyes bounced around. "I've got these maps I want you to see." He held up a sector map with marks all over it. Sergeant Xuan strained his head around to look at it. He gasped, but he did not scream.

"Oh, are you in pain? See this strip here? From Saigon up to Bien Hoa? This is where we think the main development is going to happen. Tan Son Nhut will be an international airport."

Xuan craned his head around. His back was aflame, but he had to see the map of Bien Hoa with marking all over it. Stevenson thoughtlessly held it up too high and moved it all around as he spoke. But even so, Xuan could see roads penciled in and squares marked *parking lot* and *hotel* and *access road*. Near the airfield there was a series of squares and rectangles with the words *high rise* and *mall*. What was a mall?

Mercifully, Stevenson came to the point. He described the investors as amazingly shrewd American businessmen who were ready to put money in back of their words. They would send money to the Chase Manhattan Bank Saigon branch to get things rolling. They wanted options on land and commitments,

and titles and agreements and deeds. If Xuan worked for them, there was no end to the money. Stevenson took out the wad of Kit's father's money and flashed it.

"See?"

He looked around to see if anyone was near. Only the American sergeant was, drugged and asleep.

"Sergeant, you'll be a rich man someday, mark my words. Mark my words."

Xuan knew nothing about real estate, nothing about the laws of buying and selling land. But he knew Americans wanted answers quickly. He knew the South Vietnamese would sell the land under their own homes for American money. What the South Vietnamese wanted was Japanese motorcycles. It didn't seem like much of a job at all. And there was the matter of Captain Lam.

"Well, I must go, but I want you to think about it. Think about it, Sergeant. This is an opportunity . . ."

Xuan interrupted.

"Can you get me out of here, *trung-uy?*"

"You mean *here?*"

"To somewhere where no one knows."

"To hide?"

"Yes," Xuan said, "to hide."

Stevenson wondered where this might be.

"And . . ." Xuan said, in a weaker voice.

"What else?" Stevenson bent down closer. Xuan's skin was pale and waxy. Stevenson looked closely at him.

"And I will need some money. Now."

• • •

Stevenson stepped outside the hospital. The rain had stopped. The steam was already rising from the road. Water ran down the cracks in the broken blacktop. The odors of damp canvas and creosote rose in the humid air. Stevenson walked away from the hospital with the odd feeling that at last he had taken the first step. The secret boiled inside him. He had done something. He had hired someone. He was, or rather, they were, in business.

He stopped in the middle of the main street that led to the operations center. The junk and disarray of the base, the insolent attitude of the damp, angry enlisted men who passed him, the crazy tilting and sinking attitude of the buildings, the disorder, the mess, the noise, and the filth, all disgusted and revolted him. The war was smelly and noisy and confused.

But the idea of business was clean and orderly. Business would clear away the disorder of the war, and business would raise up clean, gleaming buildings, straight white roads, and a country in which things worked.

He felt a good deal better for a few minutes. Then the doubt and annoying fears began to rise slowly. What had he done? Could he trust Xuan? What if he were found out? Was this what business was like? He went over things in his mind as he walked slowly toward the sandbagged trailer where the general lived.

Kit, his business partner, came toward him on his way to the hospital. Kit had finally decided that he must conquer his guilt and go see Xuan.

"Um . . ." Kit said.

"What?"

"I got something from my father."

"Do you have it?"

"Here." Kit put a large manila envelope in Stevenson's hand. Stevenson looked at it. It was still sealed.

"Haven't you read it?"

"Well, no. I guess I should read it."

"No, no," Stevenson said lightly, "I'll do it. I have to do everything."

"Anyway," Kit said, "I was just going to go over and see if . . ."

Stevenson ran his thumb under the flap.

". . . if Sergeant Xuan was okay."

"He's okay. He now works for me. I mean, us."

Stevenson pulled a sheaf of legal papers out of the envelope. He walked on slowly, looking through the prospectus and state of New York corporation filing.

"That's good," said Kit. "I . . ."

But Stevenson had walked on, lost in the legalese.

Kit paused a moment. He scanned the sky for signs of incoming mortars and listened for any sounds of firing anywhere. The

North Vietnamese, out in the forest, were still bailing the rainwater out of their bunkers. It would take them at least an hour before they could begin mortaring the base.

Kit went to the hospital. But unfortunately, he didn't get to see Sergeant Xuan.

The nurse wouldn't let him.

CHAPTER

SIXTEEN

A KIDNAPPING

Lieutenant Starret sat drinking warm beer in the officers' club, which was falling off its foundation.

"I'm gonna *die* in this place," he said to Lieutenant Stevenson.

Stevenson said nothing.

"I'm gonna die in this place."

"Shut up. I'm trying to write."

"It's gonna fall in on my head."

During the monsoon season, it rained in torrents every afternoon. Enlisted men had to go around after each rain and refill sandbags or repair bunker walls. But the supply of enlisted men was growing short. Vietnamese were hired to do the job, but even they were hard to get.

The water had washed the dirt out from under the cement piling under the corner of the officers' club near the door. The corner sunk down into a hole, the building sagged mournfully, the door sprung out and popped off its hinges. It was replaced with a blanket. The bar itself wobbled meaningfully.

Lieutenant Starret was in scarcely better shape. He had been drinking all afternoon. He was out of money again. His unit was standing down for good. They had orders to be ready for a drop, a cut in their number of days of duty, a return to the States.

"This building is going to c'llapse in on our heads, Stevenson. D'jou know that?"

Stevenson looked at him. Starret's eyes were red and fogged, and his burned face was filthy with salt and Phuoc Vinh dirt. His face was puffy from drinking. Stevenson's face was puffy from fatigue.

"We're going to be crushed to death in the fucking officers' club. D'jou know that?" Starret slurred.

"I am trying to write a letter."

"Y' gonna die . . ."

"Leave me alone."

Starret leaned over Stevenson's shoulder, and tried to read his letter.

Dear Father,
There has been an accident. The man we hired has been . . .

Starret breathed a long sigh of beery breath.

"I don't wanna get crushed t'death in a fuckin' officers' club, like some kind of . . ." He couldn't think of anything.

"Like what?" Stevenson asked, still writing.

. . . wounded. There may be a slight delay. As soon as he is bet-
ter . . .

"Like a . . . you know . . ."

"What?"

"Like a . . ."

"Right," Stevenson said. "Listen, Starret. Snap out of it. I may need you to help me. Do you have any more money?"

"No."

"Good. I am going to need you to help me."

"Why?" Starret said.

"I want you to stay right here until I need you. Sober up a bit," Stevenson said, looking into Starret's clouded eyes.

"Why?"

"I need you to help me. I'll pay you."

"Okay."

"Don't forget. Stay here."

"Okay."

"Okay."

"But listen," Starret said, "you got any money now? 'Cause . . ."

"Not a chance. Stay here till I get back."

"What if the officers' club falls on my head?" Starret called after him. But Stevenson was on his way back to the general's trailer.

• • •

That night they stole Sergeant Xuan from the hospital. They tied him to a stretcher and put a blanket over him, face and all. Stevenson grabbed all the medicine on the table next to Xuan's cot and put it in his pockets. Then he grabbed all the pain pills he could find on the tables next to the other wounded soldiers. He picked up a medic's kit and stuck it under the blanket. In a drawer of the dispensary he found morphine bottles.

"Mmmmm," he said pensively.

They carried the stretcher out the door to the medevac pad. A medevac pilot and two medics were sitting under a hanging light. They were playing cards, and paid no attention.

Down the division street they went, Stevenson in front, almost at a trot. Starret had the other end of the stretcher. A little more sober now, he struggled to make one foot go before the other.

"Who is this guy?"

"Shhhh!"

"What d'you want this guy for?" Starret said louder.

"Shhhh," Stevenson hissed.

In Stevenson's room they uncovered Xuan's head and untied the straps that held him on the stretcher. Xuan's face was white with pain. Sweat rolled off his brow and he moaned softly to himself.

Stevenson rolled him over and checked his bandages. Starret held the light closer.

"Christ," Starret said, "we shouldn't have been running with this guy. Jesus, look at that."

Xuan's long wound had torn away from the bandages and some of the stitches had parted. The entire wound was bleeding again.

"Shit!" Stevenson said.

"What d'you want this guy for?" Starret asked again, his thoughts coming clearer.

"Never mind."

"Never mind, my ass, you're gonna kill him."

"Okay, I'll tell you, but not right now."

Stevenson rolled Xuan over. He broke the guard off the morphine needle.

"Jesus, what the hell are you doing?" Starret was getting more sober by the minute.

"I'm giving him morphine, see?"

"Morphine?"

"See, it says here *morphine.*"

"I know, but . . ."

"This man is in pain," Stevenson said matter-of-factly.

"No shit he's in pain!"

"Have you ever done this before?"

"Gimme it," Starret said.

There was a noise outside the bunker. Stevenson stopped. He placed a hand on Starret's arm, quieting him.

"Shhhh . . ."

"Okay," Starret whispered, "but . . ."

"Just do it."

Starret blinked and took the needle from Stevenson.

"This is bullshit. This guy needs a doctor."

"No, he doesn't," Stevenson said. "Give him the shot."

"He doesn't? Like hell!"

"Shut up."

"He should be back in the hospital."

A faint voice interrupted.

"No, no doctor. No hospital," Sergeant Xuan said, barely loud enough to hear.

Starret gave him the needle. Stevenson daubed peroxide on the open parts of the wound. Then he doused it with merthiolate. Xuan jumped a little.

"Give him another," Stevenson said, working on Xuan's wound.

"What the hell are you doing?" Starret asked.

"Do you think he's had enough?"

"For what?"

"I have to fix this."

"You can't . . ."

"I always wanted to be a doctor."

Stevenson took out some silk thread from the medic's kit and opened the seal on a curved needle.

"Hmm . . ." he said.

"You idiot!" Starret said in wonder.

"Hmmm . . ." Stevenson said, making the first stitch, where the others had torn.

"Can you even see what you're doing?"

"Hold the light closer."

Stevenson tied off the first stitch and admired his work.

"How's that look?" he asked Starret.

Starret looked at the stitch. He looked closely. He had seen a lot of quick surgery in the past ten months.

"Well . . ."

"Huh?"

"Actually," Starret said, "not bad."

As he made four more repair stitches, getting better with each one, Stevenson explained Xuan's status as his employee and about the real estate enterprise. Starret listened in amazement.

"We will buy Saigon land now when it is cheap, and after the war is over we will develop it and sell it for hundreds of millions

of dollars," Stevenson said, placing fresh bandages over Xuan's stitches.

Starret paused to think about it.

"Crazy." Starret sighed.

"Oh?" Stevenson said absently, neatly taping the bandage in place, "and how *exactly* is it crazy?"

"We're leaving."

"I don't think so." Stevenson grinned at him. "And my partners don't think so. And my employee here doesn't think so. Do you, Sergeant Xuan?"

Xuan scarcely had the strength to lift his head.

"No."

"You think we'll win the war?"

"I . . ." Xuan's voice trailed off. He closed his eyes.

"So," Stevenson said, "there you have it. Incontestable proof. We will win. I say so and my partners say so and my employee says so."

"Well . . . I say . . ."

"What *do* you say?"

Starret would have said that Stevenson was full of shit. If he had still been drunk, he would have told Stevenson a piece of rude truth. But as he sobered up and thought about it, he had to admit that he didn't know.

"I don't know," he said.

Stevenson was silent, his face wrinkled in concentration. He looked down at his patient. He wiped Xuan's forehead with a towel, gently.

"So," he said slowly, "do you want in or not?"

"In?"

"In as a partner, you know? An investor?"

They sat still for a few minutes in the light of Lieutenant Stevenson's desk lamp. His fan droned on, pushing the air over them. Xuan drifted into unconsciousness.

"I hope you didn't give him too much morphine," Stevenson said.

"Nah, I don't think so," Starret said. They both listened to Xuan's labored breathing.

"He's still breathing," Stevenson said, wiping Xuan's brow again.

"Poor bastard," Starret said.

"What? I am going to make him a rich man," Stevenson said, looking at his fingers, which had Xuan's blood dried on them.

"Yeah. Sure," Starret said.

"I could make you a rich man, Lieutenant Starret."

"Really?"

"Certainly. So. Do you want to invest?"

Starret thought about it.

"I don't have much money," he said seriously.

"How much?"

"Well, I got a Chinese pistol. I'll invest that. You gimme half of Saigon and I'll give you a Chinese pistol."

Stevenson looked at him. All he could see in the half light was the glare of Starret's grinning teeth.

C H A P T E R

S E V E N T E E N

RADAR MAN

Major Dow had seven en-
listed men who kept the maps and the enemy order of battle
records up-to-date. And he had Specialist Dilby who ran the anti-
personnel radar.

The anti-personnel radar was a truly magical thing. An operator sat in a small trailer at the base of each radar tower dialing
different coordinates, listening with enormous earphones to the
sounds that came to him over the returning radar signals. To the
untrained ear the returning signals sounded like endlessly rushing
water, but within the rushing sound an experienced operator
could distinguish the sounds of motors, human voices, and even

footfalls. In the early mornings, Dilby could hear some of the villagers miles away rising and going to church. He could hear bells on the necks of the water buffalo and the bell in the church tower. Later in the day he could pick up the sounds of the woodcutters' trucks and chain saws.

Specialist Dilby also plotted the locations of sensor reports from the thousands of little sensors strewn throughout the jungle, ingenious devices that could sense movement, noise, and even the acid odor of human beings. The sensors were disguised to look like plants and animal turds. Each sensor's signal was coded so the location could be plotted accurately. They were clever little things, and it was really a shame that the war's unpopularity was denying the inventors of all these things the credit they should have received. Did we not heap praise on the physicists who brought Japan to its knees, and the intellects who broke the Nazis' codes? Yet the inventor of a turd that could smell humans was unknown. Unsung, poor devil.

Specialist Dilby put a colored pushpin on the map for each signal. Then he could analyze trends and movements from which conclusions could be drawn, or so the Pentagon thought. But the system required more attention to detail than the army could find the motivation for. In the confusion the signals didn't mean very much, and no one trusted them.

"Be careful, Dilby," Major Dow counseled, "be careful when you report those radar sightings."

"Yes, sir, I will."

"I'd hate to report some woodcutters by mistake."

"Yes, sir."

"Or some ARVNs. We give them maps, but they don't know how to read maps."

"I know, sir."

"As a matter of fact . . ."

"I know, sir," Dilby said.

"What was I going to say?"

"That our own guys don't know how to read maps, either."

"Well, yes." Major Dow was impressed by Dilby. He said, "Better not report any of those sightings."

"Yes, sir," said Dilby.

"Better see me first."

"Yes, sir."

A year before, a series of signals had been reported—enemy troops moving things around, digging in the earth, presumably some bunkers, bold as brass. One night the area was shelled for about twenty minutes by American artillery. After the barrage it was reported in horror that the target was, in truth, a government New Life hamlet crowded with some of the refugees from Tay Ninh, an already pathetic portion of the war's unfortunate. Everyone in the New Life hamlet had been killed.

Dilby had been writing songs before he was drafted about the evil of war and the sins of large corporations. His songs had too many numbers in them, like how much the war was costing on a per capita basis. Hardly good ballad material, and he had to make up most of the numbers.

Now, when time permitted, and it usually did, he speculated idly on the full cost of his radar map and sensor operation, with the idea that there might be the makings of a song in it. There were tens of thousands of sensors, maybe hundreds of thousands of sensors, which must have cost a few thousand dollars each, and there was the cost of flying out and dropping them in place, and there was the cost of the radio that picked up the signals, and there was the cost of the radio operator, and finally, there was the cost of Dilby himself.

In the song he was working on, he was called *radar man* and the lyrics so far portrayed him as a lonely individual caught in the military machine. In the lyrics, radar man realizes that he is responsible for the deaths of millions. But in the nonmusical reality, Dilby had yet to sight anything that the army had been able to kill or capture. He didn't know how he felt about this.

Dilby had the tact to at least appear busy in the presence of his superiors. Superior officers always appreciated this. But he was ruinously bored. His tact was wearing thin and he had tried to write a song about how bored he was. Not surprisingly, it was a boring song.

"Dilby," Major Dow said one evening, "I would like to ask you to do something for me."

"Anything, sir."

"It's Lieutenant Toomey," Major Dow said. "I want you to let me know if he does or says anything out of the ordinary."

Dilby had been watching Toomey. Out of the ordinary? Toomey, who wore a pistol to the shower? Toomey, who carried around a Chinese submachine gun? Toomey, who had a knife in each boot? Toomey, who read the Good News for Modern Man Bible in his spare time? Toomey, whose squinty eyes were getting squintier because he ate constantly? Toomey, who tried to engage him in conversation about how amazing it was that the human body, which was mostly water, could stop bullets, which were metal and were going so fast? That Lieutenant Toomey? Out of the ordinary?

"What do you mean, sir, like weird things?" Dilby asked earnestly.

Major Dow placed the tips of his fingers together.

"Uh . . . Before he came here he . . . was a prisoner for three weeks. But he escaped."

"Jesus, that's amazing."

"Yes," said Major Dow, thinking about the story he had just concocted, "it is."

A POW song, Dilby thought.

"He's desperately in need of psychological help," Major Dow went on, "but . . . well . . ."

"What do you want me to do, Major?"

Major Dow looked down at his pudgy hands.

"Nothing," he said. "I don't want you to *do* anything. But I do want you to keep your eyes open. And the minute you see him do anything strange, let me know immediately."

Dilby had a finger in his teeth, and his eyes were wide open.

"So," Dilby continued, "he was a prisoner, huh?"

"Yes, but you can't say anything to anyone about it, understand? Nothing is to be said to anyone. Very few people even know."

"Okay, sir, I understand."

"Because," Major Dow paused. "Well, you know what might happen . . . don't you?"

"He might go right off his head, right?"

"Yes."

"Jesus."

"Yes," said Major Dow. "You never know."

• • •

Lieutenant Toomey had been given permission to move out of the bunker Kit slept in. He was told that since he was going to be working at headquarters and for Major Dow, it would be a better idea if he were in the same bunker. That way, Major Dow said, they would know just where to find him.

By this time, Lieutenant Toomey had figured out that the general was not going to bring charges against him, a development that weighed more on his mind than if charges had been brought. Since the meeting when he had told the general everything, no one had said another word about it. Every day, twice a day, when Toomey mounted the platform in front of the maps and gave the briefing, the general looked at him for a split second, and then he looked away.

In fact, no one spoke to him very much. He was convinced that they all knew about the men he had killed, and the idea grew in his mind that there was a conspiracy of silence against him. Sooner or later, he thought, some sort of action would happen.

One night Toomey had a strange dream about writing a letter home to Blackwell's mother.

Dear Mrs. Blackwell,
As your son's platoon leader, it is my sad duty to write to you of his loss in battle. Your son was a brave soldier, of the type this nation has always counted on to defend her freedom and honor.

That part was standard commander's letter home verbiage from the *Officer's Guide.* Then he went on:

As you probably know by now, it was necessary for me to shoot your son in the back. He was running away and had just given me a lot of shit, so I had to shoot him . . .

It seemed a natural thing to write. Mrs. Blackwell appeared to be sitting across the table from him. She looked like a sad but

understanding woman. She held one of Blackwell's childhood
toys, a red metal truck, now chipped and rusted.

*Your son has helped to pay part of the cost of our nation's free-
dom, and helped ensure that the traditions we all enjoy and value
will persist.*

The only tradition that came to mind was Thanksgiving. Mrs.
Blackwell looked like the sort of simple woman who enjoyed
holidays, and for whom big meals with lots of grandchildren filling the house with their happy laughter was payment enough for
the hardships of being a mother. She would now have to do without Blackwell's children. He saw that she picked idly and sadly at
the plate of turkey, vegetables, and mashed potatoes in front of
her.

Those of us who had the fortune to know your son (he never
knew Blackwell's first name) *as a comrade in arms have been en-
riched by the memory of his brave and cheerful spirit. I'm sure that
if the circumstances under which I had to shoot him had not occurred, he would have been killed or wounded in a completely hon-
orable way, a way we could all be proud of.*

Mrs. Blackwell got up from the table and began to pace.

*The cost of maintaining the freedom we enjoy as Americans is
great, but it is a cost which men, like your son, pay willingly . . .*
The *Officer's Guide* with the suggested phrases for commander's
letters home was gone. Someone had taken it. He tried to continue from his own memory. . . . *so . . . of the tradition of
something and liberty under God and for which truth is the something which something else. And . . .*

Mrs. Blackwell was no longer there. She had left. It was a very
strange dream. Especially considering that Mrs. Blackwell was
white and the Thanksgiving dinner was being prepared in an old
farmhouse, whereas Blackwell himself had most definitely been
black, and had been from East New York.

He had other dreams, all of which seemed to involve a group of ghostly women. Sometimes they were stewardesses on the Flying Tiger planes going home, tending to the bodies of their sons, straightening their uniforms, combing their hair, and even, despite the fact that they were dead, trying to feed them in their coffins. Sometimes they strode across a landscape toward him while the wind drew their white gowns out behind them.

In his loneliness, Toomey began to eat more and more. He didn't dare drink. Food became his only companion. He ate through most of the day, and he took more food to his room at night. He ate the mess hall meals and then ate C rations later. He drank can after can of preserved milk. When his worst depression was upon him, and when the tall, motherly ladies in the flowing gowns were coming over the horizon, he seemed to be able to find oblivion only in eating.

• • •

Thi Tuan helped Toomey move. He helped him carry his uniforms and possessions from Kit's bunker to Major Bedford's. He helped arrange things in Toomey's new room, made up his bed, and hung up his uniforms neatly. Lieutenant Toomey sat on the side of the bed and opened a C ration can with a cinnamon roll in it. He dug the roll out with his knife and jammed it in his mouth. Then he washed it down with a can of milk. He flopped back on the bed and fell asleep with both hands folded over his distended stomach.

Thi Tuan tidied everything up. Then he quietly closed the door and left.

Lieutenant Toomey dreamed he was in the rubber plantation. The pieces of the other men were all over. A shallow flood of rainwater and latex flowed up around him. And there were little chevron cuts in his own legs like the cuts in the rubber trees.

He woke in a bath of his own perspiration, barely able to breathe in the heat. He strapped on his pistol and grabbed his submachine gun and stumbled out of the bunker into the afternoon heat. He started across the base toward the operations center in a state of confusion and depression, making his way down the road that circled by the Korean bunker to the rear of the

operations center. Everything was Blackwell's fault. If Blackwell hadn't run, none of this would have happened. Blackwell was a deserter. He deserved what he got.

He began to mumble as he walked along.

"He deserved it. He deserved it. I can't do anything about it and I won't do anything about it. I'm getting the hell out of here."

Specialist Dilby spotted Toomey in the road. He circled a building and followed Toomey, straining to hear his mad mutterings.

"I'm getting the hell out of here. God damn the fucking army," Toomey went on to himself. He would never forgive the army. Not a chance. If he saw men in uniform back in the States he would go out of his way to bump into them and say whatever derogatory thing came into his mind. He would knock them into the gutter and throw food at them if he happened to be carrying food. If he were carrying an ice cream cone and he saw a general or . . .

Lieutenant Toomey stopped in the street and shook his head in a spasm. God, he had to stop this. Throwing food. Talking to himself about throwing ice cream balls at generals.

He began walking again, looking from side to side with his eyes wide open. Did he have to put up with this treatment?

You tell me, he would demand of the judge advocate. Tell me what I should have done. Let them retreat? Let them go back? Go back with them? Is that the order? Retreat and file paperwork?

No, by Christ, it was not. And if he were wrong, and if he did the wrong thing, then fine, put it in writing for all to see. First we go out and look for the enemy, and then, when we have found them, we retreat and take a quick vote.

I was right to shoot Blackwell. And the others, but mostly Blackwell. I was right. I was right. I am not ashamed. Blackwell was a deserter. Yes. He was running away. He got shot. Yes. By me. Deserters will be shot. On the spot. By me. Yes. By God. By me.

You want to fight a war? You want to fight a war? Hey? You

want to fight a war? Then deserters will be shot. By me. Yes. By me.

He stopped again. He had raised the submachine gun up. Someone had said, "Shot by me, yes." He had heard it distinctly. He shook his head.

Ten steps behind him, Specialist Dilby cleared his throat.

Toomey whipped around. He raised the submachine gun barrel at Dilby's chest. Dilby's eyes popped.

"Sir, Major Dow wants you to . . ." Dilby stared at the stubby barrel. The hole in the barrel seemed enormous. Was Toomey going to shoot him?

"Sir?" Dilby's long face turned white.

"Who are you?"

"Dilby, sir, Specialist Dilby . . . Jesus, sir, could you put that thing down?"

"Dilby?" Toomey asked as his eyes searched for conspirators. "I don't know you."

"Yes, sir, I'm there in the office, over at Division. I sort of sit in the corner and I . . . take care of the map."

"How long have you been following me?"

They were standing in front of the Korean liaison office where the Korean forces kept a staff to arrange for transport and air support, since they had very little of their own. Two Koreans had come out on the tilting porch to watch Toomey and Dilby. They stood with their hands on their hips in the insolent manner peculiar to Koreans. They were both smiling broadly and, he thought, viciously, in a way also peculiar to Koreans. One of them laughed. Toomey hated Koreans. But then, everybody hated Koreans.

"Shoot him!" one of the Koreans called and laughed again. And Toomey realized that he was holding the Chinese submachine gun on Dilby. Slowly he turned and swung the gun toward the Koreans.

"What?" he called.

The two Koreans laughed all the more, a high, punctuated laugh like two magpies or jackals. *Hyenas,* thought Toomey. *They are hyenas. Koreans, the hyenas of the Orient.*

"Shoot!" they called back. "Shoot him! Shoot. Shoot!"

He straightened in a quick motion, raising the submachine gun at them.

"Shoot?" he asked.

"Shoot!" they laughed back at him.

He pulled the stubby trigger while pointing the gun directly at them and braced himself for the noise and the recoil from the spray of bullets.

Nothing happened.

"For God's sake, sir . . ." Dilby said.

There was no clip in the gun—something the Koreans had seen, that Dilby had not seen, and that Toomey had forgotten.

Where was the clip? Back in his room, dammit. The Koreans were laughing, slapping each other. This was real Korean humor.

"Sir, you're late," Dilby said. "I'm supposed to get you there on time."

Toomey lowered the gun.

"Your job is to watch me? To follow me around?"

"No, sir. It's just that Major Dow said . . ."

Toomey put his hand on Dilby's shoulder.

"Did you hear me talking to myself before? DID YOU?"

"I . . . may have, sir."

The Koreans were shouting something else now, and a third had joined them on the porch.

"Tell me what I said."

"I couldn't hear you, sir. Sir, you'll be late for Major Dow."

"Tell me, dammit," he shouted.

"Really, Lieutenant, for God's sake, I don't know!"

"I'll cave your face in! You tell me!"

The Koreans were shouting at him.

"Something about . . . that you shot somebody," Dilby croaked.

"I said that? Did I say that?" Toomey squeaked. He held the machine gun high in the air over Dilby's terrified face.

"Yes, sir . . . I think that's what you said."

Toomey lowered the gun. The Koreans were calling something.

"Here," he said. "You hold this for me."

He handed the submachine gun to Dilby, unstrapped the pistol on his hip, and began walking toward the Koreans on the porch.

Dilby came after him. *Was there ever a song in this!*

"Wait, Lieutenant, stop!"

Toomey drew out the heavy, clumsy automatic. He smiled. He pointed at the Koreans and pulled the trigger. The gun jumped in his hand. He put the first shot into the door of the building. Then he fired the rest of the clip into various points of the building while the Koreans scattered.

God! It felt good to be shooting at something again. It felt wonderful to feel the stupidly heavy pistol jump in his hand and see the windows break and the wood splinter, and see the Koreans diving for cover all over.

Nine shots, nine holes in the Korean building. A great relief flooded over him. The smoke of gunpowder and hot gun oil drifted back toward him through the humid air, the sweet smell of having done something, of having scared the hell out of those miserable little mimics. He dropped the gun to his side and blinked at the damage he had so happily created.

"Sir," Dilby said softly behind him, "let's get out of here."

"Yes," said Lieutenant Toomey, wanting to savor the moment just a bit longer. "Let's get out of here."

"Run, sir, or you'll be late."

"No, Specialist Darby," said Toomey. "We will not run. We will march with pride. Nobody runs. Nobody fucking runs. Get your head up, Darby!"

But Dilby dropped the Chinese submachine gun and took off.

CHAPTER

EIGHTEEN

THE GREEN LINE

Despite Vietnamization and all
the other interruptions, the war went on. The infantry wandered
in the jungle looking for the North Vietnamese, found them, and
tried to kill them. The Army of the Republic of South Vietnam
tried to stay out of the way. The American artillery fired shells,
the American air force dropped bombs, and the American Corps
of Engineers continued to build roads for Japanese motorcycles.

Kit did his part, sort of. His name came up on rotation rosters
for several special duties. He was often assigned to investigate
missing or stolen things, usually vehicles. He was assigned once a
week as a malaria control officer, to stand and watch long lines of

enlisted men take their Monday morning quinine pills and then run to the outhouses. He was a finance control-day officer to exchange all the military scrip.

He was a failure as an investigation officer since he believed nearly all of the reasons given for why things were missing. He wrote "taken by person or persons unknown," which was the approved army way of saying that no one cared.

He was a failure as a malaria control officer, too, because the men often palmed their pills. Kit wasn't quick enough to see whether the pill went down their throats or down their sleeves. Many were ready to risk malaria, even though it was a court-martial offense, because it might get them out of the fighting.

And he was a great failure as a finance control-day officer on the secret day when all the *old* design military scrip, with the astronauts and the submarine on it, was exchanged for a *new* design, which featured famous landmarks in American history. Such duty meant hours of counting the wrinkled, sweaty little pieces of scrip turned in and keeping meticulous records. Kit made mistakes in reissuing the new scrip. The enlisted men got mad and put on an act of profound umbrage in front of Kit's scrip-counting table. Some of the soldiers ranted and swore that the army was trying to cheat them. Kit felt, as usual, that it was probably his fault, and tried to make up the claimed difference from his own money. After he ran out, he tried borrowing from the pile of money for those who hadn't come to his table yet. This led to a substantial shortage for the men at the end of the line. After lengthy and heated discussion they accepted a partial payment he was able to borrow from the Finance Corps captain and Kit's personal IOU for the rest. The Finance Corps captain agreed to the loan only after the men offered as an alternative to beat the hell out of him and Kit and anybody else on their side of the table and wreck the building and gas the place and so on.

But his most warlike duty was his assignment as Officer of the Day on the Green Line, a twenty-four-hour stint checking on the infantry troops who manned the bunkers and towers along the perimeter. He was given a jeep and a driver, and he had to go around inspecting all the rifles, grenade launchers, mines, flares, starlight scopes, flashlights, searchlights, and radios that would be the first line of defense in case of a ground attack against the base.

Fortunately, for the past few years, the North Vietnamese hadn't made any ground attacks. The Viet Cong used to do it all the time in the early 1960s. But the Viet Cong had been crazy. The North Vietnamese were far more clever and patient. Even so, there was always the chance of an attack, and a perimeter had to be maintained. All around the base were sensors, barbed wire, and hundreds of flares and claymore mines, some manually operated and others on trip wires. Altogether this perimeter was about three miles long, with fifteen towers and more than thirty machine gun bunkers. In between the bunkers a berm of earth had been pushed up with a chain-link fence running along the top.

Three men were stationed in each bunker—infantry troops who rotated in from two weeks of field duty for a one-week stand-down on the base. Kit's job was to check on them every two hours. He was supposed to check on the condition of their weapons, sign the reports attesting to their readiness, and pass out any intelligence or special orders. Since it was only a twenty-four-hour stint every three or four weeks, he didn't take the time, and in truth he *couldn't* take the time, to learn the job properly. In various parts of the army, there was an assumption that an officer only has to be present to make things operate, even if he has no idea what is going on.

Kit knew very little about rifles and machine guns. He knew nothing about grenade launchers. He knew nothing about the web of wires and cables that operated the flares and mines. He worried that something was likely to short out in the mud or that he would step on some sort of trip lever snap gizmo buried and forgotten, and things would blow up around him. For these reasons, he inspected the mines and flares from a safe and respectful distance, which amounted to inspecting them not at all. Which he also did sometimes.

The only skill he had improved on was the skill of appearing to know what he was doing without having any idea. He wore sunglasses to hide the worry and indecision in his gaze. Since he had nearly perfect vision, they only made things less distinct. His act included a strut and quizzical, high-handed attitude that he copied from Lieutenant Gallagher of the 18th Armored Cavalry. Lieutenant Gallagher had copied this strut from someone else, who had copied it from someone else, and so on, in an unbroken line of mimicry probably stretching back to the Civil War.

• • •

The infantry troops in the bunkers had rotated back to Phuoc Vinh from patrol duty. Patrols were the worst duty in Vietnam. In the jungle they got fired on purposely by the enemy, accidentally by their own helicopters, accidentally by their own artillery, and accidentally by that greatest of all hazards, the United States Air Force, whose pilots were blind and whose navigators were crazy, or so it seemed if you were on the ground.

Duty on Phuoc Vinh base was something of a vacation for the infantry. In the field, there was no music allowed, no freedom of action, no PX, and sometimes not even smoking. There was no beer, and for most, there was no sex. By comparison, Phuoc Vinh base seemed like Pleasure Island. Men on green line duty were supposed to get six hours of sleep during the day so that they would be able to stay awake for the better part of the night, but no one checked that this was done.

An enlisted man's life is cursed. There are so many people who can waste his time—uninspired, thick-headed sergeants and misanthropic, pretentious officers. There are so many people who outrank him and can give him orders which, technically, he has to obey or at least consider obeying. And these orders can be countermanded, reissued, and contradicted on a daily basis, creating endless confusion.

Not every conflicting order wastes time. Orders to shoot and not shoot someone or to march north and south at the same time are quickly resolved. But orders of the housekeeping variety, orders about when to be at a certain place and how long to wait for something to happen, orders about whether or not another order is coming and whether or not preparation is necessary, orders to hurry up, orders to wait, orders to hurry up *and* wait, all can take time to resolve. Conflict in these orders results in hours spent in

tiresome suspension, in angry ignorance of what is going on, and in certainty that you are under the control of idiots.

All manner of time-consuming orders and countermanding orders were issued. Orders came to clean weapons, orders came to prepare weapons for inspection, to turn in weapons for repair, to draw weapons out again, to move from one bunker to another, and then not to move but to await further orders. Orders came to attend physicals, reenlistment counseling, chaplain's counseling, and obligatory training films on venereal disease made in the 1950s, in which the men were cautioned to avoid German whores. The list went on. There was no choice but to ignore all orders. A court-martial was much better than more patrols.

There wasn't much to do. There was beer. And for those who needed something more than beer, there was more beer. Most of it was warm. The rest was hot. The beer was delivered and left to stand for hours in the sun. It developed a sour, already-drunk flavor, cooked in the can for a few weeks. To drink it required a morbid desire to get drunk. Bouts of drinking were followed by bouts of vomiting. This cycle was repeated over and over, twice, and even three times, a day.

Heroin and marijuana were considered more desirable than beer by most company commanders. Soldiers on drugs tended to go off quietly somewhere and disappear for a time. But those who got drunk and sick were seized by a traditional desire to fight with one another, or with their sergeants or officers, or to steal a vehicle and drive off to Saigon in search of fleshpots. Trips to Saigon, begun while drunk, and without any clear idea of which roads led to Saigon, usually ended in a chase along the roads around Binh Duong Province, most of which led disappointingly back to Phuoc Vinh. The American MPs turned out gladly for such chases and so did the National Police.

· · ·

After days like this, those soldiers who showed up for duty on the Green Line under Kit's one-day command did so in a state of either ascending or descending inebriation. Those still drunk were stupidly cheerful; those in decline were mean, sullen, and morosely careless. They thought it was grossly unfair that they who had just finished two weeks in the jungle should have to stay up all night as the perimeter guard for those rear-echelon scum who would be safely asleep in their relatively clean beds.

Kit was actually in charge of these men, for twenty-four hours, anyway. He was most bothered by the possibility that there might actually be some fighting. Suppose, he thought, while he was the Officer of the Day, the North Vietnamese tried to attack the perimeter. Suppose they lifted the barbed wire, cut the trip lines, crawled across the sand, and actually gained access to the base, running around shooting people while they slept. And him with his guard troops either drunk or asleep or drugged or not there at all.

He went from bunker to bunker with the duty sergeant, Sergeant Roxy, who was his driver. They would come up to a bunker in the line and park the jeep. They would walk up to the door of the bunker, met by no one. These were old bunkers, made of decomposing sandbags and rotten lumber. Each one had a dark little room with an observation slit window. Each had a telephone, and each was supposed to have three men.

Sergeant Roxy would shout, "Attention," and an embarrassing moment followed while the men in the bunker looked at Kit and at each other to determine whether or not they were going to go through the motions of standing up. When that happened Kit quickly said, "As you were," to save what face he could.

Once they interrupted a card game, to the obvious annoyance of the five men in the bunker, two of whom had walked down from the neighboring bunker. There were only three rifles to inspect, stacked in the corner. The card game went on while Kit was left to inspect to his heart's content.

"But where are *your* rifles?" he asked the men from the neighboring bunker.

"Back up the line, L-T. What kinda sorry-ass deal is that? I got six cards, motherfucker. Deal again."

"You're supposed to have them with you at all times," Kit said in his most military voice.

"Yeah, well, look, L-T, we just came down for a little cards. We'll be going back in a while."

But no one was supposed to abandon his rifle and his post and go off wandering around for card games. Kit was right up against the rules. What should he do? Obviously these men knew more about staying alive than he did.

"You men better get back up to your bunker," he said to the cardplayers, trying to sound determined.

"Is that an order, L-T?" asked one of the visitors, looking at his hand. "God damn! These cards are the same as I had. You shuffle this time, slick?" he asked the dealer.

"It might be," said Kit, "if it has to be." Something he had heard Gallagher say. He adjusted his sunglasses. "If I were you, I'd do it."

"Why don't you, then? You can be me," said the man, a tall, heavily built black man, smiling. "Be fine with us, slick. Ain't that so, mens? Two cards."

Discipline in war is driven by two forces. Either the need for the discipline is apparent to all parties, or the penalty for disobeying is swift and sure. But you can't punish men with disciplinary action who have faced jungle combat and would much rather face disciplinary action. The situation was rapidly degenerating into a contest to see who would make a fool of whom.

"Tell you what, L-T," said the dealer without looking up, "whoever wins the next hand will walk up and get our rifles and bring 'em back here. Fair enough? Fair enough."

He looked around at the other players, who all began nodding and saying, "Fair enough? Fair enough."

"Kinda makes the game interestin', don't it?" said another of the men.

"Certainly does," said a third.

"Okay with you L-T? Pair o' kings bets."

Kit would have gone along with this, but Sergeant Roxy interrupted, his face red with anger.

"Forget it, gentlemen. *I'll* go pick up those rifles, and you can reclaim them from our commanding officer!"

The black man with the mean smile was counting his money.

"Another good idea," he said. "You just full of good ideas."

He looked around at the others.

"It *is* a good idea, slick. You take them rifles back to the company. It'd be real helpful, 'cause we wasn't planning on

shooting' any tonight. We'll be gettin' some sleep, as soon as this game's over." He looked around the table. " 'Less we got some *women* comin' in."

"I'll be turning your goddamn name in, soldier," Roxy spat out at him, and turned on his heel to leave.

"You do that little thing. Give the rifles to Captain Turner. He's my man. Turner's a good man. He don't care about nothin'. You want sit in a hand, L-T?"

And they all returned to their game. Roxy was furious and Kit bewildered.

"C'mon, Lieutenant, we'll see about these assholes," Roxy said loudly in a final idle threat.

"That's right, slick," said the man after him, "if I wasn't a asshole I wouldn't be here."

• • •

They drove from bunker to bunker as the light of the day faded. In some they inspected everything. In others they simply counted heads. They climbed the towers and checked on the binoculars and searchlights. Some of the towers were well-equipped, others were not only poorly equipped, but so rickety as to be a hazard to the inhabitants.

Kit signed a log that said that he had checked everything. Even the claymore mines. He had a dread of claymore mines, and even the *idea* of claymore mines bothered him. Being somehow caught in the racing curtain of little steel balls was too awful to bear. So he didn't bear it, and he didn't inspect the mines. He reasoned that he wouldn't have known what to look for, and that the inspection of the previous day could be relied on for another twenty-four hours.

In one tower they watched for a time while a short skirmish took place on the horizon in the twilight. Helicopters were dropping flares and tracer fire arced into the sky. The soft thud grenades and the muted chatter of rifles drifted across the fields to them. Kit felt as if he were watching fireworks in a neighboring town. He worried again about someone sneaking on the base through the perimeter.

"Sergeant Roxy?"

"Sir?"

"What he said about having women in . . ."

Sergeant Roxy paused.

"Sometimes, sir. I believe they get in sometimes."

"Who?"

"Well, from the village, I guess."

In fact, they got in all the time. It was an enterprise run by noncommissioned officers from the Army of the Republic of South Vietnam. In the evening, when the cleaning girls went home, a number of the older girls hid on the base and were led to the bunkers on the Green Line. Periodic crackdowns to stop this were carried out by the military police.

"They caught some this morning," Roxy said.

Day-to-day identification cards had been given to the cleaning girls. They had to be turned in by four o'clock every evening or the girl would lose her job, and that would mean no income of any kind. Ten girls from B Mua Village had already been caught. Sergeant Roxy had seen them arrested. They had cried and carried on rather pitifully, all the more so because they were very young and small and probably needed the money badly.

It was a pathetic trade. There was no secluded place on the base a man could disappear to with one of these girls. The men lived in bunkers that were little more than hovels lined with rocket boxes. There was no privacy as an enlisted man. And besides that, these whores weren't actually whores; they were young girls from rural villages. They were ashamed of what they were doing. They took the money and cleaned themselves up in a state of bewilderment that this was what they had to do in the world.

The only Vietnamese woman Kit knew was the old woman who brought his laundry. And, of course, Miss Tuyet, who was also from Bo Mua. He remembered her fondly and wondered if he would ever see her again. She was very pretty and so small that he had been able to carry her on his shoulders all the way home from the place where Sergeant Xuan had been shot. She hadn't weighed a thing.

The thought of a girl, a young girl, about the age of Miss Tuyet, copulating or worse with a soldier as mean-spirited and dirty as the one who called everybody "slick," was almost beyond him. Of course these infantry would want women, but Kit had always thought they would want women like the German whores in the VD film. How could they want someone like Miss Tuyet?

He pictured Miss Tuyet home with her family, safe and well cared for, being tucked into bed, saying her prayers. It was part of the way the war should go. She should be home in bed, and the Americans and their Vietnamese allies should be standing guard against the forces of evil.

"Have you ever been around any of these girls, Sergeant?" he asked Roxy after thinking for a while.

"What d'you mean *around them?*" Roxy returned carefully.

"I mean," Kit started, then faltered, "you know. I mean, it's none of my business. I'm just curious and I just wondered."

"Look, Lieutenant, I know what you mean."

"Really?"

"You wanna get fixed up with one of them, right?"

"Oh, no."

"No?" asked Roxy.

"No, no."

Well, yes, he thought. But not for sex. Just because he thought they would be nice to know. They all seemed to look like Miss Tuyet, and he wondered what had happened to her. He liked Miss Tuyet. He liked her smile and her long, straight black hair. He liked the feel of her thin brown legs and the feeling of her bony, little girl's bottom on his shoulders as he had carried her back home. She was like a toy—a wonderful, pretty little toy.

"You don't want to get mixed up with them, Lieutenant. They only take a bath about once a year. They smell like fish sauce." Sergeant Roxy wanted this conversation to end.

"No, they don't."

Miss Tuyet hadn't smelled like fish sauce. She smelled like a little girl, even though she had been hot and sweaty. It was a pleasant little smell.

Sergeant Roxy gave up. He wasn't going to argue about such subjective matter.

• • •

After going completely around the line once, they returned to the bunker reserved for the Officer of the Day. Roxy went inside to call base headquarters and report that all was in order. Kit, having nothing else to do, wandered out into the humid evening and stood leaning up against the jeep, looking up into the clear blue-black sky.

As he often did on such evenings he thought about the round globe of the earth, spinning languidly through space, on its way from nowhere to nowhere, a ball with everything stuck to it—dirt, rocks, water, air, people. At night he liked to try to comprehend the endless void above him and the huge ball of rock, water, and fire under his feet.

He had nearly an hour before they had to begin their second trip around the line. The air was heavy with humidity and the sour smells of the base. Roxy stayed inside the bunker and read.

Kit wandered down the line a short way by himself. The next bunker he came to was empty. It should have been manned by three men. He stuck his head in the door and looked around. A lantern had been left burning as a ruse. There were no rifles, so the infantry who had deserted this post had been at least dedicated enough to take their weapons.

He walked on, slowly, thinking vaguely about himself and his father and Stevenson and wondering where his father was. There hadn't been any letters for a week, or was it two weeks? Was his father actually coming here with his lawyer? He thought of speaking to Major Dow about this entire business, but Major Dow was busy now, trying to turn the base over to the Vietnamese army. Kit wished he could help somehow. And Major Bedford, who was nice to him, but who was busy with the psychological operations helicopter.

In the next bunker music was playing. This was also against the rules. The music was loud and raucous. A faint odor of marijuana drifted past him. Voices rose over the music.

Kit stood in the darkness trying to decide whether or not he would go forward and enforce the rules against desertion, against music in a guard post, against drug use, against everything else, or whether he would walk back into the comfortable darkness

and rely on the North Vietnamese to maintain its tradition against ground attacks.

One man came out of the bunker to relieve himself against the side. Kit saw the man sway uncertainly.

Kit knew of the weakness within himself. He knew that what made him stop and watch all these infractions from the safety of the darkness was a simple fear of contradiction, the desire to avoid confrontation, and a lack of conviction one way or the other. In a war so confused and so probably wrong, why should anyone make an effort to enforce the rules for standing guard? Certainly he could not enforce them for long against the prevailing laxity.

But why should he be frightened of these men and their loud disrespect? They were Americans; they were on the same side. Why should they make him cower here in the dark? Besides, he was an officer, a remarkable fact he had to remind himself of constantly.

He went forward toward the bunker. The music ran out, but he could hear another card game in progress. He stopped and then went forward again. He went into the door of the bunker, into the smoky dark interior. The odor of marijuana was mixed with the smell of urine and beer. Four dark faces and two white ones turned to him.

"Hey, man, hey," said one.

"Yo, L-T," said another. The rest greeted him in not unfriendly surprise.

"Good evening," said Kit.

"What's up, L-T? What's goin' down?"

"You here for a inspection? Hey, we're ready. See them rifles? Them rifles are clean, man. My rifle is culleeee-in. Go ahead, take a look. You could eat that rifle."

"I got a rifle you can eat."

"You c' eat yo' own rifle."

"You gonna inspect, L-T?"

"Check my boots, L-T."

A boot was stuck out for Kit to look at. It was filthy.

"Jesus, I shined 'em. I don't know. Jesus, last week. Jesus, they got dirty again. Shit."

A round of laughter followed, but it was silly laughter.

"Who's supposed to be down in the next bunker?" Kit asked. "Whoever it is better get down there now."

There was a silence.

"Aw, yeah, L-T, but look, we gotta be here because . . ."

"Shut up, Cornwall," said someone under his breath.

"No, man, the L-T's cool."

"You shut up."

"Ain't you cool, L-T? I mean, you're cool to what's cool. Am I right?"

"What's cool?" Kit asked.

"Cornwall, you shut your mouth," said someone else.

"See, L-T," said Cornwall, giggling, "we gotta be here because . . ."

"Shut up, fool!"

"No, man! You don't tell me shut up!" Cornwall's musical voice was unstoppable. "See, L-T, the attack is gonna be here, so we gotta be here." He started laughing again.

"An attack?" Kit asked, looking through the slit in the front of the bunker.

"Yeah," Cornwall continued through his laughter, "an attack of the . . ."

"Shut up, I'm tellin' you. Somebody better shut up this fool."

". . . of the sapsuckers."

Cornwall doubled over in hilarity.

There was a moment of nothing but Cornwall laughing.

"Sapsuckers?" Kit asked.

"Yeah, you know," Cornwall regained a bit of his composure, "little sapsuckers."

One of his companions, in a more menacing tone, no longer quietly, said, "Cornwall. Shut your dumb mouth. I'll kick your head."

"Oh, hell, the L-T is cool."

Kit tried to figure out what Cornwall was talking about.

"You know, L-T, the little sapsuckers? See, they crawl right in here through the wire and stuff and then they come in here and they suck up all the sap they can."

He burst into new laughter.

"Through the wire?" Kit asked. He understood that much.

By this everyone realized that Kit was not cool. Everyone but Cornwall.

"The boss of the sapsuckers, he know where to get in. They smart little sapsuckers."

Nobody was supposed to get in through the wire. That was why the wire was there.

"I think you better get back to where you're supposed to be." He tried to sound as grave as he could.

There was a period of silence during which the men, including Cornwall, tried to assess the damage he had done.

"Hell, L-T . . ." Cornwall murmured.

There was another long pause.

"Okay, we're goin'," said another.

Three men got up and began to collect their rifles and gear. The gear was of a notably unmilitary nature: a radio—tape player with detachable speakers, a box of tapes, and a Styrofoam cooler.

"You leave the cooler," said one still seated.

"I ain't leavin' the cooler," said Cornwall.

"You're leavin' it, goddamn it."

"I ain't leavin' it!"

The cooler was evidently Cornwall's, but the contents had some community property value.

"What's *in* the cooler?" Kit asked in the middle of the argument.

There as an explosion up the line.

"What's . . ."

"Nothin'. Jus' nothin'."

Another explosion. Closer.

Suddenly the argument froze. He heard, over the voices, a third muffled explosion, not far away. A claymore.

"Hey, man, shut up!" one of the men shouted, a thin white kid who had previously said nothing. They stopped and listened.

The sound of several explosions came from farther up the line, then an eruption of rifle and machine gun fire, close and loud.

Kit didn't understand. They listened intently. The rifle fire came from both sides like strings of firecrackers.

They pushed past him and out the door, grabbing their rifles.

By the time he got out, they were out along the earth berm. A brilliant glow of flares was growing on the outside of the line about two bunkers down.

Machine guns in the nearest towers chugged away.

Another explosion pumped through the humid air. More claymores blew. Flares popped and hissed.

A helicopter appeared overhead, launching grenades into the tree line. The men who had been with Kit began firing into the darkness. Everywhere there were things firing and exploding.

The urge to shoot spread from one bunker to the next. The pop of grenade launchers and the crumping sound of the grenades themselves, the sputtering of the machine guns and the erratic rifle fire, went on and on.

Kit had no idea of what he should do. He stood transfixed. A ground attack? He had no weapon; he hadn't even a helmet. Someone had seen fit to toss a gas grenade and the first faint whiffs of gas reminded him that he had no mask.

A second helicopter came overhead, its searchlight pointing up and down the line. It caught him, blinding him for a second. More flares went off and lit the area brilliantly. The firing intensified briefly and then began to taper off.

Roxy, in the jeep, came bouncing along the Green Line road. Kit ran out and flagged him down, waving wildly in the headlights. He jumped in.

"Jesus, Lieutenant," Roxy yelled, "they're comin' through the goddamn wire. There must be a battalion out there!"

Kit's bowels, at this news, turned to yellow wine.

"A battalion? How many is that?"

"Jesus! Hundreds!"

Hundreds meant some would get through. Some were sure to get through.

"This is maybe only the first wave!" Roxy screamed at him over the noise.

"Wave?"

"They come in waves! Human waves! Waves and waves!"

Waves! Kit remembered about human wave attacks. Hordes of Orientals throwing themselves madly against machine gun fire.

"I need a rifle! Where can I get a rifle?! I don't have a rifle!"

"In the back!" Roxy yelled. He sped the jeep down the road as Kit rummaged for an M-16 in the back.

"Where are we going?" he asked Roxy as he tried to get the clip in.

"Fuck! I don't know! You're the fucking officer!"

They were approaching what seemed to be the hottest part of the firing. There were flares now in the sky everywhere.

"I don't know! Go up there! By that tower! Christ! I need a helmet, too! I need a helmet!"

"Keep your head down!" Roxy shouted.

A shower of grenade splinters and dirt crossed the jeep. Roxy braked to a sudden stop, his hands to his eyes.

"I can't see! Goddamn dirt!"

Kit got out and, with his head down, ran awkwardly over to the tower.

Suddenly the firing died off, except for some percolating rifle fire. Kit went up the ladder.

There was one man in the top, actively pounding the machine gun, trying to get it unjammed, swearing viciously at it. He turned to Kit with wide eyes.

"Who are you?"

"I'm the O-D. What's going on?"

"This thing jammed. Right off, it jams!" He continued to swear at it and then began to hit it with the steel top of an ammunition box.

"Wait!" Kit said. "They've stopped. Everybody's stopped shooting."

The man continued to swear.

"Stop it!" Kit ordered.

They both looked out over the no-man's-land of the Green Line. Smoke floated by in the dwindling light of the flares.

Roxy came up the ladder behind him.

"What happened? Why'd they stop?"

"Have you got some binoculars?" Kit asked.

"Never had any."

All three of them peered out of the tower, up and down the line.

"What happened?" Roxy asked again. "Why'd they stop?"

In the mess in front of their tower, mixed in the dirt thrown up by the mines and grenades, barely visible in the dull orange light of the dying flares, were some small, dark human bodies, looking more like dead mice. One appeared to move, making a pathetic effort to crawl away from the berm. There were about ten in all, but smaller than soldiers.

• • •

In fact, it was discovered later, they were ten girls from the village, whose organizer and procurer had approached the Green Line at the wrong place—unfortunately, not at the place where the wires had been left cut by the American soldiers. For the chance to make five hundred piastres, or about two dollars, they had agreed to go with the man through the pitch-black woods, to crawl up to the perimeter and come through at the prearranged place. But the man couldn't find the place, or had gotten confused. Maybe he had tried to cut the wires himself rather than turn back. They were halfway across when one of them hit a wire and the first claymore had gone off. From then on a fearful madness reigned.

They were all dead when, a safe time later, the Americans sent some men out to see. Then, as the sky grew pink in the east, the little bodies were picked up on stretchers and put in bags. The bags were put in a truck. Father Tran appeared miraculously and performed rites sadly over each one on the truck.

Kit, wandering among the clumps of majors and colonels who were assessing the situation, insisted on seeing for himself each one of the dead. Even in death, some with fragment puckers all over their faces, they had, to his eyes, the look of children in sleep. They might have been older, for the Vietnamese always looked like children, but their faces fell into untroubled repose.

Miss Tuyet was not among them.

Kit looked at each one for as long as he could. Then he wandered off by himself, where no one could see him, and was sick.

PART

TWO

. . .

C H A P T E R

N I N E T E E N

MR. HART

On the plane to Hong Kong, Mr. Christopher's traveling companion and lawyer, Mr. Alvin Hart, a member of the bar in six states, who preferred Alvin, not Al, began to consider more thoroughly what doing business in the Orient would be like. And what doing business with the Christophers, *père et fils*, would be like.

Mr. Hart, by this time, had heard enough about the commercial conquest of the Philippines after the Second World War. He did not say this in so many words because he was a tactful man. He gazed off into space. Mr. Christopher, midway through an-

other jolly rendition, realized that he was getting repetitious. He laughed at himself loudly and apologized profusely to Mr. Hart.

"I won't mention it again, Al."

"Thank you," said Mr. Hart.

"Not a word."

"Good."

"Silence is golden."

"Yes. It is."

A minute went by. Mr. Christopher gazed appreciatively at the JAL stewardess. Then he turned back to Mr. Hart.

"But, I don't care what war you're talking about, Al, the process is the same. I don't care what war you're talking about."

"Please," Mr. Hart said.

"If you're the winner. It's the same thing. Winners get the spoils. Count on it. I want you to understand what we're doing."

"I know what we're doing."

Most of Mr. Christopher's philosophy was about the victors as businessmen, and what things victors were reasonably expected to do. The businessman had a special position in the process that began with a military foray. The military victory was only a portion of the process. What good did it do to win a war for a purpose, even a highly commendable purpose, such as saving a benighted people from the scourge of communism, if you then abandoned them to the same corrupt government officials who had prompted the Communist insurgents in the first place?

"It would be like taking over Russia," he said, "and then setting up the czar again. You follow me?"

"Mmm-hmm," said Mr. Hart.

"The men who fought and died in Vietnam, like my son," he said, "ought not to be allowed to die in vain."

As far as Mr. Hart knew, Lieutenant Christopher was still alive. He had been shown Lieutenant Christopher's letters. It was alarming that anyone could write as badly as that. And Mr. Hart could read between the lines. Lieutenant Christopher seemed to be as interested in the money as his father.

"Yep," said Mr. Christopher. "A chip off the old . . ."

"I'd just like to read for a while."

Of course, if the truth were known, Mr. Hart was also inter-

ested in making money. He was getting sick of Mr. Christopher. He was sorry that he had ever agreed to this trip. Dealing with the man in Connecticut, in a nice, safe business environment, was one thing, but traveling with him was another. He had heard enough of Mr. Christopher's philosophy and didn't want to hear any more. But just suppose, he thought.

Suppose Mr. Christopher were right. He might be. Mr. Christopher had raised over a million dollars, a portion of which they carried with them now. To do so he had done a great deal of talking. Much of his talking was of the same type of protuberant economic philosophy of which Mr. Hart was now weary. But without Mr. Christopher's gift of gab, the money wouldn't have been raised. People did not invest in war zones unless they were in the company of a real spellbinder. Mr. Christopher had the nerve to charge ahead into new areas against impossible odds. When he got to talking, it seemed, at least for the immediate present, that the most exciting and gainful thing to do with your dollars was to give them to him.

Mr. Christopher fell asleep, leaving Mr. Hart alone in the white noise of the airplane.

Perhaps, Mr. Hart thought to himself, I am in the company of a financial genius. Perhaps the money we will make is staggering. Mr. Hart would have preferred to stay in the tranquillity of suburban Fairfield County, where a light late-spring snow was falling on the day he left for Kennedy Airport. Why disrupt one's life to go halfway around the world in search of adventure and chancy profit? Why take the chance of getting killed or terribly ill just to make some money?

Then again, it wasn't just *some* money. If things went even partly as well as Mr. Christopher predicted, it would be a lot of money, and Mr. Hart would never have to go back to the fabled Orient again. The corporation would remain in New York, and the profits would come back by courier pouch, and his fees would be skimmed off the top in the tens of thousands a month. All he had to do for this lordly sum was a little heroic work at the beginning.

He knew that Mr. Christopher wanted him along so he could swear to the existence of the property they were going to buy, so that when more investors came crowding in, they wouldn't have doubts about Mr. Christopher's motives. Investment overseas is the chanciest of all types of investments because the money is out of the United States. And once it has been transferred to foreign soils, it can get eaten by all sorts of foreign jackals, over whom the United States government has no power at all. For example, Mr. Hart reflected, looking over at the napping Mr. Christopher, his bulk rising and falling as they flew toward the setting sun, the United States government had no power over Mr. Christopher right now. High over the Pacific, with a wad of money and letters of credit in his case, Mr. Christopher was under the jurisdiction of no one. Once you left the United States, you played in an entirely new ball game. In Saigon there was no zoning, no income tax, no unions, and so on. In fact, all the things that made investment tedious and unbearable in the United States were removed.

It was like the Wild West, Mr. Hart thought; Saigon sounded like Dodge City. The gun ruled the day; feuds were carried on; people settled their differences with explosives; and the only currency was cold, hard cash. There was no other way to get the money there. They simply put the money in Mr. Christopher's suitcase and got on the plane in New York. No one stopped them.

The plan was to put most of the money into demand accounts in Hong Kong banks. Another portion they would put in the Chase Manhattan in Saigon.

This part bothered Mr. Hart. Saigon was a city at war, and the war was not going well. If the United States were withdrawing from the fighting, how could Christopher be so sure that the Vietnamese, who were supposedly replacing the Americans, would be able to protect their investment? Investors brought up this point to Mr. Christopher. What would happen if the Americans left?

Mr. Christopher's reply was one of incredulity.

"Do you think," he had said in a level voice, "that this country is going to abandon our allies to a bunch of Communists?"

It was a question that seemed to answer itself. The battle against world domination by Communists was to be settled here. If the United States abandoned the South Vietnamese, it would be a signal to every Communist insurgency around the world that the lid was off. Nixon was President, wasn't he? Mr. Christopher's argument was solid. Name a more dedicated anti-Communist! Nixon's got something going. There's a plan. A secret plan. A deal with China! Why of course! Why did Nixon go to China? Ask yourself. The fix was in. A settlement, like they had in Korea. And then they would build up the South Vietnamese nation, like they had done in South Korea. South Vietnam would flourish and dominate Indochina.

Mr. Christopher would launch into graphic descriptions of the land and the people, and follow with predictions that money invested now, at wartime distress prices, would multiply geometrically and astronomically. And one last thing! There had been discoveries in South Vietnam, he would tell the investors in confidential tones, of offshore oil. Offshore oil! Checkbooks leapt to the table and spread themselves, to be impregnated by the nearest pen.

But not Mr. Hart. Mr. Christopher said that was fine. In fact, he didn't want Mr. Hart as an investor. No one would believe a recommendation from someone who was already in the deal. Mr. Hart knew he was being used, but he had been a lawyer for a long time, and he was accustomed to such treatment.

• • •

They were in Hong Kong nearly a week. Mr. Hart was amazed by the city. He had supposed that he would be surrounded by Chinese beggars and wailing merchants. The sophistication and commercial pulse of the place surprised him. Mr. Christopher took it all in stride.

"Al," he said, "you should see your face. Did you think this was going to be all rickshas and opium smokers?" He laughed without malice, yet Mr. Hart was chagrined. He had always considered himself cosmopolitan, but now he saw that there were many things in the world about which he was completely wrong. Here was this busy, gleaming city, working and trading at a phenomenal pace, far more frenetic than New York, on the edge of the great red mass of China.

"Is that Red China, over there?" Mr. Hart asked, looking out of their hotel room.

"God, Al, you're so American!" Mr. Christopher said, not unkindly. "Don't you see? There's *millions* of them out there. What is it? Nine hundred million? A billion?"

A billion Chinese, Mr. Hart thought, all working and slaving under the crazy misery of communism—poor, benighted devils, subject to poverty and restriction he could barely tolerate to consider. It was a vile thing, communism. How they must hate the existence of Hong Kong on their very doorstep.

He could sense the money in the city. He saw the same tight concentration on the faces of the Chinese businessmen as they pushed their way through the crowded streets among the financial houses. It was the same self-absorbed, chased look he had seen in the American financial districts—not an expression of fear, exactly, but a look of being barely in control of events, of trying to steer a bulk of money through the hazards of investment. Mr. Christopher didn't concern himself with dangers; he was a planner and the booster of plans. Mr. Hart's job was to watch for the things that could go wrong.

Yes, well, it was one thing to sense the dangers in real estate development in New York or Connecticut, where the lines of control and the limits of risk were well known. He knew exactly what could go wrong with a purchase or transfer. He knew how to check on himself, whom to ask for opinions, whom to take into his confidence, how to insure himself and his clients.

But when they went to deposit their money in the Hong Kong Royal Charter Bank, there was no FDIC decal on the heavy brass and glass doors. There was nothing on the doors but painfully writhing dragons in heavy relief. There was something about dragons that unsettled Mr. Hart. He preferred eagles.

Mr. Fawn, a meticulously mannered and impeccably dressed Englishman, greeted them and escorted them smoothly to his office, which was heavily paneled, deeply carpeted, and furnished in dark, polished mahogany. He established their account, assuring them that their funds were in safe hands. This bank had a long and storied history of trustworthy dealings. They had never experienced a loss of confidence. He smiled serenely.

Mr. Hart hadn't expected to be dealing with an Englishman at this bank. He had expected a Chinese, and he had thought that

there would be all sorts of problems with translations. He hadn't expected things to go this smoothly. Mr. Fawn was charming and civil. He said he knew exactly what they wanted. They wanted assurance that their funds would be safe. He could assure them that there was nothing to worry about. The history of the Royal Charter Bank proved that.

Perhaps, Mr. Hart said, but were the accounts, in fact, insured by anyone? By the government, for example?

"Which government?" Mr. Fawn wanted to know. "The Hong Kong government? No. The British government? Again, no. There is no insurance by any government. Does the United States really insure the funds of its citizens in private banks?" Mr. Fawn was amused.

"Yes," Mr. Hart told him.

"Such a . . . well, you must excuse the term . . . *socialist* thing to do. Especially for the American government. Extraordinary."

Mr. Hart didn't think it socialist or extraordinary that the FDIC did what it did. He wanted a guarantee that, in the event of a collapse, someone would pay off.

"Well," said the Englishman smoothly, "the only assurance I can give is the historical fact that the Hong Kong banking establishment, including the London banks, the Chinese firms, the larger trading companies, and even the fraternal Chinese lending consortiums, which I must admit are rather a mystery to me, have always banded together whenever the financial integrity of the colony was in jeopardy."

"Of course they do," said Mr. Christopher warmly, wanting to end this part of the discussion.

"But who, in that case, would we come to for our money?" Mr. Hart asked. He liked to use as many monosyllabic words as possible. "Who will pay us," he asked, "if your bank fails?"

"The bank won't fail, Al," Mr. Christopher said through his teeth.

"Banks fail everywhere," Alvin Hart said in his most level voice. "I have to ask such questions, and this is the time to ask them."

"In fact," Mr. Fawn said, almost as if he shared Mr. Hart's

concern, "there really is no guarantee in the event of a complete reversal of fortunes. You are quite within your rights to consider such an eventuality, I'm sure, in consideration of your investors. It is completely proper." He folded his hands and smiled. "I can only say that I cannot, or rather we cannot—that is, this bank cannot—see events which would precipitate such a reversal. Hong Kong is an absolutely necessary cog in world trade." His eyes fluttered. "It is unthinkable. I think you may rely on that."

"You see, Al?" Mr. Christopher said.

"What about a war?"

"War?" said Mr. Fawn, his eyebrows darting upward. "Good heavens! With whom?"

"With the Chinese."

"With the Red Chinese?" Mr. Fawn put a finger under his chin. "Well, I certainly hope not. That would be unfortunate." He smiled. "But why?"

"I don't know," said Mr. Hart. "Wars seem to start without reasons. Especially in this part of the world."

The English banker saw what the problem was. He had laughed about it numerous times at his club with other English bankers. So consumed were the Americans with fighting communism that they saw nothing else. Communists, he had found, could be some of the most reliable businessmen—much more so than some Americans. In fact, the Chinese Communists were among his bank's largest depositors and borrowers. *Doesn't anyone read Orwell anymore?* he thought. He hesitated and then said:

"In fact, the Chinese Communists are some of our largest depositors and borrowers, but I'm sure you knew that."

"Of course, Al," Mr. Christopher chimed in. "They have to do business just like everyone else. Al, the Reds need business, you'll see that. They're businessmen, just like us. Am I right, Mr. Fawn?"

"I certainly can't see anything the Red Chinese would gain by taking armed action against Hong Kong."

"Haven't they got their own banks?" Mr. Hart asked.

"Who?"

"The Communists."

"Well, yes, they do. There are large state banks. But they still need to do business with the rest of the world. And they like Hong Kong dollars rather than American dollars, which they find a bit repugnant at this time in history." Mr. Fawn paused, smiling, looking for a way to sum up. "The Chinese are excellent businessmen," he said, "whether they are Communist or whatever they are. But they are still . . . ah . . . how shall I put it? They are still Chinese."

Mr. Fawn laughed at himself, but Mr. Hart was still not convinced. The unhindered and unguaranteed nature of Hong Kong banking was bothersome, even a little scary. He didn't think he liked pure capitalism, quite frankly.

They made their deposits and gave Mr. Fawn their letters of credit from New York, and received some odd documentation in return. It didn't look like much, and all he could do, he thought miserably as he read through it, was hope to God that they were doing everything right. Mr. Christopher suggested a drink.

"Hell, Al, we're international investors!"

"I suppose we are."

"This calls for a celebration. Champagne! On the investors!"

"Please."

Mr. Hart didn't think it amusing at all, but he needed a drink all the same. He felt uneasy that the Red Chinese would be depositors in the same bank they were in. He didn't want to sound simplistic, but weren't they, in some way, enemies? Wasn't it conceivable that some of their money might be loaned to some Communists? Weren't the Chinese supplying guns and things to the North Vietnamese—the very people working against the success of their prospective investments in South Vietnam, to say nothing of trying to kill Lieutenant Christopher? If it became known back in the United States that they banked with the Communists, how would this be explained?

"Nah, nah, nah!" said Mr. Christopher. "You've got it all wrong. And don't worry about my son. You read his letters!"

• • •

Their hotel was a glistening and expensive palace, capable of delivering every convenience. The prices were frightful. The rooms were spotless, tidied endlessly by the Chinese maids, who

chittered away like little birds as they went about their work. They seemed to know no English, but they were very pretty. Mr. Hart had never seen the Chinese as a people, only in Chinatown in New York, where they were just another odd group in a city of odd groups. Here, however, *he* had the feeling of being foreign.

When they returned from the bank, two maids were still in their room. The maids wore red silk pajamas with the hotel crest embroidered on the breast. Mr. Hart's eyes followed them out the door when they left. Mr. Christopher noticed.

"The incorruptible Al Hart," he said jovially. "God! I wish we could spend the time here the place deserves. The good time I could show you here, Al."

"No, thank you," said Mr. Hart.

"But they're dolls, aren't they?"

"Please."

"Ah, another incorruptible American falls to the mysteries of the Orient. You just wait, Al, my friend, you just wait."

He poured some whiskey for both of them.

"Wait for what?"

"You wait till you see the Vietnamese women! You've never seen women so lovely."

Mr. Hart was not interested. They were here on business.

"Have you ever seen Vietnamese women, Al?" Mr. Christopher said, glugging some Scotch.

"I . . . uh, no . . . that is . . ."

The only Vietnamese women Mr. Hart could ever remember seeing were in the news photographs of weeping Vietnamese mothers whose children had been caught in the cross fire of the war, or whose sons were delivered home dead. Their faces were disfigured in grief and they were usually squatting over a corpse in unassuageable misery. And there was Madame Nhu, but she was not attractive to Mr. Hart.

"Vietnamese women are simply lovely, Al. Small and dainty, and the ones with some French blood! Ah! The most beautiful females in the Orient! Take it from me. Little hands and little boobs and little bums you could eat for breakfast."

"Never mind."

"The incorruptible Al Hart!" Mr. Christopher laughed and

drank again. "But you might as well get used to it. Braver and stronger men than Al Hart have succumbed to the wiles of those little Oriental dolls. And when we own a chunk of Saigon, you're going to have to get a few for yourself."

"Must you?"

Mr. Christopher smiled as the liquor rose in his brain.

"Do you know something, Al?"

"What?"

"You know what they say about Oriental women?"

"No. I don't know what they say."

"You know how on American women the cracks go up and down?"

"What *are* you talking about?"

"The cracks! Their cunts!"

"For God's sake . . ."

"Well, on Oriental women, they're like this." He made a motion with his hand. "They're sideways!"

Mr. Christopher laughed and threw himself on his bed.

"Shut up, will you," Mr. Hart said.

"I'm not kidding. It's incredible!" Mr. Christopher cackled.

"You know something?" Mr. Hart said evenly. "You can be awfully repulsive at times."

"And you know what else? You have to . . ."

"Please, I'm not listening," Mr. Hart said, walking toward the bathroom with his shaving things.

". . . you have to lay 'em perpendicular! Hah!"

Mr. Christopher guffawed at the ceiling.

Mr. Hart went into the bathroom and closed the door. He arranged his shaving things on the marble sink top and looked around for the towels. The bathroom was luxurious, with solid marble fixtures and gleaming brass controls. There was an enormous green marble tub, large enough for three. He began running the water. While the water grew hotter, he looked at himself in the mirror. In his face was an expression of doubt. It was his lawyer's expression. His professional expression, doubting everything.

Perpendicular? He doubted it.

• • •

At dinner in the hotel, they met an American lieutenant colonel, newly promoted, whose name was Shift. He was tall and tan and angular, with a prominent brow, a sharp nose, and gray, narrow eyes. Colonel Shift had secured himself a Chinese escort for the evening, a startlingly attractive Chinese lady named simply Miss Pi. Miss Pi said nothing through the evening, but Colonel Shift was in very good spirits. He and Mr. Christopher got on famously.

The colonel had just been promoted at the MACV headquarters in Saigon and was taking some leave before reporting to his next assignment in Vietnam. He was still young to have risen so far. He was flushed with the wonder of his new rank and his increase in pay and his good fortune generally.

Colonel Shift had shown the army that in him they had someone with wonderful administrative skills. He had set up the system by which combat information was disseminated to the troops. Under Colonel Shift's command, printing presses ground out all manner of newsletters and advisory publications for the troops.

"The American soldier is the best informed soldier in the world," Colonel Shift loudly told Mr. Hart and Mr. Christopher at his table, and some diners at other nearby tables.

"That's great. That's just great," Mr. Christopher chimed in.

"We can get out information to every soldier in a matter of days. Changes in the regs, clothing allowances, insurance deals, R and R specials, anything. The troops need this information. You have no idea what an effect this has on morale. An uninformed troop is a defeatist troop. In fact, General Abrams himself still contributes to my publications. We get letters back from men in the field with all kinds of questions, and we answer them."

"That is amazing, Colonel, amazing," Mr. Christopher said. "And what kinds of things do they ask?"

"Oh, things like, how to ship their stuff they've bought back to the States. You'd be surprised how much stuff some of these troops go home with. They buy cameras and stereos and rice cookers and—now, here's a fact for you—the average American

soldier buys nearly five hundred dollars' worth of stuff, and most of it is shipped right here from Hong Kong. But they've got a problem, like, say, how do I get all this stereo stuff back home safely? It's a real problem."

Mr. Hart marveled, but to himself. Added to all the problems a soldier faced in a war zone was the shipping home of sensitive consumer electronic equipment. He hadn't known this.

"Some of them don't know that the army will ship home three hundred pounds. And that's just for the enlisted troops. For the officers, it's even more. I think a lieutenant gets over five hundred pounds, and then it goes up all the way to a general."

"How much does a colonel get?" Mr. Christopher asked in jest. Lieutenant Colonel Shift didn't get the joke right away. And then he did.

"Oh, hah! You see? There you are. I gotta write a letter for some combat information."

Hearty laughter followed. So infectious that even Miss Pi joined in.

Slowly, with a salesman's grace, Mr. Christopher brought the conversation around to the sort of business he and Mr. Hart were engaged in. He asked about Saigon. The colonel said:

"Of course, Saigon and Long Binh are secure and the Bien Hoa corridor is patrolled. You'll be able to go anywhere there you want to. North of Phu Loi, you better fly."

"Now, *can* we fly?" Mr. Christopher asked as their relationship warmed.

"No problem," Colonel Shift assured him. "What you'll do is," he said, lighting Miss Pi's cigarette, "you'll get into Tan Son Nhut, and then you'll ask the air battalion, and . . ."

He rattled on about the procedure for requesting aircraft in an assured voice. He was also a little drunk. He now took Mr. Christopher and Mr. Hart to be men of extreme worth, both financially and, of course, as human beings. They could expect the last degree of cooperation from the army. It seemed as though the army would welcome Mr. Christopher's business ventures as they welcomed nothing else. Mr. Christopher pinched Mr. Hart under the table. Mr. Hart tried to get a question in:

"Is there any fighting going . . . ?"

"That's great. Just great!" Mr. Christopher interrupted.

Colonel Shift's new job at the MACV headquarters was processing the reports of the transfer of assignments and equipment to the South Vietnamese Army.

"Vietnamization is as smooth an operation as I have ever been part of. Highly professional. A smooth transition of the entire effort to our allies. All ahead of schedule."

Thousands of hamlets and towns in South Vietnam were all catalogued as to their relative security and affection for the South Vietnamese government.

"The Viet Cong infrastructure is literally broken. Smashed! Destroyed! All the South Vietnamese, the ARVNs, have to do now is hold on until the settlement is reached. And we're going to give 'em the tools to do it."

"Great!" said Mr. Christopher.

"I got every village on a separate IBM card, and whether it's friendly or not."

"Computers?" said Mr. Christopher. "Here?"

"It's amazing, gentlemen!" Colonel Shift expostulated. "This is the first war fought by computer!"

The computer also knew about each piece of the hundreds of thousands of pieces of materiel the United States had shipped to the country in all the years of the war. The computer searched through all the cards again and again, printing out a plan of distribution of weaponry for the South Vietnamese army to meet exactly the combat need throughout the country. Never before had the army had the great advantage of being able to get this kind of accurate matching of mission and materiel. Never before in the history of warfare.

"Computers are amazing!" said the colonel, picking up a fresh drink.

"God," Mr. Christopher said. "They *are* amazing."

"Never before," Colonel Shift went on, "have we been able to know exactly what's going on. The thing spits out a complete analysis on a daily basis. You should see the Vietnamese when we show them. Let me tell you. They are amazed!"

Previous wars, the colonel said, depended on instinct and intu-

ition. It was a case of luck. The great generals of past wars were simply the lucky generals. With the computer, luck could be dispensed with as, he felt, it should be. Modern war was scientific.

"We know where the friendly villages are, you see, so we don't have to waste resources defending them."

Mr. Hart hadn't said much, but it occurred to him now that he would also like to know where the friendly villages were.

"Where are the friendly villages?" he asked.

"The what?" Colonel Shift lit another cigarette for Miss Pi. She didn't even know the English for "thank you." She just smiled and smoked.

"The friendly villages," Mr. Hart said. "Where are they?"

"All over. It depends. The computer list is made up from field reports."

"How do you know if it's friendly?"

"Well," said Colonel Shift, "the computer list says those villages are . . . are friendly."

"But how do you know they are friendly?"

"Because . . . well, because the IBM cards say they are."

"There you are, Al," said Mr. Christopher.

Mr. Christopher took charge of the conversation for the rest of the evening. Mr. Hart tuned himself out and thought about friendly villages defended by doughty bands of IBM cards.

Mr. Christopher spun the tale of the halcyon days in Manila and of his great success there. Colonel Shift listened closely. It was a fascinating tale the first time you heard it.

In 1945, in the confusion and revelry that followed the defeat of the hated Japanese, Mr. Christopher had moved quickly ("Quickly. That's the secret!") to buy up a number of things that would be needed in the rebuilding of the city. PT boats and army trucks and even things that had been left behind by the Japanese. He had water tankers and cement trucks. He sold all of the stuff he had back to the Philippine government, which really meant selling it back to the American government ("Hah-hah!"). He had three hotels that he ran as nightclubs and brothels for American servicemen.

The aspect Mr. Christopher found so memorable about the

entire era was the complete lack of law in the Philippines. For a time he literally ("I mean literally!") ran the liquor trade on one of the largest islands.

Then gangs of Filipino insurgents started running around in the streets. He sold his holdings to his partners and got the hell out. By the time the real fighting started, Mr. Christopher was comfortably in Westchester County, dabbling in real estate.

His timing had been perfect. He had not been blinded by greed so that he stayed overlong ("That's the secret!"). He knew when to get in and, more important, he knew when to get out.

Colonel Shift was transfixed, and slightly gassed. He sat with his mouth agape. The exact same opportunity awaited them in Saigon. The city would be wide open.

He was a military man, he said, and he had never thought about Saigon in terms of real estate. But, now that he did think about it, well, of course, he could see it was all exactly as Mr. Christopher said. And he wanted Mr. Christopher to know that if there was anything he could do to help—anything—Mr. Christopher had only to ask. Aircraft, vehicles, whatever he needed.

"You know," said Mr. Christopher in an emotional voice, looking down at his hands, "that's some of the nicest words I've ever heard." He kicked at Mr. Hart under the table.

"Hell! You just ask!" said the colonel.

"See, that's the kind of help we need."

"You can count on me!"

"This is an amazing stroke of luck. I mean, what we've got to do is get around. Find the owners. What my son is trying to do. I guess most of these owners are Chinese," said Mr. Christopher.

"The Jews of the Orient," said the colonel, completing his tenth drink. "The Chinese. Jesus!"

"Are they hard to deal with?"

"Like I say, the Jews of the Orient. You take it from there!" He laughed.

Mr. Christopher laughed, too.

"Listen," said the colonel, leaning close to him, "don't worry about the Chinese. After we get the goddamn North Vietnamese outta there, we'll throw the goddamn Chinese out as well. The

Viets hate the Chinese. We'll heave the goddamn Chinese out on their slanty asses."

He held a match unsteadily for Miss Pi, who probably didn't understand the fate in store for her countrymen in Saigon.

If she did, she was too polite to say anything.

CHAPTER

TWENTY

THE GHOST SHIP

Back in Phuoc Vinh, an unexpected thing had happened. Major Bedford had been wounded!

He had been out in the aircraft repair area to arrange for the installation of huge loudspeakers and a tape recorder on a helicopter for psychological operations. The tapes had been made in Saigon at MACV headquarters—tapes of a Vietnamese soldier's ghost, screaming an appeal for surrender. Major Bedford had taken the initiative in this project, which he hoped would show up on his evaluation report.

He was in front of the repair hangar when the afternoon mortar attack started.

Three mortars landed. Three loud whoomps. Everyone ran for cover. Then another three whoomps. Major Bedford collided into two spec fours running for the building. Together they knocked down the metal door and dived for the floor. But he wasn't wounded then.

Outside, a wave of mortar shrapnel knocked a young forklift operator off his machine as he was racing toward the hangar. The forklift was an enormous, rough-terrain version with huge tires and a powerful diesel motor, capable of lifting whole helicopters. It was still in gear, and it slowed to a crawl. But it didn't stop. It lumbered blindly down the runway.

A sergeant from the repair sheds bravely ran after the machine. He tried to get on and stop it. The forklift glanced off a revetment and made a sharp turn across the runway. The sergeant fell off, landing flat on his back. He got up and chased the machine again. He caught up with it and made a second attempt. This time he fell short, landing on his face. In his third try he was able to get on the rear engine housing, but there was no way to climb into the driver's cage to shut the thing off. He jumped off again, spraining his leg badly. By this time the mortars had stopped. Major Bedford and some of others came out of the hangar.

The sergeant who was giving chase was scuffed up, bruised front and back. He was enraged at the brainless machine. He followed wildly, screaming endless profanity at the mindless hulk, now headed for the end of the runway, where the land dropped off down to a ditch. Major Bedford and the pilot got a jeep and drove after him, through the dirt-laden air. They saw him gimping along crazily, as fast as he could, oblivious to his pain. They saw him as he caught up with the damned thing, and in a final desperate lunge caught the side bars of the driver's cage and pulled himself up, just as the forklift went over the edge of the runway. It pitched forward.

The decline was too steep. The forks dug in at an angle and the entire bulk swung around and tipped over sideways down the hill.

They scrambled down after it.

And there was the heroic sergeant, now under the machine, pinned across the small of his back by the steel roof bars of the

driver's cage. His back was snapped. The motor had stopped and he screamed, an almost inaudible rasp.

They tried, in panic, to lift, to push, to pry the machine off him. Major Bedford, having completely lost his professional control in the presence of this silently screaming man, pulled and tugged at the dead weight of the forklift. And it was then that his wound occurred. Somewhere down in his groin.

There was nothing to be made of such a wound. A Purple Heart would not be awarded for a hernia, despite the fact that it hurt like bloody hell. Major Bedford could hardly walk straight for a good deal of the time, especially in the morning. It made him terribly self-conscious. He massaged the painful muscles through the layer of fat that surrounded them. But only when he had made sure no one was watching.

Especially Kit.

• • •

Major Bedford was in love with Kit, but he didn't know what to do about it. This was the first time it had happened to him. He was happy and flabbergasted at first. Then he got hold of himself and disciplined his mind. Maybe it was love, and maybe he was just going crazy. He had been in Vietnam nearly two years, and maybe this was what happened. But he couldn't look at Kit now without feeling the loneliest joy and the sweetest terror. And to be near him was almost more than he could bear. He couldn't think about this situation except in terms of constant surprise.

There's a myth of army life which says that during war men make close friends rapidly. When men place their lives in one another's hands they form a bond that transcends anything civilians could ever understand. It's a myth that can almost make going to war seem worthwhile. Major Bedford thought it would happen to him, but after all this time in Vietnam, all he had were acquaintances. The army wasn't a closely knit fraternity facing a common enemy. It was more like an empty shelter. Men came, did what was expected, and moved on.

But Kit's fortuitous assignment to the civil affairs section gave Major Bedford some hope. After disciplining his mind, he made plans. He would let Kit get to know him slowly, perhaps doing little favors for him. In this way they would become friends. That's all. A bond of friendship would spring up between them, or something. Major Bedford felt as if he were starting to climb a ladder that leaned against thin air. It felt in a way like the first time, long ago, when he had fallen in love with a woman.

• • •

One morning Major Bedford discovered that he actually did have something for Kit to do.

"Here," he said, "listen to this tape."

"Tape?"

"It's Vietnamese. It's a lost soul."

"What?"

"It's the voice of the ghost of a dead North Vietnamese soldier."

"Really? How did they . . ."

"It's psychological."

"Oh."

Over the years of the war, repeated attempts were made to convince the soldiers of the North Vietnamese Army, through psychology, that they should lay down their arms and join the government of South Vietnam. Millions of leaflets were dropped all over the jungle. By the time Major Bedford got to Vietnam, probably billions had been served.

Major Bedford's psy war operations included requisitioning the leaflets, which were printed by the United States Government Printing Office, and arranging for the aircraft to drop them. Every month he processed the requisitions and went down to the supply battalion to pick up the leaflets when they came by truck from Bien Hoa Air Base. The leaflets were thrown out of the helicopters over supposed enemy areas which Major Bedford decided on and marked on a map.

He kept the map on the wall in his office. The idea behind psychological warfare wasn't new. Early in the war, in the mid-sixties, the leaflets had appealed to the insurgents' love of their homeland. The words made all sorts of promises about the Americans' desire to help the freedom-loving people of Vietnam to establish and thrive in a democratic land.

These early leaflets were decorated with stylish line drawings of handsome white American Special Forces soldiers with generic rural Oriental people clustered around. The American soldier was giving something away—food, medicine, clothing, and free advice.

But as the war had gone on and the North Vietnamese had become the enemy, the handsome white Special Forces soldier had been replaced by the regular U.S. Army. The leaflets now being used abandoned any appeal to patriotism or the prospect of peace and plenty. Instead, they played on the most basic of Vietnamese fears—that of being killed and left to rot in the jungle without a proper burial, far from home. The legend was that the soul, longing for such a ceremony, would wander forever in insufferable misery and loneliness, seeking the souls of other family members. The new leaflets were decorated with cartoons of skulls and drawings of skeletons walking around in graveyards.

The quest for turncoats had come down to such childish terrorism. In Major Bedford's two years of leafleting only five North Vietnamese had come in, and they were so ill that they represented a net loss to the United States. Had they remained in the jungle they would surely have died from their illnesses, or been a drain on the limited medical resources of the enemy. By remaining in the jungle, therefore, they would have helped the American war effort. But no, they had shown up at the gate of the base, as requested, with the leaflets, which also served as safe-conduct passes. Two of them had stumbled into Nuoc Vang, delirious with fever and weakened by malnutrition. The village chief of Nuoc Vang, a canny old bastard, not wanting the expense and effort of burying them, quickly gave them transportation to the American base and gave them some leaflets that he kept on hand for just such emergencies. Five surrenders in two years was not a commanding record, given the tons of leaflets he had dropped, and somehow, Major Bedford thought that he would be blamed.

But technology does not stand still. The Psychological Warfare Command in Saigon had got hold of some powerful speakers and tape recorders that could be mounted on helicopters. From a thousand feet up, the speakers could be heard distinctly. The helicopter was to be flown at night, carrying a taped message of appeal for surrender from the ghost of a North Vietnamese soldier, wandering around unburied. Major Bedford, for reasons having to do with his career, arranged to have such a system brought to Phuoc Vinh.

"The general would like to know how this thing works," Lieutenant Stevenson said when Major Bedford requested the aircraft. Aircraft and fuel were in short supply now.

"Well," Major Bedford said, "we'll play this tape on the loudspeakers at night. A tape of a dead soul."

"A dead soul . . ." Stevenson said, making a note, holding his face still.

"And the dead soul is lost."

". . . dead soul lost . . ." Stevenson noted.

"And he's sort of howling to find his way home."

". . . howling . . ."

"Right."

Stevenson's pen stopped.

"I see," he said. "And does he?"

"No," Major Bedford said. "That's the point. When you hear it at night in the jungle, well, it's very scary."

"And you throw down your weapon and surrender?"

"Yes," said Major Bedford.

Stevenson restrained a smirk.

"What does the dead soul say?"

"I don't actually know."

"I see," said Stevenson, making a note.

"Maybe I'll ask Lieutenant Christopher. He knows Vietnamese."

"So I understand," said Stevenson.

The Vietnamese fear of death without a proper burial was a serious fear, even though it made little sense to Americans. The tape was replete with the sounds of moans and shrieks and rattling bones and whistling winds. The voice of the wandering soul cried out for family and friends, children and parents.

"No one will believe this shit back home," the pilot, Mr. O'Connor, told Major Bedford.

The voice on the tape howled and cried. Major Bedford had heard it, and even though he could not understand a single word, he had to admit that it gave him the willies. He felt enough like a wandering soul alive.

"Can you understand what it's saying?" he asked Kit while he tested the tape in the office. He pulled up a chair for Kit, and then another for himself. The voice howled mournfully.

Kit gave his standard answer. "Not exactly, sir."

"It's a dead Vietnamese soul, calling out for help."

"Uh-huh," Kit said.

"You know, the soul of a dead Vietnamese who is wandering in the jungle." Major Bedford leaned closer to Kit's ear.

"I see," Kit said.

"It's a myth. The Vietnamese think if you're not buried, your soul wanders forever."

"Uh-huh."

"So we play this tape from the helicopter."

"We?"

"Well, yes, *we* are going to do it. I am going to need your help on this," Major Bedford said, his heart racing.

• • •

The Ghost Ship, as it came to be known, had to be flown at night. Most of the pilots didn't like to fly at night. The one pilot willing to undertake such a mission was Mr. O'Connor, a warrant office one, with a reputation for taking chances. He was only twenty and something of a hot dog.

Mr. O'Connor wanted to paint the ghost ship solid black, which made sense. Major Bedford said that he would go along with that. Mr. O'Connor also wanted to paint a large white skull and crossbones on the front of the helicopter in fluorescent paint. Major Bedford would *not* go along with that.

"But a skull and crossbones will scare the hell out of them," Mr. O'Connor argued, his voice rising in enthusiasm. He was getting more and more excited about the entire project.

"Can't you see it, Major, this big white skull and crossbones coming through the air. It'll be like, you know, Halloween. I remember one time on a Halloween night, me and my friend, when these guys where I lived painted a skeleton on a black sheet, and they had this light that flashed on, and my God, it

scared the hell out of us and my friend was so scared he pissed his pants."

He pounded the desk in hilarity. Major Bedford waited out his laughter.

"No," he explained.

Mr. O'Connor was disappointed. Finally, Major Bedford compromised and allowed the skull and crossbones to be painted on the front in deep blood red. The design was accomplished that very afternoon by one of the enlisted troops with some artistic ability. This made the entire project seem even more juvenile in Major Bedford's eyes, but everyone else seemed to think it quite exciting. A curious thing started to happen to Major Bedford.

Major Bedford found himself in command, as it were, of a large and dangerous piece of military hardware. He had always thought of helicopters and planes and tanks as expensive and complicated and essentially beyond him. They were something that other people ran and worried about. His career had been a tracery of desk jobs and staff positions. Nothing destructive or powerful had ever been under his jurisdiction. Now the Ghost Ship and Mr. O'Connor were assigned to him on a rather permanent basis.

The Ghost Ship helicopter could not be used for other missions, and it sat in a special place all day, waiting for its first flight. In a way it now belonged to Major Bedford, and he began to think about it in an intermittently possessive way. He went out to look at it in the afternoons and inspect things. He even sat in the copilot's seat while he looked over the log.

Back in his office, Major Bedford began spending serious time thinking about where he should send this wonderful machine. He sat with a map in front of him, and a pencil and a ruler, and some dividers, planning missions for the Ghost Ship to fly.

Missions! A wonderful word. It was rather amazing, but that's what he was planning. He was planning combat missions. This meant flight over hostile territory. It meant an Air Medal for himself and for Kit. Sort of like a present. Then there was the great amount of thinking that he now had to do about flying time and fuel capacity and altitudes and radio contact and secure codes and, well, the list went on.

He sat back and looked around his office, which had begun to take on a pleasant, cluttered look. Mr. O'Connor had swiped a flight helmet and a flight suit for him. The helmet was far from new, badly scratched and repainted several times, all of which was fine with Major Bedford. The helmet sat on a corner of Sergeant Swanson's table. Sergeant Swanson was reading the poetry in *Stars and Stripes.*

"Sergeant Swanson," he said.

"What . . ."

Major Bedford waited.

"What . . . sir?" Swanson added at last.

"We need a larger map of the area put up on the wall there."

"We do?"

"Yes, and some tacks and some acetate and some grease pencils . . . and a plotter . . . and some rulers . . . and string. And I want them today."

Sergeant Swanson could make such a project last two weeks.

"NLT COB today."

"What?"

"Not later than close of business. That means before you eat."

"Jesus." Sergeant Swanson sighed.

"I beg your pardon, Sergeant?"

"Yes, sir . . ."

• • •

It was ten o'clock in the morning. Sergeant Swanson slunk out. Major Bedford returned to his map. He had no idea where he should start the missions. Maybe north of the Bo Mua rubber plantation. That was as good a place as any. But for more locations he needed some information, some intelligence, and auspiciously, at the very moment he realized that he needed more intelligence, Kit came in the door.

"Look here, Kit," he said, "what about this area for the Ghost Ship?"

"That might be a good place," Kit said agreeably.

"Or maybe over here, by the river."

"Yup. Maybe."

Major Bedford looked up at Kit. It shocked him sometimes to

contemplate the smooth, pink-brown muscularity of Kit's neck rising from the pale green fatigues. The soft symmetry of the muscles, lying on either side, the cords and veins arranged in relaxed perfection, twisting in gentle ripples as Kit looked at the map in feigned concern. Four, maybe five, blond hairs broached the lowest point of his collar.

"Now, you have experience in intelligence. You make the decision," Major Bedford said.

"Well, did you say this would be a good place?" Kit asked, pointing vaguely.

"Yes, I did. That might be a good place."

"I think so, too."

Major Bedford looked down at Kit's hands, at his lazily laced fingers in front of his crotch. They were perfect hands—long and angular, like sculpture.

"All right, then, that's it. Tomorrow."

Kit ran a hand through his hair, pushing the straw blond shock back away from his eyes.

"Okay. That sounds . . . okay."

Kit, preparing to leave, looked around for his hat.

"And another thing, Lieutenant."

"Sir?"

"You'll need a flight helmet."

"A flight helmet?"

"Yes, by tomorrow night."

Kit looked at Major Bedford openly, thinking about this.

"Night?"

"Yes. We fly at night."

"Okay. Sir."

"That's when the ghosts walk the earth."

CHAPTER

TWENTY-ONE

SERGEANT SWANSON

S tevenson changed the numbers on the chart in General Walker's trailer. The number of Americans was now half what it had been a year ago. Walker's air conditioner was still working, and Stevenson decided to take advantage of the cool. He took out his notebook and two packs of cigarettes he had just bought, and began to write.

Dear Father,
Sergeant Xuan has been recovering nicely. He should be well enough to travel any day now. He will be able to meet you at the

Hotel Napoleon in Saigon I wrote you about. You should let us know when . . .

The general came unexpectedly through the door. Stevenson's hand moved like lightning to cover his writing. He knocked the cigarettes on the floor.

"What the hell is wrong with you?" the general growled at him.

"Wrong, sir?" Stevenson bent to pick up the cigarettes.

"Don't start that shit. 'Wrong, sir?' You know what I mean. You're gone a lot and I don't know where the hell you are."

"I'm sorry, General. I'll be more attentive."

"Answer the question. What the hell are you up to?"

"I don't know what you're referring to, sir."

"Jesus."

"Sir, I am not up to anything."

"You're up to something. You're lying!"

Stevenson willed himself to be calm. It was good training. He put the cigarettes in his pocket and stood silently. Walker slumped in his chair. He wiped his face.

"You don't smoke," he said.

"I decided to try, sir."

"Liar."

Stevenson looked at him blankly, like a mirror.

"Can I get you anything, sir?" he asked at last.

"Yes. Get out," Walker said. "No, wait . . ."

Walker sat a moment.

"What's that you're writing?"

Stevenson uncovered the letter. God, he thought, this *is* good training.

"A letter to my father, sir."

Stevenson left the general's trailer. A jeep pulled up. Sergeant Swanson was driving. His passenger was Father Tran.

Stevenson continued writing in the mess hall.

And I must tell you that I could not have gotten any of this done if it had not been for my friend David Stevenson. He has been of

great help. I think I told you about him. He went to West Point. I think he should be given a fair percentage. I think at least . . .

The mess hall smelled like a garbage strike. The mess sergeant was in back, ranting to himself. Fine, Stevenson thought. No one would bother him here.

. . . at least as much as I am in for. He is good at organizing things and getting things done. I would recommend . . .

Except Sergeant Swanson. Swanson stomped into the mess hall, his expression black and his eyes blazing. He had a map under his arm and some string and tacks and crayons. Stevenson looked up.

"Ah! Swanson," Stevenson said.

"What?" Swanson grunted back.

"What, what?" Stevenson said.

"Oh, you, too?"

"Me, too, what?"

"You 'sir'-happy, too?"

Stevenson decided Swanson was on the brink of something.

"You've brought the priest again, Sergeant?" he asked.

Swanson was glumly helping himself to some corn bread left drying in a tray by the coffee machine. His blond hair was overlong and his hands dirty.

"Mmmh," Swanson said, an expression designed to be affirmative.

"How many times this week?"

Swanson held two fingers.

"Two times?"

Swanson looked at his two fingers and counted them.

"One. Two. Yeah, two times. Ya got that? Can I put my fingers down now?"

Swanson had never reacted this hatefully to him, even when he had deserved it a great deal more. Swanson kept the two fingers in the air, and gurgled down a can of milk. Stevenson was curious.

"Does he ever say what he does with the general?"

"Nosy fucker, aren't you?"

"What?"

"Nosy fucker, sir."

"Hmmm . . ."

Swanson continued eating.

"You have no idea why he's there?"

"How do I know? Maybe he gives him blow jobs. You should know."

"I just thought you might have heard something, that's all."

Swanson wiped his mouth on the end of his fatigue blouse.

"Drivin' around all day, plus I gotta go tonight!" he spat out.

"Tonight?" asked Stevenson.

"Yeah, tonight."

"What happens tonight?"

"The black helicopter—the ghoul thing."

"With Major Bedford?"

"Yeah. Bedbug."

Stevenson had heard about the Ghost Ship, and knew that it had been painted black. But it was news to him that Swanson was part of the crew. The entire project seemed to be the strangest thing they had attempted so far. But many strange things were going on.

"You're going on the Ghost Ship?" he asked.

"Mmmph," Swanson said through his corn bread and milk.

"Well," Stevenson said, returning to his writing, "the very best of luck."

• • •

Stevenson finished the letter to Mr. Christopher, folded it in threes, and put it in his shirt pocket. He went to the serving line and took some corn bread and some fruit and a few cans of Donald Duck orange juice and left the mess hall by the back door. As he walked down the rotting boardwalk to his bunker, he saw Kit coming out of the post office. Kit ducked under the low doorway, avoiding the steel planks where the roof had sagged. He had a flight helmet under his arm and a pistol strapped around his waist. He stood up to his full height, half a head taller than

Stevenson. They do-si-doed past each other to avoid stepping off the boardwalk into the mud.

"Ah. Christopher. Uh . . ."

"Yes?" said Kit.

"Well, any mail for me . . . ah, us? Anything from . . . ah . . . our father?"

"No."

"Hmmm . . ."

"I wonder what he's doing," Kit said.

"He hasn't written in . . . ?"

"Two weeks," Kit said.

"Hmmm . . ."

"Yes. I . . ."

"Now, don't start worrying. Things are under control. Xuan is much better."

Stevenson drew out the draft letter.

"Here's a new letter for father. Get it out today."

"But . . . well, I can't. I've got to go on the . . . you know . . ."

"The Ghost Ship?" Stevenson rolled his eyes.

Kit looked at the horizon in embarrassment.

"So it's you and Bedford and Swanson?"

"Yes. Tonight."

"Look," Stevenson said quickly. "You have to send this letter tonight. I mean, you never know what will happen . . ."

●　●　●

Stevenson went into Major Bedford's stifling bunker. Xuan was now sleeping in Major Ponchuso's old room. Stevenson paid Thi Tuan, the houseboy, to take care of him. Major Ponchuso had been sent home early.

Thi Tuan, under Stevenson's instruction, kept a lock on the door. Stevenson worked the combination and went in. Major Ponchuso's room smelled of antiseptic and sweat and shit. The room was incredibly hot. Stevenson put the food down and waited in the dark. He turned on the fan, which Major Ponchuso, in his haste, had left behind. But there was no power now, and Stevenson remembered that power to the bunkers was now shut off during the day to save fuel.

Sergeant Xuan slept like a dead man.

So this was Nixon's policy. All sorts of economies had been instituted—fuel for the generators was just one. There were, for the first time, shortages of artillery shells. There was a serious shortage of bombs and napalm canisters. The air force sent bombing missions only on targets where they were *sure* the enemy was hiding, as if anyone had ever been sure. Observation flights were cut back, convoys of supplies to outlying firebases were cut back. Even beer and medicine were in short supply. Everything was in short supply, except the North Vietnamese.

What else could you expect, Stevenson thought, if you elected a former ration-control officer to the presidency?

And for every man who rotated home early, like Major Ponchuso, only half a man was allowed back. The infantry battalions patrolling the jungle around Phuoc Vinh and manning the perimeter were operating with fewer and fewer men. The chart on the wall in General Walker's trailer told the story. Some units were at skeleton crew level. Those remaining in Vietnam were at greater risk.

He picked up Sergeant Xuan's chamber pot and took it outside.

The only thing that had kept the North Vietnamese at bay was constant pounding from the bombers and the howitzers. Without that, they were able to bring more mortar rounds down the trail and lob them into Phuoc Vinh every evening. He had seen the reports. Stores of artillery rounds for the American batteries were down to a ten-day supply. Some of the supplies were being siphoned off for operations up in Laos, but the majority of them were being turned over to the South Vietnamese Army, which grabbed them and hid them. The South Vietnamese army was now utterly and irretrievably demoralized, frightened and beleaguered. And iridescent with corruption.

Stevenson wondered what Nixon would do during a mortar attack, when the explosions marched across the base and the air was so full of dirt you couldn't see. He conjured up a mental picture of Nixon trying to take cover, as it was said, up his own ass.

He took the top off the chamber pot and looked in. Inside were two tiny Vietnamese turds. He looked at them clinically. His patient seemed healthy. That was a good sign. He dumped them into the hole.

Nixon and his pals thought they were going to be able to talk the North Vietnamese into a peace agreement. And everybody back home was cheering him on. They wanted to forget, and Nixon was arranging things so they could. But the North Vietnamese were a simple people; things were divided into basic groups. There were living people and dead people. The Americans could die or to go back to America. They could not negotiate themselves out. Peace with honor. After dropping bombs on North Vietnam for years, Nixon promised Peace with Honor? He talked only as a man might who had not seen the craters and the wreckage and the corpses. The North Vietnamese would not allow Peace with Honor for such people. *Death* with Honor, possibly, but not Peace.

Hmmm . . . Stevenson thought, banging the pot against the side of the outhouse seat.

The Americans were turning over more guns and shells to the South Vietnamese Army, which in some cases was the same as dumping it all into the ocean. The South Vietnamese still had not learned to fire artillery accurately. ARVN artillery landed all over the place. It's hard to do trigonometry when you're scared.

And now that Stevenson thought about it, he was mildly scared himself. The reduction of the defenses of Phuoc Vinh bothered him. The real possibility of being overrun some night by people with grenades and satchel charges loomed in his mind. What an amusing thought. He remembered Starret's account of Firebase Touchhole. *I shall crawl up my own ass,* he thought.

He went back to Xuan's room and placed the pot under Xuan's bed. Xuan stirred. Stevenson cleared his throat. He took Xuan's lighter and lit the candle.

Sergeant Xuan raised his head a little and looked at him.

"How are you?" Stevenson said.

Sergeant Xuan had lost what little fat there was on his body and his eyes were protuberant. He smiled automatically, but he didn't look at all well.

"I am much better," he said, his voice barely a whisper.

"That's good. Do you need anything?"

"Did you get any cigarettes, please?"

"Ah, yes. I remembered. Anything else?"

"No, not anything else."

Stevenson took out the two packs and put them on the table in the midst of the pain pills and antibiotics.

"Please . . ."

"Of course."

He opened one and tapped out a cigarette for Xuan. He put it to Xuan's thin lips and lit it. Xuan sucked in the smoke and then eased himself back on the pillow.

"Have you tried standing up?"

"Yes," Sergeant Xuan said weakly. "I am trying. In a few days."

"Well, now, I don't want you to force yourself. I don't want you to hurt yourself anymore."

"Have you seen Captain Lam?"

"Don't worry, I said I would take care of Captain Lam."

"You *must* talk to him and give him the money. He can arrest me now."

"You're not going to get arrested, Sergeant. You have my word on that."

"You have to make sure that he knows I want a full release. You must get the paper from him. That is the only way," said Xuan, his voice a smoky sickbed whisper.

"All right, don't worry."

"I will go to Saigon soon."

"All right."

Stevenson opened a Donald Duck orange juice.

"Here. This stuff is good for you," he said.

• • •

Major Bedford caught sight of himself in a full-length mirror in the hall of the operations center. He had often checked the condition of his uniform in this mirror, which stood near the hall to the briefing room. But he had never seen himself in his flight suit before. He had his scuffed and scratched flight helmet under his arm. He stopped and considered the entire effect.

The flight suit, which he had gotten from Mr. O'Connor, fit him like a green sausage casing, but even so, he still looked rather dashing. The suit wasn't new and had some colorful grease stains on the knees and elbows. Some of the plastic patches were torn. He planned to get his name stitched on the breast pocket and his rank put on the shoulders.

He hadn't thought very much about the fact that he was going to be flying in a helicopter, over enemy territory, making a lot of loud noise, without much armament. At night. If the enemy troops were scared out of their wits by the recording of the ghost shrieking and screaming and the bones rattling, it might be a fairly safe operation.

But suppose, on the other hand, that they thought it all a bunch of nonsense and took it into their heads to shoot the Ghost Ship down. It might happen that way. There had been a noticeable change in the attitude of the enemy. They were bolder, more resourceful, and worst of all, better armed. They had Russian heat-seeking missiles, for example.

The Ghost Ship was armed with one machine gun, which hung out the right side. Normally there would have been two guns, one on each side. But the gun on the left side had been removed so that the speaker mounts and the cables could be bolted in the sliding doorway, and the doors were locked open.

● ● ●

Off into evening sky they went. A low band of orange on the horizon was all that was left of the daylight. Kit looked down on the receding lights of Phuoc Vinh, trying to find his bunker. The base drifted away behind them, and darkness yawned ahead. How black the night was in areas of the world where there was no electricity. He longed immediately for the homeyness of Phuoc Vinh base.

Major Bedford sat in the copilot's seat, and Kit sat in the seat behind him. Sergeant Swanson stayed back with the recorder and the sound equipment.

Swanson had been late. He had been somewhere, and when he finally showed up at the aviation sheds, he was hot and angry. Anyone could tell that he was not his normally affable self. It was past his working day, and he had not had time to get a full dinner. He had little respect for this project—certainly not enough to miss a meal over.

The helicopter sliced along through the air. Below, the road from Phuoc Vinh to the rubber plantation was barely visible, but Mr. O'Connor only needed a glimpse every now and then to get his bearings. Kit wondered how the helicopter was steered, how it stayed up in the air, and how Mr. O'Connor could tell where he was going.

Major Bedford was a dark bulk in the seat in front of him. Kit had come to like Major Bedford for the same reason he liked Major Dow—that Major Bedford liked him. He didn't fully comprehend the depth of Major Bedford's friendship, but he noticed that he was warm and helpful.

They glided on through the evening to the south, toward the rubber plantation. Below them the Bo Mua Road was deserted.

Sergeant Swanson crouch-walked up behind Kit's seat and tapped him on the shoulder. Kit pulled his helmet back a little so Swanson could yell at him over the rhythmic pop of the propeller.

"You ready?" Swanson yelled.

Kit reached over and tapped Major Bedford's shoulder.

"Swanson wants to know if he should start the tape," Kit said into the microphone on his helmet.

"Not yet," he heard O'Connor's voice say.

He pushed his microphone to the side.

"Not yet!" he yelled to Swanson.

Swanson paused a few seconds.

"When, for Christ's sake?" he yelled. "Let's get this over with!"

Kit waited.

"Sergeant Swanson wants to know if he should start the recorder up," he said into the microphone.

"Tell him to goddamn wait!" O'Connor shouted back. "We're not even there."

"Where are we now?" Major Bedford said into the intercom.

"Dammit, we're . . ." Mr.O'Connor stopped.

"Where are we?!" Swanson yelled next to Kit's helmet.

"Wait," Kit said back to him, holding up five fingers.

"Is that the plantation house?" Major Bedford asked.

"I don't know. Where?"

"Over there, see those lights?"

The plantation house, where M. LaPorte conducted affairs for the Michelin Company, was the only place with a generator for miles. The house had a fence around it with some dim security lights, and they could see it coming up on the right. The woods north of the rubber trees where Lieutenant Toomey had shot his men were to their left.

Swanson tapped Kit again.

"You ready now?!" he yelled.

"Are we ready now, Mr. O'Connor?" Kit asked.

"Tell that fucking moron to wait," Mr. O'Connor said in irritation. "I'll tell him when."

Kit held up another five fingers.

"Wait!" he yelled to Sergeant Swanson.

Swanson said something in disgust and crouch-walked back to the door where the recorder was mounted.

"I think that's it, over there," Major Bedford said.

"All right. I'll go over to the north, and then we can make a couple of slow passes to the south."

"Fine, fine," said Major Bedford.

They passed over the house in a long, slow arc and started west. Major Bedford looked out the window to his right and straight down into the blackness below.

In those woods, the North Vietnamese were sleeping, hiding, healing their wounds, cleaning their weapons, planning their operations, maybe even having babies. Some of them had been living in the jungle for years, since there was almost no way for them to get back home until the war was over.

Kit felt Swanson at his shoulder again.

"Okay? Now?!" Swanson bellowed.

"Are we ready to start the tape?"

"Tell that fucking goddamn jackass to get back there and stop

asking every five seconds," Mr. O'Connor said loudly over the intercom.

Major Bedford turned his body in the chair, as much as he could.

"Kit, tell him to get back there and put his strap on and wait till we tell him to turn it on."

But Kit couldn't yell all that over the noise of the helicopter. So he simply held up five fingers again and jerked his thumb backward.

"I didn't even have any goddamn dinner!" Swanson yelled. He stood up and walked, doubled over, back to the door. "Bunch of fuckin' corn bread . . ."

Major Bedford decided that since he had turned himself around, he might as well reward himself with a secret glance at Kit. Kit was looking at the control panel lights, a look of mild concentration on his face. He bit distractedly at his lower lip.

Well, Major Bedford thought to himself, *things are, for the first time in along time, working out.* The nicest thing, of course, was that he was able to be near Kit, and he could see that Kit was regarding him in a friendly way.

"All right," Mr. O'Connor said as they went into another curve, back across the black woods, "tell him to start the tape."

Major Bedford made a round-and-round motion to Kit with his hand.

Kit swung around and made the same motion to Sergeant Swanson, who was sitting on the floor of the helicopter by the recorder with his legs dangling out into space. But Sergeant Swanson was looking out into the darkness. Finally, Kit had to unbuckle himself and crouch-walk to him.

"About goddamn time!" Swanson bellowed into the noise of the rotors. Kit went back to his seat.

There was so much noise in the helicopter, the pop-pop of the rotor and the whine of the turbine, that it didn't seem that logical that the ghost tape would be heard on the ground. But the speakers were below the fuselage. Perhaps on the ground, in the dark woods, the tape did indeed sound like a wandering soul.

The tape began screaming and howling.

Perhaps if you had been living in the open for several years,

surrounded by fighting and death, your mind would begin to lose
its sense of reality and you might be further destabilized by
ghostly noises from above. Perhaps if you hadn't seen your family
for years, if you didn't even know if they were alive or not, if you
didn't even know whether your home had been blown up in an
American air raid, or whether your son had been drafted and
killed in another part of your army, perhaps you might be pushed
over the edge into morbid insanity by the suggestion that ghosts
were coming for you.

Or perhaps it was all a waste of time. It would be good for
Major Bedford's career no matter how it turned out. He sat in
the darkness while the tape moaned on in back of him and, for
the first time in a very long time, began to entertain the possibility of making lieutenant colonel.

Quite suddenly, the helicopter sliced off to the left and dived in
a wrenching curve toward earth. Major Bedford's stomach rose
into his chest like a huge bubble. He glanced in horror at Mr.
O'Connor, who had pushed the stick forward, his face locked in
fear.

"What . . . ?"

"Shit comin' up! Didn't you see?" O'Connor screamed into the
intercom. He worked the pedals. The helicopter heeled to the
right and seemed to fall forward like a stone. Major Bedford felt
his full weight held by the seat belt and felt his neck strain with
the added weight of the helmet. He felt Kit's arms bang against
the back of his seat.

The ghost voice screamed, chasing them.

O'Connor dived for treetop level, even though he couldn't
clearly see where the trees were. It was the only way to avoid
being a target in the sky. The horizon tilted first one way and
then the other. He raced downward, then pulled up in another
curve so sharply that Major Bedford thought the ship would go
end over end. His stomach hit bottom, and for a few seconds, he
thought his heart had stopped. He had no idea helicopters could
do such things. Off to the right he saw a dim orange streak rise
out of the trees and wander around the sky.

"Christ, Christ . . ." he heard O'Connor say over the intercom.

"What?"

"A missile, a heat seeker. JEE-sus Christ!"

The helicopter raced along the tops of the dark trees, escaping the range of the heat-seeking missile. Major Bedford looked out and back. Two more rose in the sky.

The ghost tape howled.

"Turn that goddamn thing off!" Mr. O'Connor yelled at him.

O'Connor pulled the helicopter into a turn and the ship bounced as if it had hit a wall. Major Bedford's helmet fell forward. His straps strained.

"Kit!" Major Bedford tried to tell Kit to do something, but O'Connor brought the helicopter around in another sharp turn that took his breath away. Who cared about the ghost tape now?

"Can you see a light?" O'Connor yelled.

"Where?" Major Bedford returned.

"I don't know, goddamn it!"

"Where are we?"

"I don't know! I don't know! JEE-sus!"

Major Bedford looked from side to side. There was nothing but dark forest and the deep purple night above.

"Go north! Just go north!"

O'Connor made another wide swing, dived, and then climbed in a crazy spiral. The machine groaned. The pops of the rotor became explosions. He pointed the helicopter due north at its highest speed, heading for Phuoc Vinh base, which was somewhere in that direction. The voice of the wandering soul went on and on below them, the rattling bones like derisive laughter now.

"TURN IT OFF! For Christ's sake!" Mr. O'Connor bellowed into the intercom.

"KIT! Tell him to turn it off!" Major Bedford yelled.

He grasped the sides of his seat. He looked for the Russian rockets. Where had they gone? He looked back to the right, but he could see nothing. The rockets were seeking heat. The helicopter was the hottest thing in the sky. Right behind them. Gaining on them. Seeking the turbine exhaust to fly into and explode. And the entire helicopter would come apart at the seams. Major Bedford imagined the pieces falling and himself shooting ahead alone, with nothing but his seat.

The ghost shrieked. Still, as they raced home, and as they waited for the rockets to catch them and blow them out of the sky, the ghost shrieked on.

"TURN IT OFF!" O'Connor bellowed, his voice cracking.

"KIT! Tell him to SHUT IT OFF!" Major Bedford said, straining in his seat to look backwards.

"I can't stand it!" O'Connor yelled. "TURN IT OFF. SOME-BODY SHUT THAT GODDAMN THING OFF!"

Kit twisted around in his seat. He turned back and struggled with the clasp of his seat belt. He unplugged the helmet and stood, just as the helicopter went into a curve. The floor became the wall.

"Oh!"

Kit fell and stopped himself only by grabbing cargo straps in the ceiling. The ship turned the other way, slamming Kit's legs against the seat. He held on to the cargo straps with a death grip.

Something red blazed by outside.

"JEEEEEZUS!" O'Connor yelled. He threw himself at the controls and the helicopter plunged over a waterfall in the sky and down into the night.

"Ah!"

Kit's legs flew into the air and he lost his grip. He sailed back through the aircraft, slamming into the padded back wall. His fingers gripped on some wires. O'Connor pulled back. Kit sprawled against the floor. The wires gave, and in terror he scratched at the bare metal of the floor. The open side doors loomed like caverns.

Major Bedford twisted around. O'Connor tried to climb suddenly, and Kit came sliding back across the floor like a load of laundry, slamming into his seat.

"KIT!" Major Bedford called, his voice breaking.

Kit, hugging the seat, crawled around it, got in, and pulled the straps tight.

"WHAT . . . ?" Major Bedford tried to see into the back of the ship.

The ghost still howled.

Kit's face was white and his eyes were wide. He plugged in his helmet. His voice came over the intercom like a bleat.

"Sergeant Swanson. He's . . ."

Major Bedford twisted around more so he could see.

"Kit! Tell . . ."

"I can't. He's . . ."

"Good Lord . . ." Major Bedford said to himself.

He could see back into the interior of the helicopter.

Kit had tried to tell Sergeant Swanson to turn the tape off. He had been bounced off both sides of the ship, against the rear wall, and back to his seat.

But Swanson was gone.

Fallen out.

Through the open doors, out into the night air. Surprised, then screaming, then gone.

Back there somewhere.

• • •

When they landed back at Phuoc Vinh, it was Major Bedford who finally had to turn the tape recorder off, although it was nearly at the end of the tape. For a few minutes, until he found the power switch, the tape had gone on at full volume, howling and crying from beyond the grave. When he turned the switch, it stopped. O'Connor killed the engine.

A silence fell on the three of them.

"Well," Major Bedford said at last to Kit, who stood beside him, wondering and looking at nothing.

Mr. O'Connor was angry. "Well . . . it was his own fault!"

"Can they find him?" Kit asked Major Bedford.

"I don't think so. I don't know."

"We'll just leave him there?"

"He should have had his goddamn strap on!" Mr. O'Connor spat out.

"Well," Major Bedford said, and couldn't think of anything else to say.

It wasn't an unheard-of thing. People did fall out of helicopters. If Sergeant Swanson had put on his safety strap, he wouldn't have fallen out when the helicopter went into its first sharp, evasive turn.

But now he was gone. He hadn't even had time for his dinner

before the flight. He had been tossed out in the dark over the enemy forest.

And now, if there were any truth to the Vietnamese traditional fear, Swanson's soul would wander the woods north of the rubber plantation looking for a way back home, lonely and miserable.

Hungry, as well.

C H A P T E R

T W E N T Y · T W O

THI TUAN

The lonely misery that now pervaded Phuoc Vinh base was never as palpable as in the late afternoon, when the red sun fell toward the horizon, glowing dully through the haze that rose from the waste. A gray fog crept in from the cooler depths of the surrounding forests. In the orange half light of the early evening, the fog gathered around the dark, squat buildings like a rising flood of circumstance and time.

The South Vietnamese soldiers had few lamps and no source of light bulbs, except what they could steal from the remaining Americans. They stole light bulbs from the American mess hall and from the officers' club. Objections would have been made,

but for the order from the general that nothing was to disturb the process of getting the Vietnamese army in position to take over the base.

The two allied armies were distant and rapport between them was strained. The Americans had always accused the Vietnamese of cowardice, but the Vietnamese had no way of knowing that Americans accuse everyone of cowardice. And now that the Americans were leaving, the accusation seemed circular.

Two South Vietnamese colonels, who insisted they be housed with American officers of equal rank, had been billeted in Major Bedford's bunker. They also insisted that Thi Tuan help them move their belongings into their rooms. Thi Tuan checked the lock on Major Ponchuso's room, where Sergeant Xuan was recuperating.

As soon as all the heavy work was done, the two Vietnamese colonels turned angrily on poor nervous Thi Tuan and demanded to know how old he was. Thi Tuan lied unconvincingly, and they flew into a rage of accusation. They accused him of dodging the draft. Thi Tuan, who had indeed been dodging the draft, was driven into a shaking fit of fear. The two colonels slapped him around in the narrow hallway in front of Lieutenant Toomey's room. The noise of their high-pitched obloquy, Thi Tuan's crying, and the bumping of his head against the wall, finally disturbed the afternoon slumbers of Lieutenant Toomey.

Lieutenant Toomey welcomed being awakened. The ghost of the murdered Blackwell chased him through the rubber plantation, shooting him and killing him time after time. He staggered through endless rows of rubber trees while his own latex blood ran, soaking his clothes. Upon waking he sat up and listened to the noise from the hall.

In his green undershirt, which now clung to his round, sagging stomach, he stumbled out through his door, blinking away the perspiration salt that had collected around his eyes. The two Vietnamese colonels stopped their beating of Thi Tuan and looked at him.

It took a few seconds for Lieutenant Toomey to figure out who these two strange soldiers were. The low afternoon sun entered the bunker hallway in horizontal orange shafts. In the dim light

he had a difficult time finally determining that these silhouettes were indeed allies of his country. Thi Tuan was weeping, and one of the colonels had his head held back by the hair.

Lieutenant Toomey took a moment to consider what was going on.

"Th' fuck are you? What's the fucking noise?" he said thickly.

The South Vietnamese colonels looked at Toomey. He did not look like any sort of American officer they had ever seen before. Thi Tuan's weeping struck a chord in Lieutenant Toomey's troubled soul.

"Get your hand off him," Toomey mumbled. "L'gove 'im."

The colonels looked at each other.

"You live here?" asked the one holding Thi Tuan's hair.

Everything in the colonel's voice was objectionable. It was high, reedy, and laced with the Oriental lilt that Lieutenant Toomey hated.

"Let GO of him, I said."

"You ah American officah?"

And there was an arrogance in the question. Who were these little worms to wake him, to beat up Thi Tuan in his hall? He rubbed the salt out of his eyes.

"Get your fucking hands off him."

Thi Tuan heard the makings of new trouble and stopped his sobbing. The colonel held Thi Tuan's head back at a terribly uncomfortable angle, but by straining his eyes, he could just see Lieutenant Toomey's face.

"This man under arrest," the colonel began to say. "This man mus' come with us. This man . . ."

"Listen, you get your fuckin' hands off him before I knock them off!"

There was an uncomfortable pause.

"You officah?"

The second colonel stepped forward gingerly.

"What your rank?"

"Didn't you goddamn HEAR ME?!" Toomey said, his voice rising to a bellow. Thi Tuan jerked his head away, as much to avoid his savior as his captor. The colonel struggled to grab him again.

Toomey lunged forward. He pushed the second colonel ahead of him, grinding him against the wall. He grabbed the other colonel's head, knocking his helmet off, and held him up until he was nearly suspended.

"I told you, let him go! Who the HELL are you?" He forced the colonel, whom he outweighed by no less than a hundred pounds, against the wall. The colonel struggled oddly, not to push him away, but for something else. Then Toomey realized what he was trying to do. He was trying to get to the pistol on his belt.

Toomey slammed the colonel's head against the wall three times, hard.

"You shit! You shit! You shit!"

Thi Tuan tried heroically to get between them.

"Stop!" he wailed. "He colonel in ARVN!"

The other colonel had taken out his pistol. He hesitated, and then switched off the safety. Thi Tuan turned toward him.

BOOM!

The gun went off, and the shot thudded into the wood. In the hallway the explosion shocked them all. Then Toomey brought a fist down across his colonel's face and went for the one with the gun.

Thi Tuan barely got out of the way. Toomey hit the second colonel in the shoulder with his meaty fist, and the small man went down, glancing off the wall. He struggled to his knees and Toomey kicked him hard in the rear, sending him sprawling again.

The first colonel, whose face now ran blood, fired his pistol.

BOOM! A wild shot went up through the ceiling and into the sandbags.

A stream of sand ran out of the hole. Toomey turned and looked at the colonel through the roiling orange smoke and the cascade of sand.

He walked toward the colonel. His hand shot up, knocking the pistol out of his grasp. He grabbed the man and began to beat him rhythmically, with his teeth clenched. The colonel struggled with his free hand, striking at Toomey with no more effect than

to make him angrier. Toomey hit him again and again. Blood streamed out of the man's mouth and nose.

"You bastard, you gook bastard," he went on, punching again and again at the distorted face.

"Stop!" the second colonel screamed, a rasping scream of fear and hatred.

Toomey stopped his beating and looked around. The second colonel had recovered and now held his automatic pistol with both hands, pointed at Toomey's head. The gun barrel shook. Toomey looked into the fearful eyes, wide and dilated in the fading light. He felt very tired again. He let his victim drop from his grasp, unconscious, to the floor.

"YOU! YOU PUT UP YOU HANDS!" the second colonel screamed, his voice breaking.

Toomey looked at him but did nothing.

"UP! SON OF BITS!" the colonel screamed.

Toomey looked at his hands, sandy and bloody.

"Son of bits?" he asked.

The second colonel screamed at him in Vietnamese.

And then, from behind, Thi Tuan hit the Vietnamese colonel in the head, hard, with the length of steel pipe he used to pound rats to death. The second colonel toppled forward and lay next to his fellow officer.

Lieutenant Toomey looked at Thi Tuan and wiped his hands on his shirt, surveying the mess in the hallway. Looking at the blood nauseated him. Vietnamese blood. He turned to the still shaking Thi Tuan.

"Who are these guys?" he asked.

Thi Tuan, still shocked with the enormity of what he had done, and now remembering that he had been discovered as a draft evader, looked down at the steel pipe in his hands.

"What were they doing here?" Toomey asked him again.

Thi Tuan looked up at him.

"They ARVN. ARVN *trung-ta.* Colonel."

"What the hell d'they want?"

Thi Tuan turned and put the pipe up on a shelf. Then he looked back at Toomey.

"They move in here," Thi Tuan stammered, wide-eyed. "They now *living* here."

Toomey looked down at the two pathetic bodies in the bloody sand.

"Here?"

"Yes," said Thi Tuan. "They living here now."

"Shit," said Lieutenant Toomey. "Nobody tells me anything."

And he suddenly realized he would be late for the briefing.

"Shit," he said tiredly, and he went to get cleaned up.

Thi Tuan collapsed against the door to Major Ponchuso's room.

Inside Major Ponchuso's room, Sergeant Xuan decided that it was, at last, time to go to Saigon.

• • •

Kit had fewer than three months left in the obligatory one-year tour. He had begun counting the days on a calendar Major Dow had given him. Major Dow had little more time than that left himself.

"I put you in on the drop list. You'll be gone in a few weeks," Major Dow told Kit.

"What? A few weeks?" Kit said. He had been counting, but three months seemed like a very long time—even three weeks seemed long. It seemed only days ago that he had nearly been killed out on the road with Miss Tuyet and Sergeant Xuan.

He wanted to see Miss Tuyet again. The last view he had had was of the back of her, her short, slim little being trudging off to the school in Bo Mua, after her wild driving lesson.

Was this all there was to a war? A few screwed up actions, and as soon as you got used to the noise and the stink, they sent you home. Home to his family. His mother would be happy to see him. His father . . .

"But," he said, "I can't . . ."

"What? Now what?"

"I can't. I have to stay here. I don't . . ."

But Major Dow didn't have time to listen to Kit. His mind was cluttered with the endless detail of trying to make sure there were no holes in what was left of the defense of Phuoc Vinh base. Things that Major Ponchuso used to think about.

The Americans were leaving on time, as Nixon was telling the American people, but the South Vietnamese units were not arriving on time, as Nixon was not telling the American people. The ones that did show up were lacking everything. Their junior officers were young and scared, and the senior commanders were planning for the future. They looked at the maps he prepared with glazed eyes.

"Sir . . . can I talk to you?" Kit tried again.

"Kit, for God's sake," said Major Dow, trying to make sense of the lists of units he had been given by the ARVN command and the computer printouts from Saigon.

"Here's a printout from Saigon Command," Major Dow had told them. "It has all the information. And here are maps." They hadn't listened. He had tried to tell the general.

Major Dow was inordinately tired. He had noticed that in the past weeks his girth had shrunk. He was losing weight, sweating it off physically and mentally. His jowls hung flaccid, dark circles ringed his quick black eyes, and he hadn't shaved all day. In addition to all the other fears he had about things going wrong, there was a new fear. For all intents and purposes, they were undefended.

"Sir," Kit tried a third time.

"Not now . . ."

"I have to talk to you."

"Later, for Christ's sake."

"It's important."

"I'm sure it is. Later."

Had anyone performed any sort of careful check of the mines and flares on the base perimeter? Had anyone reviewed the condition of the sensors in the jungle that were supposed to warn them of approaching enemy in the middle of the night? He had tried to explain this system to everyone, including the ranking Vietnamese officers. But they couldn't seem to keep their eyes on the map.

"Here, where I'm pointing," Major Dow had told them, "are the three rows of sensors. The rows are ten meters apart. Their

batteries last about six months. Some last only about three months."

"And see? Here," he told the Vietnamese, "the sensors are marked, each one with a number. You have to match the number with the dates and then see which of the sensors are still active. You have to assign somebody to this so that they'll know when the batteries fail . . ." Major Dow had wanted to grab them by the shirt.

Specialist Dilby tried to train six young Vietnamese soldiers to work the radar. Then, one day, a surprising thing happened. The six young Vietnamese soldiers were gone. Vanished. Deserted. Major Dow himself went to find out what had happened to the radar trainees. They are gone, was the answer from the Vietnamese. Where are they gone? They have gone home. Home? You mean deserted? Yes. When will you send more for training? Soon, was the answer. Soon.

And the general listened to Major Dow's fears with almost the same glazed expression as the Vietnamese commanders.

"Look at this," the general said, tossing a newspaper at him. It was a *Washington Star* clipping. The headline said Vietnamization was going well. A man holding a computer printout was smiling from a picture. It was Melvin Laird.

General Walker looked dead tired. His uniform hung loose around his shoulders. On the wall in his trailer, the troop strength chart showed less than three hundred Americans.

• • •

Father Tran had given Major Dow the most worrisome news. Father Tran was getting into a jeep outside the general's trailer.

"I cannot come every night to see him. Have you not got a priest here?"

"We have a chaplain. We have a chaplain who's a priest. I think we do."

"He can come then."

"You come every night? What for?"

"You do not know?" Father Tran asked.

"I . . . no, I do not know."

"Ah," said Father Tran.

"What is it?"

"Ah, well . . ." said the priest.

"Tell me. What or why."

"Ah," said the little priest, and his eyes moved to the side.

"Tell me!" Major Dow pleaded.

Father Tran looked at him.

"He confesses to me."

"Confesses?"

Major Dow for a few seconds could not find a place to put this thought.

"He confesses?" he said.

"Yes."

"And . . . what does he confess?"

"Sins."

The priest looked steadily at Major Dow, who now felt no weight in his body other than the sweat on his brow.

"Sins?"

At a time like this?

"Yes," said the priest, "but I do not know."

"What?"

"What he confesses. They are not sins."

"Jesus!" Major Dow wiped his forehead.

"And that is why I do not want to come anymore."

Father Tran stood and waited for a few minutes. Major Dow sat down in the nearest chair.

"I should not have told you this, you know. A priest should not talk about a confession."

"Oh . . . yes."

"And I have prayed."

"Oh."

"I have prayed for you all."

"Ah, well," Major Dow said.

"And now I must go. I will see you again, *Dai-ta* Dow."

Major Dow was still wondering about the general.

"Yes, Father, with any luck."

"Ah, but God gives us luck."

"I suppose so."

The priest left with Sergeant Tabor, who barely had time to drive him to the church in Phuoc Vinh village, before his duty with the Ghost Ship, replacing Sergeant Swanson, began at eighteen hundred hours.

C H A P T E R

T W E N T Y · T H R E E

SAIGON

The Hotel Napoleon they were looking for was one of three Hotel Napoleons at various locations in Saigon. Sergeant Xuan had told Lieutenant Christopher that the one he recommended for Mr. Christopher was the Hotel Napoleon that was *really* a hotel. The other two Napoleons were whorehouses, and they didn't want to room with whores. So they couldn't stay there. And all the big hotels were packed with journalists and war contractors. So they couldn't stay there, either. For related reasons.

Mr. Christopher and Mr. Hart went through the crawling Saigon traffic in a jeep with Lieutenant Colonel Shift, who had been

their companion ever since Hong Kong. The colonel had some knowledge of the Saigon streets and proved to be a willing guide. Mr. Hart wished he would go away, but Mr. Christopher thought he was a godsend. And besides, the Vietnamese policeman they supposedly had hired, Sergeant X-whatever-his-name-was, hadn't materialized yet.

"We don't want to take up your time," Mr. Hart said to Colonel Shift privately.

"No. No," Colonel Shift assured him. "Glad to do it!"

How the colonel got all this free time was a mystery to Mr. Hart. Didn't the army need him for something—fighting or giving orders?

"I got six more days of TDY, and then I'm off north to join a unit!" said the colonel.

They drove past the American Embassy on Thong Nhut Street, then dived into the rat maze of the downtown streets.

Mr. Hart was lost. He could make no sense of the streets. They came and went at all odd angles, clogged with traffic, buried in dust and exhaust. Three-wheel Lambro 550 cabs jockeyed for right-of-way with monstrous army vehicles. Asthmatic old black Citroëns followed Japanese-built Willys jeeps. Bicycles were everywhere. Petite girls in long, flowing dresses pedaled through the filthy black clouds spewing from laboring old Renault trucks.

A two-ton Dodge Fargo truck, laden with concrete blocks, lost its brakes and nearly flattened their jeep. It caromed off the sidewall of a fountain, scattering twenty or more Saigonese, most of whom appeared to be crippled soldiers. Pathetic old women held up their hands, like twisted claws, for money. Children wandered, half naked, like tiny dolls lost in a quarter of hell.

"God! Feel this place, Al!" Mr. Christopher said. "Can you feel it?!"

"Yes," Mr. Hart coughed, hanging on to the sides of the jeep.

This was the Far East Mr. Hart had expected to find. He hadn't thought he was going to like it, and now that he was in the middle of it, he didn't like it. The smell and the crowding, the noise and the constant human misery. How could these people stand this, day after day, year after year? Why didn't their government come to some sort of terms with their enemies and set about improving the way they lived? What vicious insanity it all was. Women pulled at his clothes, desperately skinny old women, whose brown faces all had the same expression, halfway between pleading and accusation. He hated them to touch his clothes. Mr. Christopher shouted at them to go away.

And when they finally found it, the correct Hotel Napoleon was a disaster. There were beggars in the moldy lobby. The front windows, where an explosion had taken place recently, were covered with sheet metal printed with American beer can labels. A man with one leg was trying to sweep the lobby floor. The purpled stump of his missing leg stuck out of his short pants. Mr. Hart had never seen a stump before. He stared at it in horror. Mr. Christopher pulled him toward the desk.

"We should buy *this* place, too!" Mr. Christopher said loudly. "This place will go for a song. We could make a *fortune* off this place."

The plaster ceiling of the lobby had been blackened by a fire and hung from the frame of the building, threatening to fall momentarily on their heads. The fans were dead. Two pieces of wrought-iron furniture, a sort of a chair and a sort of a chaise longue, were arranged in front of a table made of boards and cement blocks. A radio played endless Vietnamese music.

Mr. Hart's doubts had by this time swelled into complete and undeniable fears. Saigon was far worse than he had thought it would be. He could sense the impermanence and insecurity in the air. He could see nothing for them here. This place was lost. He must talk to Christopher and do it now. They must get back to the airport.

The man with one leg turned out to be the porter, as well, and no one, not even Mr. Christopher, seemed troubled when he hobbled over with his crutch and tried to lift one of their bags to carry it up to their room. Mr. Hart could not bear this.

"No, for God's sake, wait," Mr. Hart said, trying to get the bag away from him. "I'll take it!"

The man held it tight.

"I'll take it. You can't!" Mr. Hart pleaded.

But the man insisted, croaking some words at him. He went to the stairs and labored grotesquely upwards, with his crutch under

one arm and the bag in his other hand. And Mr. Hart, held back
by Mr. Christopher's assurance that this was the way things were
done here, went up the stairs behind him, with an even closer and
more frightening view of the man's stump.

There were two iron beds in the room, a small table, and a
chest of drawers with a brownish mirror propped up on it. Mr.
Christopher flopped down on one of the beds, as he might have
done in any motel room back in the States, and grinned at Mr.
Hart, who stood in the middle of the room and waited for the
one-legged man to leave. The room was hot and moldy and pissy-
smelling.

"Al, you should see your face!" Mr. Christopher said, but now
without his usual bonhomie.

"Shut up," said Mr. Hart, who had never told anyone to shut
up before in his life. He was sickened by his own filth and sweat.
His cotton suit was a mess and his tie hung like a noose.

"Look, Al, take it easy. My God. Can't you see the potential
here? Can't you . . ."

"I asked you to shut up! I don't want to hear about the potential anymore. Just shut up about it. I want to get the hell out of
here. And right now I want to wash."

"Okay, okay, just calm down."

"Don't tell me to calm down," Mr. Hart spat at him. "This
place is a mess. I've never been in such filth. I don't want to hear
any more about potential."

"You just need a drink, my friend. You just need . . ."

"I KNOW what I need! And don't address me as your friend. I
don't feel like being sold any more of your . . . your . . . your
bullshit!" He had never used that term in his life, either.

"Al. Al, listen to me."

"SHUT UP! For the last time, shut up! And where's the bathroom?"

Mr. Christopher made a gesture of resignation with his hands.
"It's down the hall."

Mr. Hart wasn't sure about going out in the hall by himself.
But he was angry enough, and he desperately wanted to wash. He
looked out the door in both directions, and then walked quickly

down until he found the slatted door of the bathroom. He went in.

There was a toilet, a sink, a large porcelain bathtub, and, laughably, a bidet. The bathtub was full of water. *How disgusting*, Mr. Hart thought. He pulled the chain to the plug. The water ran out slowly. He stood watching it, thinking about whether or not he should go home alone if Mr. Christopher refused to accompany him. This entire mission was ridiculous. The idea of buying land, of investing money in this cacophonous sink-hole of disease and danger, was beyond him. The filth and the noise—and the heat! Let the Communists have the place; they deserved it.

When the tub was empty he turned the hot water tap. Nothing came out. He turned the cold water tap. Nothing there, either. The sink had no water. There was no water at all.

It wasn't his fault. He had had no way of knowing. The tub of water was the water supply for the entire floor for the day, drawn during the odd hours when the water ran.

He clumped back to the room, pretty much defeated.

Mr. Christopher watched him slump on the other bed.

"I thought you were going to wash up. Something wrong?"

"There's no water."

"No water?"

"That's right. No water. You heard me. I said there was no water."

"No water? Well, I just can't believe that. I'll go see about this."

"I JUST TOLD YOU!" Mr. Hart shouted. "I just told you," he said, catching himself. "You don't have to go see. And I'll have to sleep like this."

"Ah, gee, Al, I can't begin to tell you how sorry I am."

"Don't bother."

"Al, listen, you're just hot and tired. We'll get to someplace better tomorrow. And we'll get you to someplace with water and air-conditioning and everything and you'll feel better."

"I'm going home tomorrow morning," Mr. Hart said, looking up at the water-stained ceiling.

Mr. Christopher paused. He looked down at his hands and breathed a long sigh of resignation.

"Oooooh-kay."

The sweat ran down Mr. Hart's face into his ears. He couldn't remember ever being this hot for this long. Even when he played long bouts of tennis, even when he was caught in the excitement of slashing court competition, in the middle of the summer with their friends in Pound Ridge, he couldn't remember ever being this hot. And here he was, just lying still on a bed.

He had made a mistake. And any good lawyer knows that when a man has made a mistake, the best thing to do is to simply correct the mistake as soon as possible.

Mr. Christopher went down and made some sort of arrangement with the desk clerk. And a few minutes later the man with one leg brought Mr. Hart a pitcher of water, enough to wash his face.

"There, now," said Mr. Christopher cheerfully, hopefully, as Mr. Hart splashed the water on his brow, being careful not to let any run down into his mouth. "Doesn't that feel better?"

Mr. Hart said nothing.

"Al." Mr. Christopher injected a slight tone of pleading.

"I don't want to hear it," Mr. Hart said. "I've made up my mind. I'm going home tomorrow. You can do whatever you want. This entire plan is stupid. And worse than that. It's a bad investment."

"Oh, come on."

"It's a lousy investment. You're crazy. This place is lost. This city is lost. Can't you see those people out there? They haven't got the slightest ability to fight. They don't care. They're animals. They'll welcome the Communists or whoever comes along next."

"You're wrong, Al."

"I'm NOT wrong. You expect me to sanction the placement of investors' funds in a place like this, teetering on the brink of defeat. You listen to *me* for a change. Grab what money we can still get our hands on, and let's get back while we have enough to stay in the good graces of all those people you conned!"

"Conned?!"

Mr. Hart paused.

"Maybe not conned, I'm sorry I used that word, but . . ."

"Conned is it? Conned?"

"I said I didn't mean that. I'm sorry . . ."

"No, you're not sorry. You think I'm a con artist, do you? You think I'm just here to defraud investors. You really think that, don't you?"

"I don't want to argue . . ."

"Well, what the hell did you come along this far for? Why the hell didn't you stay back there in New York? I'll tell you what's the trouble with you, Al. I'll tell you what's the trouble. You've got no guts. NO GUTS. Here we are on the brink of one of the greatest opportunities ever put before anyone. A whole goddamn country and you all of a sudden lose your goddamn guts. One day without your goddamn bath and you're ready to go goddamn home. You're a goddamn coward, goddamn it! God damn you! Go the hell home. I'll just get myself another lawyer. Who the hell needs you?"

He had worked himself into a lather by this time. Mr. Hart was slightly worried.

"Look," Mr. Hart began.

"No! You shut up now. You've shown your true colors. You want to go home? Okay. Go home. I'll finish this deal myself. I'll do it because when I start something, I finish it, you, you pussy jackass. I'm going to stay here. And I'm going to make a god-damn fortune. And I'm going to help a lot of these pathetic people while I'm doing it!"

There were footsteps in the hall.

"Who the hell needs you, Al? You're just a goddamn lawyer, another summer soldier, another gutless wonder . . ."

Mr. Christopher paused. Someone was outside their room. A soft knock fell on the door.

"Come in," Mr. Christopher said.

Colonel Shift stuck his head in the door. Mr. Christopher mopped his face.

"Am I interrupting anything, gentlemen?" the colonel asked.

"Noooo . . ." Mr. Christopher changed his attitude immediately. "Just a business discussion." He smiled.

The colonel took a few steps in and looked around.

"Have a chair, please, Colonel." Mr. Christopher gestured.

"Thank you," the colonel said gracefully, smiling behind his sunglasses. "I felt a little bad about leaving you here. This place, I mean. I thought I'd better check."

"I appreciate that!" said Mr. Christopher.

"I wanted to invite you both to dinner at the officers' club over at the MACV headquarters tonight. I think you might find it a good place to meet some people. Great food. And even some entertainment."

"Colonel, you're too good. Too gracious." Mr. Christopher beamed. "We'd be delighted. Although, I don't know . . . uh . . . my partner is feeling a bit of old jet lag, I guess. Al? You up to some good army chow tonight?"

The colonel held up a finger. "Now, I'd hardly call this army chow. We do things right at headquarters."

"What about it, Al?" Mr. Christopher pestered.

"It's a very kind offer," Mr. Hart mumbled. "I don't know . . ."

"Well, I'll accept your offer, Colonel. Maybe Al could do better with a good night's sleep."

"Well, good, good," Colonel Shift said and paused. He had something else on his mind.

"You've been so helpful, Colonel," Mr. Christopher said, "I just can't begin to thank you enough."

"Yes, well," the colonel pressed his lips together, "I wanted to . . . uh . . . ask you something."

"Yes?" said Mr. Christopher.

"It's a little awkward, of course. But I've been thinking. And of course, I'm not a rich man. Colonels don't make all that much money. But . . . well, I just wondered if . . ."

Mr. Christopher smiled. A very pleased smile.

"What is it, Colonel?"

"Well, let's say that a man such as myself wanted to . . . uh . . ."

"Invest?"

"Well, yes."

"You want to invest with our group, Colonel?"

"Yes. I mean, it just seems to me that everything you've said makes a hell of a lot of sense . . ."

Mr. Christopher shot Mr. Hart a glance.

"Colonel, say no more. It would be an honor to have you—or, for that matter, any American fighting man—invest in our enterprise. Who deserves more to profit from the great efforts that have been made here?"

"Now, I don't have a great deal of money, you know—actually, only about ten thousand . . ."

"That's fine Colonel. It makes no difference . . ."

Mr. Hart, hot and tired, had to sit and watch while Lieutenant Colonel Shift became an investor in Mr. Christopher's real estate consortium for the sum of ten thousand dollars. The colonel was very happy. He thanked Mr. Christopher. He thanked Mr. Hart. How much the colonel really understood of the operation was anybody's guess. He kept thanking Mr. Christopher.

"Al, here, will send you all the papers to sign," Mr. Christopher said sweetly.

"Fine, fine," said the colonel.

"Won't you, Al?"

And if there were other officers who might want to invest, Mr. Christopher said, they would be welcome, as well. Only, as he would surely understand, they would want to limit knowledge of the entire enterprise to a select number of persons.

And Mr. Hart could think of nothing to say. The colonel had worked in the Saigon headquarters, the headquarters of the entire country, with access to all the information and intelligence the army had. And if he were convinced that the Republic of South Vietnam was not a lost cause—if he were convinced enough to put his own money, his own *soldier's pay,* into the scheme—then who was Mr. Hart to voice doubts?

The colonel talked on about the secure villages and hamlets, about the indisputable evidence that the Viet Cong and the North Vietnamese had lost in their attempts to subvert the government, that the government had indeed won the hearts and minds, that Vietnamization would work like clockwork. Nowhere, he said, in the entire headquarters, in all the multitude of commanders and advisers he had spoken to and worked for, was there any doubt that in the final analysis, the Republic of Vietnam would be, well, the unthinkable word—lost.

Journalists? Fuck 'em. Journalists knew nothing.

Mr. Christopher shook the colonel's hand.

"Shake hands with Al here, too, if you would."

Colonel Shift stuck his hand out to Mr. Hart.

"See, Colonel, I have to disclose something," Mr. Christopher said earnestly. "Al, here, has some doubts."

"Doubts? About what?" asked the colonel.

"About the U.S. cutting and running—you know, giving up. Bugging out."

"Bugging out? Out of Vietnam? After all this time? And all these Americans killed?"

"See, Al?" Mr. Christopher said softly.

"Well . . ." Mr. Hart said, his soft white lawyer's hand trapped in the colonel's meat hook.

The colonel removed his sunglasses and looked at him directly. His eyes were clear blue and radiant.

"Never happen, sir," said he confidently, even sweetly. "Never happen."

"Well," Mr. Hart said, "I just wonder."

"Sir." The Colonel squinted and addressed him in a formal, earnest voice. "What you see here . . . it's the start of a new life for all these people. We're going to turn this place into a new city, a city like you've never seen."

"Perhaps . . ." Mr. Hart tried to think of something to say.

"Never mind what you see here, sir," the colonel went on. "What you see here is the wreckage of war. Sure, it looks like hell. But as soon as this war is over, the rebuilding is going to start."

Mr. Hart felt uncomfortable and powerless.

"Well," Mr. Hart faltered, "it just seems so . . . so impossible."

"Sure! But when this war ends, with American help, this country is going to be reborn."

"It'll rise like the Tucson!" said Mr. Christopher.

"Exactly," said Colonel Shift.

Mr. Hart had been looking at his hands. He looked up at Mr. Christopher.

"What?"

"It'll rise like the Tucson!"

"Like the *what?*" Mr. Hart asked.

"It's a bird, Al," Mr. Christopher explained. "It's a Greek bird."

•   •   •

Mr. Hart went along with them to the officers' club because the prospect of staying by himself in the Hotel Napoleon filled him with dread.

The officers' club at the headquarters where Lieutenant Colonel Shift took them for dinner and an evening's entertainment was splendid on a scale not even imagined by the lonely, crazed enlisted troops on Phuoc Vinh base. Not in their wildest dreams.

They drove, in the colonel's jeep, through the streets in the main center of Saigon, out through the dilapidated suburban areas, and finally out along the highway to the U.S. Vietnam Command Headquarters.

Along the way Mr. Hart stared at the mess and confusion, the people and animals, the vehicles and bicycles, the rickety buildings and numberless naked children. They went through hastily thrown-up refugee villages, pathetic and forlorn in the late afternoon heat and dust. Some of these areas went on for miles. Mr. Hart couldn't take it all in. On the main highway, the diesel fumes choked and blinded them; traffic jams and detours slowed their travel. The colonel's driver artfully negotiated his way around everything. Mr. Hart, who had never ridden in a jeep until his arrival in Vietnam, sat in front and held on to the roof struts to keep his balance on the hard canvas seat. Mr. Christopher sat in the back and jabbered with the colonel.

They came to a bridge that had suffered some sort of sabotage. South Vietnamese army troops and white-shirted National Policemen looked at them in tired anger in the fading light. Mr. Hart saw how young the Vietnamese soldiers were; he also noticed the ever-present weapons. Everyone had rifles. No one seemed to be in control.

At long last they came to the headquarters and passed through the gate, where a military policeman rendered a white-gloved salute. Once inside the fence, Mr. Hart felt a little better.

The officers' club was not, as Mr. Hart thought it might be, some sort of temporary military affair. It was a large permanent building of concrete block, painted white, spreading comfortably out behind a stretch of mowed lawn, and ringed with parking lots filled with more staff cars than military vehicles. In front, three flagpoles presented the American flag, the South Vietnamese flag, and a red flag with white stars to indicate that general grades might be there. And coming and going were staff officers, some in fatigues, some in green dress uniforms.

Inside, soft music was playing. The entire expanse was carpeted, paneled, and peacefully dim. The air-conditioning wrapped its caress around him; Mr. Hart breathed deeply. The cool air was delicious. He felt it seep into the hot, sweaty crevasses between his body and his clothes. The clink of silverware and china reminded Mr. Hart that he was hungry.

Colonel Shift swelled with pride at being able to squire his businessmen guests around. They were shown to a table. Mr. Christopher hadn't spoken much to Mr. Hart directly since their flare-up in the hotel, and now he let the splendor of the headquarters officers' club speak for itself. Nothing could make the point clearer that the Americans were still in control. The colonel introduced them to an endless succession of colonels and majors, and even a general, all of them friendly and curious, confident and well met. Three of these officers, whom Colonel Shift knew well, joined them at their table.

The club restaurant was run by some Chinese restaurateurs, and the food was plentiful and delicious. Mr. Hart sat and ate in silence while the others, Mr. Christopher and the officers, talked on and on about the war and the political situation back home, and investments and brokers and money and other things. Then they got into war stories, which went on about planes and bombing runs, and napalm raids and infantry operations, and Vietnamization. They ordered plates of shrimp and beef and fish, and talked about the war in between bites. Very pretty young waitresses flitted back and forth, bringing wines and cheeses and

constantly asking if there were anything additional they wanted. Nothing was more pleasant for these officers than to have some clearly sympathetic civilians to impress with accounts of their operations and exploits. Mr. Christopher even got to talk about the Philippines.

Mr. Hart said nothing.

At about eight they had eaten themselves into a state of complacent satiation. The rest of the dining room was filled with officers. Colonel Shift suggested they go into the bar.

The bar was easily as large as the dining room, dark and cool, with a small stage and dance floor. A Vietnamese band was setting up its equipment. The Vietnamese musicians had sullen, mean expressions and long, dirty hair. They set up their speakers and drums and tuned their Japanese guitars. A small, lithe, and strikingly attractive Vietnamese girl in a glittery dress helped them. Mr. Hart wondered if she were a singer.

Mr. Hart also wondered about the officers' club itself. How could such luxury be a part of a war? He had never been in an army. To him, the army and the rest of the services were large, amorphous bodies that did something necessary for the country —bodies that he was generally in favor of but about which he had no working knowledge. He would have allowed for an amount of pomp and ceremony back in the United States, but an army at war was based on the strict, unfortunate necessity of having one, wasn't it? This, however, was a place where a man could amply enjoy himself.

Mr. Christopher was beyond a pleasant state of inebriation. He was drunk. The officers with him were drunk. They roared with laughter at everything he said, and he roared back when they replied. The conversation got looser and crazier. He had made the mistake—a stupid mistake, Mr. Hart thought—of talking about their business in Vietnam, or maybe Colonel Shift had brought the matter up. Now the other officers wanted the same thing Shift wanted. They wanted to invest. Mr. Christopher waved his hands about, talking of construction and clearing land. He asked them about where he would be able to get laborers, construction equipment, how to arrange for blacktop, how to get electrical power. How did one get permits?

Permits? The whole table roared. Permits, hell. If you want something here, you just take it. Permits? You mean bribes. You bribe the little shits. You lie, cheat, and steal. Pay the government. Pay the Chinese. More roaring. Stories poured out about the corruption and theft—theft of building materials, theft of vehicles, trafficking with the enemy, trafficking in drugs, dealing with the local Mafia, contract prison labor, contract killing, prostitution, currency manipulation, bureaucratic graft, the evil influence of the French and other European traders, and the great joke of the Thieu government. And the army! The South Vietnamese army, whose officers were corrupt and cowardly from top to bottom, who sold themselves and the lives of their troops. And the troops who deserted in droves.

"Hell, if I had to work for those squeaky little shits," said a major on Colonel Shift's right, "I'd desert tomorrow."

Mr. Hart listened to all this in silence. If he had had the vocal volume to take part over the noise, he would have asked the questions that now filled his mind. He would have asked why, in the name of God, or even in the name of common sense, didn't the United States simply tell them that if they didn't clean up this mess they would withdraw all the money? That would have been enough, surely. Why not threaten them to make them do what they should have been doing all along? It made infinite sense to Mr. Hart. Why didn't it make sense to anyone else?

The Vietnamese band had started to play, and Mr. Hart, in spite of the fact that he only listened to classical music at home, could recognize the sounds as American popular music, mangled in translation, but still recognizable.

The lead singer was not the girl in the glittery dress. It was one of the young Vietnamese men with the long, black hair. Mr. Hart had paid no attention to those songs back in the States, but he recognized them now.

". . . I am sayin' you ain't pretty . . . all I saying I am ready . . .

The lyrics made even less sense to him than they did normally. And worse, for most of the songs, the singer had only memorized

the words to one verse, so he sang it over and over. Mr. Hart
listened. No one else seemed to care; they were all talking loudly
over the music.

"Look at that little shit," one of the colonels said to Mr. Christopher. "Now, why isn't he in the army? Look at him!"

The lead singer did seem to be of draft age, and why he wasn't
in the army, instead of making money playing in officers' clubs,
was a pretty good question.

"He bought out, see what I mean? He bought out of the army.
See what I mean?"

The colonel's face was angry and ugly, and Mr. Hart wondered
if he intended to do something about this young man right then
and there. But he turned back to Mr. Christopher and talked, or
rather shouted, about something else.

Then, after a short pause, the band switched to a softer sound,
something like a waltz. It had no real melody, it just went on and
on. Mr. Hart listened. He thought it might be the "Tennessee
Waltz," but he couldn't tell for sure. Everyone quieted down.
Some of the men moved their chairs around; two of them came
over and stood right in Mr. Hart's way. The lights dimmed, and a
spotlight was turned on that cut through the dense smoke. He
couldn't see what was going on. He craned his neck and still
couldn't see. He stood up.

"Here, you can see from over here," one of the officers said,
making a place for him.

The girl in the glittery dress was dancing languidly in front of
the band. She was heavily made up but still, to his eyes, intriguing and pretty. Behind the makeup she smiled professionally but
nervously. She was very small, the size of a child. And she began
to strip.

Mr. Hart sat back down. He had never seen a striptease before.
His drink was empty. He looked at the officers sitting with Colonel Shift, whose faces, in the reflected light of the spotlight, had
dull, slack, stupid grins. Colonel Shift grinned with them, watching the girl intently, his tongue caught between his teeth. Mr.
Christopher was watching also, grinning also, his eyes heavy with
the weight of all the food and liquor he had put away.

Mr. Hart did not want to watch. He leaned forward with his

elbows on the table, now littered with ashtrays and glasses. He rested his head on his hands and rubbed his eyes. How he wanted to be somewhere else, he thought. Even back in the Hotel Napoleon. The music drifted on, slowly, mockingly. The men made grunting sounds and vulgar comments and sounds.

None of this should be permitted, Mr. Hart thought. He rubbed his eyes. He looked back down the row of gaping, grinning officers. The major to Colonel Shift's right was standing up. He had his hand in his pants, massaging himself idly. Here, right in the middle of everyone. And as Mr. Hart realized this, he recognized the music. It was the "Tennessee Waltz."

Then the music changed and the girl, down to her lingerie, walked behind the band. The singer returned and the conversation picked up.

The officers at the table had by this time fallen under the commercial spell of Mr. Christopher, who talked more rapidly and more uncontrollably as he got drunker. As he got even drunker, he bordered on rhapsody about the divinity of their mission.

And his *son*, Mr. Christopher bawled, as if he had suddenly remembered. His son, who was one of them, as he had been one of them. His son—he wanted to see his son in Phuoc Vinh. How he longed to see his son. Tomorrow, Colonel Shift promised, you will see him tomorrow.

The girl returned to the stage, and the band lapsed into their slow, directionless version of the "Tennessee Waltz." Some of the other officers, as drunk as the men at his table, called to her and offered her money. She couldn't, Mr. Hart thought, have been more than fifteen years old. Her tiny body and tiny breasts were those of a child-woman. And when she finally had cast off everything, he beheld her patch of pubic hair, small and insignificant, tiny, pretty, and, to him for some reason, precious. She strutted around nervously while the band droned on and the men waved money, calling to her to come over to the tables. Then she went from table to table, doing things that Mr. Hart had never seen before. She sat on some of the tables, and stretched out on others. On some of the tables she knelt on all fours while the officers sniffed at her and poured wine on her and licked it off.

When at last she came over to them, Mr. Christopher, now so inebriated that his face seemed to swell, laughed and hooted with the rest of them. Colonel Shift cleared away the bottles and glasses at his end of the table, and the girl danced closer. He brought a chair over. She stepped up on the chair and then on the table, which wobbled under her weight. Mr. Christopher laughed and brought out some money. She gingerly strutted down the table to where Mr. Hart sat. He didn't know what to do, and he felt everyone looking at him.

He looked up at her.

She knew. He could see she knew. Here was the weak man. Here was the one whose embarrassment and fear made it worth all the embarrassment and fear she felt. Here was the man who thought he was better than all of the rest. She could see it in his set face, his straight back, his tense bearing. She looked down at him with the mocking smile and the tiny breasts and pubic hair directly over him, moving back and forth in what were supposed to be sexual undulations.

He wanted her to go away, to stop it. He wanted to ask her why she was doing this. Why any of them were doing this in this drunken, filthy shame? Why they pretended to enjoy what was so demeaning and rotten, so unspeakably vile. Why, given the joy and beauty in the world, the peace, the wonder, all the good, clean, healthy things in the world, had they chosen to do this with themselves, and with this girl, this child?

Then someone pushed the table, or pushed her, and she fell with a squeal on top of Mr. Hart, soft and squirming, wet with liquor, reeking of perfume, slathered in makeup, her hair in his face, in his eyes, in his mouth, while the raucous laughter and derisive shouts of the men and the droning music filled his brain. He tried to push her back, but she held him, pushing against the table and his chair as he tried to get up, to get away, fell backward, and he and the girl went over with it. And Mr. Hart wound up on the floor with her on top of him, pushing him down, trying to kiss him, her tongue out, her child's face still grinning.

And over the noise and the music and the laughter, as he groped to get her away, pushing at her wet naked skin, pushing at her breasts and shoulders, he heard Mr. Christopher's voice, rasp-

ing and gravelly from too much talking and too much smoking, but still as loud as ever.

"Al! Goddamn it! Al! YOU SHOULD SEE YOUR FACE, AL!"

C H A P T E R
T W E N T Y - F O U R

DESERTERS

In the other officers' club, back in Phuoc Vinh, now sinking so badly he had to hold his bottle in his hand, Major Dow bought Starret several beers and asked him about the South Vietnamese who had relieved his company.

"How many men were there?"

"No men," Starret grinned. "Just boys."

"Come on, goddamn it," Major Dow rasped at him. "I know they're boys, but how many?"

"Major," Starret said, after giving the matter no thought, "I have no idea. They were all running around."

"What did they have?"

"Rifles," Starret said. "I think most of them had rifles."

"God damn you, Starret, will you tell me what they are going to do?"

"We gave them our M-60s, but our M-60s were junk. And they think they're too fuckin' heavy. An' you know *why?*"

"I don't give a damn why. Why?"

" 'Cause they're too fuckin' little!"

"Starret!"

"Next war we gotta get some bigger guys."

"What else? Radios?"

"I didn't see any."

"No radios at all?"

"I said I didn't see any. Maybe they got invisible ones."

• • •

Did anyone know how poorly equipped the Army of the Republic of Vietnam was? After six years of fighting alongside, or slightly to the rear of, the best equipped army in the free world, the South Vietnamese still struggled along without most of the basic things an army needed. Of course, they had other things the Americans didn't have. They had their wives and families who followed them around the country, and even now were setting up a squatter camp in Phuoc Vinh village. Some were living in the Phuoc Vinh church.

Starret could tell him little more.

"Here, Major," Starret said, fishing something out of his blouse pocket. "You can have these." He handed Major Dow four duplicate Polaroids of a dead Vietnamese.

"I killed this guy four times."

Major Dow took the Polaroids and ripped them in half. He left Starret sitting alone at the officers' club bar, grinning.

Starret had his drop orders. Home in four days. Fifteen contacts with the enemy, not counting Touchhole, and he hadn't been touched. And now no more chances. He had survived the enemy. He had survived his own side's artillery. He had survived the United States Air Force. And helicopter accidents and exploding machine guns and other American platoons who might mistake his platoon for the enemy. And his own men. He had

survived it all. Three more days. It was, all in all, nothing short of amazing that he was still alive.

So he turned Kit down flat when Kit asked him later if he would go out to Bo Mua with him to try to find Miss Tuyet and see if she was all right. He refused to even consider the idea. Kit looked sad. Starret offered to buy him a beer in mitigation.

"No," Kit said, "I'll buy."

"Why, thank you, lootennen," Starret said foggily, "that is a very nice thing for you to do."

Kit had had no money, and since the Phuoc Vinh officers' club had stopped all charge accounts, he had to go and secretly borrow some money on the pretext of having to take a leak. He borrowed five dollars from Mr. O'Connor, the Ghost Ship pilot, who was sitting in the corner writing a poem about the Ghost Ship to send in to *Stars and Stripes*.

Kit had a beer, and then legitimately had to go and take a leak. Starret had four beers, and his mind changed.

"Lissen, Crissover," he said with his hand on Kit's arm. "Shit. You wanna go to Bo Mua? Shit. I'll go with you."

"No," Kit said. "No, it's not that important . . ."

"What's her name, this girl's name?" Starret asked, slurring his words and breathing beerily in Kit's face.

"Oh, it's not anything important. I mean, I barely knew her. She's . . ."

"Whassername, though, this girl?"

"Tuyet."

"Whassit?"

"Tuyet. It means 'snow,' " Kit said. Sergeant Xuan had told him.

"Toot?"

"Too-yet."

"Toot-it? Does she like to toot it?"

"What?" Kit said.

"Oh . . . nothin'."

"I just know the one name—Tuyet. I don't know her last name."

Starret polished off the rest of his beer.

"Toot-it. Well, so. We'll go see ol' Toot tomorrow."

"No," Kit said. "It's not important. I only knew her for one day."

"She cute?" Starret asked, his eyelids at half staff. "Toot? Cute?"

"Oh, she's just a little girl. I mean, she wasn't . . . she's just a sweet kid."

"Toot sweet?" Starret said.

"What?"

"Toot sweet! Donshagettit? Toot Sweet! Hah-hah-hah!"

He laughed crazily, and slapped Kit on the back.

"Toot sweet! Jesus Christ!"

In the succeeding hour, Lieutenant Starret had two more beers. Beer made Kit tired, and he wanted to sleep. But Starret felt better.

"So, I gotta know something. See. I'm a married man, but you guys . . . You and this . . . this Tootsie . . . you got it together and . . ."

"Oh, no," Kit said. "She's just a little girl. But I've just been thinking about whether she's all right."

"Y'gottit together," Starret slurred.

"No, no."

"Well," Starret looked at him, "well, tomorrow we're going to go over t' Bo Mua. I gonna to take you over t' Bo Mua . . . an' see Toot."

"Oh, it's not important. And she wasn't . . ."

"Hell, lissen, you wanna see her again, right? Am I right? Am I? Course I am. I'm right. Right?"

"Yes," Kit said.

"Okay. Goddamn. I'm gonna take you. And we're gonna see her."

"If you're sure," Kit said, "okay."

"But only," Starret held up an unsteady finger, "only if you do somethin' for me."

"What?"

"Buymeenotherbeer."

• • •

Lieutenant Toomey finished the briefing and sneaked back to his bunker, dodging any South Vietnamese soldiers he saw. He peeked around the hallway of the bunker. The two ARVN colonels he had beaten were gone—where, he had no idea. But they might be back at any time. He wasn't going to be sitting here waiting for them. He went into his room and picked up a few essentials: his pistol and belt, his AK-47, all the ammunition bandoliers he had, four grenades, and a handy knife that fit into his boot.

And some soap and his razors. Razors were now in short supply. Two days earlier, the North Vietnamese had dropped a mortar on the PX. One wall of the building was blown flat and part of the roof collapsed. The American military police were slow in getting there, and by the time they did show up, the newly arrived South Vietnamese troops had looted what little inventory was left. They took the few unsold cameras and the soap, and for some odd reason they also stole all the razor blades, hence the shortage. Weird, Toomey thought, since they didn't even have to shave.

• • •

Kit's drop orders came through. Major Dow went looking for him to tell him he could go home.

His first stop was Major Bedford's office. Major Bedford was working over his maps. Major Dow hadn't been in this office for some time, and the place had changed. Major Bedford had done some redecorating. There were maps everywhere on the walls, and one rather small nude. Major Bedford was working on a map on the table.

"Where's Kit?"

"I don't know," Major Bedford said, concentrating on his map.

"Well, he's got a drop. He can get the hell out of here any time he wants."

Major Bedford's face fell.

"Really?"

"He's going home just as soon as he gets cleared," Major Dow said.

"I'll miss him," Major Bedford said, without thinking.

"Yeah, so will I."

Major Bedford started to go back to his map. "I'll tell him when he gets back," he said.

"What's this map?" Major Dow asked.

"Oh, this . . ." Major Bedford tried to affect a yawn. "You know, it's the psy ops bird."

"The Ghost Ship?"

"Yes . . ."

"Any results yet?"

"Results?"

"Any North Viets shit their knickers and give up yet?"

Major Bedford wasn't sure if Major Dow were making fun of him. But it was a good question. After several nights of running the screaming ghost tape, no one had surrendered.

"Ah, well . . . no."

"Where are you flying now?" he asked.

Major Bedford made a sweep with his hand of the area north of the great curve of the Song Be River, where Lieutenant Starret's unit had been.

"Where do you think I should go now?"

"Hell," said Major Dow, "don't ask me. I have no idea either. One place is as good as another."

"Really?"

"They could be anywhere."

• • •

Stevenson made two piles of five hundred dollars each and secured them with rubber bands, stuck them in his pocket, and left for Major Bedford's bunker.

In Major Bedford's bunker, Sergeant Xuan put on the set of ARVN colonel's fatigues, whose owner was safely out back, buried by Thi Tuan in a wall of sandbags. The wound to Sergeant Xuan's back had healed, but it still hurt, especially when he bent to put his arm in a sleeve. Thi Tuan helped, gingerly drawing the blouse over the bandages. Sergeant Xuan looked at himself in Major Bedford's little mirror. After three weeks of recuperation, Sergeant Xuan looked like a wraith.

"They should be there by now," Stevenson said, handing him papers and the keys for a jeep. "I've written all the names and so on here in this notebook. Make sure they're taken care of and tell them to stay there in the hotel until they hear from us."

"This man is your father?" Xuan asked.

"Yes. Actually, no," Stevenson caught himself. "It's what's-his-name's father. Christopher's."

"Ah."

"This money is for you. It should be plenty. If you need more, you ask him for it. He's got money."

"And you have seen Captain Lam?" Xuan asked.

"Yes. Of course. I said I had."

"But you have not."

"I've been busy. I will do it today. Without fail!"

Sergeant Xuan winced, putting the money into his breast pocket.

"Can you drive?" Stevenson asked.

"I think . . ."

"It's sixty kilometers."

"I . . ."

And so when Sergeant Xuan finally took off for Saigon into the foggy early morning, in the stolen jeep, in the dead colonel's fatigues, Thi Tuan went with him. Partly for security, partly for companionship, but mostly to get the hell out of Phuoc Vinh.

• • •

The sun rose and Kit with it, remembering that Starret had promised to go with him to Bo Mua, and wondering if Starret would remember. Starret was still dead asleep. He looked in at Starret's immobile shape in the room at the far end of his bunker. Kit went to get some breakfast, but he didn't get very much, because the mess hall was crowded with Vietnamese officers drinking coffee.

The mess sergeant hated them all, but there was nothing he could do. General's orders. No South Vietnamese soldier was to be denied food at the mess hall. The South Vietnamese officers amended this policy to prohibit any of their enlisted men from eating in the American mess hall. Their enlisted men could go eat with their families, now crowding into Phuoc Vinh village.

Kit went back to the bunker, but Starret was still comatose. He went to his room.

He had put together a few things that he wanted to give to Miss Tuyet. There was a decorated comb he had bought, intending to give it to his sister, his travel alarm clock, a T-shirt that said "San Francisco" that he had bought his last day in the States. And last, there was the glass snowstorm globe with a snowman and a Christmas tree he had bought from Starret. Now that he looked at it, it wasn't really glass; it was plastic, and there were very few flakes. But he thought she would like it. After all, her name was Tuyet, and that meant "snow." There was no snow here, except for her.

He put all these things in a green canvas gas mask bag and sat on his bed and waited until he thought of the next thing to do.

• • •

Lieutenant Toomey woke early, as well. He had spent the night sleeping on the floor in the operations center, and he hadn't slept well. He had found a part of the supply office where no one was working and had put some chair cushions on the floor. But it was uncomfortable, and he rolled off the pillow onto the floor several times. At about five in the morning he gave up and stumbled out to find a shower.

The showers were heated with small diesel oil fires that warmed the water stored in airplane wing tanks propped up above the shower huts. At five in the morning all the fires had been out for hours, so his shower was ice cold. He tried to shave in the cold water but wound up looking worse.

He went back to the operations center, and as he sneaked in the back way, he heard something that made his already cold blood freeze.

In the heart of the building, Vietnamese voices were yelling and screaming. And there were American voices bellowing. Lieutenant Toomey stopped and listened, his eyes wide. He couldn't understand what the Vietnamese were saying, but they weren't the only ones yelling.

They were after his hide. They had found out about the colonels, the one Thi Tuan buried and the one who still couldn't talk. Now the Vietnamese would want to have him court-martialed for striking superior officers. A Vietnamese court-martial! And maybe, he thought suddenly, this would be the way the army got rid of him. They would just shovel him over and forget all about him. He would end his days as a prisoner of the South Vietnamese government. Was there a fate more unimaginably horrible? He heard Major Dow shouting.

Major Dow and Major Daugherty, and even General Walker were arguing with the Vietnamese. Horrible profanity rent the air. Six in the morning. What an odd time for all this to be going on. Bizarre people!

"Cowards! Goddamn yellow shit!" Daugherty yelled.

"Liars!" Walker yelled.

Toomey turned and walked gingerly back out of the operations center. The first light of morning was flooding the familiar clutter of Phuoc Vinh base—the tipsy buildings, the wire fencing, the leaning communication poles, the tangled cables, the wreckage of supplies and equipment that had been blown up and not cleared away, the stale residue of the previous day's odors, and the fumes, only slightly diminished in the cool of the morning. He was hungry, and he figured that if the complaining Vietnamese officers were in the operations center, they wouldn't be in the mess hall.

But, God! There were Vietnamese in the mess hall, too; they were everywhere. He went in through the kitchen and grabbed some rolls and some cans of milk. The mess sergeant was busy hooting at the enlisted cooks and no one noticed him.

The only safe place, he decided, was over in Kit's bunker.

Kit had never seen Toomey so disheveled and wild looking.

"Are you okay?" he asked.

"The gooks are after me," Toomey mumbled through a mouthful of soda biscuit. He emptied a can of milk into his mouth.

"The gooks?" Kit said. "Why?"

"Because . . ." Toomey looked at Kit. What the hell good would it do to tell Kit about anything?

"I beat some of them up the other night. I gotta get out of

here," he said, more to himself. He looked at Kit again. "How can I get out of here?"

Kit was certainly the wrong person to ask. But he tried to think of something.

"I don't know," Kit said, and then a thought popped into his brain, "unless . . ."

"Unless what?" Toomey looked at him. Milk ran down his chin.

"You want to go to Bo Mua today?"

Toomey was under orders not to leave the base unless he were accompanied by another officer. And despite numerous opinions to the contrary, including his own, Kit was an officer.

• • •

There was no morning briefing that morning. Not only had Toomey failed to show up to give the intelligence part of the briefing, but the general had failed to show up. And most of the few remaining officers who did show up were immediately swept into the crisis that gripped the operations center. Major Dow sent aircraft out to the area where Lieutenant Starret's company had been relieved by the South Vietnamese.

"Look for anything," he told the air battalion, "and shoot at anything. This is a mass desertion. Anything that moves is to be hit."

It was a crisis. Three South Vietnamese companies that had been put into the area where Starret had been were gone. The previous evening, terrified by something, they had all disappeared, deserted.

Some of their officers had tried to stop them and had even drawn weapons against them. But a handful of officers couldn't stop a full-scale desertion of terrified men, especially when some of the officers were equally terrified.

But why? Why had all of them vanished? Major Dow had never heard of such panicking. He couldn't understand it.

And he couldn't understand what the Vietnamese officers were screaming at him. One of them had a bullet wound in his arm. He waved his bandaged arm at Major Dow. Somehow, these ARVN officers were blaming him. Him! Of all people!

Major Daugherty drew him aside.

"Wait a minute," he said, his hand over his eyes.

He whispered to Major Dow.

"Oh, no!" Major Dow looked at Daugherty. A thought flickered by that this was almost funny.

Daugherty was right.

Major Dow sat with his head in his hands. He wanted to laugh, and the only thing that kept him from laughing was the grim reality that there was now even less between him and the North Vietnamese than there had been before.

• • •

Major Bedford had been up late with the Ghost Ship and he had overslept. Thi Tuan had not been there to wake him. Thi Tuan was gone somewhere. Major Bedford hated to be late, even though now no one seemed to care about what he did. He washed quickly and scraped uselessly at his face.

He hurried into the operations center in the midst of the yelling Vietnamese officers and the general confusion.

Daugherty and Dow looked up at him.

"What's going on?" he asked.

Major Dow finally found the strength to laugh.

"Your Ghost Ship," he said, "finally scared someone."

Major Bedford knew something was wrong.

"It scared off three companies of South Vietnamese."

C H A P T E R

T W E N T Y - F I V E

BO MUA

Major Dow was now operating out of his own brain, telling the general what he decided, but usually after he had done it. Walker nodded and mumbled, "Yes, yes," or simply waved his hand. Walker spent his time arguing with the Saigon command for more men and more shells.

Major Dow didn't want to be in charge of anything. He and Daugherty, the operations officer, and Oakin, the supply officer, huddled together as much as they could and tried to figure out what their situation was. There had been two deputy commanders but they had been assigned somewhere else nearly a

month ago, due to a shortage of brigadiers. Oakin wasn't much help.

Now the only things worth anything on the base at Phuoc Vinh were the fuel depot and the ammunition stores. The huge rubber fuel bladders had been spread out. So far the North Vietnamese hadn't hit them with the mortars they fired in every evening. And the chance of them doing any real damage was slight. Unless.

Unless, Major Dow thought, *unless they decide to come on the base and do it right.*

Walker wanted more artillery, but supplies of shells were low. Walker wanted more bombing done, but the air force was slow to respond to his pleas. They wanted to know if he had a contact with the enemy in progress?

"You bastards!" Walker yelled at the air force colonel in Saigon.

Major Dow knew these calls were useless.

"You cowardly, miserable, stinking bastards!" Walker screamed into the phone.

He held out his glass. Major Dow looked at him. Walker shook the glass to demonstrate its emptiness and glared at Major Dow.

The general raged into the phone, and Major Dow poured into his glass.

He had to tell the truth. He had no contact, no fighting in progress. He just wanted some bomb runs to demonstrate that they still had the ability to deliver bomb runs, to lift the jungle floor up and drop it back through the trees. But that wasn't enough. The air force replied politely that they were running short of everything—bombs, planes, fuel, and even pilots.

Major Dow cruised the Green Line with Major Daugherty in the late morning, especially the sectors that had been turned over to the South Vietnamese. The Vietnamese soldiers in the towers and bunkers watched them drive by with the look of dead men. They stood by the side of the Green Line road holding their rifles at slack angles.

"I heard these guys haven't been paid for months," Major Daugherty said.

"They look like they haven't been fed, either," Major Dow said.

"I don't want to drive around these people anymore," Daugherty said. "This is my last time on this part of the road. I don't like this."

"Yes," Major Dow agreed.

"Send that goddamn Toomey out here to check it out," Daugherty said, "or goddamn Starret. I'm sick of his mouth."

"Yes," Major Dow said, and wondered where the hell Toomey was. And Starret.

• • •

"Liar!" screamed the general, later in the afternoon when Stevenson told him he was sick and needed some time off.

"I . . ."

"What are you doing?! You goddamn liar! I need you here."

"Sir, I . . ."

"Time, my goddamn ass!"

General Walker's face was purple. Even under his thinning gray hair, his skin was purple. His trailer stank of old man's sweat and laundry. The air-conditioning had broken down. The laundry soap was in short supply.

"You're up to something! I'll ruin you!"

"Sir . . ."

"I hate you, Stevenson. You know that?"

Stevenson said nothing.

"I HATE YOU!"

Walker held the whiskey bottle tight. Whiskey was in very short supply.

"I hate all you smart fuckers . . ." He unscrewed the cap and took another drink.

"I'm leaving, sir," Stevenson said.

"I know all about you smart young fuckers."

"I said I'm leaving, sir."

"YOU STAY RIGHT THERE, YOU FUCKING LIAR!"

Stevenson turned and opened the trailer door.

"YOU . . ." Walker started, then dissolved in a fit of coughing and wheezing.

290

• • •

As he closed the trailer door behind him, Stevenson noticed a three-quarter ton truck across the division street. It was an older model of Korean war vintage, slower and heavier, but famous for reliability. Two boots stuck out of the driver's window. Stevenson went over and shook the boots.

"Soldier! Wake up!"

"What?" the young black soldier said groggily, sitting up.

"I need you to drive me somewhere."

"I'm *short,* man. I ain't driving nowhere."

"Listen to me. I'm the general's aide . . ."

"I don't care if you the lemonade."

Stevenson opened the truck door. He reached in and grabbed the man by the blouse. He pulled hard, and the man came through the door and fell in the dirt.

Stevenson got in the truck and started it. The soldier got to his feet.

"Where you takin' ma truck, man?!"

"Where's your weapon, soldier?" Stevenson asked him.

"Fuck ma weapon! You can't steal ma truck!"

"You're supposed to have your weapon with you at all times."

"You . . ."

"Shut up! Now! Where's your weapon?!"

The man paused, looking at Stevenson with murder in his eyes.

"Under the seat."

"Under the seat?"

"Yeah."

"Good," Stevenson said.

And he drove off.

• • •

"You got any money with you?" Toomey asked Kit as they walked past the now empty Korean bunkers.

"No," Kit said.

"Shit."

"How much do you need?"

"A lot."

"Why?"

"I need it."

There were no jeeps that worked at the motor pool. There weren't even any Americans at the motor pool. It had been turned over to the South Vietnamese. And there were no South Vietnamese there, either.

Kit and Toomey began walking back.

"Well, that's okay. I guess I don't have to go to Bo Mua," Kit said.

"We'll get something," Toomey said.

"I appreciate you helping me," Kit said, "but maybe it's just not that important."

"Yes, it is," said Toomey.

Behind them a truck wailed in low gear. The truck slowed down.

"Come with me! I need you," Stevenson shouted to Kit, stopping beside him.

"Okay," Kit said.

"Okay," Toomey said.

"Not you," Stevenson said to Toomey.

But Toomey had already gotten in the front seat, his rifle across his lap.

"Drive," he said.

"I said *not you,* Lieutenant," Stevenson repeated.

"And I said *drive,*" said Toomey.

Stevenson hesitated a moment. Kit got into the truck and slammed the door.

"Right," said Stevenson.

They had no trouble at the gate. The military police were busy with other problems. Hundreds of South Vietnamese Army wives, grandmothers, children, and babies who had taken up residency in Phuoc Vinh village crowded the base gate, chattering and crying and making a fuss. The three lieutenants in the old truck went through the gate and out on the road to Bo Mua and Nuoc Vang.

That morning was, in spite of all the human problems and self-produced misery, a beautiful morning. The sun drifted in a crystal clear blue sky; the fields were a lovely yellow green where the first crop of vegetables poked through the rich soil. A blue-gray water buffalo with handsomely arched horns watched them as they bounced noisily by. The only other motor vehicle they met was a tiny motorcycle carrying three Vietnamese women and several chickens.

Out of a corner of his eye, Lieutenant Toomey thought he saw something in the trees.

"Stop."

Stevenson pulled the truck to a halt, turned off the engine, and scanned the wood line.

"What's wrong?" Kit asked.

"What did you see?" Stevenson said.

"Just checkin'," Toomey said. "Look all around and see if you see anything moving."

Stevenson looked around uneasily. The fields baked happily in the sun. The warmth of its rays felt hot and dry and good on Kit's right arm.

"I don't see anything," Stevenson said.

"Keep lookin'," Toomey said.

"Maybe we should go back, if you think anything's wrong," Kit suggested.

No sound disturbed the tranquil day. The Vietnamese countryside was as lovely and peaceful as a summer day in Virginia.

"Maybe we should just forget it and go back," Kit offered again.

"Yeah, well, Bo Mua's only half a mile more. And Captain Lam is just beyond."

"Well, if you want to go back, I mean, it's okay with me."

"Quiet," Stevenson said.

Kit was silent. Stevenson started the truck again and they continued.

"Where are you going?" Kit asked finally.

"You and I," Stevenson said, "are going to the National Police to see Captain Lam."

"Oh."

"Now, pay attention. You have to talk to this Captain Lam. He doesn't speak any English. You have to tell Captain Lam that Xuan is working for us now."

"He is?" Kit said.

"Yes. He's gone to Saigon to meet your fa . . . ahem . . . our business partner."

"My father? *He's in Saigon?*"

"Christ," Stevenson hissed. "Yes. Your father's in Saigon."

"Your father's in Saigon?" Toomey asked Kit.

"This is none of your business, Lieutenant," Stevenson said to Toomey.

"What's the deal, anyway? Who's your father?" Toomey said to Kit.

"He's . . ."

"Just *shut the fuck up,* will you, please. Listen to me," Stevenson said.

"What the hell is going on here?" Toomey asked.

"You have to explain to Captain Lam," Stevenson continued, "that he is to release Xuan from his National Police obligation and that we will pay him. I have the money."

"Money?" Toomey asked.

"Will you *please* shut up—*please?*"

"But, listen . . ." Kit stammered.

"What's wrong?"

"I can't . . . do that."

"Why not?"

"I can't say all that," Kit said.

"What do you mean? I thought you spoke Vietnamese."

"But I've . . . forgotten."

"What?!"

Toomey began laughing. An unpleasant sound.

The village of Bo Mua was directly ahead.

"You mean to tell me that you *can't* speak Vietnamese?" Stevenson asked Kit, giving him a withering, burning glare.

"Yes, but, not . . . like that. I . . ."

"Jesus!"

Toomey laughed some more.

"Shut up. WILL YOU SHUT UP!"

"I'm sorry . . ." Kit began.

"You shut up, too!"

They pulled up to Bo Mua village, by the school—a wispy

frame shelter with open sides. Stevenson leaned his head on the
wheel and thought furiously.

"Oh, hey, this is Bo Mua," Kit said looking around. Stevenson
looked up.

"So what?"

"Well . . ."

Lieutenant Toomey asked, "Is this the place you wanted?"

"Yes," Kit said. "I'll just be a minute."

He got out of the truck with his bag of gifts and walked slowly
toward the center of the village.

There were only six houses of any substance in the village of
Bo Mua. They were bamboo framed, covered with grass, with
metal roofs, and arranged around a dusty village center, a sort of
square but more oval. In the middle there was a flagpole from
which flew, or rather hung, the yellow flag with three red stripes.
At the present time the village was a loyal part of the republic.
But the loyalty of Bo Mua was probably as tattered and faded as
its flag, and somewhere, folded under the village chief's bed, was
a Viet Cong flag with a red and blue stripe and one big star, ready
to be run up the pole at a moment's notice.

In the truck, Lieutenant Toomey looked around, and finally at
Stevenson.

"What about this money, Stevenson?" he asked suspiciously.

"Nothing that concerns you."

"Stevenson? I think you're up to some crooked shit here. Bribing the White Mice? What is this? Like drugs or . . ."

"If I were *you*, I wouldn't . . ."

"Oh, you wouldn't, huh?"

"You forget something, my dear Lieutenant Toomey. I know
all about you."

"And now I know about you. And I'll tell you something . . ."

Stevenson put his hand on Toomey's arm to silence him.

"Jesus! What's he up to?"

Kit was standing in the middle of the village square.

He stood and waited. There wasn't a soul in the village.

Then an old man appeared in a doorway of one of the houses,
across the center from the truck. He watched Kit for a few min-

utes, and then walked out toward him. He had a half smile stuck on his face.

Toomey shifted in his seat and poked Stevenson.

"See? Look?" he said quickly under his breath. "Shit!"

"I see him. Who is that old bastard?"

"Not him. Look!"

"What? *What?*"

"There! There's somebody in back of that hooch."

Stevenson looked.

In the rear of one of the houses was a cluster of at least twenty men, obscured by the foliage, standing very still, looking at them. They didn't move; some of them had uniforms on and others were standing bare-chested. Some of them had rifles.

"Easy, easy," Toomey said.

"Let's . . ."

"Easy, easy, you idiot," Toomey growled at Stevenson.

"Who . . ."

"ARVNs. Deserters."

"Let's get out of here," Stevenson hissed. He reached for the key.

"No. No. No. Just be quiet."

Out in the village square the old man came closer to Kit. At about ten paces he stopped and waiting, smiling. He had on a black shirt, and his short hair was streaked with gray.

He made a moaned greeting and held out a limp hand, brown and bony.

"Chao thua ong," he said.

"Chao," Kit said.

"Manh gioi?" the old man wheezed.

"Xin cho toi biet," Kit began, searching his memory for some words. "Please tell me . . ."

"Yess, yess?" the man said. *"Ti-ti* English."

"I am looking for a little girl."

"Yess, yess."

"Her name is Tuyet."

The old man still nodded.

"Do you know where she is? She lives here in Bo Mua."

The old man's smile remained unchanged.

"I am leaving. I want to give her something. A present," Kit said, holding out the gas mask bag.

"Yess, Yess. I know. Yess," the old man wheezed.

"Do you know where she is?"

The man stood a minute and thought. He looked up at the bright sun, squinting his face like an old apple.

He gave a long moan, indicating a thoughtful pause.

"She go away."

"She's gone? Well . . ."

Kit turned and looked back at Lieutenant Toomey and Lieutenant Stevenson, two white faces in the dark truck cab.

"Well," Kit said, "well, is she coming back here?"

"Yess, yess."

"Well, will you give this to her?"

"Yess, yess."

The man took the bag.

"My name is on the bag, see?"

The man looked at it. Kit had written his name and his address in Connecticut.

"I am leaving soon."

"Yesssss." The old man looked in the bag.

Kit heard Toomey in the truck give a low whistle.

"Well, good-bye," he said, and turned back to the truck.

"No. You . . ." the old man said. "You wait."

Kit turned.

The old man shuffled back to the house next to the one he had come from. Kit stood and waited.

He heard Toomey whistle again.

The old man appeared in the door of the house and looked at Kit. Then slowly, behind him, a small figure appeared.

It was Miss Tuyet.

She walked with the old man across the dusty village center. And as she came toward him, and as he recognized her face, he felt an unrecognizable emotion rise within him, a combination of loneliness and uselessness, of love and stupidity.

She squinted at him. She was still so pretty and delicately formed with her hair drawn back, glittering like onyx threads in

the clear sunlight. The old man had her by one hand, and in the other he carried Kit's bag.

Kit, for a moment, forgot all about Toomey and Stevenson. He wanted to pick Miss Tuyet up and carry her away with him, to take care of her, to take her home where it was safe, to take her to a place where she could live peacefully and learn things and where he could watch her grow. He wanted to take the rest of his life and make up for having hit her that day in the jeep with Sergeant Xuan, to buy food for her and clothes for her, to treat her as a man treats a daughter, to see her grow. He wanted, even now, to pick her up and hug her and then fly up and out of this place with her under one arm. He wanted to take her up and give her everything he could, to teach her to talk to him and understand what he said in return. He wanted to give her so much—ice cream and car rides and summers and movies, and everything he could think of. He wanted to give her all the presents that children should have. And of all presents, peace.

The old man gave her the bag. She took it and stood still. Kit reached down and unsnapped the flap. He put his hand inside the bag and took out the plastic snowstorm. He shook it so the few little flakes darted around the plastic snowman and the Christmas tree. She looked at it wonderingly.

"See?" Kit said, going down on one knee. "Snow. *Tuyet.*"

The flakes swirled down. He put the snowstorm in her hand and closed her fingers around the plastic base. Then he shook her hand gently. The flakes flew up and around in the hot Vietnamese sunshine. Miss Tuyet smiled, a thin little smile that crinkled her eyes and showed her little pearl teeth. A smile so soft and bright Kit knew he would never forget it. Oh, why couldn't he have brought one of the Polaroid cameras that they had by the hundreds?

He stood up and leaned over her. She watched the flakes for a second and then looked up at him. He gave her a quick kiss on the head.

"Good-bye, Tuyet. Write to me?"

She said nothing.

He turned to the truck.

"Tell her to write me a letter!" he said to the old man.

The man moaned something in Vietnamese, something lost.

Stevenson started the truck engine. Kit walked back to the truck, paused another moment, and then got in, squeezing next to Toomey. Stevenson put the truck in reverse and backed into a turn. Then he put it in first and started off slowly.

Kit twisted around and waved out the window as they headed out of the village. He looked back and waved some more, as Miss Tuyet and the old man receded into the distance. *Well*, he thought, *I will never see her again.*

He turned around and looked down at his hands.

"Goddamn it!" Stevenson exploded.

He gunned the truck forward.

"Jesus!" Toomey said. "This is all you brought?"

"There's a rifle under the seat."

"Move, goddamn it!" Toomey said to Kit, attempting to reach down.

They scrambled around, crowded together. Toomey pulled the rifle out.

"Jesus! One clip!"

"Well, fuck!"

"You take this." Toomey unbuckled his holster and handed Stevenson his pistol.

"And you, asshole, you take this." He gave Kit the M-16.

"What?"

Stevenson braked the truck to a stop.

"There they are. More of them."

Kit looked forward through the dust cloud that sailed past them.

"Shit," said Stevenson. "Who *are* those guys?"

"ARVN deserters. I told you. See? Look. There they are."

Kit looked forward. Four or five men stood on either side of the road with rifles not more than half a mile ahead. One man stood in the middle.

"Well?" Toomey said.

"Well?" Stevenson said.

"What?" Kit asked.

"They want the truck," Toomey said.

"Should we give it to them?"

"No," Toomey said.

Stevenson looked at Toomey. People like Lieutenant Toomey came in handy sometimes.

"Right," he said.

"Okay, let's go," Toomey said.

Stevenson pressed down on the gas, and the truck reluctantly picked up speed.

"Lock and load, asshole!" Toomey barked at Kit.

Kit fiddled with the rifle. Toomey saw that he wouldn't make it.

"STOP!" he screamed at Stevenson. Stevenson hit the brakes. Toomey grabbed the rifle from Kit and pulled the charger. The men now only a quarter mile up the road began walking toward them, waving them to stop. The five they had seen were now twenty.

"You ready? You got the safety off?"

"Yes."

"Okay. Let's go!" Toomey said, then, "STOP!"

"What the hell?" Stevenson said.

"No! You got the fuckin' safety on. Jesus Christ!" Toomey reached over and clicked the safety off of the M-16. "Now start shooting!"

"I . . . yes, okay!" Kit said.

"GO! What the fuck are . . ."

The deserters were approaching, waving. Stevenson stepped on the gas and snapped the clutch.

"Listen, you idiot! Shoot as many as you can. UNDER-STAND?!"

Kit saw the men coming closer. He had never shot anyone.

Stevenson had the .45 in his left hand out the window.

The truck careened forward. Stevenson zigged and zagged. He began shooting. Toomey put his boot up and kicked out the windshield. Glass pellets flew. He stuck his AK-47 through the frame and fired. And the ARVNs fired back. Kit, with his eyes closed and his head down, pulled his trigger and held it back.

The truck, engine howling, bore down through the knot of deserters. And through them. One soldier bounced off the grille. Another grabbed at the truck and vaulted himself up on the hood, slamming against the window frame. Stevenson wrenched the wheel and the man was pitched off to the right. Hot shells clinked off the window frame. Bullets bounced off the hood and a shower of hot water blew up in their faces. Kit heard the men yell and Toomey holler as they roared through. He heard the thud of a man under the truck.

Another man clung to Stevenson's door. Stevenson pounded at him with the now empty pistol.

"Oh, fuck! Oh, Jesus!"

Toomey grabbed his neck. Blood leeched out between his fingers.

"Shoot! You stupid bastard! SHOOT HIM!" Toomey yelled.

Kit swung the rifle around. The barrel hit Toomey in the head. More blood spread over Toomey's shoulder.

"Jesus! You fucking . . . !"

The man hanging on the door had grabbed Stevenson's arm and the wheel. His head was in the cab with them.

"SHOOT HIM!" Toomey screamed.

Kit looked at the man's face, purple with rage and exertion.

"Shoot! GOD DAMN you!" Toomey screamed again.

But Kit couldn't do it.

Toomey wrenched the rifle from him, his hands wet with his own blood and radiator water. And shot the man in the nose.

He fell backward, out and away from the bouncing truck.

"Drive this goddamn thing!" Toomey bellowed. "Jesus!"

Stevenson pushed the truck as fast as it would go. Shortly they were out of range, and except for the damage to the radiator, unhurt. Toomey grabbed Kit by the hair.

"Jesus Christ! You are the stupidest son of a bitch alive. You weren't even on automatic. I ought to . . ." He let go of Kit. "You stupid, stupid, stupid, son of a bitch!"

Kit looked at his rifle.

"I'm . . ."

• • •

They reached a fork in the road where they had to decide whether to go on to the National Police or back to Phuoc Vinh base. Steam came out from under the hood.

Stevenson, having calmed down, brought the truck to a halt.

"Check for damage to the radiator," he ordered the other two.

"You check. I'm bleeding," Toomey said.

"He is bleeding," Kit said.

"It's not that bad," Stevenson said.

Kit got out and went to the front of the truck. Steam rolled up from under the hood.

"Well?" Stevenson called to him.

"I don't know," Kit said, referring to opening the hood.

"Will you help him?!" Stevenson whined at Toomey.

"You do it. For Christ's sake, I'm bleeding!"

"You're not bleeding that . . . oh, for Christ's sake!"

Stevenson got out and slammed the door.

He went to the front of the truck and elbowed Kit aside, pulled the latch, and opened the heavy steel hood of the truck. Steam billows rose. He searched for the support rod, found it, and stuck it in place. He couldn't see anything in the steam, but things didn't seem too serious. At least, not under the hood.

Toomey slid over to the driver's seat.

Stevenson waved away the steam and saw that a hose had been shot away, but that there was still water in the engine, which was idling without any damage noises.

"It'll be okay," he said.

"Fine," said Toomey.

Stevenson looked over the rest of the engine.

"We can make it to Nuoc Vang," he said, putting down the support rod.

"Fine," said Toomey.

Stevenson let the hood drop with a resounding clang. He wiped his hands on his pants and walked around to get in the driver's seat. Then he stopped.

"No," said Lieutenant Toomey, pointing the rifle in Stevenson's face.

Stevenson looked at the little black hole in the end of the rifle barrel.

"Sorry," Toomey said, "but I need this truck."

"You son of . . ."

"None of that, Lieutenant. Um . . . now give me that money you were talking about."

Stevenson looked at him levelly. There was no sense arguing about this.

"Now, let's stay calm."

"I'm very calm."

"I can see that."

"The money," Toomey said.

"Actually, you're in luck, Lieutenant Toomey."

"Just gimme the money . . ."

Stevenson dug into his pocket and pulled out the envelope of Mr. Christopher's money.

"There you are."

He held the envelope out. Toomey reached his bloody hand for it.

"That's five hundred dollars American," Stevenson said. "You can go quite a ways on that."

Toomey tore the envelope open with his teeth. He looked in and then back at Stevenson.

"What kind of shit are you two up to?"

"We all have our little secrets, Lieutenant Toomey, as well you know."

"Where'd this money come from? Drugs, right?"

"Just call this your lucky day."

"Is it real?"

"Absolutely real."

"Well, thank you, Lieutenant Stevenson. This is just what I need."

"Don't thank me!" Stevenson said, bitterly laughing. "Thank him!"

Toomey looked at Kit.

"It's his money! Hah!" Stevenson said.

Kit looked at Toomey.

"This is your money?" Toomey said to Kit.

"I . . . well . . ."

"I take back everything I said," Toomey said, thinking that you couldn't tell who was a drug dealer these days. He put the truck in gear. "Thanks a lot."

303

"Wait a minute!" Stevenson said as the truck started to move. "Where are you going to go? Wait!" He tried to run along next to the truck. "You can't just leave us here. Hey! HEY!"

But the truck was moving too fast.

Toomey drove off, leaving nothing but a trail of steam.

CHAPTER
TWENTY-SIX

THE MESS HALL

Sergeant Xuan and Thi Tuan drove up in front of the Hotel Napoleon. Xuan had once stayed there in happier days. It was the only hotel he knew in Saigon. He looked at the wreck it had become and knew something was wrong. He got out of the jeep and, walking slowly, carefully, went into the hotel.

Mr. Christopher and his friend had been there, the desk clerk told him, but they had left. No one knew where the two Americans had gone. Xuan was in worsening pain because the jouncy ride in the jeep down from Phuoc Vinh had aggravated his back wound. He would have welcomed morphine if he could have got-

ten any. He was dressed in the South Vietnamese army colonel's uniform. He had five hundred American dollars in his shirt. It crossed his mind that he should stay in Saigon and disappear. It was a tempting idea. He stood outside the hotel thinking. A man crawled up to him on the sidewalk and spat on his leg. *A veteran,* Xuan thought.

But one never knew how wars would turn out. He got back in the jeep. There was every possibility that the Americans would hang on here for years. They very well might do that; they had certainly shown greater tenacity than he had ever expected. Greater tenacity than even the French.

They were an odd people, the Americans. All so different. Of all the various groups that had invaded and tried to colonize Vietnam, the Americans were the only ones who really didn't want anything tangible in return. The French had wanted rubber, and the Chinese had wanted slaves, but the Americans seemed not to know what the hell they wanted, except that they didn't want to have to admit they were wrong. Maybe they would cut a deal with the Chinese and drop an A-bomb on Ho Chi Minh. Maybe that's why Nixon wanted to go to China. To get permission.

The last time he had been in Saigon, there had been fighting every night, but there had been lively street life during the day. Now the city was filled with a grinding, overcrowded misery. The pollution was a gray, hanging poisonous cloud. Wounded men, blinded and crippled soldiers, were living in the streets and parks everywhere. The people were steeling themselves against the last trial still to come, so tired, so wounded, so bloodied and sick at heart, they would have tolerated any form of government, any ruler, any system that brought with it twenty-four hours of quiet.

Xuan was a logical man. His options were dwindling. He could go back to the National Police or he could go back and work for Stevenson. Or he could disappear. It all depended on what he thought the Americans were going to do.

But they could not leave, he thought. It was unthinkable. Not after all these years and all this expense, not after having lost tens of thousands of their own young men, and having wounded hundreds of thousands more, after having spent billions of dollars

of their own money, after having poured billions more into the economy. They had never lost a war in their history. Stevenson was right. This was the same as Korea. They would hang on.

He parked the jeep across from the American Embassy and sent Thi Tuan to buy food. He was hungry after the long drive and he needed time to think. He gave Thi Tuan an American twenty-dollar bill.

"Listen to me," he said, "this is a lot of money. Be sure you get change."

"Yes," Thi Tuan said.

"Do not let anyone fool you!"

"No," said Thi Tuan.

"Be careful."

"Yes," said Thi Tuan.

The American Embassy was an enormous old colonial building, shaded with beautiful trees and surrounded by handsome iron fencing. The American flag and the Republic of Vietnam flag hung side by side, clean, colorful, and gently rippling. The solidity and decorousness of the building were unmistakable. Of course, Xuan said to himself, they will not leave. He took some pain pills Stevenson had given him and drank some water. He tried to get comfortable in the seat and take a nap. He felt drowsy in the heat. *As soon as I fall asleep,* he thought, *the boy will be back with the food.*

But by that time Thi Tuan was miles away, running through the streets of Saigon. Xuan could have slept forever.

• • •

The morning Kit had gone to Bo Mua, twenty more Americans left by helicopter to go back to the 90th Replacement for rotation back to the States. Specialist Dilby was among them. He came in and said good-bye to Major Dow. Major Dow smiled wearily at him.

"We're having a big party tonight," Major Dow said. "You sure you don't want to stay? Booze, girls, everything."

"If I had only known, sir," Dilby laughed.

"I put you on the list for a Bronze Star. You'll get the orders, unless they get lost. Watch for them when you get discharged."

"Really? A Bronze Star? Gee. Thanks."

"Yeah. Congratulations. Give it to your grandchildren."

Dilby looked at him carefully.

"Major? Sir? You look like hell, sir."

"Get out of here, Dilby."

Dilby looked at him sadly.

"So long, Major." He paused. "Say good-bye to Lieutenant Kit for me."

"I will."

"Thanks for the Bronze Star. I don't know what it's for."

And Dilby bounced his duffel bag up on his shoulder and left.

"Neither do I," said Major Dow to no one.

• • •

The four South Vietnamese Dilby had trained on the radar had deserted. No one was listening for the enemy soldiers. Major Dow had his grease pencil in hand. His hand quavered.

The maps he had been keeping, the situation reports he had filed, the accounts of enemy movements he had tried to catalog over the past year, the intelligence reports about caches and discoveries of weapons, the reports he got from other units, from higher commands, from the air force, and even from the ARVN—all this information, from which he tried to determine the number and nature of the enemy forces, faded in accuracy until they were of hardly any value.

The large map in his office, which covered the entire wall, had pins and stickers and grease pencil lines and stars and all manner of other markings, not one of which was even remotely reliable. And without constant radar coverage and constant aircraft observation flights, and without people like Sergeant Xuan and the Cambodian Scouts and the village spies and the high-level air force flights and the people sensors out in the jungle and American infantry units turning in captured documents, it had become more dangerous for him to guess where the North Vietnamese were massed than to freely admit that he didn't know.

"They say we will have thirty companies of ARVN replacements, General," he told Walker.

"Liars!" Walker wheezed.

"Saigon says expect half that."

"Liars!"

"I don't know," Major Dow said.

And now Major Dow feared that he might be called on to fight this war in a way he had never planned on. He had always seen his role as the man who did the clever thinking, which, when given to braver and more warlike people, resulted in victory. Now things were getting closer to his door.

At least Kit would be getting the hell out of there. He would have to tell Kit he could go as soon as he saw him. Kit would be happy, and they would say good-bye. Then Kit would leave, probably with some promise to look him up back in the States. Kit would never know that his pathetic performance as an officer was the one luxury Major Dow had allowed himself in this war.

My God, he thought, *what a wreck this army is.*

He put his head down on his desk and fell asleep.

• • •

The mess sergeant had rebelled late that morning.

"Fucking thieves!" he screamed at the Vietnamese.

In a fit of rage, he had ordered them out of his mess hall. He claimed they were stealing food. They were, of course, and selling it to their troops with families in Phuoc Vinh.

The mess sergeant couldn't stand any of them. He threw a wonderful fit. He chased one Vietnamese major out of the chow line. Then he threw a chair after him. Then he threw another Vietnamese major after the chair. And while he looked around for even larger things to throw, he heaped racial and qualitative abuse on the entire Vietnamese nation. He had fewer cooks than ever before, and no American troops would show up for KP, even when they were ordered to. If they weren't going to obey orders, the mess sergeant was damned if *he* would obey orders.

The mess hall was quiet after his cataclysmic rage, but it was still in a state of general confusion and disorder.

Lieutenant Stevenson entered the mess hall, another rage in subsidence. It had been three miles, at least, walking back to Phuoc Vinh base in the hot afternoon sun. Stevenson continued

to curse himself inwardly for ever having gotten into a business deal with someone like Kit.

Now he wanted food and something to drink. He came in the mess hall and stood, expressionless, in the middle of the clutter of trays of half-eaten food and the overturned furniture.

"What happened here?" he muttered.

The mess sergeant came barreling out of the kitchen.

"I AIN'T servin' GOOKS no MORE," he said threateningly.

"I see."

"No, you don't see. I AIN'T servin' NOBODY less I get some PEOPLE here."

"Um-hmm," said Lieutenant Stevenson, while the mess sergeant went through a belligerent little dance of anger like a prizefighter.

"I AIN'T got no KPs and I gotta feed GOOKS? Never happen, L-T. NEVER HAPPEN!"

"All right, all right."

"You don't get me some KPs, and there ain't gonna be no more goddamn food for anyone. I AIN'T FEEDIN' NOBODY!"

"All right, all right."

"You . . ."

"I HEARD YOU, Sergeant. Now, shut up. Is there any coffee?"

"I been shuttin' up TOO LONG. I don't get some KPs, you AIN'T GETTIN' NO COFFEE!"

The fans in the mess hall pushed the hot air and the odors around in circles. Stevenson was sweaty and tired, and he didn't want to talk to this fat man with the food stains all over his belly. Two American enlisted soldiers came to the door, looking for food. They peered in hesitantly.

"You two," Stevenson said, pointing at them. "You two. Come here."

They didn't move.

"How about giving the sergeant here a hand straightening up this place?"

"Uh, we gotta go, sir."

"No, you don't. You have to help here."

"No, sir, we gotta go." They turned to leave.

"Come back here!" Stevenson shouted.

"Get fucked," said one of the men, and they both took off running.

Stevenson looked after them, then turned back to the mess sergeant, who was grinning a mean grin. He pulled his filthy apron back and forth over his stomach.

"See?"

"I want some coffee, Sergeant."

"YEAH? Well, I want some KPs or nobody's gettin' anything. You hear? NOBODY!"

• • •

Late that afternoon, Sergeant Xuan got back. He drove up to the barbed wire gate of Phuoc Vinh base through a crowd of perhaps a hundred Vietnamese women and children trying to get in, to get work, to get money, to get messages to the men stationed there. The American MPs still manned the gate, and if he hadn't still been dressed up as a colonel he wouldn't have gotten in. He blew the horn and shouted at the women to get out of the way.

Children got up on the front of the jeep and tried to climb up the back onto the roof. He was weak and in pain, but he screamed at them to get off. They paid no attention. He was finally forced to let the clutch out violently and hit the brake to shake them off. It was a terrible thing to do. Those who still stuck to the car were pulled off by the MPs.

The trip had been excruciating. His back wounds had opened and his shirt was soaked with blood where the bandages had come loose. He drove as quickly as he could to the base operations center, looking for Stevenson.

ARVN soldiers were everywhere. The place was starting to look like a South Vietnamese base. He went into the operations center. Major Dow stood in the hall in front of his office.

"My God, what happened to you?" he said.

"I look for *Trung-uy* Stevenson," Xuan said.

"But you're bleeding! Christ! Look at your shirt."

"It is all right. I need a new bandage. It comes loose."

"Come on, I'll take you to the hospital."

"No, later. I have to find Stevenson."

"I don't know where he is," Major Dow said, still gaping at the stains on Xuan's shirt. "I don't know where anybody is."

• • •

Stevenson was in his room in the bunker, lying on his bed in the dim light but not asleep.

"You couldn't find him?" he asked Xuan, propping himself up on his elbows.

"He was there and the lawyer, but they left. They came and they left."

"What do you mean? They came and they left? Where the hell would they go?"

"I do not know. Nobody knew."

"Jesus!"

He fell back heavily on his bed.

"Trung-uy," Xuan said after a pause. "My bandages."

"What?"

"I must go to the hospital. I am bleeding."

"Lie down," Stevenson moaned. "I'll do it. I'll take care of it. God! I have to take care of everything."

• • •

It was one thing to chase Lieutenant Stevenson out of the wreckage of the mess hall, but quite another to chase Major Bedford.

"What the hell happened here?" he asked.

"I ain't feeding no GOOKS!" The mess sergeant began to warm to his theme, looking up from the pots he was washing violently in the kitchen.

"What gooks?" Major Bedford asked. "I don't see any gooks here."

"I AIN'T FEEDIN' NOBODY 'LESS I GET SOME HELP!"

"Don't yell at me, Sergeant!"

"I AIN'T KIDDIN', MAJOR!"

"I SAID," Major Bedford yelled over him, "DON'T YELL AT ME!"

The mess sergeant looked at him. In one fat, soapy hand was a

large bread knife. They both looked at the knife, the mess sergeant as if it were in someone else's hand.

Major Bedford was hungry. It was nearly five o'clock.

"I would—please—like something to eat," he said in a low, polite growl. "Please," he repeated, in honor of the knife.

He saw a tray of corn bread, a flavorless yellow compound. Slowly and deliberately he spoke to the red-faced mess sergeant. "Would it be okay if I had a piece of corn bread, Sergeant?"

"I'll tell you one goddamn thing! I'll tell you what! When I get back to the world, I'm gettin' out of this sorry-ass goddamn army! Look at this pig hole!" He threw the knife down in the sink.

"I'm sorry, Sergeant," Major Bedford said, walking over to the corn bread. "I am really sorry."

He put some corn bread in his mouth. It had a salty chalkiness. He looked around for a can of milk.

"Okay if I get some milk, Sergeant?"

"How the hell am I supposed to get this chow ready? I'll tell you! I ain't doin' it! You goddamn officers can starve! You can all goddamn starve. LOOK! Here's another one! GET THE HELL OUTTA HERE!" A figure peeked in at the door.

Kit had been sent to get food for Xuan.

"Come here," Major Bedford called to him. "Here in the kitchen."

Kit came into the kitchen lights, keeping an eye on the mess sergeant.

"You . . . uh . . . don't . . . uh . . . wouldn't mind helping me help the sergeant here, would you, Lieutenant? A few pots and pans? Some trays?"

Kit looked around the kitchen.

"Umm . . . sure," he said agreeably.

And then, to the incredulity of the mess sergeant, they set to work doing the inglorious work of cleaning pots.

It was pleasant work to Major Bedford, and even more pleasant with Kit working by his side. The wash water was only pee warm, and gray with grease, but they dumped in some more soap and made some suds. They sloshed the trays and pots around and around and cast them noisily on the drying rack. Kit whistled

aimlessly and Major Bedford was happier than he had been in months.

"Have you seen Major Dow, Kit?" Major Bedford asked through a mouthful of slightly moist, soapy-tasting corn bread.

"No, sir, not today."

"You can leave."

"Really?"

"You got a drop. You can leave any time you can get a flight."

"Really?"

"How's it feel?"

"It feels great, sir. You're sure?"

"Of course, I'm sure. But you gotta finish those trays first."

Kit laughed. It was the first time Major Bedford could ever remember seeing him laugh.

And as he laughed, the lights went out.

The first mortar of the evening fell to earth on the generator shack near Kit's bunker.

C H A P T E R

T W E N T Y - S E V E N

A ROCKET ATTACK

The generator shack next to Kit's bunker had two generators. A withered old Vietnamese man attended the machinery and switched the generators back and forth and changed the oil and made notes in the service book. After he had done that, he brought out a small folding chair and, for the rest of the shift, read the Saigon papers next to the pounding, whining machine, under the single light bulb, oblivious to the maddening noise.

The first mortar round of the evening fell on the generator shack and stopped the sound.

WHOOOMP!

It punctured the tin roof and exploded between the generators, killing the little Vietnamese man on duty, knocking him off his chair and rolling him out into the muddy field in a shower of newspaper pages and parts of the generator controls.

Before the next mortar hit, eight or nine seconds, a fearful silence descended. In the mess hall kitchen, Kit and Major Bedford and the mess sergeant stopped washing pots. Little pieces of the generator shack caromed off the screens of the kitchen windows, and other pieces landed on the roof. The three of them dived for the filthy floor.

WHOOOMP! WHOOOMP!

WHOOOMP! WHOOMP! WHOOMP!

Five more rounds whoomped in a line more or less down the street to the operations center. One man, caught on the run, was thrown, clutching his face, against the front of the post office. He bounced off and continued running, now blinded by dirt, down the street until he collapsed.

There was another pause.

In the kitchen, Major Bedford got up slowly to his knees. Black smoke and dust drifted into the mess hall through the iron-red, slanting sunlight. He heard shouting and yelling outside and the sound of a truck going by.

The mess sergeant had placed his head in the field oven for safekeeping. He slowly withdrew it and looked around at Major Bedford, his eyes wide, his face white, and his mouth open like a pothole.

"You think that's it, Major?"

There should have been some artillery, some outgoing from either the American batteries or the South Vietnamese, but the Americans, short on shells, now waited to see if a full attack were planned, and the South Vietnamese waited because they rarely did anything on time. If this mortar attack had happened four months ago, helicopters would have scrambled by now and would be in the air, cruising the quadrant from which the mortars had arrived.

Major Bedford heard no helicopters, just some more shouting and jeeps running around in the distance. He waited.

"Well, I hope that's it," he said, more to himself. He stood and

looked out the kitchen window over the shelf with the now empty corn bread pan. The generators were on fire; the diesel fuel ran down through the muddy field and sullen red flames pushed clouds of smoke upward into the gloomy sky.

"Holy Jesus, Kit, I think your bunker's on fire."

"Really?"

Kit scrambled to his feet.

He couldn't tell through the smoke, but it looked that way. He heard some ammunition popping. Some artillery started—three shots, then three more, then cracks, and the ripping sound as the shells sailed off to nowhere.

They went out the back door and down the rotting boardwalk to Kit's bunker. Major Bedford was first. Then he turned and stopped Kit.

"Listen. You stay here. You stay inside. This is your last day. You stay under cover." He held him by the shoulders.

"No. I'll be all right," Kit said with a half smile. "It's over, anyway."

"Maybe, but stay inside."

"I . . ."

WHOOOMP! WHOOOMP! WHOOOMP!

Three more mortars hit the runway, and then another three.

WHOOOMP! WHOOOMP! WHOOOMP!

The humor in Kit's smile evaporated but the expression stayed. To the east, in the direction of the operations center, more mortars punched at the buildings and threw dirt and lumber into the air. Kit and Major Bedford watched for a second longer, then hunched down by the sandbagged wall of the mess hall.

"Go back inside! Stay down!" Major Bedford barked.

Now the artillery, what was left of it, started in earnest, and to the west they heard the South Vietnamese artillery begin firing erratically. The ground shook. The evening was full of explosions, and explosions answering other explosions.

Through the drifts of black smoke, a figure ran, carrying a body. Major Bedford saw that whoever it was was carrying someone in a Vietnamese uniform.

WHOOOMP! WHOOOMP! WHOOOMP!

Mortars fell to the east. The figure stopped, now confused, looking for shelter. Major Bedford recognized Stevenson.

"Over here!" he shouted.

Stevenson turned, dazed, peering through the smoke as if considering.

WHOOOMP! WHOOOMP! WHOOOMP!

More mortars hit the runway. Stevenson turned and, crouching as much as he could carrying the body, ran toward the mess hall.

Stevenson dropped down by the sandbags, holding Sergeant Xuan in his arms.

"Take him inside!" Major Bedford said as Kit looked at Xuan, whom he hadn't seen for a month. Xuan's face was contorted in pain, his head hanging back over Stevenson's arm.

"God! Let me help," Kit said, trying to support Xuan's head. Xuan moaned through his clenched teeth.

The five of them went back into the mess hall kitchen, bent over, and Major Bedford, with one sweep of his arm, sent the pots they had washed and stacked crashing to the floor from the table in the middle of the kitchen. Stevenson lay Xuan on the metal surface. The mess sergeant stared while his mess hall, his very kitchen, was host to yet another gook.

Major Bedford tore away the charred, muddy trousers from Xuan's legs.

WHOOOMP! WHOOOMP! WHOOOMP!

More mortars, much closer, sent sprays of stone and dirt against the screening.

"What happened?" Kit asked.

"What happened! The goddamn bunker fell in," Stevenson said. "On fire and it falls in. Christ! What a mess!"

"It's on fire?" Kit said, still holding Xuan's head in his hands.

"What did I just say?" Stevenson snapped back at him. "If I said it's on fire, it's on fire."

They gently rolled Xuan over on the table and pulled off the rest of his pants. His burns weren't dreadful, but he was in severe pain. Major Bedford lifted the back of Xuan's shirt, where the new bandages had again come loose and his wounds were bleeding. Kit saw, for the first time, the wounds from the disastrous

day on the road to Bo Mua—a long red crease, with pockets of swelling between the stitches. Blood ran from the black threads.

"He's gotta get to the hospital," Major Bedford said. "He's gotta get there as soon as . . ."

WHOOOMP! WHOOOMP!

Two mortars fell in the street. The blast blew the screens into the kitchen.

Major Bedford looked at Stevenson.

Mortars came in threes.

WWHHHHHOOOOOMMPP!!

Before they could think to duck, the third mortar came through the roof, into the dining room.

The roof went up in a rush of furniture and lumber. The kitchen wall, with pots, pans, and tons of cutlery, wavered for a second and fell toward them, knocking one of the refrigerators on its side, casting the shelves on them with racks of utensils, rollers, spoons, tongs, knives, and sharpeners, hundreds of cans of food, glass jars of condiments, openers, bags of rice, spices, flour, cardboard tubs of sugar, and fifty-pound bags of corn bread mix. Huge pots dropped with the ceiling, clattering and clanging. Xuan's table tilted toward Kit, and Xuan, without his pants, came down on top of him as they all fell to the floor. Sandbags from the ceiling broke apart and rained sand on them. Xuan screamed. The mess sergeant shouted in pain and bewilderment.

The table had hit Kit across the knees, which now hurt so much he thought his legs had been broken. Stevenson was on top of both him and Xuan, combined with everything else in the kitchen. Cold, soapy, greasy water drained down through the wreckage.

Major Bedford, caught under part of the overturned sink, pulled himself free and crawled forward a little on his elbows. He wiped sugar and catsup off his face.

"Anybody hurt?" he asked, thinking how he had been doing dishes not twenty minutes ago, and also realizing that he himself was not hurt.

"I think I'm okay," Kit said, but his legs still hurt under the weight of the table.

Stevenson said nothing but, puffing and grunting, began push-

ing the huge mixing pots away and disentangling himself from the mess.

The ceiling hung over them at about four feet so that they had to crawl around, pushing things out of the way, searching for the door. Stevenson pulled Xuan off Kit, out toward a small, clear place. Kit struggled to get his legs from under the table. The steel edge hadn't broken anything, but it cut at the skin as he drew his legs out.

In back of the large field oven, the wall was gone. The door was blocked, and the only way out was by crawling around the stove. They started, crawling single file, over the tangle of junk on the floor, sliding Xuan along on the corn bread tray.

When they were all outside they sat against the sandbags, listening to the artillery and the arrival of more mortars. Major Bedford hadn't been counting, but the number of incoming was fifty, at least—a hell of a lot.

Suddenly, a terrific explosion, one that pushed a solid wall of air across them, one they could feel in their Eustachian tubes, came in between the mortars.

"Rockets," Stevenson said to nobody.

The 122-mm rockets were far worse than the mortars, with the explosive power of a small bomb and the accuracy of an accident. They were heavy, requiring two men to carry all the way down the trail from Hanoi. And they were worth twenty mortars.

"I'm not staying *here,*" Stevenson said. "Let's get to someplace safe."

"Right," the mess sergeant said.

"Grab his legs," Stevenson said to Kit.

"Oh, fuck him," said the mess sergeant.

Xuan cried out when Kit touched his legs.

"I'll carry him!" Kit said.

"No, you hold the tray from the side," Stevenson answered. "Major, can you hold his head?"

"Okay," said Major Bedford, coming around on his knees through the cans of peas and jars of pickles. He put a hand under Xuan's head.

The three of them, bearing Xuan on the corn bread tray, with the mess sergeant hobbling ahead of them, made their way up the

main street toward the operations center. The street was littered with lumber and overturned trucks, one of which burned merrily.

Now is the time, a little voice said inside Major Bedford's head. *If I'm ever going to get wounded, now is the time.*

Shut up, he said to himself.

• • •

They were fifty yards from the operations center when another rocket hit at the far end of the street, annihilating the graves registration morgue. The force of it bowled them all over. Kit gasped for air, rolling on the ground, ending up against the mess sergeant in front of a pile of oil drums. He lay still for a few seconds, then crawled off the man, suddenly noticing blood on his left arm and hand. But he felt no pain, no wound. The 122-mm rockets were laden with shrapnel, and a piece had torn clear through the mess sergeant. He lay dead with his head twisted back and his eyes open. Kit wiped his hands on his pants, holding back the nausea.

Stevenson called to him, "You hit?"

"What?"

"Are you hit, goddamn it?"

"No." He got up to his knees. "No, I'm okay. I'm okay."

They felt all over the mess sergeant, shaking him, trying to get a reaction. His head flopped back.

"He's dead, for Christ's sake!" Stevenson said.

Major Bedford felt for a pulse, running his fingers down the mess sergeant's fat neck.

"Major! He's dead! Let's GO!"

Three more rockets ripped into the enlisted bunkers, smashing, tearing them apart, lifting buildings and men into the air.

"Get Xuan! Grab his arms," Stevenson said.

Major Bedford grabbed Xuan's arms, and they ran with heads down, in a galloping sidestep, the remaining fifty yards to the safety of the operations center. They weren't even sure Xuan was alive.

The force of the rockets now was the only thing that counted. By comparison, mortars seemed harmless. The South Vietnamese bunkers took five more rockets, some direct, some close. Beds,

bodies, and shards of roofing lay scattered as the dirt and pieces of cloth drifted down out of the haze.

• • •

Lieutenant Starret peeked out of the officers' club, looking around the edge of the vibrating door frame. A South Vietnamese helmet spun slowly in the middle of the street. He sat back against the jamb and tried to clear the confusion of beer and explosive shock from his mind.

Only one day left in his tour, and now this. He had planned on keeping himself safe and inebriated, but the bastards were seeking him out. He looked out again, trying to see what he could see. Artillery, outgoing artillery, fired in great number. The ground shook with its anger. This was firing like the old days, when no one counted the shells. Over and over, in hatred and unthinking retaliation, cracking and hissing out into the night, piercing the earth when it landed, casting the forest and the mud and the water and anything else up into the sky.

Starret wanted a safe place. He scanned the darkening sky. No aircraft were in sight. Not even the sound of aircraft. Where were they? There should have been something up there. There should have been gunships, spotter planes, something. Mortars popped on the runway and the helicopter maintenance area.

Jesus, he thought, *could they have blown up everything?*

Mortars kept falling here and there. Sets of three, and then six, and then so many he couldn't keep them apart. It was too many.

He started running at a bent-over lope, dodging through the junk on the ground. Around the collapsed PX he ran, dodging like a football player through the smoke. Two crumpled bodies were in his way. From sheer force of habit, the habit of the infantryman, he stopped to see if they were dead. He couldn't let a man bleed to death.

They were both dead, their blood soaking their uniforms and sticking to his hand when he sought for signs of life. He held a bloody hand up, feeling for a pulse. He touched a bloody neck. Ahead of him a five-quarter truck was on its side.

He ran to the upended truck. A man was inside, alive and awake, and frightened out of his wits.

Starret ran and slid to the truck on his knees. He looked in through the shattered glass.

"You all right?"

"Yeah," the man shouted back. "What the hell's going on?"

"Oh, the end of the fuckin' world, that's all."

"Jesus."

"Yeah, well, okay, now, can you get out the other door?"

"It's jammed!"

"Cover your face. I'll kick . . ."

WHOOOMP! WHOOOMP!

Two mortars exploded in the next street, and as the dirt showered the truck, a white panic gripped Starret. Where was the third? He hit the earth and pulled himself against the truck with a death grip. This was it. There had to be a third. He forced his head under the engine hood metal, pushing his face against the mudguard. Right now, he thought, the third mortar is up in the sky. Up in the sky looking for him, starting its plummet. Mindless, careless destruction racing down toward him.

He heard a thud in the dirt twenty feet behind him, and in a second he knew what it was. He turned his head.

The mortar, unexploded, lay on its side, a small black thing in the fading light. A dud, a stupid dud, its little brains smashed from the impact, but its explosive guts still alive. A gift from the People's Republic of China.

"Cover your eyes!" he shouted to the man in the truck, and he started to kick at the smashed windshield.

• • •

"KIT!" Major Dow screamed. "Get me a rifle!"

"Yes, sir!"

"Get me a rifle, a goddamn rifle! Over there!"

"I . . ."

Inside the heavily walled operations center, the explosions of the mortars and rockets were muted, but as clear as screams across a city. Major Dow winced at each one.

In the midst of the confusion of radios and cables, in the low lights of the operations room, Daugherty sat trying to keep contact with the air force, and General Walker paced behind him.

The air force didn't respond to every standoff attack. It had to be a special threat before they would come out with fighter bombers, and a very grave threat before they would send B-52s. The bombing in the northern areas of the country and in Laos had taken a lot of their planes. The young air force liaison officer stood nervously by Daugherty's side, listening to the hell being raised outside.

Daugherty rasped out the sectors he wanted bombed and kept his voice level only with great effort. Major Dow scribbled on a map and placed it before him. Daugherty's other officers were trying to get helicopter gunships from Tran Linh base sixty kilometers to the west. They even called for aircraft from the ARVN at Phu Trach.

General Walker watched them, chewing at his lower lip. The folds of his face hung like old lava.

"We've got five birds okay, general—seven out, one up."

The radio hissed and a voice from the one flying helicopter began to report the destruction, then broke off to evade the rifle fire from the ground. When it came back, flying farther to the south, it reported that the enemy firing was tapering off and that it appeared to be coming from the northeast. Daugherty shifted the artillery targets.

"It's not from the Bo Mua woods," Major Dow said to Daugherty.

"No," Daugherty said.

"Give the rubber to the air force, then, add it in," Walker interrupted.

Daugherty added the plantation and the woods next to it to the targets for the air force. The Michelin Tire Company would just have to absorb the loss.

The two remaining American howitzer batteries swung to the new targets to the northeast and began firing. Slowly the number of incoming mortars and rockets dwindled to a few every ten minutes.

Daugherty sat back and thought for a minute. The South Vietnamese batteries continued firing God knew where.

Kit came up to Major Dow from wherever he had been, holding two M-16s.

"Is that it, you think, sir?"

Major Dow looked at him, noticing for the first time the blood on his shirt.

"What happened to you? You all right?"

"I'm all right."

"What's all this blood?"

"It . . . it's not mine."

"What's it like outside?"

Kit brushed the hair out of his eyes.

"Pretty bad."

"I want to see. Come on, and bring them."

They went out through the outer offices and down the timbered hall that led to the door.

"You think that's it for the night?" Kit asked Major Dow's back.

Major Dow stopped just before the door and turned around to face him.

"Listen, Kit, and listen carefully. I don't think that's all. But I don't know what the hell to think. I haven't known what's going on for six weeks now. But tonight, and until you get out of here, I want you to think. Think! Do you hear me? Think like a goddamn . . . I don't know what . . . but be careful! Be careful! Shoot at anything that isn't for sure an American. You understand?"

Kit didn't understand.

"What's going to happen?"

"I don't know. But I want you to think! You hear me?"

"Yes."

"Think!"

"Yes, sir."

"Keep this goddamn thing loaded and think!"

"Yes, sir."

He stood in the hallway, and then lunged forward and gave Kit a hug. And Kit, already scared to death by Major Dow's warning, was even more scared by the hug.

"Oh," said Major Dow, letting him go, "one other thing."

"What?"

"You can go home any time you want."

He opened the door and the moist diesel smoke drifted in. "Any time you want."

• • •

It was quieter in the street now than it had been for the past half hour. The light had faded to nearly dark. A few fires burned dully in the distance. They could see the tower lights where the perimeter came to the main gate. From where they stood at the end of the walkway of the operations center, behind the concertina wire and chain-link fence, they could see the black clutter of destroyed buildings and overturned vehicles. Some men were moving about; some had flashlights and were looking through the wreckage.

Major Dow could see in his mind's eye what the street and the base would look like as the sun came up the next morning. Under the wrecked South Vietnamese bunkers, soldiers were still buried in destruction.

He put his hand on Kit's shoulder and Kit felt it shaking.

"Remember what I said."

"Okay," Kit said. "You think . . ."

"Never mind about what I think. Just remember what I said. And get the first thing you can out of here tomorrow morning. I don't care if it's a fucking bicycle, just get out of here."

"I'll see you before I go, sir."

"Well, you keep in touch," Major Dow said.

A helicopter passed overhead, one all by itself.

Major Dow watched it cross over them.

"At least we've got some aircraft coming in, so there will be some going back out. And you be on it."

"I will."

Major Dow dropped his arm.

"Listen," he said.

From the south came the whistle of jet fighter-bombers from Bien Hoa, looking for their targets.

"I hear them," Kit said.

"No, no, not that," Major Dow said.

"What?"

"Not that." His voice shook. "Listen."

And then Kit heard the noise that shouldn't have been there. Not the sound of the planes, not the sound of the artillery, not the sound of mortars, but the sound that just shouldn't have been there.

He heard the repeated pop of rifles.

CHAPTER

TWENTY-EIGHT

THE NORTH VIETNAMESE

Starret helped the man out of the upside-down truck through the broken windshield. He ran with him over to the nearest building, which was used by the Engineer Battalion for administration. They hugged the sandbags at the building's base as the ground jumped.

"You okay?" Starret asked him.

"Yeah. What the hell is going on here, L-T?"

"Rockets," Starret said.

"Those things are bad!"

"Here," Starret said. "Give me a boost."

They stood up, and the man held his hands together to make a step. Starret put a foot in them. He grabbed the wooden edge and pulled himself up on the rows of sandbags that covered the roof. He crawled up the shallow pitch to the peak and looked around.

Several buildings were in flames. South Vietnamese ran this way and that. Some carried wounded on stretchers, looking for an intact building to shelter them. Others simply ran for cover themselves. Starret could see the destroyed graves registration morgue; the wreckage of the bunkers; the charred remains of Kit's bunker, with flames still flickering in the ruins; the half caved-in mess hall; the post office, now on fire.

Running down the street past the collapsing officers' club, three men in black darted from the cover of each building to the next. They carried rifles and packages. Starret followed them with his eyes straining in the darkness. They came to the library trailer and stopped. After a moment's consultation, they threw a grenade in the door, and ran out of sight. The library trailer waited a moment and then jumped off its blocks, filled with orange flame. Starret suddenly understood. Only the North Vietnamese would blow up the library trailer. He looked around for more. And there were more.

They were everywhere.

To the west he could see the main gate, where the MPs still had lights. Rifles cracked and machine guns chugged away, spewing tracer fire in raking sweeps, sometimes away from the base, sometimes toward it. At the infantry bunkers, small knots of American troops were holed up, firing tentatively at anything that moved. How many would shoot their own men was in the hands of the brutal gods of chance. The artillery batteries, now manned by the South Vietnamese, fired out at the jungle. *Very good*, Starret thought. *They are firing away from the battle.*

He rolled over on his back, listening to the cacophony, and looked up at the deep black sky. This was a perfect place to be. The thought came to him suddenly that no one would look for him up here on the roof. The chances of the building getting hit were a lot less than if he were on the ground. And he would be able simply to lie here and watch the whole thing. He only had one day left. Perfect.

"Goddamn it," he said after a few minutes, and rolled back down the roof to join the battle.

● ● ●

The North Vietnamese came through, of all places, near the main gate to the base. In the space to either side of the gate, during that day, disguised as relations—wives, and even children of the ARVNs—they had disconnected everything. They had taken out the wires to the phones, the mines, the flares, and had carefully cut up the fencing and the concertina wire.

The MPs, weary of the whines of the women and the annoyance of the children, hadn't noticed. When the sunlight faded and the noise started, the rest of the attackers went through the perimeter on foot, standing up, through the Green Line barbed wire and across the base. They carried their charges, timers, caps, and wires for the job of the evening, and rifles and grenades for the job of getting back out.

● ● ●

Colonel Shift's helicopter also arrived that evening with his guests.

Colonel Shift had had all sorts of delays getting started after the debauchery of the previous evening at the officers' club, not the least of which was waking up Mr. Christopher, who was morbidly hung over. Then there was the problem of finding out where Lieutenant Christopher's unit was. Fortunately, Colonel Shift knew someone who had access to the personnel computer.

They had finally taken off in the late afternoon.

Mr. Hart and Mr. Christopher sat in the second two seats in the helicopter, their flight helmets connected to the intercom system. Mr. Hart gripped his attaché case on his lap. Inside it were the names of a number of officers Mr. Christopher had signed up the previous evening, all of whom wanted to become investors. Colonel Shift sat next to the pilot. The helicopter chopped through the evening air toward Phuoc Vinh.

About three miles out, the pilot radioed.

"It looks to be all right," the pilot said to Colonel Shift. "They might be having a little trouble, but we'll probably be able to land down with no problems."

"Probably? What do you mean, probably? Is there . . ." Mr. Hart asked into his microphone.

"Don't worry," Colonel Shift said. "In fact, this has been one of our safest bases. The ARVN are going to be taking over here pretty soon. Couple of weeks. It's been one of the smoothest transitions in the country. They've got the change of command ceremony scheduled."

"Well! It's great to hear that," Mr. Christopher cut in. "My son will be able to get out of here?"

"Shouldn't be any problem," the colonel said.

"That's it up ahead," said the pilot. "Something's up."

Mr. Christopher leaned in front of Mr. Hart to get a better view through the windshields of the Huey.

"Will you get out of my way?!" Mr. Hart snapped.

Mr. Hart's mind had been concentrating on the helicopter. He had never been in one before. He listened to the noise of the turbine engine, the whirling, sliding, pumping, rotating apparatus tearing away at the air as they hung here, over a strange, dark, unfriendly forest. Now he heard more explosions.

"Sorry, Al," said Mr. Christopher. Over the intercom, Mr. Christopher said, "No problem, huh? That's good. That's great. I can't wait to see my son. Can't wait to see my boy." He paused, and then he said, "You okay, Al?"

Mr. Hart said nothing.

Mr. Christopher reached over and gave Mr. Hart a reassuring squeeze on the knee. Mr. Hart jumped. Noises like distant thunder came to him.

"What's that noise?" Mr. Hart asked.

"Does he know you're coming?" Shift asked.

"He doesn't know when," Mr. Christopher said.

"What's that noise?" Mr. Hart asked again.

"It'll be a surprise."

"I hope we don't embarrass him."

"Huh?" Mr. Christopher said. "Embarrass him?"

"Sure," the colonel said, his voice tinny and electric over the intercom. "He might have some little mama-san someplace."

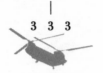

"What's that noise?"

"Hah-hah-hah!" Mr. Christopher laughed.

"There it is," said the pilot, as the scatter of lights came into view on the horizon, between the dying ocher sunset above and the black land below.

"Something's going on," the pilot said, and they began to hear the artillery firing and other noises. Mr. Hart thought he could hear explosions. He peered forward. They all peered forward.

Phuoc Vinh base came over the horizon, popping and sputtering. Tracer fire waved up into the night. The artillery flashed to the west.

"Couple of fire missions in progress," Shift said. "Look, see? That's our stuff going out. See it over there?"

The helicopter arced around to the east. The two businessmen looked down at the dark buildings and drifting smoke. Spurts of flame darted out from the artillery batteries. Other flames showed up between the buildings.

"Something's going on," the pilot said.

"I don't like this," said Mr. Hart.

They approached from the north. The pilot tried to get ground control, but no one answered until he had tried five times. Over the radio they heard other voices, some in English, some in Vietnamese. They could hear the air force, the operations center, and Major Daugherty's anxious voice.

"Maybe we ought to go back," Mr. Hart suggested in an equally anxious voice. He had only seen wars in movies.

"We have to land," Shift said. "We have to get fuel. You can go back tomorrow. Don't worry."

The helicopter came in low over the scattered buildings. Up ahead a rocket exploded. Mr. Hart blanched.

"Jesus!" the pilot said. "Colonel, I don't know about this."

Mr. Christopher held Mr. Hart's knee again.

"Get your hand off me," Mr. Hart said, forgetting about the intercom.

"What?" the pilot asked.

"Nothing," Mr. Hart said.

Mr. Christopher removed his hand.

"Al, really, don't go to pieces now," he said.

As they slowed over the runway, coming down, hovering about twenty feet above the surface, they could see the wreckage of other aircraft, tipped this way and that, some upside down, some on fire. Men running here and there, pulling and tugging at the machines. Another helicopter came in right above them and sunk to the earth farther ahead. Men ran out to it with boxes of ammunition.

"This might not be the best place for these guys, Colonel," the pilot said.

"What's going on?" Mr. Hart asked, his voice squeaking.

Fighter bombers screamed overhead.

New explosions came from the south as they let bombs fall on the rubber plantation. The plastic windows in the helicopter shuddered from the shocks in the air.

"Set it down! We can't go back!" Colonel Shift said.

"I can make it to Phu Trach."

"No, no," said Colonel Shift.

"Okay," said the pilot.

"But could we get to Phu, wherever you said?" Mr. Hart squeaked. "I'd like to get out of here."

"Oh, shut up, Al, my son's here!"

"Set it down!" the colonel said.

The helicopter descended the last few feet.

"Your son's a soldier," Mr. Hart returned angrily. "I am a civilian. And I want to go someplace safer."

"Shut up, Al!"

"Don't tell me to shut up."

Mr. Christopher glared at him.

"Why the *hell* I ever brought you along, I'll never know!"

"Why I ever came, *I'll* never know!"

"You goddamn chickenshit lawyer!"

"Just get me out of here and I won't pester you again!"

". . . and a goddamn *coward!*"

"I don't care what you say, I just want to get out of here."

"I don't give a shit what you want. You're disgusting!"

"I'm disgusting? *I'm* disgusting?!" Mr. Hart's voice broke.

Colonel Shift looked back at them.

"That's right!" Mr. Christopher bawled. "You're a disgusting coward, and you make me want to throw up!"

"You! You are repulsive, you hear me?! *Repulsive!*"

And the helicopter touched down gingerly.

There was the sound of rifle fire and artillery and grenades and mortars and rockets and the yells of men in anger, in pain.

"Listen, we'll head for that shed," Colonel Shift ordered and took off his flight helmet. He pulled back the door.

Suddenly, as if the sun itself had just come back up, a brilliant light rose on the eastern side of the base. The scattered wreckage leaped into stark relief. Shadows streaked the runway. The three passengers scrambled out of their helmets and seat belts, crouched out of the side door, and ran from the helicopter, under the hissing blades, for the nearest building. A wave of heat swept them.

In the eastern sky, a roiling mountain of flame rose ever higher against towering clouds of black smoke. It was close and hung over them. Huge balls of fire cleared the earth and shot up to the zenith like the aurora borealis. Freshets of flame uncoiled beneath the larger bursts like the breath of hell breaking through the earth's surface.

"Get over here!" the colonel screamed at the two civilians, who were standing agape in the waving orange light, Mr. Hart's eyes like two poached eggs under a heat lamp.

Mr. Christopher pulled at his lawyer. They ran for the buildings.

"My God!" said Mr. Hart. "Look at . . ."

A man in flames was running down the runway.

Colonel Shift saw the man. He took off after him.

They stood and watched while Shift tackled the man and rolled him on the ground.

"I wanna go back!" Mr. Hart howled in terror. "Let's go back! Christ! Let's go back and get the hell out of here! Let's go back to the helicopter! Please! Please! Listen to me!"

He pulled at Mr. Christopher, who pulled away. Mr. Christopher lost his balance and fell sideways. Mr. Hart fell with him.

"Let go of me! Let go, you coward!" Mr. Christopher struggled to his knees.

The colonel yelled something at them they couldn't hear.

"Goddamn you!" Mr. Christopher yelled. "Let go of me! I've got to help him!"

"Please!" Mr. Hart said in panic, holding him by the tail of his jacket. "Let's go back! The helicopter is still here! We can go!"

"Let go of me!!" Mr. Christopher tried to get away, kicking at Mr. Hart. He looked around, but Colonel Shift was gone.

"No!" Mr. Hart wailed. "Let's get out of here!"

"You goddamn coward! YOU MISERABLE COWARD!"

The wall of flame spread southward.

"Jesus! Oh, Christ," Mr. Hart pleaded, screaming, sobbing. "Please, let's go back!"

"LET GO!" Mr. Christopher's voice failed. He struggled to his feet. His jacket tore. "Let go of me!"

The helicopter rotor speeded up.

"He's leaving!" Mr. Hart wailed. "Let's go back! Please!"

"Go on, then! Go back! Go to hell! I don't care!"

Mr. Christopher flailed at him. Mr. Hart clutched Mr. Christopher's pants.

"Christ!" Mr. Hart sobbed. "Christ! Help me."

A phenomenal explosion split the air. Hundreds of 105-mm shells went off together, some all at once, some blown into the air, exploding in the sky.

Mr. Christopher fell over again, knocked off his feet by the concussion. Mr. Hart tried to crawl underneath him. Mr. Christopher rolled away from him, trying to get up.

"You filthy . . ."

"God help me!"

"Where's the goddamn case?" Mr. Christopher said, now up on his knees. "Where's your goddamn briefcase? You stupid bastard! Where is it?" He staggered to his feet. "You stupid bastard! You left it in the goddamn helicopter? I'll kill you!"

The exploding artillery shells hove each other higher and higher, borne on the waves of concussion, ignited by the raging fires.

Mr. Hart screamed, *"I've got it. I'll never give it to you! I'll . . ."*

Mr. Christopher turned, half hearing him. Mr. Hart was up.

He had the case and he began to run down the runway, toward the white heat of the flames.

"Come back here, you . . ."

Mr. Christopher ran after him. Mr. Hart danced this way and that, waving the case. Then Mr. Christopher had him by the jacket. He drew his arm back and hit Mr. Hart, openhanded but hard, with all his might, across the face.

Mr. Hart fell backwards, in pain and surprise. He put his hands up to his face for a second. Then he rolled over, rose to his knees, crazed with fear, and crawled blindly through the filth toward the light itself. He heard the noise of the rotor over all the other noises. He turned and looked back. Mr. Christopher was running in one direction with his briefcase, and the helicopter was flying away in the other, and he was on his knees, bathed in the lurid light of the burning fuel depot.

• • •

Major Dow stood at the door with Kit. They heard the combination of so many noises Kit couldn't tell them apart. But Major Dow could. He heard the rattle of gunfire and knew the North Vietnamese were on the base. He saw the flames raking the sky and knew they had blown the fuel bladders. He knew the ammunition would be next. He stood, shaking in the wonder that everything was coming apart, and listened.

The explosions began, mixed with the noise of the artillery, mixed with the thuds of the air force bombing the rubber plantations, mixed with the crackle of rifle fire coming closer and the shouts of men—shouts in English, shouts in Vietnamese.

He stumbled back into the operations center, through the heavily framed door, bordered with sandbags and steel planks. Kit looked around at the destroyed buildings, now throbbing in the dancing light. He turned and went after Major Dow, who suddenly bent double in the opening to the hallway and vomited on the sandbags.

"I'm sorry," Major Dow began, spitting and coughing. "I'm sorry. Jesus, I didn't mean to do that. I don't know why I did that."

"Are you . . ."

Kit gagged on the odor. He held himself hard against the wall until the wave of nausea passed.

"Are you all right?"

"Yes, yes . . ."

Rifle fire popped in the street.

"Get inside!" Major Dow recovered himself, and they went down the narrow hallway that led to the offices.

The rifle fire grew closer.

Kit turned toward the opening.

Four American infantry ran up and crowded into the doorway; three of them turned and looking back out. The fourth staggered up the hallway and collapsed to a sitting position. Blood ran out of his hair, down his face.

The soldiers peered into the darkness for a few seconds. One of them, a sergeant, came back and checked on the wounded man.

"Hey, take care of him. He's bleeding bad."

"Yes," Kit said, and began looking for a first aid pouch.

Bullets splattered into the doorway, ripping splinters of wood loose from the lumber and plywood. One of the two soldiers at the door fell backward and lay still. The other man turned.

"They're down the street!" he yelled. "They're down the street!"

"How many? Can you see?"

"I can't see! Fifteen, twenty, at least!"

Major Dow pushed past Kit, his rifle up and his eyes wild.

He went down the short hall to the doorway, holding on to the wall.

"Where?"

"They're down there behind the barrels!"

"Where?"

"Down there! Major, what the hell are you doing? Where the hell is everybody?"

"Where?"

"Where the hell is everybody?" the soldier yelled, pulling Major Dow back.

"Get down, Major!" the sergeant screamed at Major Dow.

Major Dow put up his rifle and fired a short burst into the dark.

"Goddamn it, Major, what the hell'd you do that for?"

"I . . ." Major Dow's nerve failed utterly, and he ran back to the end of the hall where Kit crouched by the bleeding man.

A torrent of bullets bounced into the doorway, cutting up the wood and clanging off the steel planks. Dust and sand flew everywhere. Kit pulled his helmet down and tried to shield the wounded man with his body.

In the pause that followed he could see the infantry huddling together, not even trying to fire back.

"Lieutenant!" the sergeant screamed at him. "Where the hell is everybody?"

Everybody who? Kit wondered in his confusion. But why were he and Major Dow, who now sat with his legs splayed and the rifle between them, left here in the doorway to the operations center?

The explosions of the ammunition dump reached a climax like a New Year celebration in Chinatown. The floor shook beneath them and sand rained down from above.

Up and down the main street, from the smoking ruins of the morgue to the rocket craters and wreckage of the South Vietnamese bunkers, men hid in buildings, sometimes darting around in the darkness. In the confusion the Americans shot at each other, or the South Vietnamese. And the South Vietnamese, even more confused, abandoned by their commanders, fired back blindly.

• • •

Major Bedford was in the signal room, protected by the thick walls of the operations center, helping Daugherty, trying to stay in contact with the Saigon command. He heard the noise in the offices.

He took off his headphones and set them on the table in front of the radio. He got up and walked out to the short hall that went past the briefing room. He heard rifle fire. He went around the corner into the office area, where he smelled the sharp odor of ammunition. He stopped.

"Go tell them inside," Major Dow yelled at Kit. "Go tell them we've got enemy on the base. Go on."

"You go back."

"No! I'll be all right. Just go!" He brushed the dirt out of his eyes.

"You sure?"

"Yes! I'm certain! Now go on!" He rolled around and got up on his knees.

"Go on!" he said again, standing up. And he started back down the hall.

Kit saw Major Bedford.

"What is it?" Major Bedford asked, coming through the desks.

"North Viets," Kit said. "They're on the base!"

"North Viets on the base?"

"Yes, they're in the street."

And then a flash and a punch of air as hard as concrete sent Major Bedford hurtling against Kit as a charge went off at the end of the hall, ripping loose boards and sheets of plywood. Chairs and desks flew at them and splattered against the wall. Thousands of sheets of paper were cast into the air.

Major Dow, lifted off his feet, flew through the air, slamming against the far wall in a clutter of chairs and tables. Kit fell back with Major Bedford, and they went down together, against the metal furniture and the mimeograph machine. The infantry soldiers slid back to a crumpled heap and lay motionless in the roaring silence.

The still silence held for a few seconds.

Only one bulb now burned in the offices, showing dimly through the blizzard of paper falling over everything. Kit struggled up on his elbows on Major Bedford's stomach.

Major Bedford pushed at him.

"Major Dow!" Kit called.

"Jesus!" Major Bedford gasped, his mouth full of dirt. He pulled himself up against a desk.

"Major Dow!" Kit called again.

There was nothing. Just the sound of the battle outside.

An M-16 lay in the space at the end of the hall. Kit, still numb from the blast, panting in the filthy air and blinking away the dirt in his eyes, crawled through the paper and around the furniture toward Major Dow's unmoving form. He gathered the rifle in his

arms as he went. He stopped and turned toward the door at the end of the hall. He heard voices outside, in the hard accent that, even in his present terror, he recognized as northern.

He pulled a chair out of his way and found Major Dow, still breathing, but with his arm unnaturally pinned underneath him. He tried to roll him around, but the furniture confused things, and all he could do was move Major Dow's head to straighten his neck.

"Where are you?!" Major Bedford called into the settling clouds of dust. "Who's over there?"

"It's Major Dow," Kit said. "He's . . ."

"Is he alive?"

Major Bedford looked around for a rifle.

"He's alive, but . . ."

A spray of bullets came in the door, tearing at the sandbags. Major Bedford fell to the floor, cramming his bulk under a desk.

Kit jerked around on top of Major Dow's body, shielding his eyes from the flying splinters, nearly blind from sand.

At the door at the end of the hall someone moved.

Two dark figures stood up in the swirling dust. They came forward, into the light, with rifles pointing upward, carrying dark packs.

From the end of the offices, he heard Starret's voice calling out something he couldn't understand. The first North Vietnamese fired a scattering of shots toward the light.

"Kit!" Major Bedford screamed. "SHOOT!"

In the shadows, Kit raised his rifle.

"SHOOT! FOR GOD'S SAKE!"

Kit fired.

The rifle floated upward in his grasp like a conductor's baton, but he heard nothing. He saw the two North Vietnamese, who never saw him, flail the air with their arms and hands as their faces and necks absorbed the stream of bullets, and they fell backward.

He held the rifle up for a minute longer, and then slowly let it down.

He turned back to Major Dow's crumpled form, lying there in the dim yellow light and the smoke and the dust.

He put his head on Major Dow's chest, listening for his heart, and held him with his arms for a long time, not letting go.

And some minutes later, when Starret finally came through and found them, it looked more like the sleeping embrace of two dead men than anything else.

CHAPTER

TWENTY-NINE

A PURPLE HEART

It was like Pearl Harbor, General Walker thought the following afternoon. After their initial wave of destruction, the North Vietnamese had left, like the Japanese at Pearl Harbor. At the time when confusion was their greatest ally, and they could have killed many more than they did, they ran back to the cover of the forest. Perhaps they had simply decided that they had accomplished their purpose. Perhaps, having almost no means of communication with their commanders, they were trained to follow orders and not think much beyond those orders. If they had displayed any flair for taking

advantage of what they had accomplished, they could have gone on killing Americans and South Vietnamese unrestrained.

It was of the Lord's mercy that they did not do so. Casualties among the South Vietnamese were terrible, and nearly seventy Americans had been killed or wounded. The entire fuel depot had been destroyed. The ammunition dump was a smoking ruins; no artillery shells remained intact. The electrical and communication systems of the base were wrecked. And they had tried to put satchel charges in the operations center itself, an act that would have killed the entire command, including, the general thought to himself as he was driven around the base, the commanding general.

The two dead North Vietnamese and the satchel charges they were carrying were found in the entry hall to the operations center. They had been stopped by that most unlikely of persons, Lieutenant Kit, who, according to Major Bedford, had killed both of them at point blank range, defending the unconscious form of Matthew Dow. If it hadn't been for Kit, the operations center and all the men inside it would have gone to the moon.

General Walker made a tour of his blistered patch of earth. The fires were out, and some cleaning up had been started. The perimeter, where the wires and fencing had been repaired temporarily, was now manned by the replacements and what was left of the South Vietnamese.

The dead were flown out quickly. The graves registration morgue had been demolished. The wounded were medevaced to Cu Chi, and the serious cases to Saigon. The medevac ships had been coming and going all day from the pad near the operations center, which was being used as an extra ward.

He had tried to talk to as many of the wounded as he could, but there were so many things to do. The events of the past twenty-four hours—the shock of the explosives and the severity of the destruction, and the prevalence of death itself—temporarily eradicated all the heavy doubt and the mood of guilty uncertainty he had felt before. The North Vietnamese had acted like the cruel and clever warriors they were. An attack like that bleached out all the fine philosophical arguments.

These days would be his final days in the army. He felt ill and

old. He would leave the war and the army remembering man as a warring animal, capable of little more than fighting, accomplishing nothing, and restrained only by the amount of ammunition he possessed. But he was most amazed by Kit, who had performed an act of incredible bravery, at least for him. And as the general drove around the base, among the torn buildings and the mangled vehicles, he wondered briefly why it was Kit who saved him.

The South Vietnamese struggled to look after their dead. A number of them were buried right on the base; others, in the village graveyards. The burials were conducted amid their weeping wives and children, who were now abandoned in Phuoc Vinh, having no reason to be there and nowhere else to go. The women and children wandered in the heat of the afternoon, aimless and bewildered.

The South Vietnamese sent five of their helicopter gunships to help patrol the area around the base, promising that additional infantry battalions would be brought up as soon as possible. A change-of-command ceremony, which should have happened weeks ago, according to the Vietnamization plans, might even be possible now. Of course, there was no fuel and little ammunition, but that was promised, too.

He continued his survey of the base in his jeep with Major Daugherty. They went by the fuel point where the blackened pumps were scattered about and the charred remains of the rubber fuel bladders lay in the sun like old snake skins. They did not go near what was left of the ammunition dump. No one would be able to do so safely for many years. Like the French mine field, it would be a no man's land, a testament to the American presence, after all of the other evidence had been rotted away by the weather.

We are the agents of disorder, he thought. Our disengagement was based on nothing more than sheer human weariness. It meant the breaking of innumerable promises, some made in extreme solemnity, some implied by American politicians for the best and worst of reasons, others simply lies from the beginning.

To leave meant that men were more like animals than most Americans wanted to believe. They fought until they got tired. They were much more mechanical than spiritual. Their mechani-

3 4 6

cal aspects kept them alive, and their spiritual inclinations got them killed. And this saddened him, since it went against everything he had previously believed.

Matthew Dow died the next day at the army hospital in Cu Chi. He never regained consciousness, and he was never able to say good-bye to Kit. The last time Kit saw him was when he was carried to the medevac ship a little after midnight the night of the attack. Kit didn't find out until the following day that Major Dow had died, and he didn't succumb to the need to weep until several hours later, and that was when he was alone, outside, watching the red sun fall slowly out from under the monsoon clouds toward the earth. Then he wept uncontrollably, in huge racking sobs, so violent they hurt his stomach and nearly threw him off balance.

Kit went to Major Dow's room, in Major Bedford's bunker, which had been untouched by the attack. The need for sleeping space meant that all available rooms had to be used, and the room had to be cleared. It was a surprisingly spare little room, since Major Dow had spent very little time there. His bed, unmade, still held the depression from his rounded form. A small, cheap camera hung from the wall, and a picture of him with his family—his wife and two daughters—stood on the desk.

Major Dow had been his friend and had looked out for him. An odd friendship, nearly all of which had gone unexpressed. Kit would have given himself to be killed in his place, he thought, and Major Dow would have done the same for him, and probably did exactly that. He picked up the picture from the desk, and after looking at it for a few minutes, slipped it into his pocket and left the room.

● ● ●

For reasons he didn't completely understand, Major Bedford wound up in charge of two American civilians the day after the attack. They were delivered to him by a Colonel Shift, whose uniform was burned and torn. Colonel Shift told him that he had to get back to his unit immediately and that the two men would explain everything. Their suits were ripped and filthy and their

ties twisted, and the wild look in their eyes told him that they had had a noisy evening before they got to the operations center.

"Who are you?" Major Bedford asked.

"I'm an American citizen," said the shorter of the two men.

"You're a goddamn coward. You're a piece of shit! He's a dirtbag lawyer. He's . . ." said the other.

"I want to see the commanding officer," the short man interrupted.

Major Bedford's arm was bandaged where he had split open the skin falling against a metal desk when Kit had knocked him down. He had put the bandage on himself. Only after the confusion and noise died down did it begin to hurt, and he began to worry about infection. The bandage kept coming loose.

He was so tired and bone-weary he hadn't even understood the story one of the civilians babbled to him. First he thought they might be some sort of technical representatives from some munitions manufacturer, or maybe congressional aides or journalists.

"What are you doing here?" he asked.

"I want to see Lieutenant James Christopher," the taller man said. "Do you know him?"

Major Bedford hadn't known Kit's first name.

"Yes, I know him."

"I'm his father. I want to see him. I've come all the way here to see him. To see my son."

"I want to see the commanding officer," said the shorter man again.

"You're his *what?*"

"His father."

"Did you hear me?" said the shorter man. "I want . . ."

"You yellow piece of . . ."

". . . to see the commanding officer."

Major Bedford thought about this. There were so many other things to do. This did seem like something the general should take care of.

"Come with me," Major Bedford said.

He took them to the general's trailer and knocked on the door. No one answered. The trailer had been hit with a number of things the previous night. Two windows were broken beside the door, and the normally white siding was blackened and battered.

"This is General Walker's trailer," Major Bedford said. "I don't know where he is right now. But I can let you wait here." He opened the door and looked in. The furniture was scattered around and the wall chart showing the number of American troops on the base had fallen to the floor. "You can rest here. General Walker or his aide may be back in a while. I'll tell him if I see him. It may take a while."

• • •

Stevenson was in the base surgical ward, where he had gone initially to help set up beds knocked around by a near miss. He had stayed, helping tend to the wounded, some of whom were administered to on the floor. He was getting quite good at putting on bandages and changing them, and preparing the wounded for the stretcher ride to a larger hospital. The two doctors gave him some interesting things to do, including things that would have nauseated a normal man.

He helped one of the doctors work on a young Vietnamese soldier with gruesome facial wounds. Before he knew what was happening, the doctor was cutting a breathing hole in the man's throat. Stevenson watched, fascinated. Another man had pieces of exploded wood all up and down his back. The doctor probed and pushed at the flesh, getting the pieces out. Stevenson had seen a few pieces the doctor overlooked. The doctor complimented him on his sharp sight.

He found all the cutting and patching back together extremely interesting. Perhaps, he thought, I *should* become a doctor—a surgeon. Perhaps I should get the hell out of the army and study medicine. None of what he saw made him sick, and he found that patching up the twitching, quivering bodies and administering the pacifying shots of morphine gave him a feeling of usefulness. A completely new feeling.

Major Bedford came up to him, holding his ragged bandage around his arm.

"Stevenson."

"Yes?" Stevenson said, dabbing antiseptic on the burns of a

man caught in the flames of the fuel depot. The man's shirt had been splattered with burning fuel; his neck and the back of his head were red and blistered.

"Where's Christopher?"

"I haven't seen him."

"His . . . well, there are two civilians here. And one of them claims to be Christopher's father."

"Oh," Stevenson said, unfolding a bandage. "Oh, yes."

"You *know* about this?"

"Certainly. We're all business partners."

"What?"

"Yes. Christopher and I and his father are going to develop thousands of acres outside Saigon. Shopping centers, malls, resorts, golf courses."

Stevenson looked at him and smiled. Major Bedford's face, unshaven and weary, looked sadder and far wiser than Stevenson ever remembered seeing him. He looked older, grayer, but at the same time had a deep, soulful intelligence—a man of judgment and authority, someone who should be promoted.

"What's the matter, Major?"

"What *are* you talking about?"

"We're going to be rich, Major. The richest men in Vietnam."

He broke open a new gauze pad.

"We're buying up Saigon property now, and then, after the war is won, we're going to own the place."

He applied antiseptic to the pad and placed it gingerly on the flesh, wiping the man's brow at the same time. "You're gonna be all right," he said gently.

Major Bedford watched Stevenson's careful attention to the wounded man.

"I don't know what you're talking about," he said.

"Ah, well, never mind."

"I have to go. If you see Christopher, just send him to my office."

"Yes, sir."

Major Bedford turned to leave.

"Major Bedford, wait a minute."

"Yes."

"Let me see that bandage. What the hell kind of bandage is that? Who put this on you?"

"Oh, I . . ." Major Bedford looked down at the spattered rag around his arm, "I, uh, did it myself."

"Jesus, you're going to get infected and lose your entire arm. Look at this cut!"

"Well, I . . ."

"Here, let me fix it. Let me see this." Stevenson began unwrapping the loose cloth. "Christ, this is deep. Look at this!"

Major Bedford looked down at the gash where the sharp edge of the desk had torn into his white forearm.

"This'll get infected, sure as hell."

"Really? It sure hurts like hell. I fell on something."

"Yes. Good Lord, you don't want to lose your arm. You'll get your Purple Heart without losing your arm."

Stevenson poured on a generous amount of the red antiseptic, which burned as it bit down into the wound. It was a good sensation, Major Bedford thought.

He watched while Stevenson wiped and dabbed and folded the skin back over. He put a fresh bandage on and tied up the ends carefully.

"Is that too tight?"

"No, no."

"Well, you'll need stitches. Better wait around until a doctor can see to it."

"I've got too many things to do."

"Come back as soon as you can."

"Yes, I will, and . . . thank you," Major Bedford said, and left Stevenson changing the bandages on a young black sergeant whose legs had been shot several times.

● ● ●

Kit went back to the operations center. He went in the main doorway and stood for a few minutes at the end of the hallway. Not twenty-four hours before, he had killed two men here and held Major Dow, who was dying.

He went into the personnel section, where the paperwork went

on, despite the surrounding disaster. The clerk gave him his drop orders.

"I can leave any time?" he asked the clerk.

"Yes, sir. Just let me get you your file and you can di-di."

"Well . . ."

"Feels good, doesn't it?" the clerk said.

"Well, I guess so," Kit said.

The clerk put the orders in his 201 file, which was everything the army had on him. Then he put the entire thing in a large brown envelope. He handed it to Kit with a flourish.

"Get the next thing you can outta here, L-T."

Kit walked out of the personnel office with the envelope under his arm. Ever so slightly, the base started to fade in significance, fading in intensity, in color, in volume, even in focus. He clutched the folder to make sure it was still there.

He thought about the things he had to do. He thought about going back to his room to pack, but then he remembered his bunker had been destroyed.

He thought about the people he should say good-bye to. But Major Dow was dead, and Xuan was gone.

He thought he should try to find Stevenson.

And Major Bedford.

He went down the hall to the civil affairs office. He looked in the door, but Major Bedford wasn't there. He wondered if he should wait or go out looking for him.

He sat down at Major Bedford's desk and took his file out of the envelope. He looked through it, but there wasn't really very much. All the orders he had received for all the time he had been in the service, all clamped chronologically together in a metal binder—the orders drafting him, the orders moving him around, the orders sending him to the language school, the orders making him an officer, the orders sending him to Vietnam. And on the top of the stack, the orders sending him home.

He sat staring at the papers and the forms in the folder. This was it. What a nothing he really was. Well, not completely a nothing. He had killed two men. Would they put that in his file?

Number of men killed . . . . 2.

"Hey, Christopher!"

Kit looked up.

Starret barked at him from the doorway. He grinned and waved his orders.

"Let's go!"

"What?"

"You got your orders? I got mine. And I got a deuce-and-a-half that'll take us to Long Binh. But the driver's leaving now!"

"A truck?"

"Safer than flyin'."

"Okay. Just a minute. Let me just write a note."

"One minute. That's all. I'll be out front. Don't screw around. Gettin' dark!"

"Yes," Kit said.

"One minute!"

"Okay!"

Kit took out a piece of mimeo paper and wrote:

Dear Major Bedford,

I am gone. Hope you get out soon. Maybe I'll see you back in the world.

Lt. Christopher

He propped it up on Major Bedford's desk. He stood up and took one last brief look around the sad little civil affairs office. He picked up his file and put it back in the brown envelope. Then he put on his hat and left.

He walked down the hall, through the administration area, past the briefing room, past Major Dow's intelligence office, past the supply office and the operations rooms, past the signal office and the adjutant's office, through the partially straightened up outer offices where they had fought the previous night. He stepped over the bloodstains on the floor, went down the hall and out into the twilight.

To his left was the general's trailer. It had been white originally, but now it was a dismal gray, stained by the rains and the diesel smoke, peppered by bullets and fragments. The sandbags around it were coming apart, and the chain-link fence around it had fallen away from from its poles.

If Stevenson were anywhere, he would be there, Kit thought. He adjusted his hat against the sinking sun and went toward the trailer.

Starret was waiting in the truck in the division street. He saw Kit going toward the trailer.

"Hey!" Starret yelled. "Let's go!"

Kit held up two fingers.

"Just a second!"

"COME ON!" Starret bellowed. "We ain't waitin'!"

Kit waved his file at Starret and went up to the trailer door.

And then Kit heard, or seemed to hear and feel, the sound of voices inside the trailer, coming through the broken window. Voices in loud angry contention—not Stevenson's, not the general's.

"You stinking gutless chickenshit lawyer!" said one voice.

And the other voice answered with equal venom.

Kit stopped. Then he stepped back from the door.

He stood there half a minute while the voices inside the trailer went on, cursing each other, threatening suit, countersuit, disbarment, criminal prosecution, and even physical violence.

"Okay!" Starret yelled at him from the truck. "We're LEAVIN'!"

Kit turned to him.

"No!" Kit called. "WAIT!"

"WE'RE GOIN'!"

Starret's driver started the truck.

"HERE WE GO!" Starret sang.

"I'M COMING!" Kit yelled, and he began to run.

The truck moved off slowly.

Kit dodged around the chain-link fence and chased them.

"SEE YA LATER!" Starret yodeled back at him as Kit ran alongside.

"Stop!" Kit said, out of breath.

"ALLIGATOR!" Starret laughed.

They made Kit run after them nearly fifty yards, all the way to the base gate.

Starret thought all this was very funny.

C H A P T E R

T H I R T Y

A CHANGE-OF-COMMAND
CEREMONY

Kit left Phuoc Vinh in a deuce-and-a-half with Starret, caught the vacuum of escape.

Starret watched the road ahead. But Kit, sitting by the window, craned around to look back. He watched Phuoc Vinh fade back toward the horizon, a gray smudge on the yellow-green land. With it faded the people, the noises, the odors, and the terror he had lived with for nearly a year. In little more than an hour, he found it difficult to call up from his memory the faces of many of the people he had known.

Of his friends, he remembered Major Dow's face, Sergeant

Xuan's and Miss Tuyet's, Stevenson's and Major Bedford's, and . . . but that was all, it seemed.

The reality and misery of Phuoc Vinh—with its dirt, its mud, and its smells—weakened and leached away into time. Within weeks he would have to stop and remind himself of all that had happened. And back in America he would have to remind himself that on the other side of the world, on the other side of the great ball of dirt and rock and fire, Phuoc Vinh was still there, still grinding out its destiny. He would wake in the night thinking about Miss Tuyet, who never wrote to him, and wondering if she were still alive, and realizing that in America, the middle of the night was the middle of the day in Vietnam. Miss Tuyet was still there, trying to grow up, caught in the tired, endless conflict of which she understood nothing, and for which she was not, in the least possible way, to blame. When he thought of her, he felt desperately sorry. But by that time, Mr. Christopher had returned to America, and Kit had other problems.

• • •

None of Mr. Christopher's money was ever used to buy real estate in Vietnam. The general threatened to kick him and Mr. Hart out of Phuoc Vinh. Mr. Hart said that was fine, but Mr. Christopher made a spirited argument and even offered General Walker the opportunity to get in on the ground floor of a deal that would make him a lord in the land and millions of dollars. He opened Mr. Hart's briefcase, now stained and soaked and burned and scraped. He pulled out the list of high-ranking officers he had signed up in Saigon, also destined to be lords in the land. For a moment, General Walker wasn't sure what to do with the two men.

He wanted to turn them over to the judge advocate for prosecution. But Mr. Christopher's other clients were important officers, and he wasn't sure what law Mr. Christopher had broken. Mr. Hart could have suggested a few, but he said nothing.

Lieutenant Stevenson returned from the medevac pad happily covered with blood and generally a mess.

"Oh, yes, General, I know all about these gentlemen." He smiled blithely.

Walker violently pulled Stevenson into a corner and glared at him. Stevenson could feel the heat radiating from him.

"And *how* do you know all about this, Lieutenant?" he growled.

"Sir," said Lieutenant Stevenson, cool as a cucumber, "I know all about a lot of things."

And General Walker let it drop.

But he assigned Stevenson the job of taking Mr. Hart and Mr. Christopher back to Tan Son Nhut Airport in Saigon and getting them a flight out.

Mr. Christopher was moody for a while as they went along the road to Saigon. But then he cheered up. At the airport he gave Stevenson his business card, and offered him a job when he got out of the army. He said that Stevenson could work for him doing real estate deals in southern Connecticut, making millions, working right alongside Jimmy.

"Who?" Stevenson asked.

• • •

Sergeant Xuan used his four hundred eighty dollars to get his family out of Saigon—first to Singapore, and from there to Toronto.

Lieutenant Toomey used his five hundred dollars, plus the money he got when he sold the truck in Saigon, to go to Sydney, where he lived and may still live. He discovered later that he had been reported as missing in action and that a veteran's lobby was trying to get his remains from the Hanoi government. No charges were ever filed against him. Or his remains.

He did, however, suffer an odd sort of punishment for his actions. The dreams that plagued him continued for many years, together with the fear that he would someday be tried for murder or manslaughter or something. The punishment was especially cruel because Lieutenant Toomey never really knew what crime he was guilty of, if any.

Father Tran continued as a spy for the North Vietnamese until the end of the war. Years later, he left the church and became an education official in the new government. In fairness, it must be said that as the South Vietnamese took over, his conscience bothered him more and more. He was never as effective against the South Vietnamese as he was against General Walker, whose secret troop strength charts he memorized every day. General Walker never found out that Tran was responsible for the timing of the last attack. A devout Catholic, he thought Tran helped to save his soul.

Major Bedford was later awarded a Purple Heart for his wound suffered when he fell against the sharp metal desk and the mimeograph. As a result, he decided that he would remain in the army. He still had three months in Vietnam and was reassigned to MACV headquarters, where he was promoted to lieutenant colonel. He never saw Kit again, although he kept Kit's good-bye note in his wallet for a while.

General Walker left Phuoc Vinh before the belated change-of-command ceremony finally put the base completely into the hands of the South Vietnamese army.

It fell to Major Bedford to represent the American army at the ceremony, to stand with a detachment of anxious American soldiers, saluting the American flag as it was hauled down, and the South Vietnamese flag as it was pulled up in place. He saluted the new Vietnamese base commander, Colonel Nguyen Thi Pham, who couldn't have been more than thirty. Then, because it seemed like the thing to do, he shook Colonel Pham's hand.

What that handshake meant, Major Bedford had no idea. It didn't mean congratulations, because the base was a ruins of wrecked buildings and worthless machinery. And it didn't mean good luck, because it was clear to everyone that the South Vietnamese's luck had run out.

Perhaps, Major Bedford thought as he walked away toward the waiting helicopter, *it simply means good-bye.*

Yes, he thought, *that's what it means.*

ABOUT THE AUTHOR

JEFF DANZIGER served in the First Air Cavalry Division in 1970 and 1971 in Vietnam as in intelligence officer. He is a political cartoonist for the *Christian Science Monitor* and the *Los Angeles Times* Syndicate, and currently lives in Vermont.